"Ah, Talia, h

The husky note of surrender in his voice flared her with heat, reminding her of how he had capitulated that afternoon at Floreston Manor. She closed her eyes and breathed in the sun-and-salt fragrance of his skin that summoned images of breezy tropical islands and hot deserts. His heartbeat pounded against his taut skin as she touched her lips to the hollow of his throat.

His hands flexed on her shoulders, a sudden tension rippling through him. Sensing his retreat, Talia forced herself to break away from him first, her blood racing as she tried to control the desire swirling through her. She drew in a breath and turned away, pressing her hands to her cheeks.

"I wish you hadn't come back," she whispered.

"I wish I'd never left."

Praise for Nina Rowan's Daring Hearts Novels

A Passion for Pleasure

"4½ stars! Rowan writes with a passion and compassion that reaches out to readers. Her debut garnered attention, and her latest love story puts her on the path to becoming a reader favorite. Entering the world of music, Rowan finds a rhythm and flow that moves the story quickly, never losing a beat within the plotline or character motivation and providing wonderfully emotional entertainment."

—*RT Book Reviews*

"An extremely fun book…sweet…I enjoyed seeing this relationship crescendo from a mutual adoration into a full-blown romance."

—SeducedByaBook.com

A Study in Seduction

"A rare combination of beautiful writing and hot sensuality—readers are going to love *A Study in Seduction*!"

—Eloisa James, *New York Times* bestselling author

"Here at *BookPage* we are loving debut romance novelist Nina Rowan and her new book *A Study in Seduction*. If you are a romance enthusiast with a little bit of closet nerd inside of you, then this novel is the perfect fit for you."

—*BookPage*

"Four stars! Rowan debuts a historical romance that has plenty of sizzle contained within a strong story line, featuring a feminist approach, likable characters, a mystery with plot twists galore, and plenty of sassy repartee. Readers will eagerly await the next in Rowan's Daring Hearts series so they can savor her well-crafted, sensual prose."

—*RT Book Reviews*

"[A] fabulous Victorian romance in which the mathematical puzzles provide freshness...The lead couple is a nice pairing of intelligent individuals and the siblings are fully developed...sub-genre fans will enjoy the theorem of love."

—GenreGoRoundReviews.blogspot.com

Also by Nina Rowan

Daring Hearts Series

A Study in Seduction
A Passion for Pleasure

A Dream of Desire

A Daring Hearts Novel

NINA ROWAN

FOREVER

NEW YORK   BOSTON

Copyright © 2014 by Nina Rowan
Excerpt from *A Study in Seduction* copyright © 2012 by Nina Rowan
All rights reserved. In accordance with the U.S. Copyright Act of 1976, the scanning, uploading, and electronic sharing of any part of this book without the permission of the publisher constitutes unlawful piracy and theft of the author's intellectual property. If you would like to use material from the book (other than for review purposes), prior written permission must be obtained by contacting the publisher at permissions@hbgusa.com. Thank you for your support of the author's rights.

Forever
Hachette Book Group
237 Park Avenue
New York, NY 10017

www.HachetteBookGroup.com

Printed in the United States of America

First Edition: May 2014
10 9 8 7 6 5 4 3 2 1

OPM

Forever is an imprint of Grand Central Publishing.
The Forever name and logo are trademarks of Hachette Book Group, Inc.

The Hachette Speakers Bureau provides a wide range of authors for speaking events. To find out more, go to www.hachettespeakersbureau.com or call (866) 376-6591.

The publisher is not responsible for websites (or their content) that are not owned by the publisher.

For my family—then, now, and always

Acknowledgments

I owe my gratitude to Kimberly Witherspoon and Nathaniel Jacks of InkWell Management. Thank you, Lauren Plude of Forever Romance/Grand Central Publishing, for your sharp editorial guidance and enthusiasm, and to Selina McLemore for launching the Daring Hearts series with me. Franzeca Drouin, thank you a million times over for your friendship, your support, and your inestimable research knowledge and skills. I am so fortunate to have you in my corner. Thank you always to my father, for never once wavering in your support and belief in me, and to my perceptive, fun, and savvy writing partners Rachel Berens-VanHeest, Bobbi Dumas, and Melody Marshall. Finally, I am so grateful to all the readers who have read and enjoyed the Daring Hearts books.

A Dream of
Desire

Chapter One

May 1854

*H*e was leaving. Again.

Lady Talia Hall watched from her bedroom window as James Forester, Baron Castleford, crossed the gardens of Floreston Manor. Waning sunlight gleamed on his dark brown hair. He moved with a long, easy stride, his body relaxed, at home in the glow of late afternoon with bluebells, daffodils, and lilacs blooming at his feet.

A faint hope lit within Talia at the sight of him. Though she was pained by her recent discovery that this summer James would board a ship destined for Australia, she allowed a deep-rooted, precious dream to surface. When he returned to London—*if* he returned— he would do so with a warm smile lighting his eyes, full to bursting with tales of stormy seas, snapping crocodiles, dangerous floods, and mosquito-laden treks along muddy river passages.

And perhaps upon his return he would look at Talia and finally see the woman she had become. A rich, powerful love would surge through his heart, startling him with its intensity. In that wondrous moment, he would dare to unleash the desire he had suppressed for so many years. He would take her in his arms and kiss her with tumultuous passion...

Or not.

James climbed the terrace steps and disappeared from Talia's view.

Very likely not.

Talia sighed as her daydream broke apart, as it always did. She pressed a hand to her aching chest. When James returned to London six months from now...or a year...or God forbid, two years...he would embrace Talia with brotherly affection, inquire after her health, her friends, her charity work, and then he would saunter off to a ball or a dinner party. There he would enchant the numerous guests, particularly the ladies, with more riveting accounts of his adventures.

He would swoop in and out of Talia's life for a few weeks or a few months, entirely ignorant of her abiding love for him. And then he would leave again, unless Talia dared to tempt the fates into creating a different outcome.

Unless *she* dared to create a different outcome. Ever since her mother had left and her parents divorced three years ago, Talia had struggled with her place in the world. Her four older brothers had all gone about their lives, while Talia stayed at home with her father and tried to hide from the lingering gossip.

The only person she didn't want to hide from was James. He had always been there as a childhood friend, for as far back as Talia could remember, and he was one of the few people who had stood beside the Hall family during the scandal. Now that the matter had settled a bit, Talia's father and eldest brother, Alexander, were pressing the subject of her marriage, since she was now twenty-three years of age.

And if Talia didn't do something before James left London again, Alexander would push forward like an ox with his ridiculous conviction that Lord Fulton would be an excellent match for her. And if he managed to get their father's support for the idea, then James would truly be out of Talia's reach forever.

Her stomach tightened with nerves. She turned to study her reflection in the mirror. Her dress flowed over sweeping petticoats that emphasized the tapered curve of her waist. The rich green crepe de chine matched her eyes and contrasted well with her brown hair and pale skin.

The bodice, however, dipped around her bare shoulders and showed an expanse of skin that Talia was unaccustomed to revealing. She had always worn modest evening dress, particularly after her mother's scandalous affair had prompted gossips to doubt Talia's own virtue.

She pulled a silk shawl around her shoulders to conceal the swell of her bosom, which seemed rather prominent due to the heart-shaped neckline. She took a breath and gave her reflection a firm nod.

While she had questioned the wisdom of her bold approach numerous times since learning of James's impending departure, the time was long overdue for him to see her as a desirable woman rather than the Hall brothers' little sister.

She glanced at the clock. She and her father, two of her brothers, and James had come to Floreston Manor for a few days' visit, and this was the first time everyone except Talia and James were out of the house. She had to do this before her father and Sebastian came in from their fishing trip, and before Alexander and his sweetheart, Lydia, returned from their excursion to the village.

Talia couldn't help smiling at the thought of Alexander, her rigid eldest brother, who had so obviously been conquered by Lydia and still didn't know it yet.

Talia was determined to have the same effect on James Forester, except he would most certainly *know* she had conquered him. That was the only thing that might convince him not to leave again.

Spurred by the thought that this was her last chance to be alone with him, as they were all returning to London tomorrow, she hurried downstairs. The housekeeper emerged from the drawing room and gave Talia a pleasant smile.

"Lord Castleford missed his tea, my lady, so I left a fresh pot and a platter of cakes."

"Thank you, Mrs. Danvers."

The older woman nodded and puffed toward the kitchen. Talia stepped into the drawing room. Her breath caught in her throat.

James stood beside the fire, glancing through a sheaf of papers. The crackling flames cast his tall, muscular figure in brilliant illumination. His overlong brown hair curled around his ears and the top of his collar, the dark strands etched in reddish gold light.

Shadows danced over the masculine planes of his

features, the slanting cheekbones, sharp nose, and thick-lashed eyes that Talia saw in both her waking and sleeping dreams.

"Hello, poppet." James glanced up and smiled, the warmth in his eyes mitigating the hard edges of his jaw.

"Hello, James." His name tasted like a delicacy in her mouth, his gaze alone sparking pleasure beneath her heart.

But the nickname, which Talia had always enjoyed due to its affectionate undercurrent, now reminded her all too forcefully of his indulgent view of her.

"You've passed a pleasant afternoon, I take it?" James asked.

His deep voice rolled over her like sunlight. "Yes...yes, thank you, James."

Talia moved to sit on the sofa, ensuring her shawl sufficiently covered her bare skin. She poured the tea, then watched as James walked to put the papers on the desk.

She would never tire of looking at him. She had memorized all his unconscious movements over the years—the way he rubbed the back of his neck, folded his long body into a chair, curved his hand around a teacup or glass of brandy.

A restless energy radiated from him, evident in his utter lack of idleness. He paced when he spoke, tapped his fingers on his knee when he was seated. He smiled often, laughed, and made broad gestures with his hands as if words alone could not express everything he wanted to say.

No one except Talia knew all the subtleties of how James Forester moved and behaved. She was certain of that.

"Lists of the expedition members and transportation plans," he explained, nodding toward the papers.

Unease knotted through Talia. James sat across from her and studied the tea tray, which was filled with a variety of breads, cakes, muffins, and tarts.

"You're leaving in the summer then?" Talia asked, handing him a cup of tea.

"Next month, actually."

"N-next month? So soon?"

He reached for a slice of plum cake. "I thought we'd be delayed because we had to secure a new medical officer, but we've found one and managed to book passage on board the *Ballarat*. We leave from Southampton in mid-June."

"Alexander said you were going to New South Wales." It sounded like the end of the world.

"Yes. The Royal Geographical Society requested a survey of the territory, including several rivers. I submitted a plan of exploration in November, but didn't receive word until recently that the governor had sanctioned it. So preparations have been a bit hasty."

"I thought you'd planned a trip to Asia in the fall."

"It hasn't been funded yet, so this one takes precedence. With any luck, we'll finish the survey within a few months and be able to journey directly to the Malay Peninsula."

Talia's heart sank at the thought of having to worry about him traveling. Every time he left England's shores, she worked herself into a frenzy thinking he would end up dead, or that he would decide never to come home, or that he would return and announce that he'd married a beautiful princess from some exotic land.

Thus far, saints be praised, none of those lamentable circumstances had occurred, but both time and luck were running short for both of them. Even if James returned from this particular expedition whole and hale, Talia could wait no longer.

"Well." She forced a smile to her lips and summoned every bit of courage she possessed. "Won't you need to return to London soon? What about your estate?"

A frown creased his forehead. "The estate manager handles things in my absence."

"Yes, but he can't be in charge forever, James. Surely you're expected to carry out your duties and even to...to marry soon."

"There's a distant cousin somewhere, I'm certain, who can take over the estate when the time comes." James shrugged and picked up a wedge of pound cake. "As long as there's an heir, the lineage is secure regardless of what happens to me."

Talia curled her fingers around her shawl, disliking his indifferent view of his own future. She'd often thought of little else in recent years, clinging to the hope that James's future would inevitably merge with her own. Then the scandal of her mother's affair had sparked rumors about Talia's reputation, and she'd managed to avoid all horrible speculations by remaining within the circle of her trusted friends rather than venturing into society.

James was one of the few people who had never wavered in his loyalty to her family. His loyalty to *her*.

And now Talia knew she could not hide much longer. Not if her eldest brother had anything to say about it.

Not if James was leaving again. She tightened her grip on the shawl and took a breath.

"Speaking of marriage," she said, "did you know that Alexander, the big loon, indicated to Lord Fulton that I would be amenable to a marriage proposal?"

She expected James to react with horror—Fulton, after all, was a man twice her age and as rotund as a hogshead. Though Talia had told her brother in no uncertain terms that she would never marry Fulton, she hadn't confessed that she would never marry *anyone* except James Forester.

Since girlhood, she had known James would one day be her husband. He just needed her to finally tell him that, since he was clearly too mutton-headed to figure it out on his own.

"Fulton, eh?" James frowned, a flash of darkness on his handsome face. "Pity North couldn't set his sights higher on your behalf."

"It isn't his decision, in any case." Talia set her cup down with a restless movement and walked to the hearth. Her stomach roiled with anxiety as she turned back to face him. "And I've set my own sights for marriage much higher."

"Have you now, poppet?"

"Yes." She twisted the fringe of her shawl. "My choice is what matters."

"Indeed." James reached for the plate of tea cakes yet again.

For heaven's sake. If she were a tart, he would fall to one knee and declare his undying love.

Talia glanced at the clock. Now. She had to do this *now*.

"James."

"Hmm?"

"I...I've a confession to make." She gripped her shawl close to her throat. The heat of the fire filled the air around her. A bead of perspiration rolled down her spine.

"What sort of confession?" James peered at a slice of fruitcake, then exchanged it for a muffin.

"You already know a great deal about me, considering we've been friends since childhood." Talia wiped her brow with the back of her hand. The sound of her heartbeat filled her head. "But there is...there is one thing you do not know about me. One thing you haven't yet discovered."

"What might that be, poppet?" James bit into the muffin and glanced at her.

Now.

Talia released her shawl and let it fall to the floor behind her. Hot air cascaded across her already-flushed skin.

"I want to marry you," she said.

The muffin dropped to the carpet. For one awful moment James just stared at her. All the blood rushed from Talia's head as she waited with heart-stopping fear for his response.

Then it happened. His eyes flickered to the creamy swell of her bosom. And lingered.

A surge of triumph filled Talia. She steeled her shaky courage and pressed forward with the speech she had rehearsed.

"I couldn't a-allow you to leave yet again without knowing the truth of my...my feelings for you," she stammered. "I love you, James. I've loved you since I was a girl, back when we used to climb trees and play hoops and ride horses. I loved you when you went off to university, and every time you set forth on one expedition or another. I've waited for your letters, longed for your return, and…and when I heard you were leaving again, I knew I had to tell you the truth. By rights I ought to have married already, but I've never…never wanted to marry anyone except you. Because I love you."

He managed to pull his gaze from her bosom and look at her. Shock rather than desire filled his eyes.

Talia grasped the mantel with one hand and tried to pull air into her tight lungs. "I know this is sudden, that you've always looked upon me as a friend, but I—"

"Talia."

The strangled tone in his voice caused a resurgence of fear. Her fingers tightened on the mantel. Words crowded in her throat.

James pushed to his feet and approached her, his boots soundless on the thick carpet. For an instant, Talia dared to believe her long-held dreams would come true, that he would gather her in his arms, confess to his mutual love, and then press his mouth to hers…

"Talia!"

The stench of burning silk filled Talia's nose the second James grabbed her shoulders. Instead of crushing her passionately against his chest, he yanked her away from the fireplace. Talia stumbled, her heart catching in her throat. James cursed.

She spun back around in horror. Flames leapt from the hearth and ate through her discarded shawl, the fringed edge of which had fallen perilously close to the fire.

James ran to the sideboard and grabbed a flower vase. He dumped the water, flowers and all, onto the shawl while stamping out the flames beneath his boots. Blackened water spilled over the carpet. Smoke billowed from the scorched fabric.

James coughed. He picked up another vase and doused the material again, then hurried to ring the bellpull.

"My lord?" The footman, Hamilton, opened the door, alarm crossing his features at the stench of smoke and burned silk. "My lady?"

James stepped in front of Talia, blocking her from the footman's view. He gestured to the sodden, smoldering wrap. "Hamilton, fetch Kemble and attend to this, please."

"Yes, my lord."

Embarrassment scorched Talia's cheeks. She turned away as another footman hurried into the room, though James remained standing as her shield. Male voices conferred as the servants cleaned the mess and ensured there was no further danger.

Then the door clicked shut again. Silence as loud as thunder filled the room. Talia pressed her hands to her face and wished she could disappear. She felt James's presence behind her but could not turn to face him. Cold shivers racked her body.

A wool coat slipped across her shoulders. The fabric smelled like James—sea air and a touch of something exotic. Cinnamon and cloves. Indian tea. Dark coffee. She breathed in the scent and allowed the familiarity of it to ease a bit of her despair.

"My dear Talia."

His voice was gentle—not pitying or, worse, amused. Talia forced another breath into her lungs and turned. He stood right behind her, close enough that she could see the gold flecks of his irises and the faint scrape of stubble on his jaw.

"I'm sorry," she whispered, her throat aching.

"You've nothing to apologize for." He put his hand on her cheek. "Please believe me when I say you honor me deeply with your admission."

Talia stared at him. She'd half-expected him to stammer out some sort of rot, to find a way to be rid of her and have the whole debacle finished with. While he hadn't done that, Talia sensed he had more to say...and none of it would be what she desperately longed to hear.

Fear seized her anew. Her heart raced.

He was so close to her. His palm was warm on her cheek. She stared at his mouth. How often had she wondered what his lips would feel like against hers?

Before he could speak again, Talia closed the scant distance between them and pressed her lips to his. Surprise stiffened James's shoulders. He started to retreat, but Talia gripped the front of his shirt and increased the pressure of the kiss. Heat bloomed through her at the realization of a moment that had flourished so passionately and so often in her dreams.

James jerked back, inhaling a sharp breath. Determined to prevent his escape, Talia stepped closer, nudging her breasts against his hard chest. He tensed and gripped her forearms. She curved her hand around the back of his neck and pulled him down to settle her mouth more firmly against his.

He tightened his hold on her, even as his muscles

corded with restraint. Talia dared to part her lips beneath his, both shocked and thrilled by her own boldness. Her blood coursed hot and swift through her veins as the warm, sugary taste of James filled her senses. He moved his hands to her waist, his body still rigid. His fingers dug into the fabric of her bodice as if he sought the strength to push her away.

And then, suddenly, he surrendered. A groan escaped him as his mouth opened to hers in a deep union that flooded with desire. Talia closed her eyes and sank into the kiss, savoring the sensation of being in his arms, still wrapped in his coat, his mouth locked to hers.

Sweet, delicious relief and yearning filled her heart. She unclenched her hand from his shirt and spread it across his chest, imagining what his taut, bare skin would feel like beneath her palm. She arched her body against his, emboldened by his capitulation and the coil of arousal wrapping around them...

James broke away from her. He stumbled back, his breathing hard and his eyes brewing with shock and un-fulfilled passion.

Talia stared at him, her heart thumping. She pressed her fingers to her reddened lips, where the taste of him lingered.

"Bloody hell, Talia." James's voice was hoarse, jagged. He turned away and dragged a hand through his hair. "This cannot happen. This *will not* happen."

Somehow, she managed to speak. "It did happen, James."

He spun around to glare at her, his jaw set with frustration. "You are Northwood's sister, for God's sake!"

Tension lanced through Talia's spine. She lifted her

chin and sought the enviable pride that her mother had
always embodied, the cool dignity Talia knew that she,
too, possessed somewhere deep inside.

"I am far more than Northwood's sister, James," she
said, leveling her voice to a flat, composed tone. "I am
Lady Talia Hall. I am the only daughter of the Earl of
Rushton. Even in the shadow of scandal, my hand in
marriage is sought by any number of peers, but I am offering myself to you without reservation. I want to be
with you, James. I've wanted nothing else for—"

"Stop." The command snapped from him with such
force that Talia retreated a step. James cursed again and
pressed his hands to his eyes. He paced to the windows.

"I'll never get married, Talia, to you or anyone else,"
he said, clenching and unclenching his fists at his sides.
"Even if I did wish to wed, how could I subject a wife
to a marriage in which her husband is gone months or
years at a time?"

"You don't..." Talia swallowed past the growing
lump in her throat. Her future began to unfurl before
her, bleak and empty. "You don't have to leave so often,
James. And someday you'll have to—"

"I'll have to what?" He spun to face her. "I have
charge of the estate, yes, but I never intended to beget
my own heir because I won't stay in England. I'm not
meant for marriage, Talia, no matter how...appealing
the offer might be."

An ache constricted Talia's heart. "You mean to tell
me you'll never return to London to stay?"

"I've no intentions of doing so." Some of the irritation appeared to drain from him as he approached
her. His voice softened. "Talia, there's so much to see

in the world. So much to explore. I want to find the source of the Nile. I want to journey to Greenland one day. I want to map the interior of Australia and head an expedition to find geological specimens in China. It will take years to do everything I want to."

"And then when you're finally finished with your expeditions, you'll be a lonely old man with no one to care for you or love you," Talia snapped.

Her hand flew to her mouth. Shocked by the vehemence of her own words, she stared at James in mute apology.

A smile tugged at his lips. He reached out and brushed a tendril of loose hair away from her neck. The light touch of his fingers sent tingles of awareness through her blood.

"And you," he said, "will be a cherished wife and a beloved mother. You will have an enormous circle of friends who value you beyond measure. You will be married to the love of your life."

You are the love of my life.

Her heart crushed like a piece of paper within a tight fist. Nothing would keep James in England. Not even her.

"Please, Talia." James lifted her face so she had to look at him. Self-directed anger darkened his brown eyes. "Don't give me the gift of your love. I won't do anything good with it. Save your heart for a man who truly deserves it."

Talia clenched her back teeth together, fighting a sting of tears. Never before had James indicated he thought himself unworthy of anything, least of all a woman's love. Part of her wanted to argue, to force him to understand that she would not have offered herself to him had she not known his value. But Talia did have her mother's pride, uncultivated though it might be. If James did not want her heart, then she would take it back.

"Very well." She pulled away from the burn of his touch and crossed the room, clutching his still-warm coat around her body.

At the door, she paused. He stood by the sideboard, his hands shoved into his trouser pockets and his shoulders slumped. His hair fell in a disheveled mess across his forehead.

A twist of longing, of love, went through Talia, but she pushed it down beneath the layer of cold already creeping over her soul.

"James, I ask only that you keep my...my behavior a confidence between us."

"Talia, I would die before causing you embarrassment or shame." James cleared his throat. "No one will know of this. When...if I return, we will carry on as we did before."

"Agreed." Talia pulled open the door, turning away from him as her heart broke in half. "Best of luck on your expedition then, James. I hope you find what you seek."

Because now I never will.

Talia hurried back to her room, blinded by tears.

Chapter Two

May 1855
One year later

Clouds bruised the spring sky, heralding the possibility of a storm. A few raindrops had already fallen on the cobbled streets of Middlesex, and a straggly rooster pecked at a greasy puddle in the gutter. A newspaper man went past with a cart full of papers, and a milkmaid huddled in a doorway with brightly colored cans of milk at her feet. The greengrocer, baker, and barbershop doors were open, but only a few residents trudged through the town.

Inside the cab they had hired at the railway station, Talia held the court papers in a tight grip. Across from her, Mr. Matthew Fletcher, member of the Ragged School Union and a schoolteacher, sat beside Miss Alice Colston. Alice's face was white and pinched with concern beneath her plain blue bonnet, though not even the gray light and her evident anxiety could extinguish her angelic beauty.

Alice glanced up and caught Talia's eye. Talia smiled in reassurance, though her belly was also tight with nerves.

"Peter has served his sentence," she told Alice in a reminder meant to soothe.

"And we've got a written order for his release," Mr. Fletcher added. He'd removed his hat, and his brown hair was smoothed away from his high forehead, his narrow features calm behind his round spectacles.

"All will be well," he said, but he didn't sound especially convinced.

Neither was Talia.

Rain began to patter onto the roof of the cab as it rolled through the town. The dingy, redbrick walls of the prison came into view, only the spiked roofs of the interior buildings visible behind the enclosure. A prison van stood at the entrance, and iron grates covered every window like clenched, rusted teeth.

The cab slowed at the prison gates, and Mr. Fletcher opened the window to transfer their admission papers to the guard. The guard swung the gates open, and they rolled to a halt at the prison entrance. The huge, green doors were embedded in a stone archway capped with the inscription: *The House of Correction at Newhall.*

After descending from the cab, they entered the front office—a narrow room with a wall full of empty pigeonholes and a cupboard stacked with ledgers. The gate warder instructed them to sign the admission ledger before opening the door that led to the main yard.

"Mr. Lawford will be with you in a moment," he said.

Talia stepped to the smudged window and peered out

at the prison courtyard. A dozen warders in dark blue uniforms and leather belts stood at attention while a blond-haired man dressed in the uniform of the deputy governor inspected them for duty. After he dismissed them for work, the warders filed into the main building of the prison.

The deputy governor, William Lawford, went to the governor's lodge at the far end of the court, then returned to the yard with a tall, skinny boy of sixteen who trailed behind him with hunched shoulders. His black hair hung in his eyes, and he wore a gray prison shirt and trousers too big for his thin frame.

Talia's heart filled with guilt at the sight of the boy. She stepped away from the window, trying not to imagine all he had endured during his incarceration. The door opened, and Lawford and Peter Colston entered.

"Peter!" Alice gave a little cry at the sight of her brother and hurried forward to embrace him. Though the boy bore her touch, he didn't move to return the gesture.

"I'm so happy to see you, Peter," Alice said, her voice catching.

"Peter has been greatly anticipating this day." William Lawford gripped the boy's shoulder and gave Alice a smile. A handsome man in his mid-thirties, Mr. Lawford wore both his rank and his good looks with ease. "As have we. Always a pleasure to see one of our boys released back into the bosom of his family."

Alice brushed Peter's hair away from his eyes. "You look dreadfully thin."

"Peter's been a bit stubborn about taking his meals," Lawford said, his smile swerving to Peter now. "Isn't that right, Peter? Had him inspected by the surgeon, who found nothing amiss. Certainly it hasn't been for lack of sustenance."

"I would hope not," Talia remarked.

Peter blinked, his expression still vacant, and Talia wondered for a moment if he even remembered her. Her throat tightened. Likely he didn't *want* to remember her.

Lawford's smile remained fixed in place. "Ah, Lady Talia Hall. What an entirely unexpected surprise."

"Accompanying Miss Colston is the closest I could get to the inside of your prison," Talia said. "My application to visit was denied for a third time last week."

"Pity." Lawford wrote in a ledger and turned it toward Peter. "Sign here, Peter. Smythe, take Peter to change into his regular clothes."

Peter bent to scratch his mark in the ledger, then followed the gate warder to another room. At Lawford's instruction, Alice also signed her name.

"Since Mr. Fletcher and I are here now," Talia said to Lawford, "perhaps you might spare a half hour for a tour?"

"If I'd a half hour to spare, I would be honored," Lawford replied smoothly. "But I'm afraid we have a schedule to maintain. And seeing as your application has been denied...well, I'd hate to jeopardize my own position by allowing you access."

"You've seen the prison inspection report, have you not, Mr. Lawford?" Talia extended the papers she held. "Many of the gaols have been condemned for the wretched nature of their conditions and enforced labor. The inspection of penal institutions for juveniles is not scheduled until next year. I intend to submit to the

House of Commons committee that it be carried out this summer instead, as the results of the report will have a strong bearing on our request for government funding."

A hush fell over the room when the words stopped tumbling from Talia's mouth. Her heartbeat increased in pace. Lawford didn't take the papers, instead turning to examine the ledger before slowly closing it.

"My lady, I admire your commitment to criminals, as I'm sure they do as well. But surely there are more pressing matters for a lady of your rank to consider? Why must you lower yourself to aid the most worthless members of society?"

Talia's jaw tightened. She despised that word. *Worthless.* She'd felt that way herself in the past, when society had reviled her and she'd struggled to fit into the world again. Only recently had she discovered that she had the ability to help people who had little recourse, to prove both herself and them *worthy*. She would certainly not let Mr. Lawford—or anyone else, for that matter—belittle her efforts.

"They are not worthless, Mr. Lawford," she said. "They are boys who might become productive members of society if given a decent education or a chance to learn a trade."

"Which I have attempted to provide to boys like Peter Colston." Lawford bowed slightly in Alice's direction. "I'm sorry, Miss Colston. I did try to help your brother, but he's resisted any effort on my part."

"What kind of help did you provide?" Mr. Fletcher inquired. "Has Peter learned to read or write under your care?"

Lawford's clear, blue gaze didn't waver. "The boys received daily lessons of a religious nature, of course. We fully understand they are wayward souls whose moral corruption is not irredeemable. We also believe they must be set upon the right path before being allowed to chart their own course."

"And for you, does the right path include punishments such as those carried out at Birmingham?" Fletcher asked, his voice icy.

Lawford chuckled. "I'm afraid you draw comparisons where none exist, Mr. Fletcher. Birmingham was a prison for adult offenders. Newhall is for boys like Peter Colston who...do forgive me, Miss Colston...possess an aggravated character."

"Peter is a good boy, Mr. Lawford," Alice said, her hand at her throat. "We are a respectable family."

Lawford lifted an inquiring eyebrow. "I know you and your father have tried, Miss Colston. And I do hope Peter recognizes his good fortune and renounces his offending ways. Though I must tell you, his defiance while under my care does not give me much hope for his reformation."

"Mr. Lawford, I strongly suggest you give us access to your facility before the House of Commons meeting," Talia said. "If you are running a benevolent institution as you claim, then why not allow us to see the facilities and talk to the boys—"

"My lady, your application has been denied." Lawford's voice sharpened. "I have no further authority on the matter." He glanced at Alice. "Miss Colston, I beg your pardon for this unpleasantness on what should be a day of joy for you and your family."

"May we speak with Lieutenant Lawford, sir?" Talia asked. She had the satisfaction of seeing Lawford's features tighten with distaste.

"My uncle is ill and has returned to London for care," he replied curtly. "He leaves the responsibilities of Newhall to me in his...infirm state."

Yet another reason why Newhall crouched under a cloud of suspicion. Whispers abounded about Lieutenant George Lawford's illness, which was purported to be an addiction to alcohol. Despite the rumors, he had once overseen the prison hulks that transported convicts to Australia and other colonies, but he'd been stripped of his duties when inspections of the ships revealed abhorrent conditions and numerous deaths. Last year Lieutenant Lawford had been "retired" to Newhall to oversee the small juvenile detention facility.

Shortly after his appointment, he'd selected his nephew William as deputy governor, ostensibly as an aide to help with his own duties. Everyone knew, however, that William had quickly taken over every detail of the prison's management and, in all but name and salary, served as de facto governor of Newhall while concealing his uncle's lack of interest in governing.

"I believe my father, the Earl of Rushton, is acquainted with Lieutenant Lawford," Talia said, tugging her gloves farther up her wrists. "He's been with the Home Office for a year now. I've little doubt he'll be willing to assist me in the matter of prison reports upon his return to London."

Actually, she had little doubt her father would throw a fit of rage when he learned his only daughter was seeking access to prisons and associating with juvenile delinquents...but Mr. Lawford certainly didn't need to know that.

Lawford tilted his head. "Yes, I'm sure your father will be delighted with your latest cause, my lady."

His voice wrapped the remark in sarcasm.

Before Talia could respond, the gate warder came through the door, followed by Peter. Dressed in an old shirt, jacket, and trousers, he kept his gaze on the floor even when Alice approached again and began speaking to him in a low voice.

Talia went to the door, trying to hide her disappointment—even though she had hardly expected Mr. Lawford to allow her access to Newhall, she'd hoped to find some chink in his armor that she could use to her advantage.

She glanced toward Alice, her gaze sliding past her friend to where Mr. Lawford stood behind the desk. He was watching Alice, his blue eyes attentive and specu-lating, as if he were attempting to solve a puzzle.

Apprehension rose in Talia's chest. It was a look she was uncomfortably familiar with, having received such speculative glances after her mother had an affair with a younger man. Almost four years after her parents' subsequent divorce, Talia still sometimes had to deflect unwanted male attention.

She moved forward to touch Alice's arm and gestured to the door. Alice nodded, her face shadowed as she urged Peter to follow them. Before the boy could, Law-ford reached out to grip his hand.

"Now that you have your freedom, Peter, I hope I shall not see you again within these walls," Mr. Lawford said. "If you seek the Kingdom of God and His righteousness, you will prosper. Depend upon it. And Miss Colston…"

He moved around the desk to take her hand. "I shall call upon you and your father soon to ensure Peter's smooth return back into society."

"Thank you, sir."

Mr. Fletcher held the door open as Alice and Peter exited to the waiting cab. Just before Talia followed them, Lawford's hand curled around her arm. Though Talia wasn't particularly alarmed with Mr. Fletcher close by, her apprehension deepened.

"My lady, I strongly suggest you heed my words," Lawford murmured. "I will not have my bill for a new prison destroyed because of your ridiculous screeching about reform and juvenile criminals. And you may toss your father's name about as much as you wish. We both know he will never support your endeavors. In fact, I'd venture to suggest that he would be far more inclined to support *mine*."

"My lady." Fletcher's eyes narrowed at Lawford.

"Keep to your tea parties and ballrooms, Lady Talia," Lawford said before releasing Talia's arm. "And stay out of my prison."

"Good day, sir," Fletcher said stiffly.

"I shall be in London in three days' time to visit my uncle and meet with Lord Thurlow about my proposal for the construction of a prison at Shipton Fields," Lawford said. "Perhaps I shall see you both there… well, not *you*, of course, Fletcher, but Lady Talia in any case. I've numerous invitations already."

Though Talia did not relish the idea of encountering Mr. Lawford during the whirl of the social season, it might be a potential opportunity to gain more support for her cause. At the very least, he wouldn't threaten her in the midst of a fancy ball for fear that any unpleasantness might hinder his efforts to improve his social ranking.

Talia left the office without bidding Lawford a farewell and climbed into the cab. She sat across from Peter and Alice as Mr. Fletcher instructed the driver to return to town.

"Let's get Peter settled back at home," Talia said. "I believe the next train leaves at noon, so we've time to stop in town for refreshment. You must be hungry, Peter?"

The boy shrugged. Talia and Alice exchanged glances, and the despair in the other woman's eyes made Talia's heart constrict. They might never know what Peter had endured behind the brick walls of Newhall.

Although the boy bore no visible evidence of harsh treatment, Talia had heard about Newhall's disciplinary measures from other boys who had served time there. As much as she despised the thought of any boy enduring brutality at the hands of prison guards, she hoped that Peter would one day speak about what he had experienced. His testimony could be critical to the success of reform measures, which was the only way such conditions would change.

"Your father is looking forward to your return, Peter," Mr. Fletcher said.

"No, he ain't." Peter stared out the window.

"Of course he is, Peter." Alice patted her brother's hand, her voice light but her eyes dark with worry. "Papa's been busy with work, which is why he couldn't come today, but we've a special dinner planned for your return. Boiled ham, greens, and mashed turnips. And Lady Talia brought us a lovely apricot tart for dessert."

She might have been discussing the classified advertisements of the *Times*, for all of Peter's reaction. Talia tried to suppress another upwelling of guilt as the cab continued toward the town square. Alice squeezed Peter's hand.

They resembled each other, Talia thought as she watched them, especially around the eyes. Though Alice's irises were blue and Peter's brown, they both had almond-shaped eyes with thick, dark lashes. Otherwise sister and brother were a foil to each other, Alice's delicate blondness contrasting with Peter's black hair and sharp-edged features.

Alice pointed out the window and said something to Peter. Though he still didn't respond, a faint amusement appeared in his eyes.

Talia exhaled a breath she hadn't realized she was holding. Alice and Peter were brother and sister. No matter what Peter had endured at Newhall or even before, no matter what faced him after nine months of incarceration...at least he would always have Alice.

The redbrick walls of the prison faded into the distance. Sorrow nudged at Talia as she thought of her own four brothers, all living far from London and busy with their own lives. As much as she missed them, Talia hoped they were too busy to be concerned about her.

For the first time in her twenty-four years of life, that was exactly the way she wanted it. Without her brothers to thwart her efforts, she could finally attempt to pay

Peter Colston back for having gone to prison because of her.

The domed buildings and minarets of Constantinople gleamed in the light of the setting sun. Merchants, porters, and veiled women walked past shops stocked with both local and English-made goods. Soldiers wearing red fezzes patrolled the streets and lounged at the outdoor cafés. Colorful rugs hung from stalls of the bazaar situated across from a mosque, and the scents of smoke and spices drifted on the air.

A waiter paused by the table to refill James's cup with coffee. The brew was thick and strong, a robust difference from the watery coffee served in London's coffeehouses. After setting a plate of honey-and-rice sweets on the table, the man bowed and departed.

"A prison." Alexander Hall, Lord Northwood, frowned darkly at James from the other side of the table. "What business would my sister have in a prison?"

Though James's chest tightened at the idea of Talia anywhere near a prison—let alone actually *in* one—he tried to keep his tone politely inquisitive.

"How do you know she was there?" he asked.

"Haverton was with Lieutenant-Colonel Jebb when he was conducting a survey," North explained. "He saw Talia as she was leaving Smithton. Rushton certainly wouldn't have allowed her to visit a prison, which means he can't possibly have known about it."

"Have you spoken to him?"

"Not yet. He's visiting St. Petersburg after he finishes the Home Office business in Kiev. He'll be furious if he learns Talia is involved in something unsavory."

"You don't know that she is, North," James said, still trying to maintain a practical tone. "She's a reasonable girl who would never put herself or anyone else in jeopardy."

"So I've always believed," Northwood muttered. "But if I'd had an inkling that she was in contact with a criminal element, I'd have put a stop to her charity work long ago. I thought her work with the ragged schools involved providing education for poverty-stricken children. Nothing to do with prisons, for the love of God."

James flexed his fingers and tightened them into fists. Though it had been a year since he'd last been in London, he'd dealt with plenty of convicts in his travels, both aboard ship and on the docks. He knew what they were like, the rough, broken men who'd lost hope and didn't care whom they hurt. If it was true, if Talia was somehow putting herself in danger...a sudden fear rose in his chest, quickening his heartbeat.

"I don't like it," Northwood continued. "Rushton won't either, but he can't do anything until he returns to London in September. I know he holds out hope that Talia will have decided to marry by then."

James coughed, reaching for his cup to hide the rush of dismay at the mention of Talia's marrying. He took a sip of coffee and tried to keep his voice even.

"Heard she didn't take well to your suggestion last summer that she wed Fulton," he remarked.

"Marriage to Fulton would have well secured her future," Northwood replied. "And when I asked her if she had another prospect in mind, she refused to tell me. She did, however, make it clear that she did not want my interference."

James sat back, looking past Northwood's shoulder at the bazaar. Bright, woven shawls fluttered like giant butterflies from one of the stalls. In the back of James's mind, an image surfaced—the expanse of Talia's white skin, glowing from the light of the fire, a strand of her hair clinging to her throat as she looked at him with eyes like emeralds…

He shoved the memory down alongside the inevitable flash of heat. For the past year, he'd forced himself not to think of that night, not to remember how his blood had flared at the realization that Lady Talia Hall was not only a beautiful woman, but also an intensely desirable one.

Though he'd been somewhat successful at suppressing the memory during the day, he had been powerless at night, when salacious images of him and Talia had slipped unguarded into his dreams. Leaving him hot and aching for a woman he had no right to crave.

Northwood was still talking. James blinked and tried to refocus on his friend's words.

"…last heard he was near California," North said. "And what of your next expedition? You said you've encountered difficulties?"

James nodded, forcing his mind away from Talia and back to the reason he'd come to speak with Northwood in the first place.

"The Russian vice admiral is blocking our access to the north," he explained. "We've funding from several sources and the preparations are almost completed, but we can't set sail unless we know we can access the Amur Valley."

He pushed a sheaf of papers toward Northwood. "That is the proposal in detail, which I'm certain you'll find could well benefit your own trading company. Especially once we chart routes to the towns and harbors. I ask for your help with Vice Admiral Petrov."

Northwood leafed through the papers, his forehead creasing. James could almost see the thoughts working through his friend's mind. Even as a boy, North had never been quick in his agreement—he'd always examined issues from all angles before making a decision.

Though James often did the same thing, he now felt a twinge of impatience as he watched North study the proposal. The Russians had been making substantial advancements into the southern Siberian frontier, which was precisely the reason the government didn't want to allow a British expedition into the area. Especially if that expedition were able to assess the full scope of Russian acquisitions to the east and possibly conclude that they posed a potential further threat to the south and British territories.

James had no interest in speculating about Russian land encroachment, much less conveying military intelligence to the British government. He was only interested in charting the land and studying the region's ethnography, but Vice Admiral Petrov didn't know that.

"I've made all the plans to depart from London in June," he told Northwood. "But Petrov denied approval, and the governor-general of western Siberia revoked his previous acceptance of our proposal."

North glanced at him. "You've made the arrangements already? Secured the crew?"

"And the ships. I won't put them at risk, either, if we try to enter the valley of the Amur without permission. But if I'm forced to abandon the entire venture, then

I'll lose credibility with the Royal Geographical Society. They'll doubt my ability to carry through successful expeditions in the future."

James didn't know what he would do if he lost funding for future expeditions. The idea of being forced to stay in London and to contend with the detritus of his father's estate and the ugly shadows of the past...

He took a breath. He *needed* to travel. Needed the cold, salty air, the churning ocean waves, the pitch of the ship beneath his feet, the vast expanses of uncharted land. He needed to disappear in the world.

Urgency filled him. He leaned forward. "I need your influence, North. You have a good business relationship with Petrov. If *you* could assure him we're interested only in the ethnology and cartography of the valley, he's far more likely to grant us access."

"On my word, you mean."

"Yes. Petrov trusts you. So do I."

And his trust in Northwood was boundless. North knew why James commanded his expeditions. He was the only person who knew the truth about James's parents. And while North may have speculated about James's reasons for not wanting to stay in London, he had the grace not to press the issue.

"I'm returning to London in two days' time to complete the paperwork," James said. "If I don't have approval to access southern Siberia, I'll have to cancel the entire project. Put a number of noses out of joint, too, since I've got half a dozen financiers involved. Not to mention all the men who've been hired."

Northwood studied him, his dark brows pulling together. "How long will you be in London?"

"One month, if we have approval. We're scheduled to depart on the twelfth of June." James stifled his impatience. Northwood was analytical when it came to business decisions, but he'd also never shied away from helping a friend. "You're the only person with enough influence, North. Will you help me or not?"

"I'll help you," he said. "Under one condition."

James smothered his initial relief under a twinge of wariness. "I'm in your debt."

"Find out exactly what Talia is involved with and ensure she is doing nothing foolish."

Dammit.

James tipped his hat down against the glare of the sun to conceal his reaction. He couldn't think about seeing Talia again. About having no choice *except* to see her again.

Shame inched up his throat. He'd fully intended to return to London and leave again without seeking Talia out. Not because he didn't want to see her but because he was so tormented by the thoughts he'd had about her the past year.

Northwood's sister, for the love of God, and James had hot, restless dreams about her pale skin and the swell of her breasts, the achingly soft touch of her mouth. He thought far too often about her full lips, which he'd never before imagined pressing against his until she'd actually done it. Until her tongue had met his, firing heat and a shockingly ravenous hunger through his blood.

"Talia will listen to you," Northwood continued. "She always has. More so than to me or Sebastian, at any rate."

James pulled in a breath. His friend's request was simple and reasonable. North was right too—Talia had always listened to him, though that malleability had likely changed considering their last encounter.

Not that he could ever tell North that.

"And she's always trusted you," North added. "All the more reason you ought to speak with her."

She used to trust him, James thought. Talia might want nothing to do with him anymore, though he couldn't tell his friend that either. North didn't know of James's last encounter with Talia. He didn't know that James had spent the last year battling lurid thoughts of her. Thoughts he had no right to possess.

"Well?" Northwood asked.

James could not decline without providing a reasonable explanation...and he had none. He'd been a close friend of the Halls since he and North were nine years of age. He'd been like a fifth brother to them. And no matter the degree of trepidation he felt at the prospect of seeing Talia again, he could not bear the thought of her in possible danger.

He steeled himself. He'd once faced down a rampaging elephant and a horde of pirates. He'd been attacked by a venomous snake, fought raging floods. He could certainly muster the courage to see Lady Talia Hall again. Especially if he could somehow ensure her safety, or at least assuage both his and North's fears.

"Of course," he said. "Of course I'll speak to her."

"Good." Northwood gave a nod of satisfaction. "And I'll send a telegraph to the vice admiral tomorrow. I promise your next expedition will go forth as planned."

* * *

As James strode back to his hotel, he was unable to stop thinking about that afternoon in Floreston Manor. His entire view of Talia had changed in the span of less than an hour. She'd walked into the drawing room the same young woman he'd always known—pretty, kind, intelligent, just *Talia*.

He'd been pleased to see her but distracted, his mind half on the preparations for the New South Wales trip and the things he needed to do back in London. She'd gone on about the meddlings of her eldest brother, her desire to make her own decisions about marriage...and then she'd dropped her shawl to the floor and declared her love for him.

James remembered that the shock had immobilized him. He remembered the rush of heat and desire at the sight of Talia's creamy skin and round breasts, the way the firelight had made her eyes flare with emerald light. Suddenly, out of nowhere, she was a *woman*.

God in heaven. Even a year later, he couldn't think of that kiss without his heart pounding.

We will carry on as we did before. It had been a stupid thing for him to say. Talia had confessed her love and her desire to marry him. He'd rejected her and yet been stunned by his reaction to their kiss.

How could anything between them be the same after that?

James went into his room, the plain, whitewashed walls a welcome respite from the noise of the streets. He sank onto the bed and scrubbed a hand down his face.

It would take a week to reach London from Constantinople. He could only hope that the cold salt air and wind would clear the confusion from his brain.

Maybe he could even come up with some answers, for he had no idea how best to approach Talia. He didn't know if she would even speak to him. And he was damn certain she would never again look at him the way she used to.

Chapter Three

A week after Peter Colston's release from Newhall, Talia navigated yet another crowded ballroom, her resolve strengthened anew. This was the first time she had finally learned to appreciate London's festive season. In the years following her parents' divorce, she'd despised the endless whirl of balls and parties, all so saturated with an unpleasant combination of frivolity and vindictive gossip.

Now, however, in her desire to garner support for the Brick Street reformatory school, she'd discovered how to use the social chaos to her benefit. Weaving through the crowds, Talia could move from one person to the next with a quick mention of the school and the upcoming House of Commons committee meeting. Just long enough to plant the idea into the ear of a wealthy industrialist or a peer and hope it would take root.

But not enough time for them to reject her proposal altogether. Not enough time for them to remember her family scandal or dwell upon it or, worse, to look at her with speculation and a hint of lewdness. Not enough time for them to wonder if she was as wanton as her mother.

Without Rushton and Alexander in London—and now that she was near to being on the shelf—Talia could leave questions of marriage and matches to the younger women and their mothers. Finally, she could use the season to her advantage rather than hide from it the way she'd done for nearly four years.

"My lord, my point is that the sheer violence of flogging as a punishment only begets anger and humiliation," Talia said, tempering the severity of her words with a pleasing lilt. "The children are kept in repressive conditions and not permitted to receive any education beyond religious training. I received a report that several children have been restrained with manacles. Surely you must agree that such treatment is horribly detrimental for youth who would be far better served by learning the value of education or a trade."

The plump, balding Lord Thurlow nodded absentmindedly, his gaze slanting past Talia to the dance floor.

Talia stepped into his line of vision and smiled. "I would most appreciate your support of the proposal, my lord."

Lord Thurlow's grunt signaled neither assent nor disagreement. He reached for a glass from a passing server and turned aside.

"If you'll excuse me, my lady, I do find such discussions rather disagreeable during such a fine soiree."

He trundled off toward the card room. Talia sighed, disappointed, even though she had become accustomed to such dismissals.

She fidgeted with her pearls and glanced about the room. Thus far, she'd not been able to convince any of her father's compatriots to commit their support for her cause or for the Brick Street school, but she would not give up.

She owed it to Peter Colston and to the other boys who faced dismal futures unless they were given another opportunity. Talia could not escape being the daughter of an earl. She could not escape the trappings and expectations of society. But she *could* use her position to advance a cause that others would discount as worthless.

She circled the room slowly, the flowery scents of perfume and champagne assailing her nose. A drop of perspiration trickled down her temple. She went toward the refreshment table, longing for a glass of lemonade. New strategies spun through her mind for how she could gain more support for her proposal.

Rather than approaching the peers directly at social events such as these, Talia knew she should focus more on their wives. The ladies of the *ton* were more apt to be sympathetic to the cause, especially as many of them had young sons of their own.

Mustering support from the women, however, meant Talia would have to attend tea parties and feminine gatherings, which she had avoided for so long. And she still didn't quite have the courage to face a room full of women who would likely whisper and speculate about her the moment she turned her back. Not to mention that she wasn't at all certain her presence would be welcome, considering she received so few invitations for such gatherings.

Talia continued through the crowd, deciding to seek

out Lord Smythe as soon as she had a lemonade. The ballroom was stifling. A cacophony of voices rose in the air, and a waltz drifted from the piano.

A slender, brown-haired man passed in Talia's line of sight, near the doors leading to the terrace. Lord Margate. She'd spoken to him two nights ago, and he'd expressed interest in knowing more about the House of Commons committee meeting. Steeling her spine, Talia pushed forward to reach him.

Then the sound of a man's laugh stopped her in her tracks. Even through the noise, Talia heard it—a deep, masculine laugh that spread through the crowd and thudded right up against the walls of her heart.

James.

Talia tried to breathe past the sudden heat filling her throat. A buoyant sensation raced through her, like champagne bubbles in her veins.

He was back.

For a moment Talia didn't know what to do next. Someone bumped into her from behind, forcing her to step forward. She clutched the folds of her skirt, pulled by the sound of James's laughter like a bee drawn to the warm, sweet sanctuary of a hive.

She maneuvered her way through the crush, her heartbeat increasing with every step. Then she saw him, holding court amid a circle of admiring men and women, his tall figure and dark brown hair burnished by the firelight.

James.

Exhilaration lifted Talia's heart. For the past ten years, every time James had returned from a journey, she had experienced such a mixture of emotions—delight at being near him again, anticipation to hear about his adventures, utter joy that he had come back healthy, safe, and always with that beautiful smile that contained all that was good in the world. Despite everything that had transpired between them, those feelings had not changed, still swirling through Talia in a medley of colors and light.

She gazed at him, her breath catching in her throat as she tried to assess all the changes wrought by the past year. His skin was darker, and strands of his hair had been lightened by the sun. His lean, muscular body was sheathed in a black evening coat, and a silk cravat nestled at his throat.

He was speaking to Lady Bentworth, a plump, cheerful woman who waved a silk fan in front of her flushed face while chattering animatedly. James listened intently, nodding every now and then, a smile tugging at the corners of his mouth.

Though he appeared entirely at ease, surrounded by a commanding sense of confidence, Talia sensed his reserve, the way he held himself slightly apart from the crowd. It was part of his mystery, that reserve, making people want to dig deeper, to find out more, to get closer to him.

He wouldn't let them, though. Even now, Talia knew that.

Then James looked up and saw her. Talia drew in a breath, her pulse hammering as their gazes collided across the distance. A bolt of energy seemed to arc from him into her, filling her with crackling awareness.

Oh, no. No.

She couldn't still feel this way. She'd spent the last

year smothering the embers of her love for James
Forester. Surely one look across a crowded room
couldn't spark the flames back to life again.

Talia tightened her fingers on her skirt and stiffened
her spine. He had *rejected* her. The memory still burned
her with shame, and—thankfully—quelled the anticipation ricocheting through her. She would never embarrass
herself for him again.

James bent his head to speak to Lady Bentworth, who
smiled and nodded with understanding. Then James de-
tached himself from the circle of guests and approached
Talia.

Her throat went dry. He moved with such ease, his
stride long and his body coiled with a taut energy that
had always been an intrinsic part of his being. As he
neared, Talia found herself staring at his mouth and remembering how delicious it had felt against hers.

"Hello, poppet." His deep voice warmed Talia like a
wave of heat on a cold winter night, even as his use of
the old nickname reminded her where things stood between them.

We will carry on as we did before.

Her heart sank a few inches, but she was seized by
the wish that he would take her in his arms as he always
had upon his return from an expedition. Even now she
longed for one of his big warm embraces, ached to feel
the press of his body against hers and tuck her face
against his shoulder, inhaling the scents of sea and sunshine that clung to him.

*Stop, Talia. Stop. It cannot be that way again. It will
not.*

As if verifying her assertion, James didn't move

closer to her. He did not extend his arms, though his gaze remained fixed on her face. Talia tried to ignore the chaotic mixture of pleasure and dismay that beat alongside her heart.

"Welcome back, James." Her voice, at least, managed to remain steady. "When did you arrive?"

"Two days ago."

"I didn't even know you were planning to return."

The thought disconcerted Talia suddenly, almost more than the shock of his presence. James had always sent advance word to her father's house—to *her*—about the date of his return to London. He hadn't done so this time. He also hadn't written to her at all during the past year, save for one Christmas letter addressed to both Talia and her father.

That wasn't at all as things were *before*, those many years when James would write her long, detailed letters about his travels and discoveries. As if he knew how much she cherished his letters about storm-tossed seas, arid deserts, snake-infested jungles. As if he knew she fancifully imagined herself right by his side, his intrepid female partner, the two of them against the world.

Girlish fantasies, Talia reminded herself, even as she gazed at the sun-painted streaks of gold in James's wavy brown hair and the darker tone of his skin that evoked the heat of Pacific islands. She so wanted to step closer, knowing he would smell like sea salt and wind, that the air around him would be warmed by the tropics.

"I'll be in London for only a month," James explained, his voice breaking apart Talia's silly thoughts. "I'm heading an expedition to southern Siberia in June."

Of course you are.

She could not prevent the stab of disappointment mixed with envy—a curious combination she'd only ever experienced with James. She tried to remind herself that she ought to be accustomed to her reaction by now. After all, she'd experienced it for years, every time James announced he was leaving.

Which he usually did just after he'd arrived.

"How exciting for you." She forced a note of mild enthusiasm into her voice. "And how was your adventure to New South Wales? And the Malay Peninsula, was it? My, you've likely seen the entire world by now."

His brown eyes creased with amusement. "It will take many more years before I see the entire world. But our New South Wales journey was quite successful, as we were able to provide the Royal Geological Society with new maps and entire trunks full of geological specimens. We weren't able to secure passage to the Malay Peninsula, though I did hear Nicholas was involved with an expedition there."

"Was he?"

"Not the safest passage, from what I understand, but I've no doubt Nicholas can handle it."

So did Talia. Even as a child, her brother Nicholas had brimmed with confidence over his ability to thwart both danger and convention, leaping into the fray without thinking twice. She had always rather envied him for that, qualities so different from his twin, Darius, who took no action without great preparation and assessment.

After their parents' divorce, Nicholas took to the seas and had yet to return to London—which caused the Earl of Rushton no small amount of relief. Nicholas's penchant for rebellious behavior might have set tongues wagging all over again had he remained among the *ton*.

Though James shared the urge for adventure, he was far more methodical and careful in his approach, leaving as little to chance as possible. Where James worked to mitigate danger, Nicholas actively sought it. He'd been that way since they were children, always the boy to climb the highest tree, cross a flooded river, walk the ridge of a fence.

Nicholas, Talia thought, was the one Hall brother who was likely to actually help her recent, perilous efforts rather than hinder them. Pity he seemed to have no plans to return to London, possibly ever again.

She had a sudden longing for her brother Nicholas. She'd become accustomed to his prolonged absence over the years, but with Alexander and Darius living in St. Petersburg, and Sebastian settled near Brighton with his lovely new wife...Talia was the only Hall sibling left in London.

For all her battles with her brothers, it was a strange and lonely feeling to realize they were now so far away. And that she didn't know when she would see them again.

"Did you see Nicholas during your travels?" she asked James, hoping perhaps he had word about Nicholas's future plans.

James shook his head. "I did see Northwood, though. After New South Wales, I went to Constantinople. North was there for a fortnight, overseeing a branch of his trading company. He is doing quite well, isn't he? Couldn't wait to return to St. Petersburg to be with Lydia, Jane, and the new babe."

Talia smiled, warmed by the thought of her newborn nephew. "I hope I'll be able to visit them again soon."

"North said the same," James said. "He also mentioned you've been quite involved in your charity work this past year."

Wariness flickered in Talia at the casual note in his voice. All of her brothers, even Nicholas, were well acquainted with her ragged school charity work, but she'd purposely not told any of them about Brick Street for fear of their reaction over her involvement with delinquents. She absolutely wouldn't tell Alexander, who was certain to charge back to London and put a screeching halt to the small advances she'd made with the school.

"It's been keeping you busy, he says," James continued.

"Yes, it has. The Ragged School Union is doing a great deal of good, if I do say so myself." She straightened her spine and tucked a stray lock of hair back behind her ear. "We just opened a new school in Bethnal Green last month and already have a full roster of students."

"Very good to hear." James studied her for a moment, an assessment so direct that an unexpected tingle went through Talia at the sheer warmth of his gaze. If she didn't know better, she'd think he was scrutinizing her as he would any other appealing woman.

But of course she *did* know better.

"Have you engaged in any other charities?" he asked.

Talia shook her head, deflecting a pang of guilt. James had always supported whatever endeavor the Halls undertook, whether it was Sebastian's concerts,

Alexander's Royal Society of Arts exhibits, or Talia's charities. And she had not realized until this moment that she'd never before kept a secret from James—at least, not a secret involving her charity work.

"You'd have known all about my activities if you'd sent me a letter or two and allowed me to respond," she remarked, disliking the note of hurt in her voice.

Regret flashed in his brown eyes. "I'm sorry, poppet. I wasn't…it was difficult to post anything much of the time."

"That never stopped you before." The moment the words slipped from her mouth, Talia flushed hot. The last thing she wanted to do was remind James of the way things had been *before*, when he'd always found a way to get his letters to her even from as far away as Argentina.

Those letters had told Talia without a doubt that he was thinking of her. But now…

"Talia, I—"

Talia held up a hand before he could stammer another flimsy excuse. Or before she could confess how desperately she'd missed his correspondence. Such a confession would do neither of them any good.

"Never mind, James," she said. "I'm glad you've returned safely, and I hope everything goes well for your next trip."

She turned away, sorrow sharp in her throat. His hand closed around her bare arm. Talia's breath caught at the sensation of his fingers on her skin, the way he tugged her closer into the warm space beside him. The space few could breach.

"I saw a very strange tree in a crater on Arlington Abundance," James said. "The trunk bulged out in the

middle like a barrel—so wide that the entire tree resembled a huge turnip with the branches and leaves as the
greens."

Talia looked at him. His eyes, crinkled at the corners,
gleamed with a light that Talia had once hoped was reserved only for her. She suppressed a twinge of regret
and allowed herself—just for this moment—to remi-
nisce.

"False," she said.

James smiled. "True. I was climbing to the summit
when I saw the tree. Had to blink a few times to make
sure I wasn't imagining it. I've a drawing in my journal
that I'll show you."

Talia's heart gave a thump at the implication that they
would not only see each other again before he left, but
also that they'd sit down together and look through all
his notes and drawings. Exactly the way they'd always
done. *Before*.

"On the same mountain," James continued, "I saw a
most unusual rock, very bumpy and lined with green
streaks. I put it in my rucksack to add to the collection
and continued walking. Halfway down the mountain,
the rock started to move. I opened the sack and it
jumped out and landed on my shoulder, then scurried
down my back and ran away."

Talia narrowed her eyes skeptically. "False?"

"It was an odd kind of lizard that camouflages itself
against the rocky terrain."

"Why didn't it move when you picked it up then?"

"It was sleeping."

"No creature would remain asleep when dumped into
a rucksack."

"Excellent point." James grinned, his teeth flashing white.

"False, then?"

"False," he conceded. "Your turn."

"I have a new pet," Talia said. "A cat called Misty that I dress in a harlequin costume of black satin trimmed with diamonds and a ruffled collar. I've taught her how to dance and jump through a hoop."

James lifted an eyebrow. "False, but it sounds delightful."

"True."

"True?"

Now it was Talia's turn to smile. "When you visit King's Street, I'll show you."

"Well, then." He looked both puzzled and intrigued. "I look forward to calling upon you very soon."

"Tomorrow, I do hope!" An elderly woman with bright blue eyes and a halo of thick, graying hair stopped beside them. "You mustn't keep us waiting, you rogue."

"Lady Sally." James turned his smile on Talia's aunt with genuine affection. "I'd heard you were staying with Lady Talia in her father's absence. You look lovely, as always."

A pink blush colored Sally's already rosy cheeks. "I'm so pleased you're back in London, James. You must come for dinner one night, and don't you dare tell me you can't spare the time."

"For you, of course I can."

Sally giggled. Talia shook her head in amusement. She'd never cared for the sleek, self-satisfied gentlemen of the *ton* who tossed compliments about like shiny new pennies, but James was different. James had a way of looking at any woman, young or old, and making her believe he truly meant what he said.

Perhaps because he did.

I'll never get married, Talia, to you or anyone else.

Talia didn't know whether to find comfort in that remembered statement or not. Sorrow stung her every time she recalled that James would not marry her...but at least he wouldn't marry another woman either. There was a small measure of comfort in the knowledge that Talia would be spared the pain of seeing James wed to someone else, though she couldn't help wishing he wasn't quite so true to his word. Where *she* was concerned, at any rate.

"You're returning home, are you?" James asked Sally. "Allow me to escort you to the foyer and ensure your carriage is available at once."

He extended his arm toward Sally, who slipped her hand into the crook of his elbow and beamed at him. Then James turned a questioning eye to Talia.

Resignation swept through her. She couldn't very well approach Lord Margate with James here. If he learned she was broaching the subject of aid for juvenile delinquents, he would most certainly make inquiries that could lead him to the truth. And if James knew the truth, Talia's father and brothers would learn of it as well, and then obstruct her efforts at every turn.

She gave James a nod of assent and followed him and Aunt Sally to the foyer. She might have once considered him a trusted friend, but she knew his loyalties lay with Alexander and Rushton before her. And while that would never make him Talia's enemy, it certainly meant she could no longer confide in him.

* * *

Alice Colston set a cup of coffee in front of her father, then filled a plate with eggs, buttered toast, and two kippers. She placed that next to the coffee and took her seat. Papa's head was bent as he studied his newspaper, the points of his collar a stark white contrast to his black suit.

Alice tried to remember the last time her father had worn any other color except black and white. Certainly it had been before her mother had died more than a decade ago.

She sipped her coffee, suppressing old pain. She'd been seventeen years old when Mrs. Colston had succumbed to a bout of influenza. Peter was not yet six. Alice still wondered how much Peter remembered of their mother. He hadn't spoken of her in years. And after he'd attempted to run away from home at nine years of age... well, he hadn't wanted to talk about anything. Least of all what had set him on such a horrible path.

"I thought I might visit the new panorama in Regent's Park this Saturday," Alice remarked, trying to distract herself from the inevitable guilt. She'd all but raised Peter after their mother died, and she still felt somehow to blame for his actions. "Mrs. Richards said it was quite fascinating. I'd also like to make a stop at the library to pick up a book by Mr. Hogg that I haven't yet read."

Her father made a noncommittal noise and turned a page of the paper.

"And there's a charity bazaar near Oxford Street tomorrow, if you'd like to attend," Alice continued.

"No, but you are welcome to. I shall leave you some pin money, should you wish to make a purchase." Her father set the paper aside and pulled the plate toward him. "I'll be home late tonight. We've some accounts to set up that Mr. Vickers requires done by the end of the week."

The thump of footsteps came from the stairs. Alice looked up at Peter and smiled. He shoved a chair away from the table with his foot, his expression set and sullen.

"I'll get your breakfast, Peter." Alice rose and fixed a plate of eggs and toast. Once upon a time, she'd have offered him cocoa but in the week he'd been back at home, she'd noticed he preferred strong coffee.

She poured a cup and placed it in front of him, suppressing the urge to run her hand over his thick, black hair. The way her mother used to do with her. She tried to ignore the twinge of pain at the memory of what her brother had been like as a young child—happy, reckless, full of energy.

What had gone so wrong?

Alice still didn't know what had happened to turn Peter into an angry young man who seemed hell-bent on getting himself into trouble. He'd run away from school and started associating with vagrants who roamed the streets picking pockets and vandalizing storefronts. Twice their father had to pick him up from the police station, and then last year Peter's arrest had led to his being sentenced to Newhall for nine months.

Edward Colston hadn't attended the court hearing or tried to visit Peter while he was incarcerated. Edward also hadn't wanted Peter to return home after his release, but Alice had pleaded with him to allow her brother one more chance.

Edward had finally relented, but only on the condition that Peter attend the Brick Street school and find worthwhile work. Even now, Alice knew her father hoped that Peter would somehow prove to be the son he had always wanted. That Peter would straighten up, succeed in school, become a solicitor or a doctor...that he would one day become more successful than Edward was.

What father didn't have such hopes for his only son?

Alice stared at her plate, wondering what hopes, if any, her father had ever had for her. She was well into spinsterhood now, so marriage wasn't likely...not that she'd ever been in a position to accept an offer. She'd spent the past ten years taking care of her father's household and contending with her brother's rebelliousness. Even if she'd wanted to, she could never leave and start her own family.

"Intend to enroll at the school today, do you?" Edward asked Peter. "You ought to be able to work as well."

The boy shrugged.

"I've heard the tailor on Buxton Street might be seeking help," Alice suggested.

Peter held up one of his big, knobby-fingered hands. "You think these were meant for sewing?"

"The printer, then, whom Papa—"

"Bloody hell, Alice," Peter snapped. "You need to be able to *read* to be a printer."

Anger flashed through Edward. He pushed his chair back so fast, the legs scraped against the floor. Peter cringed. Edward lifted a hand. Though Alice had never in her life seen her father strike Peter, she froze in fear.

Taut silence stretched between the three of them. Peter didn't raise his head. The clock ticked. Edward stared at his son, then slowly lowered his hand.

Alice's heartbeat throbbed in her ears. Edward picked up his cup and took another swallow of coffee, seeming to regain control of himself.

"You will not curse in my house," he told his son, his voice cold. He straightened his lapels, then folded the paper and tucked it beneath his arm. "I suggest you pay a visit to the union offices and enroll at Brick Street first thing this morning. Good day to you, Alice."

He gave Alice a stiff nod and strode to the door. A minute later the front door closed. Peter shifted and grabbed a fork. Alice opened her mouth to defend their father, then bit the words back for fear of further rancor. Peter stuffed the eggs into his mouth and washed them down with two cups of coffee.

"Did they feed you well at Newhall?" Alice asked.

Peter lifted his shoulders in a shrug. Even confined in prison, he'd grown a good two inches over the past nine months, but he was far thinner than she remembered. He used to be big and muscular. Now he was a tall, awkward boy who didn't look as if he fit into his lanky frame.

"Would you like to come with me to Oxford Street?" she asked. "We can stop at the union offices en route."

Peter shook his head.

"What do you plan to do today, then?" She tensed as she awaited his response.

"Not look for work at a tailor's or print shop," he muttered.

"Peter, it's very important that you find suitable

work," Alice said carefully, "and attend school at Brick Street."

"I ain't going back to school."

Irritation crawled down her spine. "Peter, Papa agreed to let you come back home if you either—"

"I didn't ask to come home, did I?" Peter shoved his plate away so hard it bumped against his cup and spilled the coffee.

Alice jumped up to grab a napkin. "Where else would you have gone?"

"Wherever I bloody well please," he retorted.

"Peter…"

"I didn't strike any bargain with him," Peter snapped. "Bastard's always been ashamed of me, right?"

Shocked, Alice stared at him. "Peter, do not speak of our father that way!"

"It's the truth, ain't it?" He pushed to his feet. "I'll never be as good as him, and everyone knows it."

"That is not true."

"It is true. The only reason he's letting me stay now is because of you, right? He wouldn't set foot in Newhall the whole time I was there."

"Can you blame him?" Alice asked, anger filling her throat. "Papa has always tried to give you everything you could possibly want, especially after Mother died. You repaid him by becoming a vagrant, picking pockets, and thieving. You got arrested, sentenced to prison, and now you won't consider your future. What is Papa supposed to think?"

"What he's always thought," Peter retorted. "That he should have disowned me years ago."

"Why, Peter?" Alice hurried after him as he stomped

to the foyer. "Why are you doing this? If you don't want to go to Brick Street, perhaps we can talk to Papa about going to stay with Uncle Benjamin in Surrey. He's got a farm, you know, and…"

"I ain't going to live on a damned farm." Peter pushed his arms into the sleeves of his coat.

"Where are you going to go, then?" Alice's heart clenched like a fist as she thought of him back among the denizens of London's slums. He didn't belong there. He never had. And she hated the thought that her brother believed that he *did*.

Thank heavens for Lady Talia Hall, at least. She'd come to Alice after Peter was arrested, offering her assistance. She'd explained about her work with the ragged schools and the founding of the Brick Street reformatory school, which sounded to Alice like a much better place for Peter than Newhall prison, no matter what crime he had committed.

Unfortunately, the judge hadn't agreed. Lady Talia had been a blessing, though, calling upon Alice regularly, arranging for letters to be delivered to Newhall by courier, keeping Alice informed of the progress of Brick Street and the possibility of Peter attending upon his release.

"Peter helped me," Lady Talia had told Alice. "I'd like to do the same for him and you."

Alice had even begun to consider the other woman a friend, even if she was the daughter of an earl. And it was comforting to have someone to talk to about Peter's situation, especially since Papa wanted so little to do with it.

"Peter, please." Alice tried to grab her brother's sleeve, but he evaded her grasp.

Peter smashed his hat onto his head and stalked out the door. Alice knew nothing she said or did would stop him.

She pressed her hands to her face and tried to stanch the inevitable tears. Guilt and dismay rolled through her in an overwhelming wave. The tears spilled over, and she choked back a sob. She couldn't bear to imagine how horrified her mother would be to learn that her only son had been branded a murderer.

Chapter Four

He's back.

The thought, which had coursed through Talia's mind endlessly after seeing James at Lady Bentworth's ball last night, elicited a combination of both pleasure and apprehension.

How many times during the last twenty years had Talia thought those very words? First when James was away at school, then after he'd gone off traveling with Alexander and Sebastian before Cambridge and his eventual work with the Royal Geographical Society. Not even his father's death and James's inheritance of the barony had slowed his desire to explore.

To leave. To run.

Talia shook her head to rid herself of the uncharitable whispers that had plagued her for years, ever since she began seeing James as a man. She had always disliked her nagging suspicion that he was *running* from something, for that implied cowardice. Certainly there was nothing cowardly about battling stormy seas and trekking through crocodile-infested swamps. Talia, after all, had spent a secret part of her life wishing she too could be part of such adventures.

James is back. James is leaving again. The two thoughts were like a confluence, two rivers inevitably leading to the same point.

Once upon a time Talia would have liked to think: *James is staying.*

She no longer believed such a thought would become truth. With a sigh, she settled back into the chair and opened the book. Across from her, Aunt Sally worked a needle through a piece of cloth.

" 'Camels and California, says the critic,' " Talia read. " 'Two words that are not often used in one breath.' "

"Rather." Aunt Sally chuckled and snapped off a length of thread. "Didn't you once ride a camel when your father took you to Egypt?"

Talia nodded. Memories sparked like fireflies—the raucous sound of her brothers' laughter as they tottered in time with the camels' odd gait, the sun cascading over the sugar-fine sand, dark-skinned men with wide smiles, her mother watching from beneath a lace-edged parasol.

She gazed unseeing at the latest adventure story sent by her brother Nicholas. Ever since she'd read a copy of James Fenimore Cooper's *Last of the Mohicans*, Talia had loved the tales of the American wilderness, which were always so fraught with tension and danger. She found some copies in libraries, but over the past few years most of her books came in packages from Nicholas.

Hardly appropriate for the daughter of an earl, Talia

thought. Her governesses had schooled her well on all the appropriate literature for a young woman of the peerage—Shakespeare, Petrarch, Dante, poetry— but Talia had been captivated by her brothers' stores of reading material, especially the *Parley's Magazine* that came from America and was filled with the most wonderful stories of Persian mountains and strange creatures. And the boys' books of sports and pastimes that were always showing her brothers how to *do* something—make a kite, construct a kaleidoscope, perform feats of legerdemain.

Talia had spent a great deal of time tagging along after her brothers and trying to do what they did. And when they didn't let her, or when she couldn't join them on their adventures because she had music or dancing lessons, then at least she had always enjoyed reading about them.

Even now, Talia read the more recent *Boys' and Girls' Magazine and Fireside Companion*, which was filled with stories, poems, and articles about interesting things, like how a magnetic telegraph worked. She brought all the magazines and penny dreadfuls to the Brick Street school for the boys, of course, but not before reading them first. Not before imagining what it would be like to explore the world as one pleased. Just as James did.

"Isn't it nice that Lord Castleford has returned?" Aunt Sally remarked. "Lady Willingham said he intends to publish his journals before he leaves again. Quite an exciting life the man leads."

Talia murmured a noncommittal agreement.

"I've always found his tales so fascinating," Aunt

Sally continued as she selected a slice of plum cake from the tea tray. "Your uncle was in the Royal Navy before we married, you know, and he always had a longing for the sea."

"Part of our blood, it seems," Talia said. Her grandfather had spent much of his life traveling throughout Russia as ambassador to St. Petersburg, and her father had taken the family on many excursions to Europe, Egypt, and Russia. All four of her brothers enjoyed travel, as Talia had until her mother's abandonment had made the idea of home far more appealing.

Talia had gone to St. Petersburg last fall to visit Alexander and his family, but aside from that one trip, she had remained in London. Compared to her brothers' lives, hers was dull, but at least she knew what to expect here, and she wasn't faced with unexpected choices that called her judgment and her very nature into question. At least she could do some good here.

"He cut such a fine figure in his uniform," Sally remarked with a sigh.

"Uncle Harold?" Talia thought of Sally's portly, whiskered husband. "Er, I imagine he did."

"Oh, I know he wasn't terribly handsome, my dear." Sally plucked at a loose thread on her needlework frame. "But he carried himself with such dignity, such command, that women were naturally drawn to him. Bless his heart, he only had eyes for me. He said I was Helen to his Paris, though with a much happier ending, of course."

Talia smiled at the tender, wistful look on her aunt's face. She remembered Uncle Harold as an affable man who often remarked on his wife's beauty and goodness.

"You had a good marriage," she said.

"Heavens, yes. Would that all women were as fortunate in matrimony as I was." Sally pushed the needle through the cloth again. "Not only did Harold provide well for me, but he also never failed to demonstrate how much he admired and loved me. Both outside and inside the bedchamber."

"Aunt Sally!" Talia felt a blush crawl over her face.

Her aunt laughed. "Talia, dearest, don't believe any woman who says what goes on in the bedchamber doesn't matter. Trust me, it matters a great deal. And the happier a couple is *there*, the happier they are in every other aspect of their lives."

Talia stared at Sally, suppressing a sudden rush of questions. Certainly her aunt and uncle had always seemed happy and in love, but Talia had never imagined that pleasure in the bedchamber had anything to do with it.

Then again, she remembered vividly how arousal had bloomed through her the instant she'd pressed her lips to James's. She remembered how their bodies had fit together, how her heart had pounded, how thrilled she'd been when he hauled her into his arms and took possession of her mouth...

Talia dropped her book to her lap and pressed her hands to her cheeks. *God in heaven.* Could the matrimonial bed really be more exciting, more fulfilling, than that?

"And it's not just the husband who should be satisfied either, though of course Harold always was," Sally continued in a conversational tone, as if they were discussing the latest fashions from Paris. "When you meet a man you might want to wed, Talia, be certain you find him both physically and intellectually compelling. Ensure that he respects your needs, that you enjoy conversing with him, that he is interesting to you and allows you a degree of freedom. And yes, that he is very attentive to your desires in the bedchamber."

"I…" Talia swallowed past the tightness in her throat. She fought images of James, fought all the hopes and wishes that had taken root inside her so very long ago. The hopes and wishes that she'd tried hard to bury since that afternoon at Floreston Manor.

"I don't intend to marry, Aunt Sally," she managed to say. "I've told you that."

"Yes, well, one is always allowed to change one's mind." Sally shrugged and returned her attention to her needlework.

Talia tried to focus on the book again, but the words swam before her eyes. She couldn't help wondering if that was the reason her mother had left. Had her marriage to Rushton been that desolate? Had her attraction to the young Russian soldier been that powerful? Had he given her all that Aunt Sally described?

Talia shook her head. It didn't matter, in any case. Even if she did still harbor some fanciful thoughts about marriage to James, she knew they would never come to be.

That knowledge, at least, made it easier to contend with the resurgence of her old feelings. James would never stay in London, never marry, never be the man she wanted him to be. Whatever lingering threads of love and warmth she held for him would forever remain locked inside her heart. And there was a certain comfort in knowing exactly where things stood.

Never mind the hint of sorrow that Talia would never know the type of marriage Aunt Sally described—or, indeed, even the kind of passionate relationship her mother had with the soldier. Talia wondered how many women ever knew that kind of love or pleasure. And the two combined in wedded bliss? Rare as a blue diamond, surely.

Perhaps just as precious, too.

A knock sounded at the half-open door. The footman, Soames, peered in.

"My lady, Lord Castleford has arrived."

Talia's heart jumped. "Lord Castleford?"

"I invited him for tea." Aunt Sally set her needlework frame aside and removed her spectacles. "Didn't I tell you?"

"No." Oh, there it all was again, swirling through her like a whirlwind. Anticipation, pleasure, excitement...all echoed in the rush of her pulse, the beat of her heart.

"I wanted to hear about his latest journey, but without all the noise of the ball," Sally explained. "He's bringing his journals along with him. I remember how you always enjoyed those."

"But I'd intended to go out in a half hour." Talia looked at the clock, trying to quell her riotous emotions. "I've some errands to run."

"Well, fine, you'll have time for a cup, won't you? Do send his lordship in, Soames."

The footman nodded and left, returning a moment later with James. A thousand shivers tingled down Talia's spine at the sight of James, his lean muscular body clad in a navy morning coat and gray waistcoat, a cravat knotted at his throat. He carried several leather-bound journals beneath his arm, and he set them on a table along with his gloves before turning to greet Sally.

"Good afternoon, James." Sally's blue eyes twinkled. "We're so pleased you could join us."

"Thank you for the invitation, my lady."

James moved to Talia and extended both hands clenched into fists. Talia ignored that now-familiar twinge around her heart and reached out to touch his left hand. Her fingers just brushed his knuckles, but the light contact alone caused a shiver to travel clear up her arm. She didn't look up into his face, afraid of what she might see in his eyes.

And more afraid of what she would certainly not see.

James turned his hand and opened his fist to reveal an empty palm. Talia tapped his right fist. He opened his hand. Nestled in his large palm was a shimmering, brilliant green stone about the size of a robin's egg.

A gasp of pleasure caught in Talia's throat. She picked up the stone, struck by how the light shone on the sharp, jagged surfaces, displaying a kaleidoscope of green hues. A gift from him to her, just like he'd always given her *before*.

"Oh, James." Warmth filled her heart. He hadn't forgotten how much she loved the treasures he brought back from all parts of the world. "It's beautiful."

"Quartz, from one of the New South Wales mines," James said, a responding pleasure appearing in his eyes and curving his mouth. "Not terribly precious, but the green reminded me of you."

"Thank you so much." Talia extended the stone for her aunt to see.

She gathered in a breath, struggling against the thoughts that still came so naturally to her—imagined images of James picking the stone out of a pile of dirt and rocks, thinking of how it matched her eyes, picturing her in his own mind, then tucking the stone into his rucksack and keeping it safe for her all those thousands of miles back to London...

"Lovely, James." Sally squinted at the stone. "But why did the green remind you of Talia?"

"Oh, er, I..."

Both Talia and Sally looked at him. Talia's mouth twitched at the sight of the flush cresting on his cheekbones. James Forester was not a man who often blushed.

"Well, my lady, Talia has..." James cleared his throat, his gaze on the carpet. "Her eyes are quite green, are they not?"

"Oh, yes, of course." Sally gave a tittering laugh. "*Green* can also refer to her youth, I suppose."

Talia threw her aunt a mild glower. Sally had remarked numerous times on Talia's age rather than her youth, so she knew quite well that James had not been in mind of budding freshness when he found the quartz.

What, exactly, had he been in mind of?

Talia's heartbeat intensified at the idea that James might have just been thinking of...well, *her*. The way she looked. The color of her hair and eyes. What she might be wearing, the sound of her voice or—

Or perhaps Talia ought to put a stop to such foolish thoughts once and for all.

"In any case, it is very pretty, and thank you for thinking of me, my lord," she said, plucking the stone from Sally's hand.

"And now you promised to show me your new pet," James reminded her.

"New pet?" Sally repeated.

"Wait just a moment." Clutching the quartz, Talia hurried from the room. She went upstairs to her bed-chamber and tucked the stone beneath her pillow, then took a large wooden box, painted blue with white swirls, from her desk and returned to the drawing room.

As she neared the open door, she caught the sound of her aunt's voice.

"She's been quite amenable to attending balls and dinner parties this season," Sally was saying. "I've been pleased to see that, though she still dislikes afternoon teas and hasn't accompanied me on any calls. I heard a rumor Lord Bexley might approach Rushton upon his return to discuss a marriage arrangement."

Oh, no. Talia's heart plummeted. Not another rumor. She tightened her hands on the box, her shoulders tens-ing as she waited for James to respond to that remark.

"Northwood didn't say anything about Bexley when I saw him," he said.

"Likely he doesn't yet know." Sally made a clucking noise with her tongue. "Though knowing Alexander, he would approve of Bexley the way he did Fulton."

James was silent for a moment that seemed to Talia like forever. She desperately wanted him to state un-equivocally that Bexley would be a horrid match for Talia, and that both Alexander and Rushton would be fools to believe otherwise.

"Northwood only wishes to ensure Talia is cared for," James finally said. "I promised him I'd look after her a bit while I'm here, as he can't do so himself."

Something crumbled inside Talia. She closed her eyes for a moment, absorbing the sharp edge of disappointment over James's revelation.

"I believe Alexander intends to visit London this autumn," James continued.

And when he does, you'll be free of your responsibility.

Only now did Talia realize how much she'd hoped James had actually wanted to see her again. It was a foolish thought, considering he hadn't even bothered to write to her, but they had *once* been good friends.

Until she'd made a mess of the whole thing by telling him she loved him. Perhaps this was her penance—longing for nothing to have changed when it was so painfully obvious that everything had.

Mustering her courage, she pasted a bland smile on her face and entered the room with the painted box. "Here we are. My new pet."

James looked at the box with bewilderment. "You keep it in there?"

"Yes." Talia exchanged a smile with her aunt as she set the box on the low table in front of the sofa and opened it.

A platform extended from the box, bearing a miniature platform and hoop. A mechanical cat dressed in a harlequin costume crouched to the side, its glass-blue gaze on the hoop. Talia twisted the key at the back of the box. A tinny music began, and the cat coiled back on its haunches before leaping forward in a two-step dance, then vaulting through the hoop.

James laughed, clapping his hands together in appreciation. "What an extraordinary machine. Where did you get it?"

"Sebastian's wife, Clara, has an uncle who owns the Museum of Automata and workshop," Talia explained. "She had him make this as a birthday gift for me."

"It's a fascinating place, James; you really ought to visit," Sally remarked. "Talia, you must introduce him to Mr. Blake. He's a very dear man, if a bit long-winded at times. He made me a clock with little horses spinning around in a carousel. Extraordinary."

The door opened to admit a maid with a tray of fresh cakes and tea, and Talia moved forward to pour. From the corner of her eye, she watched James turn the key to rewind the automaton. He chuckled as the cat performed its antics. The rumbling sound echoed through Talia's blood. His laugh had always brought her such pleasure.

She handed a cup of tea to her aunt as James settled into a chair. She added two sugars to another cup before handing it to him. Their fingers brushed as he took the cup, the light touch sending another shiver coursing through her arm.

"So, James, you're publishing your journals, are you?" Sally asked.

"Yes, I'm in the process of rewriting them all now," he replied, lifting the cup to take a sip of tea.

Talia gazed at his hands, tanned from the sun and dusted with dark hair. The cuff of his sleeve inched up to display the corded muscles of his forearm. Despite the size of his hands and his calloused fingers, James held the china cup with care, as if it were a bird nestled in his palms.

Talia wondered if he would hold a woman the same way. If he would slide those large, rough hands gently over her bare skin, intent on her pleasure as much as his own…

"Don't you think, Talia?" Sally asked.

"Er…I beg your pardon?"

"We're hoping Darius will also return for a visit in the fall," Sally said. "After the season is over. Sebastian has already invited us to his new home near Brighton."

"Yes, yes. I hope so." Talia could hardly remember the last time she and her brothers had all been together.

"My lady, a…visitor to see you?" Soames stepped into the room, giving Talia a nod.

"A visitor? But I'm not expecting anyone." Talia set down her cup and stood. "If you'll excuse me for a moment, James, Aunt Sally?"

"I told her to go round the back, but she insisted you would see her," Soames murmured as she passed him in the doorway.

Talia hurried to the foyer, where the door was wide open. Alice Colston stood on the front step, huddled in her coat with a dark blue bonnet framing her pretty face. Talia's heart bumped against her ribs.

"Alice, what's wrong?" She hurried to grasp the other woman's hands, noticing as she drew closer that Alice's eyes were puffy and shot through with blood. "Is it Peter?"

Alice nodded. "My father told me not to disturb you, but I'm so worried about him."

"Talia?" Aunt Sally peered at them from the drawing room doorway. "Won't you invite your guest in?"

"Oh, no, I…" Alice shook her head and stepped back toward the door. "I'm sorry, I…"

Talia tried not to wince when James appeared behind

Sally, his gaze going from her to Alice. She did not want James to know anything about Alice or Peter Colston.

"We'll just be a moment, Aunt Sally." She took Alice's arm and went out to the front step, closing the door behind her. "What happened to Peter, Alice?"

"He left again this morning and hasn't returned yet. I'm afraid he might have gone back to Wapping."

"Did he say why he left?"

Alice shook her head. "He knows our father wants him to attend Brick Street, but he insisted he'd never return to school. Our father won't allow him to stay if he doesn't, and Peter knows that. I think that's why he's run away again."

Dismay speared through Talia at the resignation in Alice's voice. Despite their dissimilar upbringings, she had felt a kinship toward the other woman since their first meetings at the Colstons' modest Spitalfields home. Both she and Alice had lost their mothers, and Talia sensed that, like herself, Alice had felt both isolated and trapped in a position she would never have chosen for herself.

"Mr. Lawford said Peter refused all lessons at Newhall as well," Alice said.

"When did you speak with Mr. Lawford?"

"He came to visit several times when Peter was still in prison," Alice explained. "To assure my father and me that Peter was faring well, but was often defiant for no apparent reason. And he wouldn't learn to either read or write, despite Mr. Lawford's best efforts."

Talia frowned. She'd not heard of Lawford visiting any family members of Newhall's inmates. Just the opposite...considering the disciplinary measures reputed to take place behind those brick walls, Lawford sought to limit contact between the boys and their families. Even letters were seldom distributed within the prison.

"Has Peter said anything to you yet about Newhall?" Talia asked.

"No, he won't talk about anything. I hate to think he's returned to the docks, but I've no idea where else to begin looking for him. Or even if I should."

"Of course we should." But Talia wasn't foolish enough to think she and Alice could venture into the streets of Wapping alone to look for Peter. One mistake had been enough to remind her that bravery and recklessness were two very different characteristics. So who could—

James.

He knew the London docks. He knew the great port where massive barges, fishing boats, schooners, and steamers cluttered the Thames as they hauled cargo and passengers in and out of the city. James knew the warehouses packed with goods from all over the world. He knew the rhythm of the docks, the men who worked and supervised, the riggers, shipwrights, lightermen, wharf laborers. He knew the type of boy who frequented the quays.

He would know where to look for Peter Colston.

And yet Talia knew she could not ask him to find a boy who had just been released from prison. For the first time in her life, she couldn't ask James for his help.

If James knew about Peter, she'd have to tell him about her attempts to visit Newhall and about Brick Street, the temporary reformatory school they'd set up in Wapping. And if James knew Talia was working with juvenile delinquents, the big fool would run straight to Alexander, and they'd shut the whole project down right as she and Mr. Fletcher were getting started.

Not to mention what he might discover about Peter.

Talia sighed in frustration. The timing should have been perfect. Her father had left London just as she was implementing the plans for the reformatory school and finishing her report.

Rushton would be gone through the summer, which meant Talia could present her evidence to the House of Commons committee, find a patron for the school, and hopefully garner support among the peerage. When Rushton returned to London in August, he'd find the foundation of the work successfully established...and with any luck would then lend his own support to the cause.

Yes, it should all have gone exactly as Talia planned. She just hadn't counted on James Forester coming back. Much less realizing that he could actually help her, if she still trusted him enough to keep her secret.

She tightened her hand on Alice's arm. She couldn't ask James for help, but she could appeal to the director of the Ragged School Union. "Let me talk to Sir Henry and Mr. Fletcher tomorrow. They'll have an idea of what to do."

Alice swiped at her eyes. "You've already done too much, my lady, but I didn't know where else to go. If Peter gets into trouble again, he'll be lost forever."

"No, he won't. And I wouldn't have offered to help you if I hadn't wanted to." Talia pushed open the front door before Alice could protest. "Come and have a cup of tea."

"No." Alice's eyes skirted past Talia to the marble-floored foyer with its curved staircase and huge, gilt-framed mirror. "I'd best get back. My father will be home soon."

"Very well." Deflecting a pang of regret, Talia released Alice's arm and stepped into the foyer. "I'll call upon you at ten tomorrow morning, and then I'll go to the union offices to speak with Sir Henry. We'll find him, Alice."

Talia couldn't bring herself to add, *"I promise."*

William Lawford watched Alice Colston from a distance. Beautiful, she was. Delicate like a bird, but without the artificial trappings of society. So different from the women of the *ton* with their silk and ribbons. Alice wore plain cotton dresses, and the one time he'd been close enough to see her hands—when she had signed the ledger the first time she came to see her brother at Newhall—William had noticed her roughened skin and short-clipped fingernails.

But, God, she was lovely, with her pale gold hair and Madonna-like features. Blue eyes fringed with long, dark lashes. A rosebud mouth that he couldn't stop staring at as she'd stood in the front office at Newhall and told him she was Peter's sister.

Not once since that day several months ago had William been able to stop thinking of her. He'd almost petitioned for the boy's release himself just so that he could see Alice again when she came to fetch her brother. Instead he'd waited the interminable weeks until the day of Peter's release...only to have his enjoyment over seeing Alice again blackened by the presence of that interfering Lady Talia Hall and her accomplice Fletcher.

Under the guise of giving her a report about Peter's condition, William had visited Alice twice at her family's Bell Lane house. Her wretched father had been there both times, making it impossible for William to speak with Alice alone, but at least he'd been able to gaze at her and hear the sound of her voice.

Now that Peter had been freed, William had to find another excuse to be in her company.

When Alice turned the corner of King's Street, William followed. His heart beat faster as he closed the distance between them.

"Good afternoon, Miss Colston."

She startled, her head turning. "Oh, Mr. Lawford. What are you doing here?"

"I'd thought to pay a visit on Lady Talia Hall when I saw you leaving." He kept his tone politely inquisitive. "You had the same idea."

"Yes. Lady Talia has been very kind to my family, especially after Peter's arrest."

"How did she come to know Peter?"

"He helped her in some way, she once said." Alice reached up to tighten her collar around her neck. "Though she's been more of a help to us."

"And how is Peter faring after his release?" William asked.

"He's begun putting back the weight he'd lost, which is good, but he's still...upset."

William clenched his jaw. Peter had been a problem since the moment he was brought to Newhall. Sullen and defiant in a way William hadn't encountered before.

He knew Peter was afraid of him—several floggings and confinement had ensured that—but the boy had a hard shell that William hadn't been able to crack.

After he'd met Alice, William had tried to make prison life easier for Peter. He'd given Peter extra food, which went uneaten, offered to let him outside in the prison yard longer than the other boys, released him from work duty, allowed him more time in the library.

Peter refused all his efforts, which made William dislike the boy all the more. Not that he would ever let Alice see that.

"Has Peter visited Lady Talia as well?" William asked, tensing as he awaited her response.

"No." Alice's mouth twisted. "She has a place waiting for him at the Brick Street school, but Peter isn't willing to even consider enrolling. I hope it's because he simply needs some time to adjust. I suppose that's one of the reasons Lady Talia thinks boys like Peter should not be sent to prison in the first place."

William smothered a rush of irritation. "Yet incarceration teaches them the ills of wrongdoing and ensures the safety of law-abiding citizens, does it not?"

"Yes, I suppose so."

"I'm sorry Peter served time at Newhall," William said gently. "It's a very run-down institution, likely should never have been reopened. The Shipton Fields prison that I am seeking to establish will be much more expansive, with a large yard, quarters for the warders and chaplain, storerooms, visitors' rooms…and quite a grand lodge for the governor."

His pulse sped up as Alice glanced at him with those blue eyes like marbles. He'd been working on the Shipton Fields bill for more than a year, anticipating having management of his own prison and finally escaping life with his miserable uncle. He also wanted the approbation that would come with the governorship of a brand-new prison, the approval of Lord Thurlow and other peers that might one day lead to his own knighthood for service to the Crown. He wanted the salary that the position would earn, the income from his prisoners' labor.

But not until he met Alice did William realize *why* he wanted all that. He'd thought about it for himself, for the success and recognition he'd long deserved, especially after Elizabeth's betrayal.

Elizabeth. His gut clenched at the thought of her rejection. Her resistance. If she hadn't resisted, he wouldn't have had to force her. If only she'd accepted him, his love, his need for her... instead she'd been horrified by "what he did to her"—ignoring the fact that she had first *let him* touch her—and had refused to see him again.

Then she'd told everyone that he was depraved and of course she could never marry him... well, that had smeared his name all over Lewes, and he'd moved to London shortly thereafter to get away from it.

Elizabeth could rot in hell, for all he cared. The lying cow was nothing compared to the sweet-tempered Miss Alice Colston with her soft, blond hair and eyes the color of cornflowers.

She was now the reason William craved the success of Shipton Fields. With the prison under his command, his newfound association with the peerage, the salary of the governorship... he could court and marry Miss Alice Colston with nothing to stand in his way.

Except, perhaps, her brother, Peter.

"Have you considered asking Lady Talia or Mr. Fletcher for their advice about a new prison for juveniles?" Alice asked.

William choked back a laugh. "I'm afraid we are not in agreement for how best to manage criminals, Miss Colston. I believe in fair treatment, but also that one must pay when one commits a crime. Lady Talia has far too soft a heart when it comes to lawbreakers."

"I don't know that it's possible to have too soft a heart, Mr. Lawford," Alice murmured.

"Soft hearts are easily crushed, Miss Colston."

"They're also resilient, aren't they?" Faint amusement curved her lovely mouth. "Wouldn't you rather have a heart like a pillow rather than one made of crystal?"

William stared at her lips, not caring what material constituted his heart as long as he could give it to her.

"Of course," he murmured.

Her smile faded a bit as she turned her face forward again and continued walking. William stepped closer to her, his arm brushing the sleeve of her coat. As much as he disliked the idea of using her, he thought it would be helpful if she were to say good things about him to Lady Talia and whatever other member of the *ton* she might happen to encounter.

Alice would never be cruel enough to speak ill of another person—least of all William Lawford, who had been nothing but kind to her and her brother.

He just had to ensure Peter Colston did nothing to ruin that impression.

Chapter Five

James smiled and nodded in response to whatever the chit beside him was saying. He took another swallow of champagne, his eyes narrowing as he tracked Talia's progress across the ballroom. He'd been back in London for three days and had already determined Talia was definitely hiding something. Not only from her father and brothers, but now from James as well. He intended to find out what it was.

"An *elephant*, he said," the young woman went on, her eyes wide with amazement. "Is that true, my lord?"

"It is, Miss Dunnett." James forced his gaze away from Talia and smiled at Miss Dunnett. Wouldn't do to have the woman feel slighted by his lack of attention. Wouldn't do to have anyone think ill of him.

Society had been scathingly critical of the Halls following Lady Rushton's affair and the earl's subsequent petition of divorce, so James had seen the vile nature of scandal. He also knew well how people could ignore what was right before their eyes. How they could pretend nothing bad was happening so they wouldn't feel guilty for not trying to stop it.

James would not be at society's mercy the way the Halls had been. He would not be ignored the way his mother had been. He would court society with smiles and rollicking tales of adventure, never giving anyone reason to think he disliked them all. Never giving them reason to think he had anything to hide.

"Do you know, my father was once nearly trampled to *death* by an elephant?" Miss Dunnett continued. "He was in India, the Deccan...oh, perhaps four years ago, and he accompanied several game hunters—*shikarees*, aren't they called?—to hunt wild boars in the most treacherous *jungle* you can imagine. Oh, isn't that silly of me to say, though? You've probably *charted* that very jungle, haven't you?"

James chuckled, hoping he looked attentive enough as he tried to find Talia in the crush again. Miss Dunnett's musical voice drummed in his ears. He caught a glimpse of Talia's chestnut hair, smooth as silk, her dark blue gown a contrast to the lacy dresses in shades of pink and green worn by other young women.

She will listen to you. Northwood's certain words rang like a ship's bell in his mind. Even North knew of James's influence over Talia. James had known her since she was a child, yet he was not her brother. That fact alone meant that Talia had at least always listened to his advice.

Only now did he realize that her professed love had also likely contributed to her trust in him.

Regret seized him. He hated remembering that afternoon at Floreston Manor. Hated remembering how he'd hurt Talia. How he'd reacted with uncontrollable pleasure to the press of her mouth and—

His spine stiffened. Lord Margate, a young, insolent heir to a marquess, had approached Talia, his gaze on her face, a smile tugging at his mouth. She stopped as he spoke to her, but her posture was tense.

"...then hunting tigers on *foot*," Miss Dunnett was saying.

"Do forgive me, Miss Dunnett," James muttered, shoving through the crowd to Talia's side.

Just as he reached her, Margate put his hand on Talia's arm. She jerked away.

"There are you, Lady Talia." James stepped slightly in front of her, putting himself between her and the younger man. He kept his tone pleasant, but narrowed his eyes. "Margate isn't disturbing you, is he?"

"Of course not." Margate moved back, holding up a hand in defense. He glanced from Talia to James with a frown.

"Good. My lady, your aunt is looking for you." James extended his arm to Talia as the other man slunk away. "I'll be pleased to take you to her."

"I don't wish to be taken, my lord," Talia replied.

The chill in her voice did nothing to stop a blatantly provocative image from appearing in James's mind. An image of him *taking* her. He inhaled a hard breath before turning to face her. Talia's expression was set, her eyes lit with irritation.

"What do you think you're doing?" she snapped.

"Helping you," he retorted. "Margate is an insufferable rogue. You should not be speaking to him."

"You've no right to tell me what to do, James." She retreated a few steps. "I was speaking with Lord Margate about a business matter."

"Then why did he try to touch you?"

She didn't respond, but he saw the pain flash in her green eyes.

"Still?" James spoke through clenched teeth. "Men like him still treat you as if you're no better than…"

… *your mother.*

He bit off the words when Talia paled. James despised Lady Rushton for what she'd done to her family, but the woman would always be Talia's mother. James knew well how complex feelings toward one's mother could be.

He stepped closer to Talia and lowered his voice. "I'd understood the matter had been put to rest."

"The *matter* is not your concern, James," Talia snapped. "Just as *I* am not."

Anger flared in his chest. "You will always be my concern, Talia."

"No. Your concern will always lie with responsibility, won't it, James? With loyalty to my brothers? You wouldn't have even come to see me if it hadn't been for Alexander." She paused, her mouth compressing. "True or false, James?"

James fisted his hands, hating his cowardice. "It had nothing to do with you, Talia. I'm here for just a few weeks to—"

His voice broke off. He stared at her, his heart thudding. He'd looked into her eyes countless times over the years, never failing to notice how they were composed of multiple shades of green—emerald, jade, viridian.

Her eyelashes were black and glossy like the wings of a crow, a striking contrast to her pale skin.

God, she was a beauty. How was it possible that no man had moved heaven and earth to marry her? To claim her as his own?

Regret stabbed him. He couldn't give her what she sought, couldn't leave a wife behind while he explored the world. And he wouldn't allow marriage to tie him to London either, this wretched city where bitter memories lingered like smoke.

He'd given Talia an honest, honorable response, but he would forever hate himself for hurting her.

"True or false, James?" she repeated.

"False." His throat nearly closed over the lie. "Of course I'd have paid you a visit, poppet."

A shadow crossed her expression. He cursed inwardly.

"Talia, I don't want this to be difficult."

"Then don't lie to me! You said you wanted things to be as they were before, but you didn't write me one letter, and you would not have come to visit me if Alexander hadn't asked you to. I heard you say as much to Aunt Sally."

His heart sank. "I didn't mean—"

"I know what you meant, James, so stop trying to convince me you're here because you want to be." She stepped away from him. "Stop trying to pretend nothing has changed."

"What would you have me do then, Talia?"

"Go and find someone else to fulfill your responsibility," she replied as she turned and walked away. "And leave me alone."

I can't.

＊　＊　＊

James pushed through the crowd and found Margate heading toward a group of young women clustered by the terrace doors. He grabbed the other man's arm.

"What did Lady Talia speak with you about?" he asked.

Margate tried to dislodge James's grip. "Why don't you ask her?"

"She said it was a business matter. What did she mean?"

"She wants a patron for her bloody school, of course."

"What school?"

"For poor children or something like that," Margate said. "She's such a humanity-monger, always trying to pinch our pockets for one cause or another. Thinks she can escape her mother's shadow, I expect."

James shoved Margate hard enough to send the other man back a few steps. He curled his hands into fists, wishing he could strike a blow as Margate smirked, straightened his collar, and continued on his way.

Taking a breath to quell his anger, James followed the path Talia had woven through the crowd. He found her speaking to another man . . . only this time, she looked as if she wanted to engage in conversation. James eyed the man warily—tall with blond hair and a somewhat arrogant look about him.

Suppressing the urge to intercede again, he grabbed a glass from a passing server just as Talia looked in his direction. Their gazes met, a sizzling glance that jolted a rush of heat through James's entire body. He swallowed the champagne and tried to smother his desire, tried to remind himself that he had to leave her alone.

James cursed inwardly. The problem was he didn't *want* to leave her alone. Now that he was here, now that he'd seen her again…he remembered how much he'd always wanted her company.

Talia had always been the one steady presence in his life as he'd moved from one place to the next as fast as he could, never able to settle in one place, but always knowing she was *there*. She didn't even realize what a bright, pretty light she'd been in the darkness of his childhood and again in the days following his mother's death.

She didn't know how much he'd always loved writing her those long, news-filled letters. Hunched in a tent on an African plain, pitching to and fro on a ship…he'd clutched a pencil and written *My dear Talia* countless times, always picturing her curled in a chair beside the fire, her hair gleaming with gold light as she read about his adventures and mishaps.

My dear Talia…you would love looking at the sky…I have never imagined it contained so many millions of stars…I walked today to the rocky summit of Notre-Dame de la Garde in Marseille…flags of all the nations flying, with the dark blue waves of the Mediterranean Sea in the distance…I met not a single person on the path to the castle of Jedin, only timid gazelles and partridges with whom I shared my lunch of bread and cheese…a lagoon surrounded by coral sand and coconut trees…

How he'd missed writing to her this past year. Every day he'd thought of her as he reached for a pencil and his notebook.

I must tell Talia about that…Talia will laugh when I tell her…Talia will never believe it when I…Talia would love this…I'll save that pretty rock for Talia…

Then he'd fought the urge to write her a letter and scribbled in his journal again, a damned coward afraid of what he'd inadvertently tell the woman who had fearlessly declared her love for him and then borne the brunt of his rejection.

Not once had he thought his lack of correspondence would hurt her.

What an idiot he was. He'd left Talia with the dictate that everything would be the same between them, yet he'd been the one to sever contact with her because he was scared. And that had just hurt her all over again.

He had to set things right between them. Not just because of his promise to Alexander, but for the sake of his and Talia's friendship. Because he had to fix what he'd broken.

He had no idea how he'd do that while also determining what she was hiding, but he'd find a way.

He stared at her. She blinked, her lips parting, her skin flushed with warmth from the overheated room.

James wanted to kiss her again. Wanted to taste her, to strip that gown from her shoulders and expose the pale expanse of her skin and rosy-tipped breasts—

Stop. A growl spread through his chest. He would not do this. Not with Talia.

Bloody hell. It had been too long since he'd been with a woman. That was the problem. He'd never been one to frequent brothels like other young men, preferring instead to indulge in discreet affairs. Not always easy when one traveled so often, but he'd never had trouble finding a woman willing to satisfy his needs.

Except that for...what, eight months now...he hadn't even wanted to look for one. The summer following Talia's confession of love, James had tried to forget her by engaging in an affair with a nurse in New South Wales, but that had ended when he'd left for the outback. And there, in the rocky, wind-whipped plains with stars sprinkled like sugar overhead, his all-consuming thoughts of Talia had begun.

"Fancy a game of cards, Castle?"

James took a breath to get himself under control before glancing to his right, where Benjamin Walker, Lord Ridley, had stopped. A fellow student at university, Ridley was an affable young man with brown hair and a wide, open smile that made him a favorite among society's mothers.

James pointed his chin toward the blond man who was still speaking with Talia. "What do you know of him?"

"Lawford? Decent sort of chap, I suppose. He is persuading Lord Thurlow to help with a proposal for a new prison."

James jerked his head around to stare at Ridley. "A prison?"

Ridley nodded. "He's deputy governor at Newhall in Middlesex."

"What is Newhall?"

"Prison for juveniles. Old building, but they reopened it to get rid of juvenile wings in other gaols because they were getting too crowded with other criminals."

A combination of fear and anticipation flared in

James's chest. He was getting closer to finding out the truth, but he still hated the words *prison* and *criminals* being anywhere near the name *Talia*.

"Do Lawford and Lady Talia work together in any way?" he asked.

"Don't think so, though I know she's been asked to give evidence at the House meeting later this month."

"What meeting?"

"Something to do with prisons. Other than that, one doesn't hear much about Lady Talia Hall these days."

James didn't know whether to be pleased or angry about that statement. He'd kill anyone who spread malicious gossip about Talia. But how could society ignore a woman so lovely and intelligent, a woman whose qualities far surpassed those of anyone else in the *ton*?

"Cards?" Ridley asked again.

James nodded. "Just going to get a drink first."

"I'll be at the vingt-et-un table." Ridley sauntered toward the card room.

James grabbed another drink and glowered at the deputy governor, sensing Lawford was the key to unlocking whatever Talia was hiding.

And not liking that thought one bit.

The smells of fish and salt water assailed Peter Colston's nose, cleansing the lingering stink of rotten straw and waste that had permeated Newhall prison. Shops lining the streets of Wapping displayed maritime goods—brass sextants, hammocks, sailors' shoes, pilot coats, and oiled nor'westers. Provision agents hawked cases of meat and biscuits packaged for ship storage, and the sail makers' workshops emitted the burned smell of tar.

Peter quickened his pace, enjoying the freedom of being able to go wherever he wanted. The gates of St. Katharine's Docks were open, allowing a stream of people to pass in and out—laborers, sailors, butchers, clerks. A forest of masts and flags rose from the ships clustered in the basin, and the air was thick with smoke, tobacco, and sulfur.

A foreman stood on a box outside Warehouse Five, shouting out the day's work as hopeful laborers crowded around him. Knowing he was too late to be hired for a day's work, Peter stopped along the edge of the quay. He looked at a massive steamer with its gilt stern and mahogany wheels, wondering where it was going next.

The unease he'd felt since leaving Newhall dissipated a bit in these familiar surroundings. As much as he'd wanted his freedom, for the past nine months he had feared what awaited him back in London.

He still did. He couldn't go to that Brick Street school like his father and Alice wanted him to. He'd left school when he was ten because he couldn't understand the lessons, not even the alphabet. Before his eyes, the letters swam like fish beneath rippling water, always changing and escaping his comprehension. Numbers were the same, and none of his teachers had ever understood his lack of ability to read or write.

What else was left for Peter to do? He could work at the docks, but there was no guarantee of being hired...and no future in it either, as his father would say.

He couldn't even hope to be a dockmaster one day to oversee the loading and unloading of cargo. Those men were always reviewing written orders and delivery descriptions. Always tallying numbers of crates and hours for the counting house.

Guilt bit into Peter. He was either too much trouble for his family or useless. And though he was grateful to Alice for insisting he come home after Newhall, part of Peter wished she hadn't bothered with him. At least then, he wouldn't feel obligated to her. At least he'd only be responsible for himself.

Sunlight shredded the morning fog into gauzy wisps. He squinted out at the boats. For all its chaos, Peter liked the docks. He was comfortable here, knowing he could do any work required of him, from loading to winch work. He liked the huge ships and fishing boats, the passenger steamers heading off to all parts of the world, the clanking noise of rusty anchors lowering.

After checking in a few of the warehouses and being told there was no work available, Peter returned to the highway. He stopped at a fish shop and bought a cone of fried fish, which he ate while walking down the street and looking through the store windows. He tossed the empty wrapper away and pulled open the door of a shop that sold ships' instruments.

The shopkeeper glanced his way, but otherwise made no remark. Astonishing what clean clothes and a haircut could do. Nine months ago, the shopkeeper would have thrown Peter out on his ear.

He stepped toward one of the cases displaying compasses. The round, shiny faces looked up at him, etched with markings that Peter didn't understand but intrigued him nonetheless.

"Can I see that one?" he asked, pointing at a brass compass attached to a chain.

The shopkeeper unlocked the case and opened the compass lid before putting it in Peter's hand. "Inscription of the maker on the back."

Peter stared at the compass, watching the needle settle to the north. He would never be able to actually read a compass, but he liked looking at them. He liked the smooth weight in his hand, the way the needle swung around the face, the idea that if you had a compass, you could go anywhere on earth and still know where you were.

"Hello, Peter."

A shiver ran down Peter's spine. He turned to find Lawford standing in the doorway, his expression grave. He wore a fine blue coat and trousers that were less imposing than his uniform at Newhall, but still Peter felt his nerves tense.

"Sir," he muttered, his hand tightening around the compass. "How did you know I was here?"

"I remembered Wapping is your haunt and assumed you would come back here upon your release," Lawford remarked. "And your sister told me you left yesterday morning and hadn't come home yet."

Unease roiled in Peter at the idea that Lawford had spoken with Alice.

"How does it feel, finally being out of prison?" Lawford asked.

The shopkeeper glanced sharply at Peter. "I don't want any trouble here."

Peter set the compass back on the counter. "No trouble."

"You're bound to find trouble if you frequent these parts again," Lawford warned. He stepped into the shop, his blond hair darkening in the shadows. He wasn't a big man, but he was tall, and the sheer presence of him seemed to block the doorway.

Peter swallowed. Sweat pricked his forehead. How many times had he been trapped in his cell at Newhall with Lawford standing in the doorway, piercing him with that stare...

He rubbed his damp palms on his trousers. "Just...just leaving, sir."

Christ. He was *free* now. And still just the sight of Lawford made him cringe like a scared rabbit.

"Your sister told me you don't intend to enroll at Brick Street," Lawford continued.

"I...I don't reckon so," Peter stammered. The fish he'd eaten tumbled greasily in his stomach.

"I'd suggest you stay away from Brick Street." Lawford stepped toward him, reaching out to take the compass. "Lady Talia is hoping you will testify with her at the House of Commons meeting about the treatment of juvenile prisoners. Though I know you would never speak against Newhall, you would be well advised to avoid such...temptation."

Peter shook his head. He couldn't speak past the tightness in his throat.

He still didn't understand what had happened during his time at Newhall. He'd struggled to prove to Lawford he couldn't be broken, that he was too tough, but Lawford had won in the end. Months of enforced silence, hunger, confinement, and floggings had imprinted fear in every cell of Peter's body.

And then, perhaps two months before his release, Lawford had changed. Given Peter extra food, stopped inflicting the harsher punishments, offered him extra time in the yard. Peter hadn't wanted any of it, but he hadn't understood Lawford's change of heart either.

"I don't want nothin' to do with her ladyship," he muttered, which was the unvarnished truth. In fact, he wished he'd never encountered the woman.

"Good," Lawford said, tilting the compass as he watched the needle turn. "Because Lady Talia can be...persuasive. So I'd suggest you avoid her."

Peter nodded, unable to stand the confines of the shop any longer. He ducked past Lawford and back out the door, inhaling a hard rush of air into his lungs.

He glanced behind him once to see if Lawford was following. Goddamn, he hated his fear of the man. Almost more than he hated the man himself.

Chapter Six

$\mathcal{I}$'m certain he'll return soon." William Lawford crossed one leg over the other as he settled into a chair in the Colstons' front parlor, looking as if he were entirely comfortable in his surroundings.

Talia smothered a stab of discomfort. When Alice had come to her yesterday morning with concerns about Peter, she hadn't mentioned she had also asked Mr. Lawford for help. Talia wondered how many times Lawford had called upon Alice Colston when her father was at work, as he was now. The idea of Lawford alone with Alice sent a shiver of repulsion down Talia's spine, especially when she recalled the speculating way he had looked at Alice when they were at Newhall.

"You've been here often, Mr. Lawford?" she asked, glancing toward the parlor door to ensure Alice wasn't approaching just yet.

"On occasion. Consider it my duty to ensure a boy is faring well upon his release from Newhall, but I can't say I expected much from Peter, considering his...history."

Guilt flared through Talia like a struck match. She managed to keep her voice steady as she said, "Did Alice ask your help in looking for him?"

Lawford nodded. "Couldn't find him this morning, but I'm visiting the Wapping police station later today. I'll speak with the constable about Peter. He's rather well known to them. They'll keep an eye out for him, if I ask them to."

"I would appreciate that, Mr. Lawford." Alice Colston entered with a tea tray. "My father will not allow Peter another chance. If he doesn't attend Brick Street by the end of the week, he'll be forced to leave the house."

"Forgive me, Miss Colston, but perhaps that's exactly what Peter wants," Lawford remarked.

"Peter is my younger brother, Mr. Lawford. I won't give up on him."

"An admirable devotion, Miss Colston," Lawford murmured, his gaze on her face.

A pink flush colored Alice's cheeks as she handed him a cup of tea. Talia set her teeth, disliking all the implications of Lawford's attention toward Alice...and Alice's response.

"How is your uncle, Mr. Lawford?" Talia asked brightly.

Lawford's mouth thinned with disgust. "The same, my lady, thank you for asking. He intends to retire soon, after which Newhall and eventually the Shipton Fields prison will be under my governorship. Did I tell you more about the lodging for the governor and warders, Miss Colston?"

Alice shook her head, tucking a stray lock of hair beneath her cap as she settled beside him on the sofa. "Please do, Mr. Lawford. It sounds quite impressive."

Unwilling to leave her friend alone with Lawford, Talia waited for another forty-five minutes before Lawford finally left; then she told Alice she'd stop at the Ragged School Union offices to speak with Sir Henry after running another errand.

"If Peter does come home, I'll send word," Alice promised. "Though I'm not hopeful."

Neither was Talia. For some reason, Peter Colston seemed determined to make life difficult for himself, a tendency that likely had grown stronger during his incarceration at Newhall. Talia took her leave of Alice, wrestling with the uncomfortable feeling that she needed to find Peter before Lawford did.

She tilted her hat against the morning sun as she stepped outside. Her father's carriage waited at the curb, and she instructed the driver to take her to Mudie's Library on bustling New Oxford Street. Shelves of books and journals lined the interior of the shop, and several patrons sat at the desks situated along the walls.

"Good morning, my lady." Mr. Hammersmith, a tall, thin man with a fringe of white hair, stood from behind the front counter as Talia approached. "The magazines from America arrived just two days ago. We've got them packaged up for you."

He hefted a tied bundle of magazines onto the counter.

"Lovely, thank you. And do you have the recent editions of the *Boys' Journal*?"

"Yes, I'll fetch it for you. Would you care to have a

look around? We just received some new books for children."

Talia nodded and went to the shelves where Mr. Mudie kept the most recent arrivals. There were several books of stories for children, and a primer on geography. She paged through the primer, which included lessons on the shape of the earth and how to read maps. She looked at maps of the vast United States, the Russian colony in northwest America, and the continent of Africa.

She loved maps, all the curves and lines representing mountain ranges, oceans, cities, wide plains, and valleys. When James was off on his expeditions, Talia could look at a map and imagine where he was at any given moment. She could picture him hiking through a jungle, climbing a mountain peak, guiding a boat over a serpentine river.

Warmth filled her chest. She tried to smother it, tried to remind herself that she no longer felt anything for the man who had rejected her.

Then his voice spilled over her like a ray of sunshine on a chilly day.

"Good morning, my lady."

Talia turned, her heart giving a wild leap at the sight of James standing just behind her. A shaft of light gilded his brown hair, and his eyes crinkled with a warm amusement that never failed to ignite flutters in Talia's belly.

She clutched the primer to her chest, as if she could use it as a barrier between them. "How did you know I was here?"

"Soames told me you'd intended to come here during your errands."

"And why did you go to the King's Street house?"

"I wanted to apologize." He stepped toward one of the shelves and picked up a thin book of lessons. "I should have written to you, poppet. I did want to."

Talia didn't bother asking why he hadn't, then. She already knew. However, her embarrassment over that afternoon at Floreston Manor was tempered by the memory of how he had responded to her kiss. As if he'd been unable to stop himself from surrendering.

She gazed at his profile as he opened the book and studied the contents. So familiar, yet completely different. Sharp nose, strong cheekbones, and jaw dusted with whiskers. A shiver ran down Talia's spine as she remembered how the scrape of his stubble had felt against her skin.

"Do you remember 'A was Apollo'?" James asked, glancing up from the book.

Talia shook her head, even as a tendril of warmth curled through her heart. When they were children, James and her brothers had taught Talia several verses to help her memorize lessons.

"The god of the carol," James prompted, his warm brown gaze still on her, potent as a touch.

"James—" Talia swallowed hard. Memories stirred in the back of her mind, pressing for entry, asking her to remember the many cherished moments she'd shared with James. The moments that had culminated in her love for him.

"B stood for Bacchus, astride his barrel," he said.

"What is the point of this?"

"C for good Ceres," he continued, edging a bit closer to her so they were concealed by the stacks of books, "the goddess of grist."

"And D was Diana, who wouldn't be kissed." Talia stepped back, fighting the wave of nostalgia that swept through her. "Enough, James. Those days are long gone."

"Nothing remembered between two people is ever gone, Talia."

Heat flooded Talia's cheeks. A faint disconcertion darkened James's eyes as he appeared to realize what he'd just implied.

Talia turned away from him and went to the front counter, where Mr. Hammersmith was tying up her bundles of books. She still couldn't reconcile everything she'd felt since discovering James had returned—she held so much love for all their cherished childhood memories. Yet now those memories were bittersweet and tarnished with Talia's realization that her long-held dreams of James Forester would never come true.

James stopped next to her at the counter. Awareness moved through Talia at the sensation of his strong body beside hers, that innate sensation that she was safe and protected.

"That will be all, Mr. Hammersmith, thank you," she said. "Please put everything on my bill."

Before she could scoop up the books, James hefted the stack into his arms and opened the front door for her.

"The Ragged School Union offices," she told the driver as James handed her into the carriage.

As she had known he would, he climbed in behind her and shut the door.

"Lawford," he said.

Talia's heart jumped. She lifted her head to stare at James.

"I saw you speaking with him last night," James said, folding his arms across his chest. "Ridley informed me he's the deputy governor of Newhall prison."

Rather than implicate herself, Talia chose to remain silent. Her stomach tightened.

"And Northwood got word from a friend of his that you visited Smithton prison recently," James continued.

Oh, no.

Talia's breath escaped her in a rush, her pulse pounding with trepidation. She curled her fingers into the seat cushion and tried to conceal her sudden fear.

"Er, Alex... Alexander knows about that?"

James nodded, regarding her steadily. "But he doesn't know why."

And he asked me to find out. He didn't have to say the words. Talia knew her brother and she knew James Forester. Of course they would both want to know why she was visiting a prison.

"Alexander is concerned about your safety, Talia," James said. "As am I. Tell me why you went."

The faint note of command in his voice prickled her nerves. She certainly wouldn't tell him the truth simply because he ordered her to. Besides, telling James anything about Brick Street would be a huge risk, akin to having confessed her love for him. And that had turned out an unmitigated disaster.

Resolve filled her. She would not allow either Alexander or James to divert her from her path. This was the first time in years that she had actually felt useful, felt as if she could do something in the world, and nothing would take her from it.

Not even James.

"It's simply part of my charity work," she told him, gazing out the window.

"Yet you've not had need to visit prisons before."

"You haven't been here for a year, James. You have no idea what I have or haven't done."

She experienced a grim satisfaction when he didn't respond to the truth of her statement.

She looked at him again. Her breath caught. In the darkened interior of the carriage, his eyes glittered. He was staring at her mouth. Talia parted her lips to draw in a breath as heat bloomed in her chest.

No. No. Foolish girl, you can't possibly…

Her eyes lowered to his mouth—the beautiful shape of his lips that had fit so seamlessly against hers. She could almost feel it now, the hot press of their kiss and the way their tongues had met. The mere taste of such intimacy had caused all sorts of heated thoughts to deluge Talia's mind during the past year. If a thirty-second kiss with James Forester could ignite such fire in her blood, what would further intimacies do to her?

Only in a shadowed, secret area of her heart did Talia admit she would still very much like to find out.

She tore her gaze from James, aware of her increased breathing. His presence seemed to fill the enclosed space of the carriage. Even with his rejection of her hovering like a shadow between them, James still embodied all the qualities Talia so admired. Boldness, daring, the urge to succeed and carve uncharted paths.

He was still looking at her. She felt his gaze like a touch. She remembered the warmth of his large palm as he rested his hand against the side of her face.

How different her life would be if he had reciprocated her love...

Stop!

The order snapped into her brain. Talia straightened her spine. She refused to be a lovesick wench, even in the privacy of her own mind. It was over. James could bluster all he wanted about needing to ensure her safety, but Talia knew his reasons had nothing to do with her. He'd agreed to look after her because of his loyalty to Alexander. Not because he was genuinely concerned about her well-being.

And if he could use her to get what he wanted, then she could certainly use him to get what she wanted. She just had to remember that what she wanted was most assuredly *not* him.

James followed Talia from the carriage to the Exeter Hall offices of the Ragged School Union. He carried most of the books, while the footman trailed behind with the journals and magazines.

Gentlemen and a few ladies occupied the corridors of the building, pausing every so often to consult with each other about one matter or another. Talia strode up the steps to a glass-windowed door that bore a painted sign: *Sir Henry Clark, Director*. After a knock, the man's voice bade them enter.

"Lady Talia, an honor to see you here." A rotund man stood from behind a paper-strewn desk and approached, a smile breaking out from behind his whiskers. "I hadn't expected you until later this afternoon."

"It's a bit of an impromptu visit, Sir Henry." She gestured for James and the footman to put their books and journals on a nearby table; then the footman departed. "I've just visited Mr. Mudie's Library and picked up some things I thought the boys would like."

"I see." Sir Henry looked as if he didn't, in fact, see. "Er, you wouldn't care to bring them directly to—"

"Not yet," Talia interrupted, her voice bright. "I thought I might store them here for the time being, if you don't mind?"

"Of course not." Sir Henry looked inquisitively from Talia to James.

Talia made quick work of the introductions, then added, "Lord Castleford is leaving London again soon, Sir Henry. He's heading an expedition to Siberia. Won't that be exciting?"

Irritation prickled James's neck. Every time she introduced him to someone, she remarked that he was *leaving again soon* in that light tone that suggested they needn't trouble themselves by involving him in anything important. Because he'd be leaving again soon. Off on another adventure.

He turned to examine the books he had left on the table. Tried to ignore the discomfort rising in him. Talia had always respected his travels, always reacted to them with admiration and a hint of wistfulness. Now she seemed almost...indulgent about the idea, as if his taking to the sea were a childish whim they should all merely tolerate.

James glanced to where she stood across the room. She was speaking with Sir Henry in a low voice, her expression serious as she nodded in response to his remarks about the new Bethnal Green school.

James took advantage of Talia's distraction to gaze at

her for a long moment. Her chestnut hair was tucked beneath her hat, a few loose curls spilling down to caress her neck. She wore a dark blue gown that fitted her curves, but lacked any fanciful embellishments to attract attention. Her profile was lovely as ever, with high cheekbones and those full lips that had haunted James's dreams. Only her green eyes had changed, a new guardedness concealing the warm innocence he remembered from a year ago.

He hated the idea that he might have been the cause of it, though he wasn't arrogant enough to imagine Talia had been pining after him for all these months. Perhaps something else had happened to contribute to her new solemnity.

Perhaps she might even have told him what it was, if he'd deigned to write to her this past year. He smothered another surge of regret and turned back to the books.

A knock on the door preceded another man's entrance. Thin and of medium height, he wore a plain black coat and hat, which shadowed his features. The gleam of his spectacles further obscured his expression. He paused at the doorway, his gaze passing over James to where Talia stood by the windows.

"Mr. Fletcher!" Talia looked up and smiled, crossing the room in a rustle of skirts. "I hadn't expected..."

Her voice faltered suddenly as she caught James's eye. She stopped.

"I hadn't expected you to be here today," she told the newcomer.

"I'd hoped to find you, my lady."

The man removed his hat, revealing sharp, narrow features and dark brows. His hair was cropped very short, and he looked to be several years younger than James. Closer to Talia's twenty-four than his own thirty-one.

"I received your message about Peter Colston," the man continued. "I'd intended to visit Brick Street this afternoon and can—"

"Just a moment, Mr. Fletcher, please." Her smile firmly in place, Talia turned to James. "Lord Castleford, this is Mr. Fletcher. Mr. Fletcher, Lord Castleford is an old friend of the family and recently returned from a journey to Australia."

James almost gritted his teeth as he waited for her to tell the man he was "leaving again soon."

"My lord, Mr. Matthew Fletcher is one of our teachers," Talia said, her voice putting an oddly firm stop at the end of that introduction.

James shook Fletcher's hand and spoke a few rote words of greeting. "What is your subject of specialty?" he asked, out of politeness rather than genuine interest.

"I prefer the sciences, personally, but our curriculum allows me to teach everything from reading to history and geography." Mr. Fletcher glanced at Talia. "But about Peter Colston—"

"Yes, we'll discuss it later, please," Talia said.

Fletcher blinked at the order, then nodded.

James frowned. He'd never known Talia to interrupt so often. As if she feared what people were about to say.

"Lord Castleford is only in London for a short time," Talia continued. "He's leaving in June for another expedition to—"

"I'm here for the remainder of the month," James interrupted. "And I'd hoped to be of some service to your organization during my stay."

The words surprised him as much as they appeared to surprise Talia.

"You want to help the ragged schools?" she asked, as if the idea were absurd.

"You needn't sound so shocked," James muttered, irritation biting at him. "I've engaged in a number of good works myself."

"How are you able to help, my lord?" Sir Henry asked.

"Well, I...I could assist Lady Talia with whatever tasks are necessary."

Talia swiveled toward the door, her movements sharp and abrupt. "Sir Henry, Mr. Fletcher, please excuse us for a moment. A word, my lord?"

Feeling as if he were about to receive a scolding, James followed her from the room. His gaze moved to the tapered curve of her waist as she strode down the corridor in front of him. Talia opened another door and gestured for him to follow her into an empty office. She closed the door behind him, her eyes flaring with sudden ire.

"Who do you think you are, James?" she snapped.

He stepped back, startled. "I'm the same man I always was."

"You are not." Talia paced halfway across the room, her hands fisting into her skirts. "You're offering your help because you told Alexander you'd *look after* me. Not because you truly want to help."

James frowned. "You're the one who is withholding information from Northwood, Talia. Perhaps if you'd been honest with him and your father, he wouldn't have reason for concern."

"Alexander *invents* reasons to worry about me, James." She spread her hands, her shoulders tense with frustration. "Everything I do gives him cause for concern. Did you ever consider I might be protecting him by not divulging my every move?"

"How is that protecting him?"

"He's happy now." Talia spun on her heel and paced toward him, her skirts swirling about her ankles. "He has a lovely wife, a daughter he adores, and now a newborn son... certainly he doesn't need unfounded concerns about me to tarnish his happiness."

"And yet they are." James grasped her arms to prevent her from spinning away from him again. A little gasp caught in her throat, and his entire body reacted to both the sound and the sensation of her warmth burning clear through the sleeves of her dress.

Then she looked up at him, and her green eyes seared past his defenses, as if she could see right into the place in his heart that was reserved only for her. James took a breath and tried to focus, tried to pull his mind from the growing knowledge that he wanted to do anything Talia asked of him.

"Why else would Alexander have asked me to look after you?" he asked. "If you don't want him to worry, if you've nothing to hide, then you'll accept my help."

She glared at him, her features set mutinously. "I don't want the kind of help you're offering."

"What kind is that?"

"The kind where you swoop in for a fortnight, make people *depend* on you, and then leave again." Talia yanked herself from his grip and stepped back, her chest heaving. "Just like you did with Alexander's Society of Arts exhibition last year. You do the same thing every time you return to London, and this time I won't allow it."

"Why the bloody hell not?"

"Because I don't want to be indebted to you!"

"I would never consider you indebted to me," James retorted.

"But *I* would." Talia shook her head and stalked to the other side of the room again. "You can't do this and run away again, James. I won't let you."

He stared at her. "Run away?"

Talia turned, sorrow darkening her eyes. "I meant—"

"You *said* run away. Is that what you think I do?"

When she didn't respond, a foreboding filled his chest. He knew he'd hurt her—he'd spent the last year hating himself for it—but he couldn't stand the idea that she thought him a coward. Not Talia, who had always looked at him with such admiration.

Until he'd shattered whatever illusions she'd held about him.

A moment passed with the beat of forever. They stared at each other, a palpable energy crackling between them. His pulse raced. Even across the expanse of the room, James could feel the heat of her green eyes, the warmth of her body. He could still feel *her*, all the emotions radiating from her. Determination. Anger. Passion.

In three long strides, James closed the distance between them. His throat tightened with irritation and another emotion he could not name. He stopped in front of her, staring down into her vivid eyes, fringed with thick dark lashes, and the succulent curve of her mouth that had haunted both his waking and nighttime dreams.

He lifted his hand to cup her chin, tilting her face toward the light. Her skin was fine as silk, pale but for the faint color cresting her high cheekbones. A visible tremble went through her as her lips parted to draw in a breath. Heat slid into James's veins as he recalled the soft, hot press of her mouth, the crackling urgency as she fit herself against him and opened to let him inside...

A growl started in James's chest as he grabbed Talia's shoulders and pulled her to him. Before he could think, before he could stop himself, he lowered his head and captured her mouth with his. Talia gasped, a breathy little sound that jolted arousal through his entire body. Even now, even with all that lay between them, she folded herself against him without hesitation, as if she knew that their essential bond of trust was still strong and true.

James cupped her face, angling his mouth more securely over hers as the heat of her breath warmed him from the inside out. Her breasts pressed against his chest, their soft fullness evident even through the constriction of her corset. Lust pooled through his groin. Part of his mind still prickled with shock over the swiftness of his reaction—to Talia, of all people, the one steady feminine presence in his entire life—while another part of him wondered at how natural it felt, how easy.

She fit against him like a puzzle piece locking into place, her curves molding against the planes of his torso, her arms twining around his neck. She tasted sweet, like apples and sugar, and when she parted her lips under his and touched her tongue to his, all reason fled James's brain. He deepened the kiss, his erection pressing hard against the front of his trousers, his mind filling with images of Talia naked beneath him, her gasps hot in his ear and her body opening for him.

He muttered her name, hearing it break between them on an exhale of breath. He grasped the back of her neck and fought the urge to bury his hands in her hair, to yank her hat off and tug her hair from the pins. He imagined her stripped bare, letting him caress every inch of her naked flesh, her pink-tipped breasts overflowing his hands, her hips pushing forward as she begged for his touch...

Talia moaned. The soft noise filled him with heat and the urgency for more. James gripped the nape of her neck and broke away, his chest heaving as he stared into her lust-dark eyes.

A sudden anger rose in him, mingling with his shocking urgency—anger at Talia for making him want her in the most lewd and carnal of ways. For making him feel things for her that he had no right to feel.

Talia lifted a trembling hand to touch his mouth, her fingertips light as feathers. With her forefinger, she traced the line of his lower lip.

"I've dreamed of you," she confessed, her breath catching on a husky note.

James closed his eyes, fighting a resurgence of near-overwhelming urgency.

"Talia." His voice was strangled. "I will not..."

"Yes, that's what you said last time, isn't it?" She

swept her finger into the notch beneath his lower lip. A hard tremble coursed through him. "*This will not happen*, you said. And yet you were the one who surrendered."

James swallowed hard against the rising shame. He may have rejected her, but he had the sudden and unwelcome sense that Talia had been the one to gain the advantage that afternoon at Floreston Manor. An advantage that brought him to his knees.

"Yes, my lady," he said, forcing his heart to freeze against the heated look lingering in her eyes. He grabbed her wrist and pulled her hand away from him. "I surrendered to your sweet kiss and enjoyed every instant. I haven't regretted it either. Do you want to know why?"

He tightened his grip on her wrist, felt her pulse beating fast as a hummingbird's wings against his fingers.

"I haven't regretted it because that one kiss planted the seed for a thousand hot dreams of you," James hissed, grimly pleased to see trepidation creep into her expression. "Yes, I've dreamed of you as well, Talia. And my dreams have been raw, stripped of all decency. I've dreamed of you writhing naked beneath me, of feeling your legs wrapped around my thighs, of stroking your breasts and touching you in places that would shock you."

He lowered his head to look her in the eye, forcing himself to go on, to confess the unvarnished, crude truth so that she would know exactly what kind of man he was.

"I've dreamed of thrusting so far inside you I can't tell where one of us starts and the other ends," he bit out.

"I've imagined your voice begging me to plunge inside you again and again until you cry out and shatter with a pleasure so intense the world spins off its axis. I've dreamed of you on your hands and knees with me taking you from behind. I've dreamed of you riding me, of us copulating on the floor, on the table, in the goddamned bath…"

He pried his fingers from her wrist and stepped back, his chest heaving. His heavy erection still pressed against his trousers. He pulled air into his lungs and tried to calm the fire raging in his blood.

"So if you have imagined sweet, romantic kisses and courtship," he said through gritted teeth, "you will not get them from me."

He turned away, unable to look at her glittering eyes and reddened lips. The air, thick with tension, vibrated between them. James dragged a hand across his face and through his hair, thinking that any one of Talia's brothers would do well to beat him to a bloody pulp. He wished they would.

"I…I haven't," Talia whispered.

James turned, apprehension piercing him. "You haven't…"

"I haven't imagined sweet kisses…" Talia swallowed. A blush swept up from her throat to sting her cheeks. "Or, I have sometimes, but mostly I…I've dreamed about…about what you just described."

Her voice trailed off into a husky murmur. Though her blush deepened, she didn't take her eyes from his.

James's fists clenched as he suppressed yet another wave of undiluted lust. *Goddamned bloody hell.* How did Talia, of all people, know about such things? And in the face of that confession, how would he ever muster enough self-control to protect her from himself?

Coward.

The accusation burned his brain. He straightened his shoulders, infused with new resolve. He'd muster the self-control because Talia deserved better. Because he'd had his chance when she'd declared her love, and he'd all but thrown the gift back at her. Because even though he knew they would generate unimaginable heat together, he could never give her all he wished he could.

"I will not do this with you," he snapped.

"That's also what you said last time." She paused, pulling her shawl around her shoulders as a gleam of triumph lit her eyes. "And yet you haven't forgotten that first kiss, have you, James? Neither have I."

James clenched his jaw and strode to the door. He pulled it open, trying to ignore the trembling of his hand as he gestured for Talia to precede him.

"We'd best return before your colleagues wonder what became of us."

For a moment, she didn't move, that gleam still in her eyes. Then she moved past him, her arm brushing his in a caress laden with a thousand longings. James sucked in a hard breath before he followed her from the room.

They returned to Sir Henry's office, where the director and Mr. Fletcher were consulting over some papers. Both men looked up at their entrance, Fletcher's gaze going directly to Talia. Unease clenched James's chest, dispelling the remnants of his lust.

"Sir Henry." He spoke in a sharp tone and removed a card from his breast pocket. "Be assured I am at your service for the next fortnight."

He tried to ignore the cold look Talia threw him. Somehow he'd prove to her he wasn't a coward, that he wasn't running away as she seemed to think. Somehow he'd prove he was the man she once knew. A man of honor and decency.

Talia went to speak to Mr. Fletcher, the furrows on her forehead easing as she approached him. James gritted his teeth, forcing down a wave of jealousy that he shouldn't feel. He would never have Talia as he'd dreamed—as they'd *both* dreamed—but that didn't mean another man wouldn't.

And James could do nothing to stop it.

William Lawford's uncle, Lieutenant George Lawford, sat in a chair by the fire, his ruddy face damp with perspiration, the buttons of his shirt straining against his belly as he stared at the papers in front of him. The air was stale, thick with smoke and the smell of brandy.

William shifted in his own chair, impatience nipping at him with sharp teeth. When the new Shipton Fields prison was funded, plans would be made to shut down Newhall. And William would eventually be named governor of Shipton Fields.

He couldn't wait. He already had plans to send his uncle off to live with a distant cousin, thereby getting rid of him and cutting off his contact with everyone in London. William did not want rumors about his ailing uncle to threaten his pursuit of Alice Colston. Even more, he did not want his uncle to remember anything about what had happened with that bitch Elizabeth in Lewes.

"There will be separate blocks for felons and vagrants," he said, gesturing to the prison specifications.

"And depending upon the juvenile population, we might open up a wing for adult prisoners."

Lieutenant Lawford grunted and tossed the papers onto a nearby table. "Waste of time and money. Ship the lot of them off to the colonies, like we used to. Put them to work."

William sighed and stood to collect the papers. "There are some transport ships still in use. One or two are leaving this month, I believe."

"Not enough," Lieutenant Lawford muttered. "That was a worthwhile system, not like letting the bastards rot in cells."

"I'm planning several workstations at Shipton Fields," William assured him. "No reason the juveniles can't labor. Most of the work will be treadwheels, cranks, and shot drills, as I've found the boys are more docile if required to engage in hard labor." He paused. "May I count on your support, Uncle?"

"Don't owe you nothing, do I?" Lieutenant Lawford's face twisted with dislike. "You've always hated me, wantin' to get rid of me so you can have your glory…"

He reached for his glass of brandy and downed it in one swallow. William's mouth compressed. He took a step toward the door. The sooner his uncle was out of the picture, the better for all involved.

"I've another appointment with Lord Thurlow tomorrow," he said, making an effort to keep his voice friendly and even. "I expect his commitment, so we can be assured of funding."

Not even his worthless uncle could stop William from pursuing his goal. He promised to return in a few days'

time and went back to his carriage. He knew how to deal
with his uncle, but he still didn't know what to do about
Peter Colston. If the boy stayed in Wapping and worked
at the docks, disavowing any contact with his father and
sister... that might be enough to keep him out of the
way.

Might be.

The only sure method was to lock the boy back up
again, but even then William would have to keep a close
eye on him. Pity he had such a solid plan for his uncle,
and such a tenuous one for Peter.

Unless...

It wouldn't be difficult to learn when the next transport ships were leaving for the colonies. It certainly
wouldn't be difficult to ensure that Peter Colston was
on board one of them, especially if he was arrested
and convicted a second time. The superintendent of the
prison hulks had no qualms about transporting juveniles,
and if Peter were in the colonies, he would no longer be
a threat.

Buoyed by the idea, William sat back and reviewed
the plans for the prison. *His* prison. He wondered if they
might expand the governor's lodge, perhaps add an enclosed kitchen garden separate from the prison yard.

Picturing Alice Colston... Alice Lawford... working
in such a garden, William descended the carriage in
front of the Colstons' house. Alice greeted him with her
usual offer of tea. She looked lovely in a lemon-yellow
dress that made her blond hair gleam.

"Has Peter returned yet?" William asked, settling beside her on the sofa. A bit closer than he had last time.

"No, but I offered Lady Talia my assistance with

Brick Street school," Alice said, twisting a stray lock of hair around her finger. "I thought perhaps if I were more involved, I could better understand why Peter is so resistant to the idea."

Lawford had no desire to discuss that wretched boy again, but he made a few more concerned remarks before telling Alice that he'd visited his uncle that morning.

"He's going to support my plans for the new prison," William said. "Once it's under way and proven beneficial, I expect it will draw the attention of the court."

"Do you think so?" Alice didn't look as impressed as he'd hoped she would. "I hope you'll receive the recognition you deserve, then."

William edged closer. A pulse thrummed through his entire body as he caught a whiff of her scent. He paused, watching her, waiting to see if she would retreat. She didn't. He moved closer, then lifted a cautious hand to her face.

"You have quite extraordinary eyes, Miss Colston," he murmured.

"Thank you." A pink flush colored her cheeks, her gaze sliding down to his mouth.

Warning himself to be restrained, William lowered his head and brushed his lips gently across hers. Heat flared in his blood. Alice didn't move, though her quick intake of breath nearly undid him. His mind flashed with images of her naked beneath him, her legs wrapped around his hips, her skin hot under the clutch of his hands...

He curved his fingers around her arm, unable to stop himself from increasing the pressure of his mouth. Her lips softened beneath his, the taste of her so sweet he was gripped by a craving for more and more...

Alice broke away with a gasp, rising to her feet. "Mr. Lawford, I—"

William tried to rein in the lust coursing through him. He held up his hands in a gesture of apology. "Miss Colston, I do apologize. I find your beauty so compelling that I'm afraid I allowed it to overrule my reason."

He forced himself to stand. "I shall...begging your pardon, but I shall take my leave."

Though he ached for her to protest his departure, Alice nodded in assent and followed him to the foyer.

"I hope my attentions do not offend you," he said, grabbing his coat and hat.

She reached a hand up to toy with the brooch pinned at her neckline. Her cheeks were still pink, her gaze averted.

"No, Mr. Lawford," she murmured.

His heart hammered. "Then you will not refuse future visits?"

Not giving her a chance to respond, he turned to the door. "We shall see each other again soon, Miss Colston."

Chapter Seven

"Here you are, milord." The housemaid Polly stepped into the study, balancing a tray with a teapot and a plate. In her mid-twenties, she had a plump, youthful face and a faint air of worry. She set the tray on the desk in front of James with a flourish.

He eyed the offering—what appeared to be a stale crumpet and a slice of potato bread—dubiously. "Isn't there anything more...substantial?"

"I've got a mutton pie leftover from me supper last night, if you'd like."

"No." James sighed and reached for the teapot. "Is there sugar, at least?"

"We've run out." Polly twisted her apron between her fingers. "Ought I run out to fetch some?"

"No, never mind. Thank you, Polly."

The girl gave an awkward curtsey and departed. James sipped the lukewarm tea, thought wistfully of sweetening it with sugar, and returned to his letter. He reread the four pages he'd already written, then added his signature at the end before blotting the ink and sealing the page.

He set the letter aside and spent the next hour reviewing the ship's logs, the equipment lists and crew roster, and the navigation routes. He studied the budget, crossed out a few unnecessary items, and wrote a note to one of the financiers that they should arrange a meeting before his departure.

All business that he didn't particularly enjoy, but that needed to be done. Such dealings were the reason he returned to London between journeys—though he employed a secretary and solicitor, as well as a skeleton staff to maintain the family seat in Devon, James still preferred to oversee the details himself. He'd long ago learned not to rely on anyone else to execute necessary matters.

"My lord?" A knock came at the door and his solicitor, Graham, peered in. "A moment?"

James nodded and gestured to the chair in front of the desk. "I'd offer you tea, but—"

"Er, no bother." Well acquainted with Polly's lack of tea-making skills, Graham offered a smile of understanding. "You wanted to know about a Mr. William Lawford, deputy governor at Newhall. His uncle is the governor, but rumor says he's incapable of managing the place, so Lawford does it for him. Lawford is supporting a proposal for a new prison in Shipton Fields."

"Why?"

"Because Newhall is too small and rather dilapidated. And Lawford hopes to be appointed governor of the Shipton Fields prison."

"How long has he worked at Newhall?"

"Nine years. His father was a warder at Birmingham Borough, where the governor went to trial for mistreatment of prisoners. Several cases of men dying there as well." Graham studied his papers. "Lawford was born and raised in Lewes."

"Married?"

"No. Stays at the governor's lodge in Middlesex and with his uncle when he visits London."

James rubbed his jaw and tried to think of a reason Talia would associate with such a man. He knew all too well why Lawford would want to keep company with Lady Talia Hall, and the very idea made his blood seethe with jealousy.

Not that he had any right to feel possessive of Talia.

But clearly Talia's interest in prisons, of all bloody institutions, extended beyond the convicted fathers of ragged schoolchildren.

Maybe it did have something to do with Lawford himself?

"What of the House committee?" he asked.

"They're addressing the issue of prison reform and inspections of juvenile facilities," Graham said. "And Lady Talia has been asked to give testimony on the efficacy of reformatory schools in lieu of prison sentences for juveniles."

James turned that information over in his mind. It made sense that the ragged schools would somehow be associated with juvenile delinquents, but that still didn't fully explain why Talia would be called for her testimony.

"Very well then, Graham. Thank you for the information."

"I'll keep you apprised should I learn anything more, my lord. It seems Lawford is quite committed to seeing the Shipton Fields prison built."

"Lady Talia isn't one of his supporters, is she?"

"I don't believe so, no. I haven't heard that she is trying to prevent it either."

James nodded and saw Graham to the door. Then he picked up the sealed letter from his pocket and went out to procure a cab. He didn't bother keeping a carriage and horses in London, owing to the fact that they would rarely be used.

He instructed the driver to go to Piccadilly, not glancing out the window until the brick façades of the King's Street town houses came into view. The cab slowed halfway down the street in front of Rushton's house. Narrow windows blinked out onto the street, the shutters opened to the morning sun. James's heartbeat accelerated as he imagined Talia behind one of those windows.

He took the letter from his coat pocket and smoothed it between his fingers.

Just as the driver bounded from the bench, the door of the town house opened and Talia stepped out. Several books were cradled in the crook of one arm. Her father's carriage was not waiting at the curb, which seemed odd, considering she was dressed for an outing in a bonnet and cloak.

James gestured for the cabdriver to wait. Talia closed the door behind her and walked down King's Street, then turned the corner toward St. James's Square. With a frown, James instructed the driver to follow at a slow pace, then stop at the end of the street. The man nodded and climbed back to the bench.

James dropped the letter onto the seat beside him and leaned forward to peer out the window. He caught sight of Talia approaching a cabstand. After she engaged in a brief discussion with one of the drivers, the man opened the door to let her into the cab.

"Follow them," James called up to his driver, who tugged on the reins to spur the horses forward.

The carriage jolted into motion again. James looked out the window to see which direction Talia was heading. The streets of London passed on either side, filled with the clatter of wagons and carriages, the cries of street vendors, the permanent layer of smoky fog. Everything was unchanged since the last time James had frequented London. Stagnant, like a puddle of filthy water.

He experienced a sharp longing for the vast, untouched plains of the Australian wilderness and the near-perfect solitude. Or the endless expanse of the sea, where the salt air filled his lungs and dissolved the tightness in his throat.

James hated that London still made him feel like this, pulled back to the abyss of his childhood where normal things took on the cast of evil. Sometimes they were innocent—chairs in a dark room looked like skeletons, hanging coats like monsters. Other times they were not—his violent father, his mother transformed from a warm, quiet woman to a hollow shell devoid of life. The stark indifference of people who ought to have given a damn.

James unclenched his hands, twisting his neck from side to side to ease the tension. He'd leave London again soon enough. Fall back into the world and chart new territories, carve paths on land where no man had set foot before him. Places so remote that not even ghosts could find their way to haunt him. And if they did, they were swallowed by salt-laden winds and endless terrain.

He shook his head and looked out the window again. The wider paved streets of Piccadilly gave way to narrow alleys lined with tenement houses and dilapidated buildings. Torn brown paper and rags covered broken windows, and unkempt urchins and vagrants huddled in the doorways.

James frowned, unease pulling at him as the cab rolled through streets coated in coal smoke. They came to a halt in front of a smithy. The noise of iron striking iron rang in the air. James reached for the door handle the same instant Talia stepped from the cab in front of them and entered a door beside the workshop.

What the . . .

James bounded down the steps and followed her. He entered a dark corridor just before the door closed. Young male voices echoed against the stone walls. Talia disappeared through a door halfway down the corridor and half-closed it behind her.

James stopped just outside the door and pushed it open slightly. He glimpsed several tables and chairs, windowpanes clouded with grime, a few lamps emitting dim light. Boys in their teens sat at long, scarred tables. Some of them squinted at papers, others shifted restlessly, and at least one looked to be fast asleep.

Pushing the door open a bit more, James craned his neck to see the rest of the room. Cracks speared through the plastered walls, and pockets of mildew clustered in the corners. A pile of broken furniture sat at the back, and several prints of historic scenes hung along one wall in a vain attempt to cheer the place up.

Surely this wasn't a ragged school. The Earl of Shaftesbury had drawn a great deal of attention to the cause of the ragged schools, and their facilities had improved over the years. Even with higher enrollment, the union shouldn't be forced to hold classes in such a hovel. Certainly Talia wouldn't stand for it.

A rustle rose from the boys. James started to draw back just as one glowered at him.

"Who're you?" the boy called.

The sharp click of boots sounded on the wooden floor. James shut the door and went back down the corridor.

"James!" Talia's voice hissed behind him.

With a muttered curse, he turned to face her. Talia stopped in front of him, her eyes flashing and her jaw set. "What are you doing here?"

"I ought to ask you the same question, along with numerous others." Sudden frustration and anger filled his throat. He spread a hand out to indicate the street. "How often do you come here alone? Why didn't you take your father's carriage? What is this place?"

"How dare you follow me?" Talia snapped.

"Answer me."

"No, *you* answer *me*, James. Have things really changed so much between us that you find it necessary to lie to me?"

The sudden note of pain in her voice startled him. "I haven't—"

"You have done, James. You didn't even tell me you

were coming back, and you've been failing miserably in trying to act as though nothing is wrong. Now you're finding it necessary to follow me."

She took a breath and seemed to gather her courage. "Let's just have it out, shall we? I spent the last year regretting my behavior at Floreston Manor. I acted in a reckless, foolhardy manner entirely unsuitable for an earl's daughter. And you'll never know how sorry I am for that. Had I known it would ruin our friendship, I'd never have told you the truth."

James swallowed. "I…the truth can never ruin our friendship, Talia."

"I'm afraid it already has."

Pain lanced through him. He stepped toward the door leading to the street, fighting the instinct to escape the stark fact that one of the few steady elements in his life had irrevocably shifted.

The only way he could put it back into place, to fix what had changed between him and Talia, was to give her the one thing that had always formed the foundation of their friendship. The truth.

"Talia, I made a promise to Alexander," he admitted.

"To look after me, yes, I know."

"No. More than that. It was a…an agreement."

Talia frowned. "What sort of agreement?"

James fought a wave of shame. "North had no idea what business you would have at Smithton prison, and he knew Rushton wouldn't have allowed it."

"So he asked you to find out." Talia's eyes hardened. "Exactly like Alexander, isn't it? Even from hundreds of miles way, he needs to interfere in my life."

"He has every right to be concerned, if you're visiting

prisons. Why didn't you tell him about this when you were in St. Petersburg last fall?"

When she didn't respond, he nodded. "Because you didn't want him or your father to know. And we both suspected you wouldn't tell me the truth, either."

Talia exhaled, her shoulders slumping. "I know my father and brothers are concerned for my well-being, James. I know they love me. But ever since my mother…it was all so horrible, and they've tried to steer my course for me instead of trusting that I can do it myself. They don't know what it's like to have one's virtue questioned, to be the subject of that kind of vicious gossip. I decided long ago that I couldn't fight it. I no longer want to. But if society cannot view me as respectable, no one can deny that I am at the very least *useful*."

"No one has ever denied that, Talia. But then why have you not told your brothers?"

"Because they'd try to stop me, just like you and Alexander are doing," she replied. "I went to Smithton prison, James, because I've been invited to give evidence at a House of Commons committee about juvenile detention and disciplinary measures. For the past eight months, I have been working with Sir Henry and Mr. Fletcher on establishing a reformatory school for boys who have committed crimes.

"This"—Talia gestured to the room behind her—"is the only place we've found in this district that will allow us to conduct lessons until we've obtained enough funds to build a proper school. That's one of the issues the committee will address—whether or not the government should fund schools for delinquents rather than send them to prison."

James shook his head, as if to clear his mind from that barrage of unpleasant information. "You mean to tell me your work with the ragged schools has extended to criminals?"

"They're boys, James, not criminals. Our proposal is to give them an education and help them learn a trade rather than lock them behind bars."

James stabbed his finger to the door leading to the classroom. "All those boys were in prison?"

Talia's mouth compressed. "They were convicted of things like theft, pickpocketing, vandalism. Several endured corporal punishment while in prison, which I'm convinced does nothing but beget more anger."

She looked away from him. "And I know that anger is an emotion that allows for no hope at all."

"Er, Miss Hall?"

They both turned at the sound of Fletcher's voice. He was peering at them from the half-open door.

"Mr. Fletcher." Talia straightened her shoulders. "I apologize for the interruption. I'll be there in just a moment."

He nodded, glancing from her to James before ducking back into the room.

"What is he doing here?" James asked.

"Mr. Fletcher volunteered to establish a curriculum for these boys. He is an excellent, dedicated teacher who will be the headmaster of Brick Street as soon as we are officially recognized. And if you'll excuse me, I need to get back. We've two new students who need a bit of extra help."

She turned and went back to the classroom. James watched her go, his anger and frustration tempered by a twinge of admiration. Though he had known of Talia's recent dedication to helping people, in his head and heart she had always been the sweet, innocent girl of his childhood. He hadn't seen this blunt, determined, courageous side of her before... or if he had, he'd ignored it.

But now, her passion echoed inside him, reflecting his own desire to explore distant horizons and unknown lands. For the first time, James thought that Talia would understand the exhilaration sparked by a storm at sea, trekking terra incognita, climbing to the highest peak of a mountain. And he wished there was some way he could share all of that with her.

He went out the front door to the street. He realized, not without a certain degree of consternation, that Talia was no longer the guileless girl he'd left behind. And he had no idea what to do with the woman who had taken her place.

The light behind the windows was beginning to dim when Talia finally left the classroom with Mr. Fletcher at her side. Her throat hurt from the smoky air, and a headache pressed like a pin right behind her eyes.

She had to find better facilities for these boys. No one could learn properly in such stifled, filthy surroundings. The only blessing was that the owner of the lodging house down the street had allowed them to rent the place for use as the dormitories. At least there, the boys were somewhat protected from the stink of the blacksmith shop.

"I'm going to ask Sir Henry about allocating space in the Bethnal Green school," she told Mr. Fletcher as they stepped outside. "Though I don't expect it would be easy getting the boys all the way to Bethnal Green for lessons."

"No, better that we find something in this district," Mr. Fletcher agreed. His gaze skirted past her for an instant. "Er, isn't that your—"

Talia turned. Her heart did a somersault at the sight of James standing beside a cab, his hands shoved in his pockets and his expression dark. As he approached, Talia saw the irritation hardening his jaw, sensed his leashed anger. Though trepidation rose in her, she supposed she should be glad he hadn't tried to haul her from the classroom in front of everyone.

"Have you been here all afternoon?" she asked.

"I would not leave without seeing you safely home." James narrowed his gaze on Mr. Fletcher, who withstood the glower with impassivity.

"Mr. Fletcher always hires a cab to return me to King's Street," Talia said, her spine stiffening.

"That will no longer be necessary, Fletcher," James said.

Talia almost resisted James's high-handedness, but she didn't want to cause a scene in front of Mr. Fletcher. She nodded a farewell to him and allowed James to guide her to the waiting cab, where the driver pulled open the door. James handed her up and climbed in after her, snapping an order at the driver. Within seconds, the vehicle jolted into motion.

Talia looked at James across the expanse of the seats. Shadows cut across his hard features and his eyes glittered in the waning light. She realized, quite suddenly, that she'd never borne the brunt of his anger before. He'd always treated her with kindness, courtesy, warmth...but he'd never had reason to be angry with her.

"I won't have it, Talia." Coldness edged his voice.

Talia suppressed a wave of responding anger and forced her own voice to remain calm. "It isn't up to you, James."

He leaned forward, narrowing his gaze on her face. "If you truly believed this was a safe venture, you'd have told Rushton and Northwood when you first started it. But you didn't because you know those boys are dangerous."

"That is not why I didn't tell them," Talia replied. "I simply knew that both my father and brother would have thwarted my efforts. They only believe these boys should be locked in prison."

"Like the criminals they are," James snapped.

Talia clenched her fists. *Exactly* what her father and Alexander would have said.

"My hope," she said, staring out the window, "is that my father and brothers will one day recognize the good we are doing." She paused, her stomach tightening with nerves. "I hope the same will be true of you, James."

He paced to the carriage and back, his shoulders tense. "I will never believe that you keeping company with criminals will do any *good*."

Talia took a breath and mustered her courage. "That is exactly why I would like to invite you to spend an afternoon at the Brick Street reformatory school."

"What?"

"I am issuing you a personal invitation to spend an afternoon at the school with me tomorrow," Talia repeated. "You can sit in on Mr. Fletcher's lessons, review the curriculum, see how the class is structured. You can even speak with the boys, if you wish."

Though Talia hadn't expected him to be overjoyed at the idea, she also hadn't expected this weighty silence to descend. James just looked at her, as if he couldn't fathom the reason for such a proposal. Talia's nervousness intensified.

"Why?" he finally asked.

"So that you might, at the very least, understand that these boys are redeemable," Talia replied.

"And if I don't?"

"I ask only that you try."

They looked at each other for a long moment. Suspicion crackled between them. Talia knew James was torn between his loyalty to both her and Alexander. But if she could convince James of the usefulness of her work, perhaps he might persuade Alexander to let her see it through.

Perhaps he might even help her.

It was a frail hope at best, but Talia did know that James possessed an innate sense of fairness. He would, at the very least, allow her to make a case.

"I shall accompany you," he finally said. "Not because I want to, but because I've no intention of letting you go there alone again."

Talia controlled another simmer of irritation. "I'm not asking you to come as a protector. I'm asking you to come as my friend."

"I will always be both to you."

"I don't need a protector," Talia said. "But I do still need you to be my friend."

His jaw tightened. They fell silent on the drive back

to King's Street. The cab halted in front of Rushton's town house. Neither she nor James moved. She felt his gaze on her, the slow drain of his anger.

"What am I going to do with you?" he muttered.

For a moment, they looked at each other. A crackle of energy, red and blue, shimmered through the air. Talia's pulse thumped.

"I'm not yours to do anything with, James," she whispered.

A shutter came down over his expression. He pushed to his feet and shoved open the cab door, gesturing for her to precede him. As Talia rose, her fingers brushed against a folded paper on the seat beside her. The paper dropped to the ground, and she bent to retrieve it.

Just as James moved to take it from her, a stream of light illuminated the front of the paper. The name *Lady Talia Hall* was scrawled on the front in James's distinctive penmanship, the letters joined together like string. Talia would know that hand anywhere.

She held the paper away from James as he tried to grab it again. His fingers grazed her wrist, the light touch sparking a shiver all the way up her arm.

"What is this?" she asked curiously.

Even in the dim light, she saw his face burn with a flush.

"It's just a note, Talia." He reached for the paper again, and his hand closed around her wrist, the space of bare skin between her glove and her sleeve.

Talia drew in a breath at the clasp of his strong fingers, knowing he could feel the racing of her pulse beneath her skin even through his glove. She tightened her grip on the paper, sensing it contained something momentous. Her heart pounded.

"Did...did you intend to deliver it to me?" she asked.

"I was bringing it this morning when I saw you leave." He took hold of the paper with his other hand, and then they were so close together that she could feel the heat of his body radiating into the space between them.

Talia looked up at him, struck by the intense way he was looking at her and seeing herself reflected in his brown eyes. They were both holding the paper, and Talia thought that nothing in the world could make her release her grip on it. James flexed his fingers against her wrist, and she swore he was seeking the rhythm of her heart.

"I...won't you let me read it?" she whispered.

He let out his breath in a warm rush that stirred the fine hairs at Talia's temple. She wanted almost desperately to lean into him, to press her forehead against his neck where she knew his pulse beat as rapidly as hers. She felt his surrender before he spoke, just as she had that afternoon at Floreston Manor.

"I suppose." His voice was low and hoarse, rumbling through his chest.

Talia twisted her hand slightly, and then he let go of her. She moved back, her breathing shaky. His chest heaved, his eyes glittering.

"Th-thank you." She tucked the paper beneath her cloak and descended the cab. "Good night, James."

She managed to keep her voice cool, her stride sedate, as she went up the steps to the front door. She felt James watching her as if he were touching her. Only when Soames closed the door behind her did Talia hasten to shed her cloak and hat. She tossed them at the footman and rushed upstairs to her room.

Her hands trembled as she broke the seal on the paper and unfolded it.

My dear Talia…

Talia's breath caught. She closed her eyes for a moment and pressed the paper to her chest, her heart beating swift as a wind-whipped leaf. For ten years, James's letters to her from the four corners of the earth had all begun the same way.

My dear Talia.

She blinked back unexpected tears and settled in a chair beside the fire. After smoothing out the paper, she read the words sweeping like a crescendo across the page.

Then we took a steamer on an excursion down the Parramatta River, passing the barren, rocky islet of Cockatoo Island where stone is quarried. The other islets off the river abounded with vegetation and orange groves that supply the city markets with enormous fruits a lovely golden color…

Talia drank James's descriptions as if they were the finest wine, picturing the winding rivers, the architecture of Sydney, the colorful cockatoos and parrots with lemon-colored crests, scarlet tail feathers, and speckled wings.

A lovebird with beautiful plumage of soft, vivid green…

The letter, filled with evocative tales of his travels, was four pages long and ended with his usual signature.

Very truly yours, James.

Very truly mine. Talia let the paper flutter to her lap and gazed at the waning fire.

Her heart would always know the truth, no matter how hard she tried to convince herself otherwise. Her love for James was the reason she would never marry. She couldn't be with one man while still feeling this way about another. It would be unfair to both herself and him.

Talia folded the letter in half and pushed up from the chair. She went to her desk beside the window and opened the bottom drawer.

Inside, bundles of letters lay tied with ribbons, the colorful satin bright against the creased pages, all bearing rows of James's bold handwriting. Talia tucked James's newest letter beneath a blue ribbon and closed the drawer.

Peter stopped across the street from his father's Bell Lane house. Tidy place with its white shutters and flowers lining the front walk. He shoved his hands into his pockets and tried to quell his nervousness. He'd left the house two days ago and wasn't sure he'd be welcomed back. His father had given him until the end of the week to attend Brick Street. If Peter refused, he'd be kicked out on his ear.

At least his father would be at work now. Good thing, since he wouldn't be pleased to see Peter returning. He didn't feel so bad about his father—the old man had never been happy, no matter what Peter did.

His sister, though...she'd always tried hard to be good to him. Always tried to take their mother's place. Always blamed herself because he went wrong, even though none of it was her fault. For her sake alone, he'd try again.

Peter crossed the street and went up the steps. Took hold of the door handle and let himself in. Silence greeted him, broken only by the tick of the foyer clock. He thought Alice would be home now. She liked to have her tea precisely at four. Peter remembered that. He took off his coat and hung it on the rack, noticing an unfamiliar greatcoat hanging near the wall.

A man's voice came through the half-open door of the parlor. Peter frowned. Not his father. He tensed, his footsteps silent as he made his way toward the parlor. He couldn't understand what the man was saying, but something in his voice made prickles break out on Peter's neck.

Who...?

He eased open the door farther. Seated on the sofa, his back to the door, was a man with blond hair. He had a rigid, straight-backed posture, and a gold-braided hat rested on the table beside him. Alice sat across from him, leaning forward to pour another cup of tea.

Lawford. Bile rose in Peter's throat. The bastard was in his father's house, speaking to his sister...

"I would greatly appreciate your testimony on the matter," Lawford said to Alice, his voice polished as a jewel. "Everyone knows my uncle does not actually govern Newhall, so if you were to write a letter to Lord Thurlow telling them of my concern toward your brother, that would greatly aid my proposal for the Shipton Fields prison."

Peter's stomach swirled with nausea, pooling into the fear that had become part of him at Newhall.

"I'll consider it, Mr. Lawford." Alice extended a plate of cakes. "Though I won't testify to anything until I have Peter's consent."

Peter saw Lawford's shoulders stiffen.

"When did you last speak to Peter?" he asked.

"Three days ago."

"I assume his absence means he still has no intention of attending Brick Street," Lawford remarked.

"If he does not by week's end, my father won't allow him to return home." Alice lowered her head, her face shadowed. "Though I don't suppose Peter cares anymore. If he ever did."

Shame scorched Peter. He dug his fingers into his palms. Tried to find some semblance of courage beneath the layers of fear. He suddenly realized why Lady Talia had sought him out after he'd inadvertently helped her—when someone did something for you, you wanted to return the favor. He'd never done that for Alice.

"Well, perhaps it's time Peter finds his own way," Lawford said, setting his cup back on the table. "Certainly I did all I could at Newhall to set him on the right path. And it seems to me that you and your father have done all you could as well."

Alice didn't respond. She looked older than her

twenty-six years. Shouldn't have had to spend her life dealing with a younger brother who would never measure up.

"In any case." Lawford shook his head, as if to dismiss the subject of Peter. "Please do consider my request, Miss Colston. May I call upon you on Thursday?"

Call upon...? Surely Alice wouldn't...

"You may," Alice said after a moment's hesitation.

Cold trickled down Peter's spine, his fear intensifying. He shifted. The movement caught his sister's eye, and before Peter could duck into the shadows like the coward he was, Alice looked past Lawford's shoulder to the doorway.

"Peter?" She stood, hurrying across the room to him.

Lawford swung around, his gaze narrowing on Peter like an arrow. Peter started to sweat, retreating a few steps.

"Peter, where have you been?" Alice grasped his arm, as if she sensed he were about to flee.

Which he desperately wanted to do. He could barely restrain himself from yanking his arm from his sister's grip and running back out to the street. Self-disgust rose in his throat. He tried to steel his spine and meet Lawford's gaze.

"Just...out looking for work," he muttered.

"Even Lady Talia has been wanting to find you," Alice said, still holding his arm. "Please don't run away again."

Why the hell not? It was what he was best at.

Alice moved closer to him and lowered her voice. "If you do not come home now, Peter, you'll never be able to. Papa won't allow it. Is that what you want? To end up begging for food or a place to stay? All because you didn't want to go back to school?"

Peter tried to look at his sister, aware of Lawford's presence like a sickness. His teeth clenched.

For the love of God. He was *free*. This was not his prison cell. This was his father's home. If Peter were to regain any hint of self-respect, he could not allow Lawford to drive him from his father's house. Or worse, let Lawford use Alice for his own purposes.

He swallowed hard. Concentrated on the feeling of his sister's grip on his arm. She would not let go. She had never let go of him, never given up on him. Not even when he was sent to prison.

He couldn't bring himself to meet her eyes, staring instead at the brooch she always wore pinned to her collar. The oval frame encased a painted image of a blue flower with a slender, green stalk. Alice had told him the brooch once belonged to their mother.

"All right." His heart pounded as he felt Lawford's gaze, sharp as a pin. He tried not to think about what would happen if he went back to school. "I'll go to Brick Street."

He sensed the relief coursing through Alice and was even more ashamed of it. He tugged his arm from her grasp, finally glancing at Lawford. Though the man smiled at him, his eyes were filled with the coldness that had pierced the dark cells at Newhall.

"Lady Talia will be delighted with your decision, Peter," Lawford remarked.

Peter wished to God he'd never run into that alley ten months ago. If he hadn't, he'd never have met Lady Talia Hall or learned anything about her godforsaken school.

He ducked back into the foyer. Alice and Lawford followed.

"Peter, Papa will be home by six, and I've supper planned at eight," Alice said. "I'd like you to tell him yourself. He'll be so pleased."

Peter doubted that. His father might be cautiously pleased, at best, but he'd know in his heart that Peter would never succeed at any school, even Brick Street. And the old man would be right about that.

"I'd best be off, then." Lawford paused by the rack and shifted the coats around to retrieve his greatcoat. "Glad to know you are setting foot on the right path, Peter."

"Won't you stay for dinner, Mr. Lawford?" Alice asked, her voice lit with an expectancy that made Peter's stomach twist again.

"Much obliged, but I've a few errands to run, Miss Colston." He shrugged into his coat and tucked his hat beneath his arm. "Perhaps another time."

"Perhaps," Alice echoed.

"Or perhaps I shall see you at the Brick Street school." Lawford's gaze slanted to Peter, as if warning him that he would never fully escape the shadow of Newhall. "I'm quite interested to learn more about the school myself, if it might help to reform boys who have found themselves on the wrong path. We might consider such an institution as part of the Shipton Fields prison."

Peter watched his sister as she watched Lawford leave. Her eyes had an anticipation and warmth that filled him with dread. He had to protect her from Lawford and his blade-sharp cruelty. Peter owed it to his sister, and he could not fail her again.

Chapter Eight

James knew these boys. They frequented the docks and shipyards, scavenging for food and occasional work, clad in threadbare clothes that hung on their skinny frames. They picked pockets, stole food, fought, vandalized, and hoped for passage on an expedition to some faraway land that they were certain had to be better than London.

They were boys on the cusp of manhood who had seen far too much of the vile nature of humankind. Who'd either been victims or victimized others, sometimes both. They'd committed crimes—theft, begging, conning, fighting, and those at the very least.

If any of the Hall brothers or Lord Rushton knew exactly the kind of company Talia was keeping in her charity work, they'd either lock her in her room or send her off to live with Aunt Sally in the country.

Pity James didn't have either option. That would solve a great deal of his problems.

He glowered at Talia from across the room. She stood with Mr. Fletcher beside the desk, her expression serious as they discussed something he'd written on a piece of paper.

James pushed to his feet, shaking off the sudden rustle of unease. He strode across the room, his boots ringing out against the wood floor. The boys glanced at him as he passed. A wadded-up paper ball hit his ear. Talia looked up, her eyes narrowing on the boys.

"Mr. Norvell," she said, her voice sharp but with an undercurrent of warmth that needled James. "Should you wish to throw something at Lord Castleford, I suggest you choose flowers. That might go a long way toward sweetening his disposition."

The boys guffawed. James frowned. Even Fletcher cracked a smile as he returned to his desk and called for the boys' attention.

"Open your books to page fifteen, please," he said.

James caught Talia's eye and jerked his chin toward the corridor before stepping out of the room. He reminded himself that he could not allow his resolve to soften, no matter how much he might want to acknowledge Talia's...belonging here.

He couldn't help but notice how at ease she was in this hovel of a room, how the boys actually listened to her, how assured she was in surroundings that would unsettle any other woman of her status.

Yet Talia's status was precisely the reason she shouldn't be here. James kept his frown in place as Talia joined him.

"Surely you can see the—" she began earnestly.

"Talia, do you think these boys don't know who you

are or what you have?" James asked. "That you're fooling them by wearing plain clothes and no jewelry? Boys like this can spot wealth a mile away, especially with a woman as refined and lovely as—"

The words stopped in his throat. Talia blinked. A taut silence descended.

As you.

It was a simple truth. Talia was refined, and she was lovely. It was like saying a giraffe has a long neck, or a parrot is colorful. A basic fact that not even the most militant of the Hall family detractors could dispute.

So why—standing here in a badly lit corridor with Talia before him in a plain gray dress and bonnet—did her loveliness sear through his chest and fill him with sudden heat? Why did her green eyes seem more vivid than ever? Why did he notice yet again that her mouth was quite lushly full and—

The door leading to the street opened, hinges screeching and wood scraping against the floor. James turned, suppressing the direction of his thoughts. A man with dark, graying hair and a black coat entered the corridor, followed by a tall, lanky boy who appeared to be around fifteen or sixteen years of age.

"Peter!" Talia hurried forward, surprise and relief lightening her expression. She grasped the boy's arms, seeming to restrain herself from embracing him. "Peter, where have you been? What happened?"

"My son has agreed to enroll at Brick Street, my lady," the man said, giving the boy a sharp tug forward. "I would like to request that he reside in the dormitories for the time being, at least until he has proven his commitment to his word."

"Yes, of course. This is wonderful news." Talia opened the classroom door and ushered them both inside. "I'll have to fetch all the paperwork from Sir Henry, but in the meantime we'll get you situated here, Peter."

James watched as the boy Peter slunk to an empty desk at the back of the room. His shoulders were hunched so far forward, it looked as if he were trying to hide in himself. James experienced a strange discomfort as he recalled having felt that way himself once, after he'd discovered the truth about his father.

The other boys rustled with interest over the newcomer until Mr. Fletcher rapped his desk to call for attention.

"Page fifteen of the geography text, gentlemen," Mr. Fletcher called.

Peter Colston just slouched lower in his chair and glared at the books as if they were his enemies. James crossed the room, avoiding a boy who stuck out his foot to try to trip him. He sat down on the bench beside Peter Colston.

"Might be interesting if he talked about opium robbers," James muttered.

He felt Peter glance at him. "What do you know about robbers?"

"Had a caravan attacked by them in the Yunnan valley a few years ago," James said, still keeping his voice low.

Peter was silent for a moment before he said, "Really?"

"We'd entered China through Tibet and had been given an escort of Chinese soldiers from the governor of the province for that very reason."

Peter straightened, leaning forward into the space between the desks. "What happened?"

"A skirmish, though no one was hurt. Ran them off."

"What were you doing there?"

"Head of an expedition to document customs and institutions of the Yunnan province."

"I've seen those ships at the East India dock," Peter
said.

"Likely you've seen mine, then."

He almost felt questions bubbling in Peter. Reminded
James a bit of himself when he'd been the same age.
Curious about the world, always wanting to know more.
Imagining excitement, danger, adventure.

Another wad of paper hit James in the chest, followed
by a muffled guffaw. He glowered at the boy, Martin,
who sat in the last row. Martin nodded at the paper.
James unwrapped it and stared at the scrawled note on
the inside.

Murdrer.

An icy ball tightened in James's throat. He looked at
Martin, who tilted his head toward Peter.

Bloody hell.

James shoved up from the bench and stalked to the
door, grabbing Talia's arm as he passed her by the book-
shelf. She gave a little gasp. He pulled her back into the
corridor and shut the door.

"What the hell is this?" James snapped, thrusting the
creased paper at her.

She took it from him, her face paling as she read the
scribbled word. "Who gave this to you?"

"The boy Martin Norvell." Anger sank claws into James's neck. "Is it true? Did Peter *murder* someone? Is that why he was in prison?"

"Keep your voice down, James," Talia hissed. "I don't want the others to hear you."

"Answer me!"

Talia crushed the paper in her fist and turned to stalk outside.

"That boy murdered someone and you're determined to see him reformed?" James felt his rage building like a stoked furnace as he followed her to the street.

"I don't have a choice," Talia replied curtly.

"You do have a choice! How many others have committed violent crimes? And why do you think you have to be the one to help them?"

"Who else would it be?" Talia faced him, her hands balling into fists. "You don't understand, do you, James? These boys are lost. The ragged schools have done brilliant work educating poor children, but what are we to do with children who have committed crimes?"

"Keep them in prison," James retorted. "Especially if they've *murdered* someone, for the love of God."

"No good will come of Peter rotting in prison, James," Talia said, "being flogged for disciplinary offenses or kept manacled. It's my duty to help boys like him."

"Why *you*?" James snapped. "Why must you, Lady Talia Hall, be the champion of miscreants?"

"Because no one else will! And I've learned well over the past four years that I cannot fight the speculation about my respectability, but not a soul can argue my efforts to be useful."

"What is *useful* about trying to help a person who has committed such a heinous crime?"

"It's not as straightforward as you think, James, but it is always useful to help someone who has no other recourse."

James's heart clenched with anger and regret. If he'd agreed to her proposal a year ago, he could have at the very least provided her with the respectability of marriage. He hadn't even thought of that at the time, too intent on his latest expedition, too convinced he could never be the kind of husband she deserved.

Nothing had changed.

Except…*her.*

He stared at Talia, struck by the sudden realization. Determination glinted in her green eyes, and her jaw was tight with frustration. She returned his gaze with a steady one of her own, as if daring him to oppose her resolve.

"It's like trying to stop a broken dam, Talia," James said, aware of a hard-edged desperation beginning to grow inside him. "Plenty of other young criminals will go through the courts and be sentenced to prison. Do you intend to rescue them all?"

"James, that is the very reason we need support for the school!" Talia said, turning to stride toward the waiting cab.

James went after her, hating the words crashing together in his brain. *Murder, discipline, criminals, prison, flogging, manacles…Talia.*

Her name didn't belong anywhere near such words. The name *Talia* belonged alongside *flowers, silk, tea parties, laughter, kisses.*

James grabbed Talia's arm and pulled her to a halt.

"Talia, stop this foolishness, and I'll give your bloody school a fortune," he hissed.

She threw him a withering look. "Oh, I'll take your fortune gladly, my lord, but don't you dare think you've a right to tell me what to do."

"Dammit, why, Talia?" James snapped. "There are a thousand boys like Peter Colston on the streets."

"That does not mean he is not worth helping."

"If Martin is telling the truth, Peter is a *murderer.*" The word tasted like rusted metal in his mouth. "Why would you possibly want to help him?"

Talia stopped. She turned to look at him, a sudden darkness suffusing her eyes.

"Because he saved my life."

Chapter Nine

"Explain." James slammed the carriage door behind them, his features set and his eyes burning.

Talia tightened her hands on her lap as the carriage started forward.

"It happened last year, shortly after I returned from Russia," she said. "There was a girl at one of the ragged schools whose mother was sick, and I went to her house near Queen's Theatre one afternoon to offer my assistance. I hadn't expected to stay, but I told the girl's brother to fetch the doctor. By the time he arrived, and we'd procured some medicine...well, it was dark when I left to return home."

"And why did you not take Soames for protection?" James asked through gritted teeth.

"Soames is loyal to my father, James, you know that. And as I said, I didn't intend to stay very long. I'd gone halfway back to the cabstand when a man...well, he pushed me into an alley and intended..."

A DREAM OF DESIRE 151

Her throat closed, her skin crawling at the horror of what might have happened. The memory assaulted her—the stink of the alley, the man's rough voice, the panic flooding her. The glint of a knife.

James cursed. Anger radiated from him. "What?" he demanded. "What did he do?"

"I managed to scream before he could do anything." Talia put her hand on her chest. Her heart thumped against her rib cage. "Next thing I knew, a boy ran into the alley, crashed straight into the man so hard he nearly fell to the ground. There was a scuffle, and they...the man was killed. The boy was Peter."

She looked down at her entwined fingers, tight from the pressure of being squeezed. She felt the sudden, tense stillness surrounding James. Images flashed before her, the fear that had immobilized her as she stared at the crumpled, blood-stained body, the rasp of Peter's breath, the unreal sensation of being in a nightmare.

"Peter had gotten hold of the knife and stabbed the man," Talia said. "I...I was shocked, couldn't even move. Someone had fetched a constable when they heard the commotion, but Peter ran off right when he arrived."

She risked a glance at James, aware of a faint relief curling through her, the sense of a burden lifting. She'd told no one about that terrible night, and confessing it all to James eased the tightness around her heart. Even now, telling him her secrets felt right.

"How was Peter arrested?" he asked.

"Another man went after him and caught him. He was taken immediately to the station, but they wouldn't allow me to speak to him. The following day, with Sir Henry's help, I discovered that his father and sister live in Spitalfields and I went to visit them, to see if I could help. They told me Peter had been getting into trouble for years, so it wasn't a surprise to them when he was sentenced to Newhall. I attended the hearing and spoke on Peter's behalf, told the magistrate he'd been defending me. That at least got his sentence reduced to nine months. He was released a week before you returned to London, and his father said he would retain custody of Peter if he found decent work and enrolled at Brick Street. Until now, Peter has refused to do so."

The carriage came to a halt outside the King's Street town house, and they went into the parlor. James closed the door, a frown creasing his face as he studied Talia.

"You don't feel guilty because of what happened, do you?" he asked. "It certainly wasn't your fault."

Talia looked away from him as she pulled off her cloak and gloves, not wanting to admit how often she'd thought Peter would have been spared Newhall if it weren't for her.

"I owe Peter my life," she said, tossing her bonnet aside, "but my motives aren't entirely selfless. I also want his testimony to present to the House committee, a personal account of a juvenile's experience at Newhall."

"Surely the other boys can provide testimony."

"Yes, several have, but none who were at Newhall for so long." She shook her head. "He's from a good family, James. His father is a clerk at the Patent Office. He's not like the other boys, whose fathers are drunkards or who have been on the streets since they were children. Peter ran away from his regular school when he was ten years of age, and he's fought all attempts to help him."

"So stop trying."

Talia's chest tightened. "If it were you, would you give up on him?"

"I wouldn't try to help someone who doesn't want my help."

A few petals from a bouquet of flowers had fallen to the glossy surface of a table. Talia swept them into her hand and rubbed the silky petals between her fingers.

"Aside from his troubles, he reminds me of Nicholas," she finally said.

The frown lines on James's forehead eased.

"Nicholas never liked school either," Talia continued, knowing James shared the same memories. "Couldn't sit still long enough to pay attention to lessons. His tutors were constantly exasperated with his utter aversion to learning. Nicholas always wanted to be running about, chasing birds, riding horses...so different from Darius. Opposite sides of the same coin."

She lifted one of the bruised petals to her nose to smell the fragrance. "Peter reminds me of the way Nicholas once was. He even looks like him a bit, don't you think? All dark, snapping eyes and black hair. Big, too, like he'd be good at sports."

For a moment, James didn't say anything. Talia crushed the petal between her fingers. A pang speared through her. She missed her brothers. For all their arguing and bluster and interfering, she missed having them all nearby. Always there if she needed them.

Oh, but she was still glad that James was back. Even with all the tension between them, it was easy to tell him the truth, easy to hope that he would understand.

She lifted her head to look at him, almost seeing the thoughts shifting through his mind.

"Talia," he finally said, "if you think you can change these boys by making them read primers and learn sums, then you are sorely mistaken."

"And you have no faith, James."

Frustration flared in his eyes. "Talia, suppose one boy proves successful. He leaves behind his thieving ways, he learns how to read, how to add, learns a trade. Then what? If he's lucky enough to find work, his employer will toss him a few pennies as compensation and work him to the bone. Then the boy will become embittered and realize all the learning he did wasn't worth it. It will only be a matter of time before he thinks to steal from his employer, which will either send him to prison anyway or put him back on the streets. Right where he started."

Talia stared at him. "You really believe our work is that ineffective?"

James sighed. "No, Talia. I believe people cannot be forced to change. Or even to *do* anything."

"Why on earth would you think such a thing?"

"Because I've seen it!" he snapped, his body lacing with tension. "My father was a violent man, Talia. He beat my mother. My whole life, it was the same...he was a bastard and she...she spent every waking minute trying to hide it from the world. And even when people...family, friends...even when they found out, they didn't do anything about it. No one did anything. Not even the police. *Nothing changed.*"

Pain seized Talia's chest. A fierce urgency filled her to go to him, wrap him in her arms and soothe the anguish from his features. Instead she tightened her hands into fists and remained seated.

"I . . . I'm sorry, James. I didn't know."

He shook his head. "I wouldn't have wanted you to."

"Was that why you spent so much time away from home when we were children?"

James shoved his hands into his pockets and stared at the floor. "My mother often sent me away. It's one of the reasons I didn't know how bad things were until it was too late."

Talia frowned. "Too late?"

Bleakness entered his eyes, cold as a frozen plain. Talia dropped the broken petals to the floor and rose, crossing to him in three steps. Without thinking, without questioning the wisdom of her actions, she slid her hands around his waist. He tensed, resistance lacing through him for an instant before his arms closed around her.

Their bodies pressed together. Talia closed her eyes and breathed in the familiar exotic scent of him—cinnamon; strong, sweet tea; cloves. An old longing tried to wind its way around her guarded heart, but this time she didn't let it. This time, she wanted only to erase that bleakness from his eyes, to ease the cold that seemed to have infused his entire body.

"After my mother left, I didn't think there was anything good, either," she whispered. "But I was wrong. There was vile gossip and bitterness, yes, but there were also people who stood by us and lent us support. People like you, who gave me hope."

His grip on her tightened, his breath tickling the strands of hair at her temple. "Exactly what you've always been for me, Talia. Exactly why I spent so much time with you and your brothers when we were younger. You were a . . . a light."

A light. How lovely to think she had been a light for James, especially when she'd spent the past three years feeling as if she were living in the dark.

She closed her eyes as images of her beautiful, elegant mother swept through her mind like a cool breeze. Her mother, who had risked everything and lost. Who had fallen so wildly in love that she'd abandoned her family.

That was not the kind of love Talia wanted, a desperate love that would ruin both her and those around her. She wanted a love that blossomed, one that spread warmth like the rays of the sun. A love rooted in strength and certainty, not despair.

She pressed her cheek against James's chest and breathed him in, unable to deny that a small part of her still wished to share such a love with him. To prove that it existed, that it was stronger than anything.

"We have to change things ourselves, James," she whispered. "If my mother was so unhappy in her life, her marriage … why didn't she do something else? Why didn't she try to change her situation? Why did she just wallow in her misery until a man rescued her from it?"

She shifted and looked up at him. "If there's any lesson I learned, it's that I can't simply *wait* for something to happen. And I won't give up on something … or someone … because it's too much of a challenge. I won't do what my mother did. I won't be weak."

His expression softened as he gazed at her, his brown eyes tender with affection. "Even before she left, no one would have accused you of weakness, Talia."

"It's not the *before* that has plagued me, James." Dismay tightened her throat as she thought of all the barbed gossip and insinuations that had filled the wake of her mother's abandonment. "It's always been the *after*."

After her mother's affair…

After her parents divorced…

After she confessed her love to James…

After her brothers left…

After James returned…

All too soon, it would be *after he left again…*

James cupped her cheek in his hand. Talia's breath caught in her throat. She looked up at him, felt his gaze sweeping her face like the glide of fingertips. Her heart pounded, the warmth of his body still clinging to her.

The first time at Floreston Manor, she had kissed him. The second time, he had kissed her. This time, they met each other halfway, each closing the distance with a sigh of surrender. Heat bloomed through Talia at the press of his lips, the way he tilted her head slightly so their mouths fit together without a seam. She spread her hands across his chest, feeling the warmth of his body burning through the material of his coat.

Dangerous, she knew, and yet so utterly delicious the way his tongue eased past her lips to glide against her teeth. A moan escaped her, arousal unfurling like ribbons in her blood as she swept her palms up his stubbled cheeks to tangle in his hair. She gripped his hair tightly and stepped closer, her breasts nudging against his chest. James muttered something low in his throat, moving his hands down to her hips, his fingers closing into the material of her skirts.

He deepened the kiss and urged her mouth open with the gentle pressure of his lips. Sinking into the heat of their union, Talia let him in, her mind filling with all the thousands of images that her dreams had conjured. She eased her hands into the opening of his coat, the heat of his torso sliding up her arms. His tongue touched hers, and a firestorm of sensation exploded in her blood.

She tightened her fingers in his hair, loving the sensation of the thick strands brushing her palms. Even through the material of his coat and her bodice, she swore she could feel the heavy beat of his heart thumping against hers. She drank him in, her mind swirling with a thousand wishes and dreams that would forever flourish, no matter how often she tried to deny them.

When shadows had descended on Talia's life, when she'd wanted to hide from the world, James had been the one to remind her of all that was good. With his warm smiles and easy affection, the promise of an adventurous future that always radiated from him... with him as her bright, shining example, Talia had mustered the courage to chart her own path once again. To dare to be part of the world.

She eased her lips from his, sliding them over his whiskered jaw to the pulse throbbing at the base of her throat. His breath escaped on a hiss as he pressed his mouth to her temple.

"Ah, Talia, how you undo me..."

The husky note in his voice flared her with heat, reminding her of how he had surrendered that afternoon at Floreston Manor. She closed her eyes and breathed in the sun-and-salt fragrance of his skin that summoned images of breezy tropical islands and hot deserts. His heartbeat pounded against his taut skin as she touched her lips to the hollow of his throat.

His hands flexed on her shoulders, a sudden tension rippling through him. Sensing his retreat, Talia forced herself to break away from him first, her blood racing as she tried to control the desire swirling through her. She drew in a breath and turned away, pressing her hands to her cheeks.

"I wish you hadn't come back," she whispered.

"I wish I'd never left." His voice was rough with dismay.

Talia lowered her hands and turned to look at him. "Why?"

"Because if I hadn't..."—a flush of heat still crested his cheekbones as he stared at her reddened mouth—"if I weren't always seeking another expedition, I could have married you."

He didn't sound the remotest bit pleased at the thought.

"And then you'd have an easier time monitoring me," Talia said, her heart tightening when he didn't deny her remark.

"Marriage to you would not have stopped me." Talia took a breath and lifted her head to look at him, needing him to understand the depth of her commitment to her charity work. "I need a patron for the Brick Street school, James."

"It cannot be me." He shook his head. "It *will not* be me."

Although she had expected that response, disappointment stabbed through her. Regret darkened James's face.

"Talia, I would do anything for you, as long as—"

"As long as it's what you want," she interrupted. "I

know, James. My brothers are the same way, which is exactly why I haven't told them. But if I have support, if I have a patron before my father returns...perhaps the school will have a chance. And if the House committee agrees to fund the school as well, that means the boys will have an alternative to prison."

"I still fail to see why you cannot do all of this work without venturing into dangerous territory."

"For the same reason *you* cannot do *your* work without trekking into deserts and navigating jungles," Talia retorted. "How would you chart the course of a river without traveling it, James? How would you create a map of the outback without going there? Would you have thought to bring back a piece of green quartz for me if you hadn't found it yourself?"

...because you looked at it and remembered the color of my eyes...

She cupped her hand around the bump in her pocket where she kept the stone wrapped in a handkerchief.

"Do you think I've not worried about you every time you've left?" she asked, her throat aching. "Do you think I haven't prayed for your safety, hoped you wouldn't be hurt? Do you think I haven't wondered whether or not you would even return?"

"You...you are a *lady*, Talia, the daughter of an earl..."

"Who believes change is possible." For a heart-stopping instant, she thought she saw him waver. She tightened her grip on the quartz. "Won't you help me?"

James looked at her, tension lacing his shoulders. "You could be hurt, Talia. I don't trust any of those boys farther than I can throw them. And while your motives are admirable, even if I hadn't made the promise to North, I would still insist you stop."

Talia's spine stiffened with a combination of irritation and disappointment. "And do what instead, James? Host afternoon teas and church bazaars? If you think such activities would suit me, then you don't know me at all."

He turned away from her, his hands curling into fists. "I do know you, Talia. And it is precisely because I know you that I cannot bear the idea of you associating with criminals and murderers. It's like putting a diamond in a pig's trough."

In spite of herself, Talia almost smiled. "Diamonds are hard, James. They can cut glass."

"They should also be treasured."

The guilt in his voice sent a pang through Talia's heart, though she tried to steel herself against it. He'd had his chance. She'd been prepared to give him everything, body and soul, and he hadn't wanted it.

Well, she thought, remembering his undeniable reaction to her... he'd *said* he hadn't wanted it.

"This is me, James." She spread her hands, willing him to remember that he knew the core of her heart. "Do you remember what a recluse I became after the divorce? How I wanted to hide from everyone so I wouldn't have to face the gossip and speculation? Then I found the ragged schools and Brick Street... I found a purpose, a way to be worthwhile. People depend on me. I can't let you take that from me, no matter what you've promised my brother. I won't. If I asked you to stop traveling because I didn't like it or because it put you in danger, would you do so?"

"That is entirely different," he snapped.

"Is it? How?" She paused, knowing her next words would hurt him and yet wanting to make him see the truth. "At least I'm not running or hiding anymore."

James muttered a noise of disgust and stalked to the foyer. The slam of the front door seemed to echo through the entire house.

Alice shaded her eyes and looked at the dilapidated building that housed the Brick Street school. Smoke and noise billowed from the blacksmith's shop beside it, and the clatter of wagon wheels and horses' hooves filled the air. Alice opened the door and went into a narrow, dark corridor that stank of mildew.

She rattled the handles of another couple of doors before pushing one open. She looked at the classroom, her heart sinking. No wonder Peter didn't want to attend Brick Street, if this was the only classroom. Lady Talia had said it was temporary, but such conditions were hardly conducive to learning.

Alice tested the doorknob. Even the lock was broken. She went inside and examined the tattered books, the papers scrawled with rudimentary writing. The odor of coal smoke hung in the air, and torn brown paper covered cracks in the windows.

"I thought I'd find you here, Miss Colston."

Alice turned, alarmed at the sudden male voice. Her apprehension eased a bit when she saw Mr. Lawford standing at the door.

"How…how did you know?" she asked.

"A fortunate guess," he replied smoothly, stepping into the room.

Alice frowned. Several times over the past week

she'd had the odd sensation of someone following her, but surely Mr. Lawford wouldn't...

He moved closer. His eyes were a rather brilliant blue in the smoky sunlight. He paused, a crease appearing between his eyebrows. "Are you well, Miss Colston?"

"Yes, I..." Alice clasped her hands together. She felt as if she could still feel the kiss he'd given her the other day. "I wanted to see the school since Peter has finally agreed to attend. Lady Talia said there were no lessons this afternoon, so I thought to stop by."

"And how is Peter faring since his reappearance?" Lawford asked.

"Well enough," Alice said, not wanting to tell him that their father still refused to allow Peter to return home from the dormitories until he'd proven his commitment to staying enrolled at Brick Street.

An unwelcome sense of helplessness rolled through her. For all she'd tried to do to keep their family together after her mother's death, Alice could not rid herself of the feeling that she had failed.

Mr. Lawford was still looking at her. Never had a man given her the kind of attention that he had these past two weeks. As if he actually *saw* her, when for so much of her life she had felt utterly invisible.

"I'm leaving next Thursday," Mr. Lawford said.

"Leaving?"

"I must return to Middlesex. My uncle is...unwell, and so I'm forced to oversee the situation at Newhall. We've several new inmates who require my attention."

"Oh." Disconcerted, Alice didn't know what to say. "Er...will you return to London soon?"

"I shall make the most valiant effort." He lifted a hand

to her chin, tilting her face toward the light. "For no other reason than to see you."

Something softened inside Alice. Though nervousness wound through her, she allowed herself to move forward when he leaned in to press his mouth to hers.

Curiosity flared in Alice's belly. Before William, she'd been kissed maybe twice...and even then, it had been years since she'd experienced the affection of a man. His lips were dry, slightly rough, and when he moved his hands up to cup her face, she felt as if electricity were flowing through her veins. Her mind fogged as his lips moved gently over hers, eliciting her response, her desire, which had been dormant for so long...

His hands tightened on her face. Alice startled as tension seemed to roll through him. He lifted his head, his eyes twin blue flames of lust as he stared at her.

"You are a paragon," he whispered hoarsely. "I have dreamed of a woman like you."

Alice tried to smile and ease away from him at the same time. "Mr. Lawford, I—"

He slid his hands to the back of her neck, holding her in place. His mouth descended on hers again, this time with a force that caught her off guard. She gasped, shocked when he attempted to pry her lips apart with his tongue.

Her alarm turned to outright fear. Alice pushed her hands against the solid wall of his chest. He didn't move, his fingers digging into her neck.

"Stop!" Panicked, Alice brought her hand up and scratched her fingernails down his face, hard.

Lawford cursed and released her. Alice stumbled

backward and pulled a breath into her tight lungs. She turned and hurried toward the door, fear still burning through her.

"Miss Colston, I'm sorry!" he called after her.

Alice didn't look back. She went out to the street, relieved to be in the safety of public surroundings again. She stopped and took a few more breaths to calm her shaken nerves.

"Miss Colston?"

She looked up to find Mr. Fletcher approaching, a stack of books in his arms.

"Oh, Mr. Fletcher. I was just…just wanted to see the classroom."

"Of course." He looked at her with a hint of puzzlement. "Are you quite all right?"

No, she was quite *not* all right. Sorrow and anger boiled in Alice like a sudden firestorm. She shook her head and tried to speak past the constriction in her throat.

"Mr. Lawford is—" She broke off when the door opened and Lawford stepped out, his expression hardening as he saw them.

Instinctively, Alice moved closer to Mr. Fletcher. Her fear eased a bit, an inner voice assuring her that he would prove a safe haven. Though Mr. Fletcher was not a particularly tall man, he carried himself with a degree of assurance that Alice found comforting.

As if sensing her unease, Mr. Fletcher moved in front of her and eyed Mr. Lawford, his gaze sharp behind his spectacles. "You wish to see the classroom as well, sir?"

"Already done so, my good man." Lawford seemed to

force a smile as he bowed in Alice's direction. "Thank you, Miss Colston. We'll meet again soon."

He turned to leave, his back straight as an arrow as he walked to the cabstand.

Alice shivered. Dismay filled her as she thought of how she'd succumbed to Mr. Lawford's attentions, *welcomed* them...and she had tried to ignore the stark fact that her brother was afraid of Lawford. Now Alice had a sick feeling she knew why.

Chapter Ten

James paced to the windows and back, rubbing the nape of his neck. For the past day, he'd been wrestling with all that Talia had divulged, and he kept coming back to the same conclusion.

He was bound to tell Northwood about Talia's involvement with this new school. He'd always been honest with North, the one person who knew the complete truth of his parents' marriage. North had never betrayed that confidence and never would.

So how could James break a promise to his oldest friend?

At the same time, how could he look into Talia's green eyes and tell her he couldn't keep her secret? That he *wouldn't*?

James cursed and went to the sideboard to pour himself a brandy. He downed it in one swallow and wiped his mouth with the back of his hand.

He didn't like the idea of Talia's disappointment over failure, but that would be easier to bear than watching her venture into London's slums to consort with criminals, young though they might be. Even if Peter Colston had killed a man in self-defense, that didn't mean the boy wasn't dangerous.

His spine tensed at the memory of what Talia had told him. He hadn't been here. He couldn't have protected her. And he couldn't bear to imagine her terror as some bastard forced her into an alley with the intent to . . .

Rage speared him.

"Milord?"

James took a hard breath to calm his turmoil before he turned to face Polly. The girl hovered uncertainly in the doorway.

"There's a lady here to see you, sir," she said.

"Who is it, Polly?"

"She didn't say."

James sighed. "Would you ask, please?"

Polly blinked, as if the thought hadn't occurred to her, and went back to the foyer.

"Lady Sally Shaw 'ere to pay you a visit, milord," she announced as she returned to the drawing room.

"Show her in, please." James ignored a flicker of disappointment, which told him he'd been hoping his visitor was Talia.

He pasted a smile on his face as he crossed the room to greet Lady Sally, who bustled into the room like a little white-haired squirrel. Her bright blue eyes sparkled as she took his hands in greeting. She glanced around at the furnishings—the dusty curtains, worn sofa, frayed rug—with an air of disapproval.

"I don't pass much time here," James said by way of an explanation.

"Yes, I know." Lady Sally settled back in the chair. "Does your maid intend to serve me any tea?"

"Of course. Please forgive me." James went to ring the servants' bell, but Polly didn't respond to the call.

"She seems a bit…inexperienced," Lady Sally remarked.

"She is, rather," James agreed. "She was the wife of a crewmember who accompanied me on an Arctic expedition three years ago. The poor man died in a wagon accident shortly after our return, so I offered Polly the maid position."

"You could find someone far more skilled, James," Lady Sally said.

James shook his head. Though Polly wasn't terribly adept at her job, she was pleasant enough to have about the place, and he felt a certain degree of obligation toward her.

"I'm not in London long enough or often enough to require a skilled housekeeper," he told Lady Sally as he went in search of Polly.

He found her eating a slice of bread and jam in the kitchen and asked that she bring in a tea tray.

"Aye, milord." Polly wiped her sticky fingers on her apron and went to the stove.

James waited until she'd actually made the tea before accompanying her back to the drawing room. Polly left the tray on the table, gave Lady Sally an awkward curtsy, and departed.

James leaned forward to pour the tea and extended a cup to Lady Sally. She took it with a frown.

"You know, James, you wouldn't need to contend with inexperienced servants if you had a wife to manage a staff for you."

Startled, James fumbled with the teapot, spilling the tea into the saucer. He looked at Sally. She dropped a spoon of sugar into her tea and stirred.

"Er, I've...I've no plans to marry, my lady," James said.

"Oh, I know." Lady Sally blinked at him. "Merely a statement."

He rather doubted that. Sally was a bit too cunning to make *mere statements*.

"But speaking of marriage..." Sally sipped her tea and continued looking at him. "I'm certain you're aware that my lovely Talia is getting rather...on in years, yes? She should have married quite some time ago."

James tried to deflect a pang of guilt and regret, even as an image of *lovely Talia* appeared in his mind with no effort whatsoever. As if she were a part of him, natural as breathing.

"Er..." He scratched his chin. "Earlier you said Rushton might give Bexley his approval if—"

"Really, James." Lady Sally set her cup down with a clink, her frown deepening. "Do you honestly think Rushton would find Talia a husband whom she would actually want? He's just like Alexander! He'll think someone like...like Lord Kingston would do."

James tightened his hands on his cup at the extremely unpleasant thought of Talia marrying the obnoxious, fifty-year-old viscount.

"Of course Talia would vehemently refuse, which would cause all sorts of strife between her and her fa-

ther, not to mention leading to gossip," Sally continued.
"That is the last thing our family needs, James. And with
both Alexander and Sebastian settled down... well, it's
about time Talia does the same."

James cleared his throat, sensing this conversation
was heading in a direction he definitely did not want
to go.

"I consider it my duty to ensure that Talia also mar-
ries a man with whom she will be genuinely compat-
ible," Sally said. "A young man of the peerage with
a secure future and a good reputation, someone who
will respect her and treat her well. A handsome man,
of course, but not one of those vain dandies who struts
about like a peacock. A man who appreciates literature
and travel. A man who will give his wife a good bit of
freedom, but not allow her to run wild. That is the kind
of husband my Talia needs."

Lady Sally nodded, as if the matter were already settled. James shifted, placing his teacup back on the table.
His stomach tightened with nerves at the idea of now
having to tell Lady Sally what he'd told Talia a year ago.
And realizing that he didn't want to recount all those
flimsy excuses. That he didn't want to believe they were
still true.

"My lady, I have always wished the best for Lady
Talia," he began.

"Of course you have."

"But I do not... I've never intended to marry, not that
Talia isn't ideally suited as a wife, but with my career
and—"

"Oh, for pity's sake, James." Lady Sally actually
rolled her eyes. "I wasn't referring to *you*."

He looked up with a frown. "You weren't?"

"Certainly not. I know quite well you'd never do as a husband for Talia. No offense intended," she added.

"None...er, none taken." He was somewhat baffled to realize he actually *was* rather offended.

"No, no." Lady Sally waved her hand again, as if she were batting away a pesky fly. "You and Talia? Perish the thought!"

She gave a little laugh, the tinkling sound of which grated on James's nerves. The idea of him and Talia wasn't *that* ridiculous.

Was it? And why should he care anyway what Sally thought?

"James, I've another man in mind for Talia," Sally said, leaning forward to fix him with her blue gaze.

Another man.

A fierce possessiveness speared through James at the mere mention of another man. He couldn't bear the thought of Talia with anyone else. Certainly not the likes of Fulton, Bexley, or Kingston. *No one.*

His jaw clenched. He could not be the man for Talia either, undeserving fool that he was. And he could not wish for her a life of lonely spinsterhood. Not warm, generous Talia, who deserved a good man, a family of her own, children on whom she could shower her love...

"What other man?" he asked Lady Sally through gritted teeth.

"Lord Ridley."

"Ridley." James didn't know whether to be relieved or further irritated. Ridley was a friend of his. A good man from a good family. Honorable. Decent. Everything

Lady Sally wanted for her niece. Ridley would be an excellent match for Talia.

Of course he would. Better than Fulton or Bexley, at any rate, even if the idea did still make James want to hit something. And he didn't dare examine *why*.

He rose and went to the sideboard to pour himself another brandy. He took a swallow, appreciating the burn as it spread through his chest.

"That's the reason I've come to see you, James," Lady Sally continued. "I'd hoped, given your long-standing friendship with my brother's family, that you might assist me in this matter."

"What... what is it you wish me to do, my lady?"

"I'd like to secure Talia's engagement to Lord Ridley... or at the very least, set it on the right course, before Rushton returns to London," Sally said. "That way, he won't have any reason to interfere. And Talia won't have reason to refuse, if she's the one actually making the decision."

"And you believe she will?"

"If Lord Ridley approaches her in the right way, of course she will," Sally said. "Even women as headstrong as Talia are not immune to masculine attentions. Especially when they are designed to suit one's disposition."

James frowned. "I don't understand."

"That's where you come in, James. I want you to tell Lord Ridley about Talia. I know they are acquainted, but he doesn't know her nearly as well as you do. So if you were to *educate* him on Talia's temperament, the things she likes and dislikes, her pastimes... well, then he could court her in a manner she will not be able to resist."

"How am I to *educate* him, my lady?"

"Just inform him about all the things that interest Talia, what she likes to do, her favorite books and music. The fact that she likes currant muffins and detests lobster, loves Petrarch but thinks Boccaccio is horrid. You know everything about Talia, James. All you need to do is tell Lord Ridley."

"What if Lord Ridley does not wish to court Talia?" James asked.

Sally laughed again. "You haven't seen the way he looks at her, have you, James? Or if you have, of course you wouldn't notice. He can't take his eyes off her when he sees her, but he hasn't yet mustered the courage to approach her. So it's your duty to fortify his courage." She raised her fist, as if galvanizing troops into battle. "Give Lord Ridley the confidence of knowing exactly how Talia wants to be courted."

James felt his spine tighten. "And what if Lady Talia doesn't wish to be courted?"

"Oh, she will," Sally said. "Once she discovers just how perfect Lord Ridley is for her, how well he knows her ... I daresay, her heart will begin to flutter every time he is near. And once a woman's heart flutters for a man, James, then no one else will do."

She reached to pour herself another cup of tea. James paced to the windows and stared out at the garden. Talia's heart had once "fluttered" for him. Did that mean no one else would do for her?

He inhaled a hard breath. He wanted Talia to be happy. And if that meant smothering his own feelings for her ... then so be it.

Before James could dwell on all the implications

of Ridley's courting Talia, before his mind could start imagining them kissing, touching, marrying... he turned back to face Sally.

"You've determined an excellent match for Lady Talia, my lady," he said. "I admire and respect Lord Ridley and would be most pleased to help however I can."

"Wonderful!" Lady Sally clapped her gloved hands together. "I knew I could count on you, James. I'll begin making a list of ideas as soon as I return home. You won't regret this, I promise you."

James forced a smile as he saw her to the front door and into her carriage. Then he returned to the drawing room and headed straight for the brandy decanter again.

Peter squinted at Miss Hall and Mr. Fletcher. They were hunched over the front desk, explaining a lesson to Daniel, a fourteen-year-old boy who actually understood everything.

Not like Peter, who couldn't make heads or tails out of the bloody primer or, worse, the sums. Resentment flooded his chest. He squirmed, tapping his pencil on the desk. That other bloke... Forester... was slouched in a chair near the windows, his arms folded and his face etched with a frown. He didn't look any too pleased about this whole endeavor either.

Peter picked at a hangnail, wondering how long before he could get the hell out of here. He wanted to go back to the docks, where at least he knew he could do something. He was good at engine work. Strong, too. All the foremen wanted to hire him for loading cargo, pulling sails, working in the warehouse. Didn't earn a pittance, but it was better than sitting here trying to get his sorry brain to grasp written words and numbers.

He glanced at Forester again, startled to find the man watching him. Wariness shot through Peter. He knew certain nobs stalked London's slums in search of boys to satisfy their predilections...as if dealing with the kidsmen weren't enough of a bother, the street boys had to contend with the bastards of the *ton* too.

Just let Forester try to mess with him. Get a stick in his eye, he would.

"Peter?"

Peter glanced up at Miss Hall. His shoulders tensed.

"Did you finish the first lesson?" she asked, looking at him with all that hope and expectation, as if she truly believed that *one day* he would suddenly be able to read and calculate sums. As if one day he would prove her success story.

He slammed his book shut and glared at her. "Waste of time, *my lady*."

Who was she fooling, having everyone call her Miss Hall? As if it weren't obvious just by the way she looked at you that she was one of those fancy women who had everything at her fingertips.

Unlike Alice, with her rough hands and shadows under her eyes.

Shame filled his throat. He looked away from Miss Hall. He felt the uncertainty radiating from her, and he was glad of it. He wanted to make her nervous and uncomfortable. Then maybe she'd leave him the bloody hell alone.

She opened his book again to the correct page. "If you've read the first part of it, I can help you with—"

Peter shoved the book to the floor. *Read the first part.* He couldn't even read the first letter, stupid things constantly twisting in front of his eyes. He bolted to his feet, hating the dismay crossing Miss Hall's face as she stepped back.

"Peter, don't—"

He pushed past her and headed for the door, his boots stomping on the worn wooden floor. He sensed the other boys rustling behind him, murmurs and chuckles rising. His shame deepened. No wonder his father was always so embarrassed by him. Peter wasn't good for much but hefting coils of rope and crates, like a dumb ox.

He hurried out onto the street, sucking in a lungful of smoky air. He started for the docks, where he could lose himself in the chaos. No one paid attention to him there. Not like the school, where he couldn't escape scrutiny.

Apprehension shot through him again. He glanced over his shoulder and cursed. Forester was coming after him, his face set with determination.

Peter ran, darting around a fruit vendor and nearly crashing into a rubbish wagon. His foot skidded on the muddy paving stones. Surely he knew his way around the streets better than Forester did, so it wouldn't take much to lose him.

Peter raced around a corner, aware of Forester chasing him. He turned into an alley, then back out to a side street. The bustle of Ratcliffe Highway lay ahead. He raced toward it, knowing he could navigate the tangle of carts and wagons before disappearing into the crowds heading toward the dock gates.

A hand suddenly grabbed the back of his collar, yanking him to a halt so fast he skidded backward with a grunt.

"Bloody fool." Forester gave him a hard shake, his chest heaving with exertion. "Where do you think you're going?"

"Away from *there*." Peter squirmed, trying to pull away. He was bigger than most boys his age, but Forester was bigger and stronger. And he wasn't about to let Peter go.

"Not good enough for you, is that it?" Forester shook him again.

Peter scowled, his fists clenching. "Let go of me."

Forester's grip tightened. Peter braced himself for a lecture about how the reformatory school board, about how Lady Talia, just wanted to *help* him, that he was running from *opportunity* and a *better life*, how . . .

Forester shoved him away. Peter stumbled in shock. He righted himself and spun to stare at the man, who had a glare that could cut you like glass.

"Where are you going?" Forester demanded.

"The . . . the docks."

Forester frowned. "What for?"

"First one picked for work when the gates open." His fists curled in instinctive defense, his chest heaving as he sucked in a breath. Forester's eyes narrowed.

"What happened to you?"

"What . . . ?"

"In prison."

A prickle of fear raced over Peter's skin.

"I know why you were there," Forester said. "But is it true that you were flogged and manacled?"

Peter couldn't respond. His back stung as he almost felt the pain of the lash again.

"If you go now, you won't come back," Forester said.

Peter tilted his chin in challenge. "Why d'you think I left in the first place?"

Forester studied him for a long moment, then jerked his head toward the docks. "Go speak to Jim in Warehouse Two. Tell him Castleford said to hire you on board the *Defense*."

"What...what's the *Defense*?"

"A ship leaving for Africa in a week. Don't expect to be on it, but you can help load the cargo. Do a decent job, and I'll talk to Miss Hall on your behalf."

"What's the catch?"

"You'll owe me." Forester began striding away.

"Why are you doing this?" Peter called.

"Because you remind me of someone," Forester replied without turning around.

Peter chewed on his lower lip as he watched the man round the corner and disappear.

A ship heading for Africa. He'd often wondered about the destinations of all the schooners and barges clustered at the London docks. Wondered if he'd ever be aboard one of them, but unable to imagine ever leaving his sister and father.

A hard rush of pain filled him. Didn't much matter anymore, did it? He could go to the ends of the earth and his father wouldn't care.

He trudged toward the dock gates. Tried to ignore the very faint twinge of regret over leaving Miss Hall again.

For all her humanity-mongering, she'd been decent to him and was a kind enough lady.

But she had no duty to him, owed him nothing. He was alone now and could take care of himself.

The dock gates began to close. Peter ran.

Chapter Eleven

$\mathcal{S}$he likes mulberry preserves." James spoke through the tightness of a clenched jaw as he stood next to Ridley in Lady Hamilton's ballroom. "Reading novels, especially adventure stories. *The Last of the Mohicans* is one of her favorites. She enjoys ice-skating in winter. Going to the theater. The Egyptian displays at the British Museum."

Ridley listened intently, as if he were preparing for an exam. He glanced past James to where Talia stood with Lady Sally beside a potted plant.

"Ice-skating," Ridley repeated. "Egyptian displays. What about music?"

"Mozart is her favorite." James struggled against the urge to lie so that Ridley couldn't possibly succeed in this venture that Lady Sally had concocted just yesterday.

He stepped back, following the line of sight toward Talia. She looked strikingly lovely in a forest-green gown with a strand of pearls encircling her slender neck. James let his gaze wander to her bodice, the swells of her breasts that he'd imagined bare more times than he wanted to remember—

"Go on, then," he said gruffly, gesturing Ridley toward Talia. "She doesn't like inane gossip, so you'd best start with an interesting topic of conversation."

Ridley gave a nod and straightened the lapels of his coat. He took a breath, as if mustering his courage, and approached Talia. Both she and Lady Sally greeted him with smiles of welcome, though Sally quickly excused herself and headed for a group of women at the hearth. She caught James's eye and winked.

He clenched his jaw harder. He watched Ridley speaking to Talia and waited for the inevitable flash of wariness to cross her features. Ridley was a good fellow, and James had no reason to disapprove of him courting Talia—just the opposite, in fact—but Talia had an armor about her. She didn't let anyone get too close. Especially men.

Talia laughed at something Ridley said. James heard the sound from halfway across the room, a gentle laugh like a breeze rustling through trees. That laugh had permeated his dreams this past year.

His hands tightened into fists as he watched another smile light up Talia's green eyes. He forced himself to turn away from them. Well enough that Ridley had managed to strike up a conversation that Talia seemed to be enjoying. Lady Sally would be pleased.

And maybe James could get the bloody hell out of London before the sight of Talia with another man drove him mad.

He dragged a hand down his face. He suspected he would always wish *he* were the man who was worthy of Talia. He wished he could give her everything she both wanted and deserved.

"Have you managed to convert the world's heathens, my lord?"

James suppressed his turmoil of emotions before looking at a delicate, older woman dressed in a lavender gown, her hair a puff of snow-white around her head. She smiled, her features creasing with warmth and a sense of youthfulness despite the fact that she was past sixty years of age.

"Lady Byron." James pressed her gloved hand in greeting. An old friend of his mother's, Lady Annabella Byron was a welcome respite from the women fluttering about in their silk gowns, hiding whispers behind lacy fans. "Always a pleasure to see you."

"You as well, James. Whenever you're away, I fear you will fall prey to the devil's talons."

James lifted an eyebrow. "You believe I'm so hopeless?"

"I believe you should hold fast to Christian charity," Lady Byron replied, her eyes twinkling, yet sharp with intelligence. "You've an opportunity to do good works in the world, but I've yet to see you approach your journeys with benevolence and a sense of spiritual duty."

"I must leave spiritual duty to ladies like yourself," James admitted. He felt the same way toward religion that he did toward London society—tolerant, but unwilling to extend himself beyond the most superficial involvement. Both society and religion had failed him and his mother once too often.

Lady Byron tilted her head to study him. "Restless still, aren't you, James? You'd find peace in extending brotherly love, I assure you. When we view and treat our fellow man as equal, we secure our position in God's kingdom."

Though James never intended to dedicate himself to Christian charity the way Lady Byron wished he would, he found a strange comfort in the repetition of her speeches. For all her disapproval of society's frivolity, the baroness never wavered in her devotion to social causes and action, having been one of the few women to attend a world antislavery conference fifteen years ago. James wondered what it would feel like to be so devoted to something.

Or someone.

He glanced at Talia again. She and Ridley were still in conversation. They looked handsome together. Ridley wasn't so tall that Talia had to tilt her head to look up at him, and his fair hair and broad, open face were a striking contrast to Talia's Slavic beauty.

Talia turned her attention from Ridley suddenly, as if sensing James's gaze on her. She met his eyes, and from clear across the damned room, energy crackled through the air and straight into his chest. He swallowed, fighting the rush of awareness.

"Lady Byron, I'm having a dinner party this coming Friday," he said, surprising himself with the remark. "I'd be honored if you'd attend."

She pursed her lips, but nodded. Though she continued to disapprove of the excesses of the *ton*, Lady Byron was no fool. She knew well that her continued association with the peerage kept their attention on her causes.

And she never gave up hope in her belief that each and every person could be saved.

James excused himself from her ladyship's presence with a promise to call upon her the following day. He realized now that he had to actually plan a dinner party. He mentally put Talia and Ridley on the list, as well as Lady Sally and a few other friends whom he hadn't seen since his return. Twelve people, perhaps, enough for a small gathering intended to bring Talia and Ridley together again.

That ought to be enough to keep his promise to Lady Sally.

He sought Talia out again, then frowned as she excused herself from Ridley's presence and started toward the foyer.

"You're leaving already?" James fell into step beside her.

"I've an appointment at the Bethnal Green school tomorrow morning, so I thought I'd retire early." Talia stopped in the foyer as the footman went to retrieve her cloak. "And I need to call on Alice again. Find out if Peter has contacted her."

"You'll never convince him to do something he doesn't want to do, Talia."

"And you'll never convince me of that, either." Her eyes flashed with a challenge as she looked at him. "I do appreciate your giving him work on the *Defense*, James, but it won't be enough to appease his father. Mr. Colston doesn't want his son working as a dock laborer...not because of the work itself, but because of the company he kept in Wapping. People who would set him on the wrong path."

"What do you want of the boy, Talia?"

"To be back with his family and have a good future. And the only way to achieve that is for Peter to attend Brick Street and find respectable work." Dismay crossed her face. "I admit I never imagined it would be so difficult to help him."

A surge of guilt filled James's chest.

"He doesn't want to go, Talia," he muttered.

"I will not stop trying."

Of course she wouldn't. The woman was nothing if not tenacious. James had personal evidence of that fact. He just hadn't expected to encounter it to such a degree upon his return to London.

He saw Talia into her carriage, then returned to his own town house. He spent the next few hours reviewing his expedition journals and fighting the urge to write Talia another letter filled with details of his adventures.

If he were going to encourage the attentions of another man toward Talia, he would have to maintain as much distance from her as he could...even though that was already proving nearly impossible.

When dawn broke, James procured a cab and ordered the driver to the Wapping docks. He squinted against the glare of the morning sun as he strode past the basin, the ships' masts casting long, fingerlike shadows over the wharf. Men and boys in stained clothes and hats scurried past him, hefting cargo onto the ships, loading wagons for the warehouses, winching the wheels. Noise swam through the air—shouting, clanking machinery, horses, engines.

All familiar. All reminders that this was his departure

point for the world, that here he could leave London and all its bleak memories behind.

And still take the good memories with him.

He shook his head hard to dislodge *those* memories, the ones clinging like cobwebs to his mind. The ones that surfaced only when he was asleep and couldn't push them away.

"Jim." He increased his pace as the foreman of Warehouse Two lumbered from the front doors. "Have you seen a boy called Peter about?"

"Lots of boys called Peter about." Jim Bitner clamped his yellowed teeth around a pipe and inhaled a breath of smoke. "What're ye wantin' wit' him?"

"Peter Colston. Told him to see you about working on board the *Defense* before it sets out. Tall boy, dark-haired. Doesn't speak much."

"I remember him. He did some loadin' yesterday, but this morning Sam down at Three had a barge come in. Got some boys to unload for the warehouse. Told Peter to go there this mornin'."

James thanked him and went to the third warehouse. He found the foreman, who verified that he had hired Peter as soon as the dock gates opened.

"Found out he's good with engines, so I sent him to work on the steamer." The foreman jerked his head toward the steamer docked at the end of the quay. "Would hire him again, if he comes back tomorrow. Good worker."

James strode along the quay, skirting pallets filled with crates and wheelbarrows. Gulls dove through the air on the hunt for bits of food, and the smell of tobacco wafted from one of the warehouses. After finding the ship's captain and speaking with him, James boarded the steamer and went to the engine room.

His sleeves rolled up to his elbows and covered with grease and coal dust, Peter Colston was cleaning the furnace and checking the engine's feed pipes. His brow was furrowed in concentration, his movements sharp with assurance. He appeared so intent on his task that he didn't notice when James approached.

James cleared his throat to get the boy's attention. Peter straightened, swiping his forehead with his sleeve. He looked at James, a hint of fear coloring his expression.

"I ain't goin' back," he said.

"So you'll keep hiding?" James sat on a bench and studied the boy. "Miss Hall feels she owes you for helping her."

"She don't owe me nothing." Peter's mouth thinned as he stabbed a poker at the dead coals.

"She said you saved her life in that alley."

Peter shook his head. He tossed the poker aside and grabbed a shovel.

"You certainly saved her from getting hurt," James continued.

"No." Peter hauled a load of ashes from the furnace and dumped it into a wheelbarrow. "That's the problem. She thinks I ran to save her, but I didn't."

"What did you do, then?"

A dull flush colored Peter's face. He turned and shoveled up another pile of ashes. Sweat dripped from his brow.

"There was . . . couple of fellows I knew were wantin' to pick pockets from the Queen's Theatre crowd after the play," he said. "We nabbed a few quid; then someone saw us and called for the police. One of them grabbed my collar, but I got away and ran. Ducked into an alley and crashed right into the bastard who was trying to hurt Lady Talia. He had a knife...I didn't see it at first, but we started brawling and I got hold of it...didn't mean to do it, but he got killed. Then the police came, and Lady Talia was sayin' that I'd saved her..."

Peter pulled the stokehole plates from the furnace and dumped out the remaining ashes before turning back to the engine.

"Didn't even know what I was doing," he muttered, peering at the safety valves and boiler gauges. "Was running away, is all. If I'd known anyone was in the alley, I'd have gone the opposite direction. So her ladyship's been thinkin' all this time I'm some kind of hero, when the whole thing was a bloody accident."

James was silent for a minute. Talia had once seen *him* as a kind of hero, or at least a man worthy of her love. And he still hadn't done anything to prove to either her or himself that he actually deserved her belief in him. In fact, he'd probably crushed it with his rejection and evasion.

"Is that why you've not wanted to attend Brick Street?" he asked Peter. "Because you don't think you're worthy of her help?"

"I'm not." Peter grabbed a rag to wipe his greasy hands. "Can't do it in any case neither."

"Why not?"

"Too thickheaded." Peter tapped the side of his head. "Can't make sense of letters or numbers."

James watched as Peter began cleaning the rivet screws. "You're a good worker, from what I hear."

Peter shrugged.

"I can help you find work your father would approve of," James suggested. He didn't know what kind of work yet, but he had enough resources. He could even hire Peter himself, if he were so inclined.

"If I go back to Brick Street, right?" Peter said. "What's the point of going back when I can't learn anything?"

"It's better than running away again." An uncomfortable pang struck James as he realized he was echoing Talia's own words about himself. He pushed to his feet and headed for the entry port. "Think on it, Peter. Perhaps it's time to stop running."

Peter gave a humorless laugh. "Don't know how."

Neither did James.

Talia could not remember a time when James Forester had hosted a dinner party. He attended them often when he was in London, enjoying the good food and drink as much as the next man, but never had he organized one himself.

"Do you need any assistance?" Talia asked him as they left Wapping the day after Lady Hamilton's ball. Talia was hardly one of society's renowned hostesses, but she'd organized several parties for her father over the past year and knew all the proper rules of etiquette.

"I don't think so." James frowned, a vague look of worry crossing his features. "My housemaid assures me she can make all the preparations."

"Polly?" Talia tried to think of a way to phrase her concerns delicately. "Er, James, she's not organized a dinner party before, has she?"

"No."

Talia chewed on her bottom lip as they settled into the cab. Considering how trying James had been since his return, she didn't necessarily want to *help* him at the moment. But she also didn't want to see his first foray as a host end up a complete disaster. She couldn't bear to think of people laughing at him.

"Perhaps you'll allow me to consult with Polly?" Talia asked carefully. "I arranged a party for fifteen people just before my father left London, so I'm quite capable of ensuring all goes smoothly. If you'll allow me to help," she added.

Rather than be appreciative or even relieved at the offer, James only frowned more deeply. "You're invited as a guest, Talia."

"I shall be a guest. I'm merely offering my assistance for the preparations. To plan the menu, arrange the seating, order the flowers. That sort of thing. Unless you'd rather leave it all to Polly. Or do it yourself."

"All right," James muttered. "I'll tell her you'll arrange it, then. Thank you," he added grudgingly.

Talia gave him an amused look. "You're quite welcome."

He looked so...frustrated. He'd been that way ever since he returned. So unlike the warm, cheerful James he'd always been.

Talia's heart tightened. He'd changed because her declaration of love had put a wall between them that had never been there before. If she hadn't confessed her love, perhaps everything *would* be the same as it once was.

"Ask the driver to take us to Old Bond Street," she said.

"What is in Old Bond Street?"

"Something you'll enjoy," Talia promised.

James called up the order to the driver; then the cab lurched into motion. A half hour later, they came to a stop.

"It's just a short walk," Talia said as James descended before her, then extended a hand to help her down.

As she always did, Talia relished the moment his fingers closed tightly around hers, the warmth of his grip evident even through the layers of both their gloves. And, also as she always did, Talia loosened her grip first, the moment the ground steadied beneath her feet. She didn't want to give James reason to believe she might want to cling to him. And she certainly didn't want to feel as if she'd never want to release him.

She preceded him along the street, leading the way to a narrow town house whose front garden was enclosed by a wrought-iron fence. A hanging sign proclaimed the establishment to be the residence of *Blake's Museum of Automata.*

"Wait here." Remembering the stall on the opposite side of the street, Talia gestured for James to stay where he was as she hurried across to the vendor. She dug into her pocket for a few pennies and purchased a small bag of sweets before returning to James.

"Almond toffee," she said, extending the bag. "I gather you've still got a taste for toffee?"

"Indeed." He looked at her somewhat oddly, as if not quite fathoming why she would remember such a thing.

"Well, come along, then."

Talia opened the front door of the museum and

stepped into the foyer. A hint of trepidation rose in her as she caught sight of the formidable figure seated behind the front desk. The museum secretary, Mrs. Fox, stood and approached, her handsome features made stern and pallid by her high-collared black gown and severe hairstyle.

"Good afternoon, Mrs. Fox," Talia said. "Is Mr. Blake in?"

"I'll see if he is available, my lady." Mrs. Fox swept her gaze over James in a rapid assessment before heading into the depths of the museum.

"Bastian met his wife here?" James asked in faint wonderment as he peered into the front parlor, which was cluttered with tables and shelves displaying various mechanical toys and moving clocks. "Seems more of Darius's sort of haunt."

"Oh, Darius and Mr. Blake have engaged in quite a correspondence, from what my father tells me," Talia said. "Something to do with a cipher machine and encoding alphabets. All rather beyond me, I'm afraid."

"Lady Talia!" A blond-haired man in his mid-forties hurried into the foyer, his eyes bright with welcome behind his spectacles. "What an unexpected surprise. I was telling Mrs. Fox just yesterday that I ought to pay a call on you and your father."

"My apologies, Mr. Blake." Talia smiled at the sight of his wrinkled jacket, crooked tie, and grease-covered apron. "My father is still traveling, and I've been quite busy lately. I stopped by to introduce you to Lord Castleford, an old family friend. I'd hoped you might have a moment to provide us with a tour?"

"Yes, yes, of course." Mr. Blake wiped his hands on

his apron, looking a bit disconcerted for a moment at the unexpected request.

"If you'll both please follow me." Mrs. Fox stepped forward and extended her hand to the drawing room door. "I'll tell you the history of the museum, then fetch tea while Mr. Blake explains the mechanics of the automata to you."

Mr. Blake's face cleared with relief as he nodded. "Beg your pardon, for just a moment," he said, hurrying back to his workshop lair.

Amused, Talia followed Mrs. Fox into the drawing room, forcing herself to listen politely as the woman droned on about Blake's establishment of the museum. When Mrs. Fox left to see about the tea, Mr. Blake came in and showed her and James how the various machines worked—a twist of a key prompted a frog to hop onto a lily pad, a bear to spin on one foot, a pair of birds to whirl around a tree at the top of a clock.

James was fascinated by the inventions, peering closely at the painted figures and requesting permission to turn the keys himself.

"How extraordinarily clever," he said, the sound of his deep chuckle filling the room as he watched a pair of ice-skaters glide over a glass pond. "You made all of these yourself, Mr. Blake?"

"Most of them," the inventor replied modestly. "Some were sent by my colleagues." He stepped forward to turn the machine around and unlock the panel at the back. "Let me show you the machinery, which gives you an explanation of how the figures operate and—"

James shook his head. "Much obliged, Mr. Blake, but I'd rather not know the details of the mechanics."

Mr. Blake blinked, as if he couldn't fathom such a statement. "You don't wish to know how they work?"

"No, but thank you. They're such charming creations, I'd rather disregard any evidence that they're controlled by wires and gears."

Mr. Blake looked at Talia. She gave him an apologetic smile and a shrug. "Sometimes illusions are best left intact, don't you think?"

"I suppose." Mr. Blake looked as if he thought no such thing.

"Mr. Blake, a word, if you please?" Mrs. Fox entered with the tea tray, bustling about rearranging the automata on a table so she could set the tray down.

"Beg your pardon, again," Blake muttered to Talia and James as he followed Mrs. Fox from the room.

Talia watched James twist the key on another machine. A tinny music wafted from the base as a mouse lifted a flute to its mouth and began piping the tune. James shook his head in wonderment, his features creasing with another smile.

"Astonishing, isn't it?"

Talia nodded. His pleasure was like a ray of sun, lightening the darkness that had collected around her heart over the past week. Reminding her how easy it had always been just to be with him. She watched his hands as he picked up another automaton. He had strong hands, tanned and calloused from his work on so many expeditions. His fingers were long, his wrists dusted with dark hair that disappeared into the snowy white cuff of his shirt.

He motioned for her to come closer, in that *come share with me* gesture that she would recognize forever.

She moved beside him, her heart vibrating like a viola string as she sensed the warmth of his body. With a dexterous flick of his fingers, he turned the key on the automaton, and they watched a hummingbird flutter over an open flower.

James looked at Talia, his eyes creasing with a smile that spread warmth through her blood.

"What was that verse we used to recite?" he asked. "The one about the hummingbird? Tea is brought from China..."

"Rice from Carolina," Talia said, intensely aware of his gaze, her skin prickling with the urge to feel his hands on her. "India and Italy..."

"Countries far beyond the sea."

"Coffee comes from Mocha..."

"Wholesome tapioca..."

"Is from the West Indies brought..."

"Where the hummingbirds are caught." James touched the hummingbird, its feathered wings moving back and forth.

"The same land produces fruits of richest juices..." Talia stopped, remembering the rest of the verse about Portugal, Spain, Africa, and Peru. She forced a smile to hide her sudden disconcertion. "That must have been the verse that sparked your desire to explore the world."

James shook his head, still staring at the hummingbird.

"What did, then?" Talia asked curiously.

He didn't respond. She remembered, with a twinge of pain, what he had told her about his father's abuse of his mother. About how no one had tried to help Lady

Castleford. It was hardly a wonder that he bore such ill will toward society.

It was hardly a wonder that he sought to escape.

She wanted to touch him again. Wanted to cover his hand with hers and slide her fingers up his forearm, into the cuff of his sleeve, where his skin would be warm and taut with muscle.

Their gazes met with that now-familiar energy that seared through Talia like an arrow of light. *Oh, James. Why couldn't you believe in us?*

She suppressed a wave of sorrow and stepped away from him, turning her attention to a toy train.

"The...the boys at Brick Street would enjoy such amusements." She tried to keep her voice steady, tried to calm the pounding of her heart. "I'll have to ask Mr. Blake if he would consider loaning or donating several automata to the school."

"Ridley accepted the invitation to Friday night's party," James said suddenly.

Ridley? The abrupt shift in conversation almost startled Talia. Why would James mention Ridley?

She turned to find him still watching her. "Oh?"

"He's looking forward to seeing you again."

"That's very kind of him."

He nodded, as if glad he'd gotten that message across. Talia quelled a rush of unease. She knew Ridley and James were good friends, but surely James wasn't...

"Well, then." Blake reentered the room and clapped his hands together. "Come along then, my lord. I'll show you my workshop."

Before James could protest again, Blake ambled off.

Talia smiled at James's resignation as they followed the inventor down the corridor to the depths of the house. As they walked, James opened the bag of candy and held it out toward Talia. She accepted a piece, and they shared a brief glance of enjoyment as they each bit into the sticky-sweet candy.

They went into the workshop, where dozens of greasy machine engines and parts lay scattered about the tables. Wires, gears, and bellows cluttered the floor, and the smell of oil filled the room.

"This is the mechanism that supports the interior engine," Mr. Blake said, pausing beside an automaton of a dancing couple. He opened the base to show them the machine inside and the cranks that controlled the couple's movements. "If you position this lever to control the main axis, then attach it to the crank wheel with..."

He went on about the details of the mechanism, his words becoming a drone in Talia's ears. She glanced at James, expecting to see him looking equally bored. Instead he was not only listening to Mr. Blake, but even seemed...interested?

How odd. James relished the outdoors, nature, the mysteries of the natural world. He'd never expressed interest in machines or inventions—not like Talia's brother Darius, who would take apart a train engine if he could, simply to learn how it operated.

By the time she and James took their leave and returned to King's Street, it was nearing teatime, the sun glowing behind a layer of fog. They went inside and found Aunt Sally bustling around the drawing room.

"Oh, how lovely that you visited Mr. Blake." Aunt Sally gestured for them to sit as she poured them tea.

"Aren't his inventions wonderful, James? And, Talia, Lord Ridley's mother sent an invitation asking you to join her at her luncheon next Saturday."

Talia couldn't help glancing at James to gauge his reaction to that remark, since he'd found it necessary to mention Ridley earlier. His eyes were steely as he frowned down at his cup. Talia didn't dare hope that his irritation might be directed not toward Ridley, but the fact that another man seemed interested in courting her.

As much as Talia had tried to tell herself she no longer felt anything for James, her heart still gave a little leap at the idea that he might be jealous. Because if he were jealous, surely that meant—

Stop.

"You're leaving in a fortnight, aren't you, James?" Sally asked brightly.

"The twelfth, my lady, yes." He was still staring at his cup.

"Pity Talia can't accompany you," Sally continued. "I assume you'll stop in St. Petersburg en route, will you not? It would be lovely for her to see Lydia and Alexander's new babe."

James looked at Talia, something flickering in the depths of his gold-flecked eyes that made her heart tighten. She still knew him. He was thinking the exact same thing she was...even with all that had passed between them, it would be an undeniable pleasure to visit St. Petersburg together.

She frowned, annoyed with him for eliciting such a thought. Annoyed with her aunt for suggesting it, especially after mentioning Lord Ridley...

An unpleasant speculation bit at Talia. Both Sally and

James seemed rather intent upon assuring her of Lord Ridley's attentions. Though Talia had nothing against the man, she was not interested in pursuing the matter— especially since Sally had now planted the idea of a passionate, blissful marriage in Talia's mind. She would never have such a union with Lord Ridley, no matter how kind he was. The only man with whom she could imagine such a—

Talia stopped that thought before it went any farther, even as her blood warmed with the ever-present memory of James's kiss. She bit down on her lip with frustration. Perhaps all this talk of Lord Ridley was to her benefit. Perhaps if she were to turn her attention to him, she could finally smother these lingering thoughts of James Forester.

Though sorrow filled Talia at the idea of eradicating any part of James from her life, she knew she had no choice. Not if she wanted to keep her heart intact.

Chapter Twelve

$\mathcal{P}$eter grabbed a greasy rag and wiped his hands, pleased with the fact that he'd fixed the engine. A piece of coal had gotten jammed under the snifting valve, allowing air to pass into the condenser and destroying the vacuum. He'd managed to clear the valve and prevent far more serious damage to the engine by stopping the flow of air. After telling the captain what he'd done, the man asked him to return the following day to see if he could determine the problem with another steam engine.

Peter had promised to return at dawn, thinking he had a far better chance at success with another broken engine than he did by agreeing to Forester's proposal to return to Brick Street. Fixing machines made Peter feel good, like he could actually *do* something. Like he had abilities, could solve problems, and make things right for people.

The sun was starting to set over the basin, reddish

light reflecting off the high masts and gently rocking boats. At times like this, the place almost seemed peaceful—water shimmering like diamonds, the noise lessening as workers trudged home.

Peter went to collect his meager pay from the foreman, then stopped at a water barrel to splash cold water on his dirty face and hair. He swiped his forehead with his sleeve. His stomach growled again, an ache he'd tried to ignore all day. Likely the boys at Brick Street were having supper now.

He went toward the gates. Crowds of weary workers were going through. The clatter of wagons and cabs rose from Ratcliffe Highway. Peter joined the queue leaving the docks. He touched the pennies in his pocket and tried to calculate what he could buy with them. At least he'd no trouble figuring numbers in his head, only when they were spread on paper in front of him.

"Hungry, Peter?" A man stepped into his path.

Peter looked up, expecting to see Forester. Instead William Lawford peered down at him, his expression friendly beneath the brim of his hat. Peter suppressed a surge of fear, hating that Lawford could still make him afraid. He reminded himself that, by law, Lawford had no control over him anymore.

Though given the look in the man's eyes, Lawford didn't care about the decree of the law.

"Hungry?" Lawford repeated.

"Maybe."

Lawford tilted his head toward the highway. "Come on, then. Fancy a meat pie?"

Peter's stomach rumbled in response. He rubbed two pennies together in his pocket. If Lawford bought him something to eat, he'd have enough to pay McGinty to let him sleep in the tavern kitchen that night. He tried to shove aside the memory of his own bed at his father's house.

He nodded his assent to Lawford. Followed him toward a pieman's stand and accepted a steaming, fragrant pie. Trying not to appear starving, he bit through the flaky crust as the hot mutton filling dripped down his arm.

"On your way back to Brick Street?" Lawford asked pleasantly.

Peter took another bite of the pie and spoke around the mouthful. "Why d'you care?"

"I'm merely curious since Lady Talia went to rather great lengths to defend you and ensure your well-being after Newhall," Lawford remarked. "Yet you don't seem grateful for her kindness or even willing to take advantage of it. Why is that?"

Peter didn't answer. He didn't owe Lawford any explanation.

"Your sister is still concerned about you," Lawford went on.

Peter jerked his gaze to the other man. Unease filled him along with the ever-present shame.

He'd never live up to his father's hopes, but Alice had never demanded anything of him other than he do the right thing. She'd tried hard to take their mother's place for him. He'd failed her too, when he'd started filching. When he couldn't *learn* anything.

"I'll take you back, if you'll come with me," Lawford suggested, nodding to a cab at the edge of the street. "You'll be doing what your sister wants."

"How'd you know what my sister wants?" Peter snapped.

"I've spoken with her, Peter, of course. Your father wanted nothing to do with you when you were released from Newhall. Do you not remember that your sister came alone to pick you up...well, her companions notwithstanding? Alice asked...no, she *begged* me for help."

Peter stepped back, dropping the remainder of the pie crust to the street. He hated hearing Alice's name in Lawford's voice.

"You leave Alice alone," he said, well aware of the hollow futility of the command. He had to tell Alice the truth about Newhall. But then she would tell Lady Talia, and they'd both want him to stand before a House of Commons committee and relive the torture.

Peter knew he didn't have the courage for that.

He turned, shoving his hands in his pockets and hurrying away from Lawford. Before he'd gotten halfway down the street, another man stepped in his path. He looked up at a constable.

Dread swamped Peter's chest in a wave. He turned to find Lawford standing with another constable who must have been waiting nearby. The man lifted his head like a bloodhound on the scent, then started toward him.

Fear bolted through Peter. He stumbled backward. The constable made a grab for him, but he managed to evade the grasp. He turned and ran. He didn't dare look behind him, but he sensed both authorities gaining. He darted around a stack of crates, a wheelbarrow filled with fish, a cart loaded with rubbish. His breath became short and choppy, his leg muscles failing to move fast enough.

He gritted his teeth and pushed forward. One of the constables shouted his name. Before he could put on another burst of speed, a barrel-chested butcher stepped in front of him, clamping a large hand around his arm and yanking him to a halt.

"Let go!" Panicked, Peter tried to pull himself away but the man held fast until the police officers approached.

"Peter Colston." The constable grabbed his other arm. "You're under arrest."

Three days after coming up with the idea of a dinner party, James walked into a disaster. He stopped in the foyer of his town house, his hat dangling from his fingers, and stared at the carnage surrounding him. The faded paper had been torn from the walls, the furniture was overturned, the rugs pushed aside, the curtains gone. Voices rose from the drawing room, and a skinny boy of about fourteen years of age darted past with a flower vase clutched in his arms.

"Stop!" James broke from his shock and chased the boy into the dining room. He had few possessions of true value, but he certainly didn't want to be the victim of theft.

"Perfect. Put it right on the sideboard, please, Daniel."

James skidded to a halt. Talia stood in the dining room wearing a dusty apron with her hair tucked beneath a cap. The boy put the vase on the sideboard next to her and returned to the foyer.

Pushing a lock of hair away from her forehead, Talia gave James an apologetic smile. "Good afternoon, James."

"What on earth—"

"I'd *only* intended to have the curtains and rugs cleaned," she explained hastily. "But the wallpaper was already peeling off, and the furniture was in desperate need of a good polish. Not to mention the *dust*, James, really..."

"You're...you're doing this all for the dinner party?"

"Well, it needed doing anyway, so I thought we might as well take care of it beforehand, yes." Talia put her hands on her hips and looked around. "I've arranged for my father's staff to do the cooking and serving Friday night. If you've time later, I'd like to discuss the menu with you."

"I'm sure whatever you plan will be fine." James frowned as another boy trotted through the room with a pile of sofa pillows. "What—"

"I asked a few of the boys from the school to help me this afternoon."

Of course she did. James was painfully aware that he was fighting a losing battle with this woman. And worse, he was beginning to want to surrender.

Talia turned away to direct two maids into hanging the curtains, effectively dismissing James. He suppressed a surge of impatience and stalked to his study. He locked the door behind him, sat at his desk, and ignored the bustling activity through the house until the rumble of his stomach told him it was teatime.

Wary, he stepped back into the corridor. A faint hush lay over the house. He went to the drawing room and stopped. He blinked. New velvet curtains draped the sparkling clean windows, and the rug patterns and oil paintings shone bright without the layer of dust. The mahogany furniture was polished to a shine, the upholstery tears repaired, the mirrors and hearth gleaming. Fresh-cut flowers bloomed from vases, perfuming the air with fragrance. Even the chipped edge of the side table had been repaired.

Pleasure and gratitude filled his chest. A home. Talia had swept out the detritus of his house and turned it into a place of welcoming light and order. James knew without a doubt that Talia could do the same for him, if only he could give her all that she deserved in return.

"Is it all right?" Her voice sounded anxiously behind him.

He turned. She was holding a tea tray, her expression worried.

"I'm sorry," she said hastily. "I went a bit pell-mell, but if you intend to host a party you really must—"

James shook his head to stop her apology. "It's fine, Talia. More than . . . I mean, it's quite lovely. I'm . . . thank you."

Her smile hit him right in the middle of the chest. He watched as she moved past him to set the tray on the table and pour the tea. A lock of dark hair fell across the curve of her cheek. Her movements were unconsciously elegant and graceful, yet as familiar to James as his own. The rhythm of Talia's body was like a song he'd heard countless times before. And yet still he thought he could simply gaze at her forever and be happy.

Talia added sugar to a cup of tea and passed it to him. His fingers brushed hers as he took the saucer, and it was as if currents of electricity traveled through skin and into his blood. Revitalizing every part of him. He sat back, letting her pleasant chattering fill his ears.

"I've requested a menu of soup...Cook makes a delightful consommé...salmon in a vol-au-vent, and lamb cutlets with asparagus and beet root," Talia said. "Followed by duckling, and I'm hoping to order some plovers' eggs, because they're lovely in aspic. I'm also considering a shrimp salad for those who prefer a cold dish. Dessert will be lemon and cherry ice, candied nuts, and chocolate cream, of course."

She shot him another smile. This time, it twined right around James's heart like a bright green ribbon. *Chocolate cream, of course.* She knew it was his favorite. She hadn't forgotten. Just as she hadn't forgotten his fondness for almond toffee.

He took a sip of tea, which was strong and sweetened with at least two sugars. Exactly the way he liked it.

The knot in his chest loosened. She remembered so much about him, all the little details of his likes and dislikes. She paid attention, cared for him in the exact manner of a loving...wife.

For a moment, an instant, James could not resist the dream of him and Talia together. Days of shared laughter, quiet companionship, easy conversation. Nights of heated passion. Everything they already had, but magnified a thousandfold and untainted by secrets and mistrust.

He forced his attention back to Talia, the pleasing lilt of her voice. She was talking about the seating arrangements of the guests. She handed him a plate with a slice of pound cake and a cranberry muffin. James looked at the platter on the tray, which was near overflowing with cakes and breads.

"Did Polly make all that?" he asked. If so, a miracle had been wrought.

"No, I brought them from home," Talia said. "I know how much you like Cook's pound cake. There's a whole loaf in the kitchen for you."

She poured her own tea and settled against the sofa cushion. She'd removed her apron and cap, and she looked entirely at her ease seated in his drawing room with her chestnut hair curling around her neck, her eyes bright as she discussed their upcoming dinner party.

Their party. The word speared into James, breaking apart all the pleasure he'd just felt. Dammit. He couldn't think like this. Couldn't enjoy Talia's presence or, worse, become accustomed to it. He couldn't appreciate the fact that she remembered how sweet he liked his tea.

He was leaving in two weeks. Before his departure, he had to ensure Talia's engagement to another man and convince her to stop her work with the reformatory school.

If he didn't, he'd have to tell Northwood about it.

He put the cup down with a clatter, cursing inwardly. None of this was going as he'd planned. It should have been easy—all he had to do was report to her eldest brother, and his duty was done. So why hadn't James done that yet?

Because of her.

He pushed to his feet with an abrupt movement. Talia looked up at him.

"Are you all right, James?"

"No." He dragged a hand through his hair and paced

to the window. "No, Talia, I am bloody well *not* all right."

"What's the matter?"

"You." He spun to face her, angry at himself for feeling so conflicted and divided in his loyalties, angry at her for making him feel this way. "You are the matter, Talia."

She blinked, a flare of hurt darkening her eyes. "I don't understand."

His fists clenched. An image burned in his brain of the dreams he'd had about her—dreams in which she lay naked and panting beneath him, her hair tangled over the pillows and her hands gripping his shoulders.

James forced in a breath. Such lusty dreams had permeated his nights in the outback, but at least those he could attribute to loneliness, the rigors of travel, the sheer isolation of the expedition. But this...Christ, he'd had that dream just *last night*.

"You are the reason I'm incapable of fulfilling a promise," he snapped. "You are the only reason I want to return to London again. You are the reason I can't look at another woman without seeing you. The reason I promised Northwood I would ensure your safety."

Her eyes narrowed. "Why were you in Constantinople in the first place, James? Why did you visit Alexander?"

"I needed his help securing passage to the Amur Valley. The Russian vice admiral had rejected our expedition proposal, and I asked North to intervene. He agreed, with the condition that upon my return to London—"

"You *spy* on me," Talia snapped. She fisted her hands in her skirt. "That's why you followed me, isn't it,

James? That's why you came to see me again. Because you made a bargain with Alexander."

"No, I..." The protest died in his throat. He hated knowing that he would *not* have come to see Talia had it not been for his promise to Northwood.

"I would expect such high-handed conduct from Alexander, even from thousands of miles away," Talia continued. "In fact, I've become accustomed to it. But...but *you*?"

"I'm sorry." Desperation rose in him suddenly. Never before had Talia looked at him with such disappointment, not even during that life-changing afternoon at Floreston Manor. "I wasn't trying to deceive you."

"But you did."

"I wanted to protect you."

"No, you didn't! You wanted to honor your bargain with Alexander, which might as well have involved balancing his accounts, for all it would have mattered to you." She held up a hand when he tried to protest again. "James, please. I...that day at Floreston Manor, I meant what I said. I truly did. *At the time.* But now? You've spent the last year avoiding me, you wouldn't have come to see me on your own, you're running off again in less than a fortnight, you offered your help with the ragged schools yet you refuse to commit your support to boys who desperately need someone like you..."

She shook her head. "I loved you when you were brave and honorable, James. But you've changed. And somehow you've become...the opposite of the man I once knew."

No. I'm not. I'm the same.

The words stuck in his throat because he knew they

were a lie. And he couldn't stand it, couldn't bear this evidence that Talia Hall no longer loved him. Not only that, she didn't much *like* him anymore.

Given all she'd recounted, why should she? And wasn't that what he wanted, for her to keep the wall firmly between them?

"Go ahead and tell Alexander, if you must." Talia's voice dulled as she turned away from him. "I've butted heads with him and my father before. I've hoped I wouldn't have to do so again, but make no mistake. I will if I must."

James dug his fingers into the edge of the mantel to stop himself from going after her. *Let her go. If she hates you, you've no excuse to go near her. Maybe you'll finally be ashamed enough to stop thinking about her.*

"My father's kitchen staff will be here at noon on Friday," Talia said as she walked to the door. "My aunt and I will be here at five, ostensibly for tea, but of course to ensure everything is going smoothly. Your guests should arrive around eight."

The door clicked shut behind her. James scrubbed his hands over his face. He suddenly couldn't wait to get the hell out of London again. Nothing good ever happened here.

Peter woke to a gray light shining in parallel bars across from him. He rubbed his sore eyes and pushed to a sitting position on the narrow cot. His brain prickled with fear and dismay. He'd never thought he would ever be the success his father wanted, but he certainly hadn't expected to end up in prison again.

He dragged himself to the bucket in the corner and

splashed cold water over his face. He wasn't in Newhall again; he could determine that much from the cell itself and the street noise filtering through the barred window. The constable had told him he'd been accused of stealing from the mariner's shop on Ratcliffe Highway, and they'd found the compass in the pocket of the coat he'd left at his father's house.

Peter didn't give himself much credit for being intelligent, but even he could figure out that Lawford had arranged this.

He turned as a key twisted in the lock. His heartbeat kicked up as Lawford stepped into the cell. For an instant, Peter was thrown back into Newhall, the countless times he'd been trapped in his cell while Lawford loomed over him.

"Hello, Peter." Lawford's voice was deceptively friendly.

Peter fought the urge to cower. He folded his arms in front of him and lifted his head to meet Lawford's gaze. "You did this, didn't you?"

"I can't have you getting in my way." Lawford bent to pick up a tray from just outside the door and placed it on the foot of the bed. "You'd have been better off if you hadn't agreed to attend Brick Street."

The mention of Brick Street sparked something inside Peter. Lady Talia Hall had helped him before, so maybe...

Lawford shook his head. "She's finished with you, Peter. They all are. Your father and sister want nothing to do with you anymore, not now that you've gotten yourself locked up again. And Lady Talia has exhausted her efforts on your behalf, hasn't she?"

Peter swallowed to try to ease his dry throat. "What...what's next, then?"

"You'll be scheduled for a hearing, though I wouldn't expect much sympathy considering your past. I've already spoken to the magistrate myself."

Lawford didn't have to say any more, Peter thought. He'd be going back to Newhall in due course, and if he—

"Ever wished to travel, Peter?"

The unexpected question sparked new wariness. Peter eyed Lawford and shook his head, though that wasn't quite a true response. He had thought about traveling once, imagining the destinations of all the docked ships, but he suspected Lawford was speaking about a very different kind of travel.

"Where're you sending me?" he asked. He hated the sound of his voice, thin and reedy. Scared.

"There's a ship bound for Australia next Wednesday. The prison hulk supervisor assures me there's a cell available for you." Lawford straightened, his hands on his hips. "Shouldn't be too difficult a journey, likely one of the last convict transports. And I'm certain the colony will appeal to you more than Newhall."

"I want to speak to my sister."

"She won't come, Peter. Neither will your father." Lawford turned and headed back to the door. "You're alone."

Just as he was all those months in Newhall. And like then, Peter had no idea what to do next.

Chapter Thirteen

One day it will stop hurting.

Talia repeated the thought to herself again as she turned to let the maid fasten her corset. She looked in the mirror as Lucy tightened the stays, then helped her into a forest-green gown with russet trim and a heart-shaped bodice that, only now, Talia realized was reminiscent of the neckline of her gown that afternoon at Floreston Manor.

No matter. James certainly wouldn't remember.

One day...

She hoped that day dawned sooner rather than later. She sat at the dressing table while Lucy arranged her hair, adding green satin ribbons that trailed over her bare neck. A few puffs of rice powder on her skin, and Talia felt ready to face another evening in James's presence. He hadn't been at home that afternoon when she went to his house to oversee the final preparations.

Tonight would be more challenging, however, since she wouldn't have the crush of a crowd to hide in.

Well, she wasn't the one who ought to hide, in any case. James was the fickle friend who would rather lie to both her and himself rather than admit he was a coward.

"Will that be all, milady?" Lucy asked, clasping a strand of pearls around Talia's neck.

"Yes, thank you. Please tell Lady Sally I'll be waiting downstairs."

"Oh, she's feelin' a bit poorly, milady, didn't she tell you?"

Talia frowned with concern. "No, she didn't. What's the matter?"

"Headache, I think, milady. I don't know if she's planning to accompany you tonight."

Talia rose and went down the corridor to the bedchamber where her aunt was staying. She knocked once and opened the door when Sally bade her enter. She was sitting beside the fire, a book open on her lap and her glasses perched on her nose.

"Are you all right?" Talia hurried across the room. "Lucy said you were feeling ill."

"Just a bit of a headache, my dear." Sally pressed a hand to her forehead. "I'm terribly sorry, but I would hate to attend the party and then make you leave early if I begin to feel worse. Do convey my regrets to his lordship."

"Well, I can't leave you alone if you—"

"For pity's sake, Talia, it's a headache, not the plague," Sally remarked.

Talia hesitated, torn between her duty to her aunt and her promise to James.

"Go, go." Sally waved her hand in dismissal. "I'll just take a nap instead of having supper, Talia. If I'm feeling better later, I'll take myself to James's house. In the meantime, please don't worry about me."

"All right, but I'll be back early." Talia kissed her aunt's forehead, then went downstairs.

"I asked Soames to assist at Lord Castleford's tonight," she told the housekeeper as she pulled on her cloak. "So please send Kinley to fetch me if my aunt's condition worsens."

Talia had the driver take her to Arlington Street, where Soames opened the front door of James's town house.

"Everything is progressing well, my lady," the footman assured her. "Lord Castleford is in the drawing room."

"Thank you, Soames." Talia stopped in the dining room to ensure the table was set properly, then went to the kitchen for a last-minute consultation with the cook.

Smoothing her skirts, she went to the drawing room. Another footman opened the door for her and stepped aside to allow her entry.

Talia stopped for an instant to absorb the jolt of awareness that shot through her at the sight of James. Her heart thumped.

He turned from the sideboard, a glass of sherry in his hand, his figure so tall and striking that Talia's breath caught in her throat. He wore a beautiful, black superfine evening coat and a snowy white shirt that made his skin seem even darker in contrast. A green silk waistcoat hugged his lean torso, the silver buttons gleaming in the light. His hair, which had been unfashionably long, was now cropped short—a style that emphasized the masculine planes of his face and wide mouth.

"You've cut your hair." It was the first thing she could think of to say.

James blinked, as if he'd forgotten. "Yes. Paid a visit to the barber this afternoon. Had a shave, as well."

"It looks very...distinguished."

"Thank you." He gestured to the sideboard. "Sherry?"

"Please." She accepted the glass he poured, determined to ignore the awkwardness shimmering between them. Just as she finished telling him about Aunt Sally's absence, the front bell rang again.

James moved forward to greet Lord Ridley and his father, Lord Greenburg, a robust man with bristling side whiskers and a merry twinkle in his eye. Ridley came to Talia's side almost immediately after his arrival. For once, she was grateful for his presence, as it allowed her to try to ignore James.

She admitted, too, that she liked Ridley—unlike so many other young men, he didn't look at her with that faint gleam of curiosity, as if wondering whether or not to ask about her mother. As if wondering if Talia, too, had those same immoral urges.

She blushed suddenly, remembering what *else* she had confessed to James about the thoughts that had blossomed vividly in her dreams. Heavens, would she never learn to keep her secrets locked away from him?

"Lord Ridley, you told me you had a fencing match on Wednesday." She pulled her attention back to the young man. "Do tell me how you fared."

"Quite well, won two bouts with a riposte and parry." He launched into a discussion of the details of the match before pausing to take a glass of sherry from a footman. "My mother had another engagement this evening, but instructed me to ask if you might be available for a call next week."

Unease flickered in Talia's belly. She was well acquainted with the rituals of courting, though she had never carried them through to their anticipated conclusion.

"Of course."

She glanced over his shoulder to find James watching them. Their eyes met. Her heart jumped as that inevitable current of energy passed between them. Then a shutter came down over his expression and he turned away.

Talia deflected an arrow of hurt and tried to focus on what Ridley was saying. She would no longer struggle to understand James Forester's strange moods, as capricious as the sea these days. Especially when another man was making such an effort to engage her attention. She spent the next half hour talking to Ridley about his recent trip to Italy before Soames informed them that dinner was served.

The dinner went beautifully—Cook's food was succulent and delicious, and Rushton's staff served with crisp precision. Though Talia's feelings for James were still in utter turmoil, she was pleased that she'd been able to help with the dinner party. No one could fault him for being a shabby host. Even if she still couldn't fathom why he'd wanted to have a dinner party in the first place.

And she mustered all her efforts to serve as an excellent hostess. She spoke with all the guests, ensured everyone had what they needed, and was pleased to make the acquaintance of Lady Byron, a diminutive elderly woman with a birdlike face and sharp blue eyes.

"I've heard of your good works and admire your dedication, Lady Byron," Talia told her. "Was that how you became acquainted with Lord Castleford's mother?"

"We met through our church." Distress darkened Lady Byron's eyes. "Kind lady. Deserved more than she received."

The pained note in her voice struck Talia, reminding her of the other day when James had spoken of his mother.

"That's the case with most women, isn't it?" Lady Byron continued. "We deserve more than we receive."

Talia wondered if the other woman included herself in that statement. She had heard plenty of rumors about Lady Byron's brief but tumultuous marriage to Lord Byron, the beautiful, selfish, eccentric poet who had died some thirty years prior.

"Lord Castleford tells me you're involved with the ragged schools," Lady Byron remarked. "Do tell me about them."

Talia did, pleased by the other woman's interest and her intelligent understanding of the need for social reform. After dessert, the men drank port while the women had tea and chatted. Finally when the clock neared one o'clock, everyone prepared to depart.

"May I call upon you tomorrow?" Ridley asked Talia as they stood in the foyer.

"Oh, I . . ." Talia hesitated. She couldn't refuse him in

front of the other guests. She shouldn't *want* to refuse him, she reminded herself. "Yes, both my aunt and I will be at home tomorrow afternoon."

"Good." Ridley smiled and bent to brush his lips across the back of her hand.

Talia tugged her hand from his with a murmur of farewell, then went toward the foyer. James stepped in front of her, blocking her path. An odd emotion radiated from him, one that Talia could not identify.

"It was a lovely party, my lord."

"Yes, it was. Because of you."

Talia shook her head. "My father's staff did the work, James, but I'm glad I was able to help you."

"That's what you do, isn't it? Help people."

Talia looked up, puzzled by the faint note of irritation in his voice. Only within the past few years had she discovered a new avenue in her charity work, one that allowed her to finally stop living in the shadow of scandal.

"I find great satisfaction in helping others, yes," she admitted. "It's a valuable way to live one's life. Being useful."

He slanted his gaze past her to where Ridley stood. "What does Ridley think of your work?"

"We haven't spoken much about it, but he finds it admirable, I think." Apprehension flickered in Talia as she studied him—the set of his jaw and the coldness in his eyes. She'd thought he and Ridley were good friends. "I'd best be going home now, James."

"Wait here and I'll see you home safely."

"There's no need. I can—"

"Wait." He snapped the order at her before striding to say good night to the last of his guests.

Talia suppressed a surge of irritation as she went to the foyer to retrieve her cloak. The clatter of carriage wheels echoed on the street as the guests either returned home or went off to another event. Since she'd sent her father's carriage back home for Aunt Sally, Talia waited for James to fetch a cab.

He reached past her to open the door, then extended a hand. Talia grasped it without thinking as she climbed into the carriage. As usual, a shock jolted up her arm as his gloved hand closed strong and firm around hers.

Oh...

How often in the past had James clasped her hand? How often had she thought, "He will not let go of me." And he hadn't.

She remembered ice-skating on the pond at Floreston Manor when they were children—James's hand gripping hers tightly as they skated over the ice with increasing speed, before he'd taken hold of her other hand and spun her in dizzying circles, so fast that the world spun around her and their laughter floated on white clouds.

He won't let go, she'd thought then. *He will never let go.*

And he hadn't. No matter how fast they skated, no matter how many times her brothers darted past them and around them, no matter how rutted the surface was...James's grip remained tight and secure. He caught her when she skidded, stopped her from falling, guided her back to the safety of the shore.

She hadn't feared anything when James was holding her hand.

Now she pulled her hand from his as she sank onto the bench, her heart beating too fast. A painful longing rose within her—a wish for the return of those bygone days when her brothers had filled their house with boisterous laughter and teasing, when James had smiled at her with warm affection, when her parents had been...well, if not happy, at least together. In those days, they'd still been a family.

Now they were fractured beyond repair, flung to all corners of the world, and Talia didn't even have the security of her friendship with James to hold on to anymore.

He sat across from her, his features still hard. They didn't speak on the drive to King's Street, but he thanked her again for her help as he saw her to the door.

"You've gone above and beyond what I deserve from you," he said, his voice roughening with the admission.

"I still consider you a friend, James, no matter what else has changed. Good night." She went into the house, tossing her cloak on the rack before trudging upstairs.

She stopped at Aunt Sally's bedchamber to check on her aunt. Sally was still awake, sitting up in bed with a book.

"How do you feel?" Talia sat on the edge of the bed.

"Much better, my dear, thank you. How was the party?"

"Successful. Everyone appeared to enjoy themselves, and the food was excellent. It won't be the talk of the town tomorrow, but everyone will speak highly of James."

"They do already. He is very well respected."

Talia kicked off her shoes and drew her legs up beneath her. "He'd invited Lady Byron. What do you know of her?"

"Oh, heavens, she's a bit of an odd bird, isn't she? Hardly a wonder, given her marriage to Lord Byron. One can only surmise what that relationship must have been like."

"Why do you suppose she married him?"

"Because he was mad, bad, and dangerous to know, as Lady Caroline Lamb remarked," Sally said. "Some women think they can save men like that. Lady Byron said as much herself, I believe. She spoke of Byron having an angel inside him." Sally shook her head. "I wouldn't imagine many others believed the same thing."

"Perhaps she loved him," Talia suggested.

"Perhaps, though by all accounts he treated her abominably. I can't imagine falling in love with a man who didn't treat me with the utmost respect and love."

"The way Uncle Harold did."

"Yes. He wasn't the most handsome of men, of course. Didn't have women flocking around his feet. He wasn't dashing, you know, but he was so very kind and caring. He valued me. And I gave him the same in return, which is how we passed forty lovely years together."

Talia drew her knees to her chest and rested her chin on them as she studied her aunt. "I never wanted to marry, after my mother left."

"I know, dear. And perhaps you won't. But if I may suggest that you don't entirely dismiss the idea just yet...marriage can be a wonderful thing, with the right man."

Once upon a time, Talia would have thought of James after hearing a statement like that. She'd been so convinced that *he* was the right man...until he'd returned to

London and shattered all her long-held illusions about him.

"And was Lord Ridley there?" Aunt Sally asked, her voice casual.

"Yes." Talia looked suspiciously at her aunt. "James seems to have a sudden...antipathy toward him."

"Does he? Good."

"What are you up to, Aunt Sally? You haven't been able to stop talking about Lord Ridley, when you know quite well I don't want a suitor."

"I know, dear. But isn't it interesting that James is so opposed to it? Especially since he knows Ridley is perfectly suitable."

"Even if I did allow Ridley to court me, he doesn't inspire all those feelings in me that Uncle Harold did in you."

"Hmm, well..." Aunt Sally placed her spectacles on her nose and picked up her book again. "Perhaps you need to look for a man who does, then."

She didn't have to look far, Talia thought in dismay as she bid her aunt good night and went to her own room. She called for Lucy to help her undress and change into her shift, then fell into a restless sleep in which her dreams ricocheted between images of James and Lord Ridley.

Talia had never imagined herself with any man other than James. For so long, she'd pictured their entwined futures, and even after the Floreston Manor debacle she had turned her attentions to work rather than to another man. So it was decidedly odd to wake up the next morning and feel as if she were somehow betraying James, for heaven's sake, by even thinking about Lord Ridley.

Especially since James, too, could not offer her love. And Talia could not ignore the secret area of her heart that still longed to both give and receive such a love, one wrapped in the marital bliss Aunt Sally still cherished.

Pushing the ideas out of her mind, Talia dressed and went down for breakfast. Aunt Sally was still asleep, so Talia ate alone and got ready to pay a visit to the Ragged School Union offices. As she descended the stairs, tugging on her gloves, the front bell rang.

Soames strode into the foyer to answer it, his back stiffening as he pulled the door open.

"Who is it, Soames?" Talia called.

"Mr. Edward Colston and his daughter, Miss Alice Colston, my lady."

Talia paused, faint alarm rising in her. "Let them in, please."

Her alarm intensified when Mr. Colston stepped inside, his features set into a grim expression. Beside him, Alice looked upset, her eyes puffy and red.

"What happened?" Talia asked, hurrying to meet them. "Is it Peter?"

"He's been arrested, my lady," Mr. Colston said, his voice edged with anger.

Talia came to an abrupt halt, shock and dismay filling her throat. She reached for Alice's arm, feeling the other woman tremble with suppressed sobs.

"A-arrested?" Talia stammered. "What on earth for?"

"Theft from a mariner's shop on Ratcliffe Highway," Mr. Colston said. "The constable informed us this morning. He's keeping Peter at the Wapping gaol until he can be transferred back to Newhall."

"Have you seen him?"

"We have not and don't intend to," Mr. Colston said. "I wished to inform you myself because you've tried to help Peter. As I suspected, however, he will likely never change his ways, and I apologize that your efforts on his behalf have been thwarted. And that Peter never appreciated them."

An unpleasant speculation bit at Talia. "Does Mr. Lawford know?"

"Likely yes, considering he's good friends with the constable." Mr. Colston looked at Alice and nodded to the door. "I apologize for disturbing you, my lady. We'll be off now. Just wanted you to know that we've washed our hands of Peter. Shame though it might be."

Talia met Alice's gaze as she followed her father back outside. The door slammed shut behind them. Talia pressed a hand to her chest, her heart pounding against her ribs. She had a difficult time believing Peter had stolen anything, but if he'd been arrested...

Apprehension sank claws into her neck. If there was evidence against him, he'd go back to Newhall.

She grabbed her cloak and went outside to the waiting carriage, then instructed the driver to take her to the Wapping gaol. The police constable agreed to allow her ten minutes with Peter, and a guard led her back to the dank cell where he was being held.

"What happened?" Talia suppressed a surge of anger when she saw Peter hunched on the narrow cot, his eyes nearly obscured by a hank of dark hair.

He shrugged. "They found the compass in my coat pocket. What'd you think happened?"

"You didn't steal it," Talia said.

Though it was a statement, not a question, Peter shook his head anyway.

"Doesn't matter though, does it?" he asked. "Lawford'll have me back at Newhall no matter what." He lifted his head to look at her, seeming to gather his courage. "You don't owe me nothing anymore, Miss. You never did."

"It's not only because I felt I owed you, Peter. I want to help you. I…" Shame nipped at her. She'd told James the truth—her motives hadn't been entirely selfless where Peter was concerned.

"You wanted me to testify with you at that meeting," Peter said.

Talia nodded. "Two of the other boys have agreed, but they weren't at Newhall for nearly as long as you were. And I've never been granted access to Newhall, so you're the only one who can testify as to the conditions."

Peter stared down at his grubby hands. Half-circles of dirt were embedded beneath his fingernails. "If I do it, will you help me again? I don't want to go back there. I can't go home neither, not even if I went back to your school…"

"How can I be assured you won't run away again, Peter?"

"You…you can't," he admitted. A flush burned his face. "But he…Lawford…he's been talkin' about my sister, and if I…if I'm back at Newhall…"

Alice.

Talia's heart plummeted as she remembered Lawford's attentions toward her friend. The very idea that Lawford might seduce Alice into doing his bidding…

Talia reached out and gripped Peter's arm. She had to

get him out of here. Now, at least, they had a common goal—to protect Alice from Lawford.

"Since you're charged with what seems to be a relatively minor theft, I can petition the magistrate for guardianship over you in lieu of a prison sentence," she said. "I will take personal responsibility for you."

Peter eyed her warily. "I ain't done anything to make you trust me."

"No, you haven't," Talia agreed. "But your sister is my friend, and I do not believe Mr. Lawford has honorable intentions where she is concerned. I need your help. So does Alice. I'll trust you, Peter, if you'll trust me."

Silence fell between them. Talia knew that Peter had far more to lose than she did. Finally he nodded. "I will."

Chapter Fourteen

This is utterly appalling." Lady Byron squinted at the small, cramped room of the Brick Street school. "How is anyone to learn in these conditions?"

Not very well, Talia thought. She glanced at James, who stood just behind Lady Byron in the doorway. After last week's dinner party, he had sent her a note that Lady Byron wished to visit the school and he would escort her that afternoon, if Talia had no objections.

Talia was pleased at any potential support for the cause, but she wondered what James thought would be the result of the visit. He would never patronize the school, and he didn't want her involved with it any longer, so why would he care about Brick Street's success or failure?

"My lady, allow me to show you what we've accomplished thus far," Mr. Fletcher said, stepping forward to indicate that Lady Byron should follow him to the front desk. She did, casting a disapproving look toward the boys seated at the narrow tables.

At least they were behaving well, Talia thought, thanks in part to a stern lecture earlier from both her and Mr. Fletcher.

She moved closer to James, trying to deflect the familiar surge of awareness.

"Thank you for bringing her."

"She has done quite a bit of work to bring about prison reform measures," he said. "She would be a staunch ally, should she approve of your own efforts."

Talia glanced at the other woman, who was examining the books and curriculum Mr. Fletcher had prepared. She could think of only one reason James had escorted Lady Byron to Brick Street. If she were to support the school, James would be relieved of his guilt over being unable to do so himself.

He jerked his head toward the corridor. Talia followed him, curling her gloved fingers into her palms as she sensed his sudden anger.

"You will be the death of me," he said, turning to face her. A pulse beat visibly in his temple. "Your aunt told me that you have petitioned for guardianship of Peter Colston."

"Yes, and the magistrate will decide by Friday." Unease filled Talia's chest at the thought of what James might do with this revelation. "Will you tell Alexander about that, too?"

James stared at her for a moment, then grasped her shoulders, his eyes flaring with both heat and irritation. "I wrote him a telegraph this morning and couldn't send it. Do you know why?"

Talia managed to shake her head, her heart racing at his closeness, the sensation of his fingers clutching her shoulders.

"Because of you," James snapped. "Even though I made the promise to him, I feel that if I told him the truth, I'd be betraying you."

"You...you would be," Talia admitted, forcing the words through a tight throat.

James let go of her with a mutter of frustration. "And yet I am in your brother's debt. Where does that leave me?"

Before Talia could respond that he was the one who'd gotten himself into this predicament, a shout broke out from the classroom.

"Bloody bastard!"

James turned and ran back into the room. Talia followed. A desk lay overturned in the middle of the room, and the boys crowded in a circle, yelling and cheering as a tall, skinny boy called Ben wrestled a bigger boy to the floor. Mr. Fletcher was trying unsuccessfully to pull Ben away.

"Stop it!" Talia rushed into the snarl of flailing fists.

James plunged forward to grab her just as Talia entered the fray. She reached for Ben's arm. The boy threw his fist back for another punch. James grasped Talia's shoulders and yanked her back out of harm's way just as the blow caught him on the side of the jaw.

"James!"

He thrust her aside, grabbed Ben by the back of his shirt, and hauled him off the bigger boy. A crash sounded as another couple of boys knocked over the benches and joined the fray. A chair leg hit James above the eye. He shoved the other boys back and pulled Ben to his feet.

"Out!"

"Lousy bugger tellin' me what I ought to—" Ben twisted from James's grip and threw another punch hard enough to knock James's head back. He shoved Ben toward the door. Blood dripped from the gash on his forehead.

"Get out," he snapped.

Ben glowered at him, swiped his nose, and headed for the door. Mr. Fletcher was bending to help the other boy to his feet. Blood trailed from the boy's nose, and his left eye had begun to swell shut.

"Henry!" Fletcher ordered. "Go and fetch Mrs. Wickers. I believe Mr. Chatham here is suffering a broken nose."

Another boy darted from the room. Talia grabbed James's arm and tried to turn him toward her.

"Never mind, Talia."

"Let me see."

A bruise was beginning to darken his jaw, blood dripping down over his eyebrow. Talia muttered a noise of exasperation and turned to Lady Byron, who was still standing by the front desk. "I'm terribly sorry, my lady. We don't often have such occurrences, but perhaps another day would be more appropriate for your visit."

"Perhaps," Lady Byron acknowledged with a nod.

Talia had the sudden sense it might not matter if she agreed to James's proposition or not, though Lady Byron was likely familiar with the rough behavior of delinquents and prisoners.

She suggested to Mr. Fletcher that they return the following day, then left him in charge of the boys for the remainder of the afternoon. James and Lady Byron had taken Lady Byron's carriage to Wapping, and she instructed the driver to leave Talia and James at King's Street before she returned to her own town house.

"Hot water, please, Soames." Talia ushered James into the drawing room, peering more closely at the cut on his forehead.

The footman took one look at James and frowned. "Shall I send for the doctor, milady?"

"No. His lordship suffers only from lack of prudence, which I fear no doctor can cure." Talia rested her hands on her hips as she watched James pace to the other end of the drawing room. "Sit down, James."

"I don't need to sit down," he muttered, shoving a swath of hair from his forehead. "That could have been you, Talia. It's only a matter of time before it will be. Then what? You're going to rely on Fletcher, who doesn't look as if he could lift a teapot, much less protect you from a gang of ruffians."

"Please do not speak ill of Mr. Fletcher."

"I don't like him."

"I daresay he doesn't like you either."

"You're changing the subject."

"Because you won't," Talia snapped. "You want me to stop doing something worthwhile and useful just because of a promise you made to Alexander, yet you keep pretending it's because you're concerned about me."

"I am concerned about you!" James thundered, his eyes darkening as he strode back to stand in front of her. "If this were only about North, I'd have telegraphed him a week ago, but I didn't. Because I don't want you to hate me any more than you already do."

Talia stared at him, her throat aching. "I don't hate you, James."

"You act as if you do."

"I'm upset with you." She paused, then again gave him the truth. "I could never hate you."

Before James could respond, Soames came into the room with a bowl of water, gauze, and clean cloths. He set the tray down. "Anything else, milady?"

"No, thank you. James, sit down, please."

This time, he did. Talia rinsed a cloth in hot water and went to stand in front of him. Though her heart pounded at being close to him, she kept her touch impersonal as she brushed his hair back to examine the scratch on his forehead, then his bruised knuckles. She cleaned the minor scrapes, taking his hand in hers and wiping the dried blood off. She glanced up to find him watching her, his brows drawn together and his expression closed.

"I'm glad you didn't tell Alexander," she finally said. "Thank you."

He frowned. "Don't thank me. I've reached the limits of my patience."

Talia released his hand and dropped the cloth back on the tray. She sank onto the edge of a chair, wondering if there would ever be a time when it was only she and James in the room. When her brothers and father were left on the other side of a closed door where they belonged.

Only once had she and James been entirely alone. Even though the memory of that afternoon at Floreston Manor still made Talia flush with embarrassment, she remembered their kiss as if it were a candle flame encased in glass—burning, glowing, crystal-clear, and utterly private.

"You've always been loyal to him," she said. "Alexander, I mean."

He nodded, studying his scraped knuckles. "He had what I didn't."

"What was that?"

"All of you."

Silence fell, broken by the crackle of the fire. An ache spread through Talia's chest. She knew little about James's childhood, save that he'd been the only child of his parents and that their marriage appeared to have been an unhappy one. When he wasn't away at school or university, he'd spent a great deal of time with the Hall brothers. As if he didn't want to be at home.

And even though Talia's parents had lived within a brittle, formal marriage that ultimately cracked apart, she'd always had her brothers to rely upon. The scandal and divorce had separated them—and, of course, Alexander had become even more overbearing in his protectiveness—but never once had Talia doubted her brothers' dependability and love for her.

She looked at James, allowing her gaze to trace the hard edge of his jaw, the strength of his profile. Firelight glinted in his brown eyes, highlighting the flecks of gold in his irises.

"What happened?" she asked quietly.

James raised an eyebrow in question.

"You told me you'd never marry," Talia reminded him. "That you're not *meant* for marriage. Why did you say that?"

He stretched his hands out, flexing his fingers. "I'd not be any good at it."

"Just because your parents were unhappy doesn't mean you wouldn't be good at marriage."

James frowned. "What do you know of my parents?"

"Not a great deal. But you wouldn't have spent so much time with us or away at school if you'd wanted to be with them." *If they'd wanted to be with you.*

James pushed to his feet, the muscles of his shoulders cording with tension. "I was thirteen the day I walked in on my parents arguing...my father slapped my mother across the face and she fell and hit her head against the corner of a table, and...well, I ran to stop him, and he hit me too. I later realized it was my mother who'd sent me away to school, who told the tutors to keep me away from my father. She knew he'd..."

He shrugged and turned to face Talia. "She died when I was seventeen."

"I remember. She'd been ill again."

"No." James shook his head. "My father *told* everyone she was ill. I was at Eton. I returned the moment I received word. She died the next day."

"Of what?"

"Overdose of laudanum." He spoke in a dispassionate tone.

The implication speared through Talia. She stared at him. "Overdose...?"

"She'd committed suicide. She knew I was going away to Oxford the following month. I was bigger than my father by then, and we'd had several brawls when I was home, though my mother begged me not to confront him. She worried about what he'd do, thought he'd find some way to ruin my future. He couldn't disinherit me, of course, but she...she waited until she knew I could take care of myself before she gave up."

The air tightened with a dark sense of foreboding. Talia gripped her hands together so hard that her fingers ached.

"Her illnesses were..."

She couldn't even fathom it, let alone speak the words aloud. James lowered his head, pinching the bridge of his nose between his fingers.

"I didn't understand until it was too late." Old anger and frustration threaded his voice. "I didn't know the extent of it, Talia, but I should have. I *should have* known. I should have done something. Instead, I—"

"How could you have known?" Talia asked. "They sent you away, James."

"But I saw him...I mean, I knew he was violent, that he beat her, and still I didn't...I didn't realize that she was hiding or...or *recovering*, for the love of God. Why didn't I figure that out until it was too late?"

"For the same reason I didn't know my mother was unhappy with my father. We can never know all that goes on between two other people, James. And sometimes I think my mother kept her unhappiness from me too, as a way of protecting me. Just as your mother did."

James expelled his breath on a hard sigh, dragging his hands over his face. "I'll never stop thinking I should have done more. That I *could* have, if only I'd paid closer attention. Other people must have known, must have seen what was occurring, but no one did anything to stop it. Myself included."

Talia stared at her hands. No words existed to ease

his guilt, just as none would ever ease the pain of her mother's betrayal.

"It was my father's fault, Talia." James turned to face her, his eyes glittering. "He might as well have killed her himself. He never paid for what he did to her. And now I bear his title and hold his lands..."

"James, they're not *his* anymore. They're yours. Don't give him such power over you."

He looked at her, something flaring in the depths of his eyes. Talia struggled for a way to make him understand that the past would fade only if he stepped out of its shadow.

"I didn't want to be poisoned by my parents' marriage and divorce," she said. "I refused to be. When I told you I wanted to...to marry you, I believed we could create something completely different. Something good."

A marriage of the type Aunt Sally described, a joyous combination of love, respect, and a wild, mutual passion that Talia could hardly even imagine.

She looked up at James. She was no longer embarrassed by her confession. She'd had the courage to tell him the truth, to prove to herself that she would not be afraid of loving him.

James watched her with a hooded gaze, his eyes glittering but his face lined with tension.

"You can't outrun the guilt, James," Talia whispered.

His mouth tightened. "I'm not trying to."

"Yes, you are." Talia rose to approach him, her heart thumping slow and heavy against her chest. "You think that by leaving London, you can escape the horror of what happened, of thinking you failed. If you're at sea or on a mountain or in a desert...you're not trapped by your title or your past. You're not Lord Castleford there. You're just...James."

He stared at her, his gaze tracing her face as if he'd never seen her quite this way before. Then he lifted a hand to touch her cheek, brushing his warm fingertips against the hollow beneath her cheekbone and stroking down to her throat. Her skin tingled in reaction. He rested his fingers against the base of her throat.

"How do you know all that?" James whispered.

"I know *you*." She swallowed hard, her gaze searching his face as certainty flooded her heart. "I've never thought of you as Lord Castleford. To me, you've only ever been James."

My James.

"God in heaven, Talia." A tremble coursed through him as he cupped her cheek. He brushed his thumb against her lips, sparks flaring in the darkness of his eyes, as if something lit within him. Then he lowered his mouth to hers, his touch hesitant, uncertain, feather light.

Talia placed her hand on the side of his neck and shifted. Warmth surged through her as their mouths settled together in a tender kiss that seemed to encompass all the years of their friendship. His lips were so warm against hers, seamless, his hand sliding around to the nape of her neck as he drew her closer. The world dissolved around them, and she fell again into this moment of lovely pleasure.

"I..." He lifted his head, his breath hot against her lips even as restraint corded his muscles. "Talia, have you any idea what you've given me over the years?

You've been the only woman I've ever relied on, the most steadfast, loyal person I know. Whenever I've dreaded returning to London, I've thought, *But Talia will be there* and then I'd anticipate seeing you again.

"I'd think of our talks and outings and games, of how you'd like whatever trinket I'd brought for you. I'd think of you inviting me for tea, and that you'd be certain to serve all my favorite cakes and you'd know exactly how much sugar to put in my tea...you've been the *one* good thing here in London, Talia, the only reason I've actually looked forward to coming back."

Talia's breath caught in her throat, her heart hammering. *Then love me, James.* The wish bloomed bright and hard again, as if the ice surrounding it had melted under the warmth of spring sunshine.

"But I..." He pushed away from her, his jaw clenching. "I've given you *nothing* in return."

Talia pressed a hand to her chest. Disbelief spilled through her.

"You...you think you've given me nothing?" She almost couldn't voice the question.

James spread his arms out, his expression dark. "What? What have I ever given you but grief, Talia?"

A lump formed in her throat. She gripped the folds of her skirt, her breath coming in shallow bursts as she turned to the door.

"Come with me, James."

"What?"

"Come." She sharpened her voice and strode from the drawing room without looking to see if he was following.

A moment later, she heard his boots ringing against

the marble floor of the foyer. She climbed the stairs, her senses prickling with awareness of him behind her. She pulled another breath into her lungs and went to her bedchamber, flinging the door open wide.

James stopped in the doorway. His shoulders were tense, his expression wary as he cast his gaze about the feminine room—the soft, airy curtains and white lace counterpane, the paintings of cloud-peppered skies and idyllic landscapes populated by languid figures in flowing Grecian robes.

James settled his gaze back on Talia with faint surprise, as if struck by the fact that she had invited him into this very private space. He took a step backward.

Talia turned and opened the bottom drawer of her desk. Her hands shook as she removed the bundles of letters and slid them from their binding ribbons. One by one, she tossed the bundles onto the bed, where the papers piled into a hill. Talia grabbed one from the top and opened it, her vision blurring as she read the first line of James's bold handwriting.

My dear Talia…

"'I wish you could hear these drums, which the Ceylonese use instead of flutes or wind instruments,'" she read aloud. "'They say it produces "a sound like thunder breaking on a rock, against which the sun rises," and I daresay that's a most apt description…'"

Talia let the page flutter back to the bed and picked up another. "'There was a storm at sea tonight, huge waves looking as if they'd swallow the ship whole before they appeared to melt away beneath us, rather like a vicious-looking dog who turns out to be docile upon approach...' "

Another letter. " 'Cape York is astonishing. I wish you could see the Crimson Cliffs, for they truly are a reddish color. Beyond was an iceberg almost perpendicular on one side, with a fringe of crystal icicles and columns slender as those one might see on a mosque. There was a gallery, too, of the most astonishing emerald-green (of course, that brought you to my mind), and with the sun glittering from above, it all resembled something from a fairy tale...

" 'The Japanese garden is beautiful in summer, with wild strawberries blooming along the walkways and water lilies floating on the pond. Amid flowering plants at the teahouse we sat at square, lacquered tables laden with teacups, sweetmeats, cakes, and bowls of rice and fruit. The tea was quite good, though somewhat bitter, and I admit to a brief longing for my oversweetened Indian tea...' "

Talia dropped the letter and grabbed another, another, another. " 'The summit of Ekeberg Hill in Oslo affords one the most lovely view, a sea of rolling pastures dotted by red and white cottages... Today I visited the garden at Fort William, where there is an abundance of raspberries, gooseberries, strawberries, and currants (I am quite certain your father's cook would make an excellent muffin with such large berries as flourish here)... The stream enters the Tigris approximately five miles below Baghdad, and the remains of a bridge and the geographical position lead me to believe it is the Isa Canal...' "

The pages fell from Talia's fingers like autumn leaves

as a thousand images crowded her mind—all evoked by the scrawl of James's writing, the allure of his adventures.

He hadn't moved, an odd stillness surrounding him as he watched her, his expression unreadable.

Tears choked Talia's throat. She went to the curio cabinet resting against the opposite wall and opened the doors. From the numerous drawers and shelves contained within, she pulled out items and put them on the nearby table. "A Greek coin. An Indian arrowhead. Shells and sea glass from the Indian Ocean. Roman pottery fragments, a tiger's tooth, a Chinese lantern, a Persian inkstand…"

She stopped, her tears overflowing, barraged by the reminder of how everything he'd sent and brought to her had filled her with so many hopes, wishes, and dreams. His letters, all the imaginings they evoked of distant, exotic lands, had even sustained her in the dark days of her mother's abandonment.

"My God, James." Talia whirled to stare at him. "Have you not known? You think you've given me nothing?" She shook her head, swiping at her eyes. "You've…you've given me the *world*."

He pushed away from the doorjamb and closed the distance between them in three long strides. Before Talia could speak again, he grabbed her shoulders and hauled her to him, his mouth descending on hers with a kiss as fierce and potent as a storm.

Talia gasped, her body softening in uncontrollable response as she parted her lips to allow him inside. His tongue swept into her mouth, a deep invasion the complete opposite of his previous hesitant kiss.

"I cannot drive you from my thoughts," he hissed, his hands moving to the sides of her neck as he angled her mouth to his. "I could be in the middle of a desert, the summit of the tallest mountain...and I would be thinking of *you*. In the outback, I lay awake at night imagining how much you'd like the land, the stars, the animals. I wondered what you were doing back in London, what parties you were attending, what dress you were wearing, if a man had requested your hand...and how I would not be able to bear it if you accepted."

He brushed her tears away with his thumbs, his gaze searching her face. "I wanted to write to you, Talia, so much. But you so consumed my every thought, I...I feared what I would say to you."

Talia swallowed hard, reaching up to skim her fingertips against his cheek. "Tell me now."

Heat flared white-hot in his eyes, even as he started to draw away from her. Talia slipped from his grasp and went to close and lock the door, her heart pounding wildly. She returned to twine her hands around his neck and pulled him back to her.

"Don't run away, James," she whispered against his lips. "Not from me."

He muttered something beneath his breath, tension still coiling through him as Talia pressed her mouth more firmly to his. She gripped his shoulders, warmth flowing in her blood and assuaging any hint of doubt.

"Tell me," she repeated.

"I feared I would confess how much I desire you." He tightened his hands on the sides of her head and stared down at her. "I *wanted* to tell you that my dreams of you were wholly indecent, that I'd wake at night aching for you... God, Talia." He shook his head. "I shocked even myself with the utter lewdness of my thoughts."

A smile tugged at Talia's mouth. Only because it was James did she experience a riotous thrill of both excitement and purely feminine satisfaction. He may have refused her love, thwarted their first kiss, but the idea of them together had flourished in the secret recesses of his mind. He hadn't been able to dislodge thoughts of what they *could be*... if they both dared to surrender.

"Kiss me again," she whispered.

He did. A fleeting hesitation warred with his desire before he lowered his mouth to hers on a groan. Talia met him halfway, her heart blooming with both certainty and pleasure, as if all the years she'd spent longing for James had led to this one moment. His hands flexed against her waist, then spread up her back as he pulled her closer.

Emboldened, Talia sank against him, absorbing the heat of his body as their kiss deepened. She knew instinctively that she had to be the one to push matters forward, as James would most certainly fight to protect her virtue... no matter how badly Talia wanted to give it to him.

She threaded her hands through his thick hair, her head filling with the warm, salty scent of his skin. She stepped forward, catching him off guard and tumbling them both onto the bed. She fell on top of him, her arousal intensifying at the sensation of his long body stretching beneath hers.

James tightened his hands on her waist. "Talia—"

"Stop fighting this." She uncoiled her legs, pushing

up her petticoats to straddle him, his hard thighs pressed between hers. A bolt of arousal shot through her. "Make both our dreams come true, James."

Finally.

She planted her hands on either side of his head and lowered her mouth to his again. Spurred by pure instinct, she captured his lower lip between her teeth and slid her tongue against his. A groan shook his chest. Talia's fingers trembled as she sat up and pulled his loose cravat from around his neck, then began unbuttoning his linen shirt.

Her heart lurched as his body was bared to her questing touch. She stared at the hair-roughened muscles of his chest, the ridges leading to the waistband of his trousers. With a hard swallow, she pushed his coat off his shoulders, then moved back to allow him to hitch the shirt over his head.

"Oh." Her breath escaped on a rush, a coil of pleasure winding through her as she drank in the sight of his naked torso, his smooth, taut shoulders, and his corded arms.

"You're beautiful," she said truthfully.

He gave a muffled laugh and shook his head. "I'm a weak, useless coward where you're concerned, Talia, but for the life of me I can't bring myself to care right now."

He pushed upward, rolling her swiftly onto her back as he came over her like a lion approaching its prey— all hot, golden skin and fierce eyes, his sun-streaked hair spilling over his forehead. Excitement and apprehension burst through her.

She parted her lips in invitation, then sank into the

kiss when their mouths met again. She dimly thought she could lie there kissing James for hours on end, even as urgency began to throb in her lower body. Her clothes seemed to constrict around her, her breath shallow against the compression of her corset.

She squirmed beneath James, sliding her hands over the ridges of his abdomen. "James, I...I want..."

He uncoiled to sit up, his skin flushed with heat. He extended a hand to touch her, then stopped.

Talia stared at him, the air between them crackling with energy. She shifted off the bed and got to her feet, reaching up to tug her hair from the pins. She held the long mass away from her neck and turned her back to him. For a heart-stopping second, he didn't move. Then she felt his hands at the nape of her neck as he began unfastening the buttons marching over the back of her gown.

She shrugged out of it, letting the printed cotton fall in a puddle at her feet, and unfastened her petticoats. She reached behind her to tug at the laces of her corset.

"Hurry," she murmured, her skin tingling with anticipation for his touch, every part of her being aching to be free of the confinement.

He loosened the ties enough for her to unhook the corset in the front and slip it off. Talia took a deep breath, her entire body softening with pleasure. She became painfully aware of her nakedness beneath her loose cotton shift, the weight of her breasts, and warmth collecting between her thighs. She crossed her arms, anxiety twisting through her suddenly.

Then James settled his hands on her hips. With an exhale of breath, he stroked the curves of her hips, around to her buttocks, down to her thighs. Talia trembled as the heat of his palms burned through the thin cotton.

"Turn around," he whispered hoarsely.

She did. Nervousness fluttered in her belly. James's eyes burned with heat as he cast his gaze over her, lingering on the swells of her breasts, the firm nipples tenting the material. He cupped her left breast in his hand and then, to Talia's shock, he leaned forward and took her right nipple into his mouth.

Talia gasped, clenching her fingers instinctively in his hair as the heat of his mouth jolted arousal straight to her core. Through the damp material of her shift, he sucked the taut bud between his lips and rolled his tongue over it until Talia's breath burned her lungs and trembles coursed through her blood. Then James grabbed her waist and brought her back onto the bed.

Talia's anxiety eased a bit as he lifted his head, his eyes filled with both lust and affection. He held her gaze as he gathered her shift and began to ease it up past her thighs, sliding his hand beneath it to touch the warmth of her torso before stopping. Talia knew what he was waiting for, and she pulled the shift over her head in one movement.

"God, Talia…" James's eyes glazed with lust as he stared at her bare breasts and the tapered curve of her waist.

Emboldened by the heat of his gaze, Talia pushed her drawers off, and then for the first time she was naked in front of a man…in front of the only man she had ever loved and ever would love. She rose to one elbow and brought her mouth to his. After another few minutes of delicious kissing, she felt James's hand probing gently between her thighs.

"James..."

"Wait," he whispered against her mouth. "If you'll let me..."

His thumb brushed against a spot that shocked her with a jolt of arousal; then he pressed his finger inside her. Talia swallowed an instinctive protest, forcing her muscles to loosen. He kissed her again, twining his tongue with hers as he pushed another finger into her and worked her with a deliberate intent toward...

Talia gasped, jerking away from him as a sudden pain spasmed through her. James withdrew his fingers, but kept his thumb circling around the knot where Talia's pleasure was centered. She tensed, bewildered by the confusing mixture of lingering pain and pleasure.

James murmured a soothing noise, his breath hot as he trailed his lips across her cheek and down to her neck. He licked the damp hollow of her throat as he worked his fingers faster, the simultaneous sensations causing heat to blaze across Talia's skin. A moan escaped her. She parted her legs wider, straining toward the completion of this mounting urgency. Then the pressure broke and she cried out James's name, an explosion of stars crashing through her blood.

He captured her cries with his mouth, his tongue sliding over her lower lip as the movement of his fingers slowed. Talia twisted beside him, gasping, already craving that incredible rapture again. She rose to her elbows, stunned by the smoldering look in his eyes.

"Is there..." She swallowed to ease her parched throat. "Is there more?"

James gave a pained laugh, drawing her to him to brush his lips across her cheek. "Oh, there's more, sweet Talia. So much more."

She pressed her hand to his chest, feeling his heart thumping wildly against her palm. "Show me."

His breath escaped on a groan as he grasped her wrist and guided her hand down his abdomen. Talia brushed her fingers against the heavy bulge in his trousers. Curiosity sparked in her as she unfastened the buttons— all apprehension fading in the wake of this extraordinary heat and pleasure. She reached into his trousers and touched the smooth, pulsing stalk.

"I want to see you."

His jaw clenched as he shifted to rid himself of his trousers. Talia stared at the length of his erection, her heart lurching with both trepidation and excitement at the thought of him pushing inside her. She took a breath and wrapped her hand around his shaft, tracing the pulsing veins and hard knob with her fingertips.

When James let out another muffled groan, Talia stopped to look at him. His face was flushed, his chest damp, and his jaw still clenched in resistance. God, but he was beautiful, all sweaty and disheveled, his hot gaze drinking in the sight of her naked body.

"Should I...?" She suddenly wanted to give him as much pleasure as he'd already given her. "What should I do?"

"Just...touch me." He reached to wrap her fingers tighter around him, then guided her hand up and down the length of his shaft. "Like that."

He shifted again to ease her onto her back, half on top of her. Talia parted her thighs, knowing at least this part of the intimate act, but James didn't move between them. He stayed at her side, one hand delving into her hair as she stroked her hand over his erection and urged him toward the same exquisite completion he'd given her.

He thrust into the vise of her fist. Talia squirmed, turning to open her mouth beneath his as her breasts crushed against his chest and the sound of their breath filled the air. He pressed his face against the side of her neck as she increased the speed of her stroking. Then a hard shudder coursed through him, his growl rumbling against her skin as his seed spilled onto her belly.

Renewed urgency coiled around Talia as she loosened her hold on him. James wrapped an arm around her shoulders and pulled her closer. She rubbed her hot cheek against his chest, her blood filling with the scent and feel of him.

"Don't you want to…" Her voice trailed off.

"More than you know." He stroked her tangled hair away from her face. Tension laced his body. "But I'm not such a bastard that I'll put you at that kind of risk."

Talia settled against him, fitting her curves to his side. She slid her hand over his chest and tried to ignore all the underlying implications of his statement.

Silence fell. James coiled a lock of her long hair around his finger.

"I'll see about procuring a special license," he finally said. "So we can marry before I leave in June."

Talia's heart froze. For a moment, she couldn't move.

"Marry?" She forced the word through her tight throat.

"I'll not dishonor you by taking advantage of your virtue without marrying you."

"Taking..." The cold spread from her heart through her veins, freezing all the lovely warmth still lingering throughout her body. She pulled away from him and reached for her discarded shift, trying to stop her voice from trembling with anger. "You didn't take advantage of me, James. I offered myself to you."

He rose on his elbows to watch her as she pulled the shift over her head. "All the more reason we should marry soon."

"And I didn't do this with the expectation that we'd *marry*," Talia snapped.

Her hands shook as she strode to the wardrobe and grabbed a dress that buttoned up the front. She slipped it on and fastened it closed, her breath coming in shallow bursts.

"Then what?" James pulled on his trousers, a current of irritation filling the air around him. "I won't be the kind of husband you deserve...I *can't* be...but I swear to you I will do everything in my power to ensure your security and happiness. You will have whatever you desire. I'll give your school enough money so the union can hire someone else to run the reformatory—"

"Stop." An ache cracked open in Talia's heart, so painful that she had to grab the wardrobe door to steady herself. "You...you think I'll agree to marry you and stop my work with the school simply because we've been intimate? Do you not know me at all, James?"

He stared at her, his hands fisting at his sides. "You're the one who confessed your love for me, Talia. You said you *wanted* to marry me."

"Over a year ago! And I haven't spent all these

months sitting in my room pining over you. I haven't been hoping you would return to London and change your mind about marrying me." A sudden, jagged thought stabbed her. She stared at him. "God, James. Did you think I was trying to *trap* you?"

"No! I thought...dammit, Talia." James paced across the room, his bare shoulders bunching with tension. "Ever since I returned, I've been trying to stay away from you, trying to pretend I haven't wanted you so badly my blood burns. But I can't fight it anymore, not with you. I'll give you whatever you want, *anything*, if you'll marry me and—"

"Do your bidding," Talia finished, her voice dull.

"My only request is that, at the very least, you work with the reformatory school at a distance that befits a woman of your status."

Talia pressed her hands to her eyes. "You sound like Alexander. Like my father."

"It is not an unreasonable request."

"And if I refuse?"

"Agree, and I give you my word Northwood will never know of your ventures to Wapping." His voice tightened. "You deserve better than me, but with our marriage you'll never again have to contend with over-familiar young men, never have to wonder what people think of you, never have to choose usefulness over respectability. You will have your own household, an unlimited allowance, the security of marriage, and I hope the approval of your father and brothers."

Talia lowered her hands to look at him. His hands were fisted at his sides, his expression dark. The ache in her heart expanded, breaking through the walls she'd tried so hard to construct. The walls meant to keep James out.

"If I truly sought all of those things," she said, "I could marry any number of men. Lord Ridley, for one."

His jaw clenched. "You will not marry Ridley, Talia, no matter what—"

He stopped, his gaze moving past her shoulder suddenly. A frown creased his forehead. Talia turned to see that he was looking at the open doors of her wardrobe. Too late, she realized what had caught his attention.

Her heart lurched. She hurried to slam the doors shut, but James reached them first. He pushed one door open and reached inside to grab a garment off a hook. He pulled it out and stood staring at it in shock.

Talia swallowed hard, crushing the folds of her skirt in her fists. Anxiety and embarrassment twisted through her stomach.

James extended the coat. "This is mine."

Certainly there was no point in lying. "You gave it to me that…that afternoon at Floreston Manor."

A blush crawled over her neck.

James looked at her with bafflement. "And you kept it?"

"It seemed…pointless to discard a perfectly good coat." Talia almost winced at the ridiculousness of the remark. Nothing could account for a woman keeping a man's coat as if it were a precious keepsake, except if she believed that it *was*.

She took the coat from him and hung it back in the closet, smoothing her hand over the soft wool that still held the scents of cinnamon and tea.

"This is why I offered myself to you," she confessed.

There would never come a time when she could be less than truthful with him. "Because I told you the truth when I said I've often thought of you and dreamed of you. Because even now, I trust you. But I will not marry you."

"You've kept my coat for over a year, Talia! Surely that means you still feel something for me."

"I won't marry you, James."

His eyes sparked. "Why not?"

"Because you will never love me," Talia said, the words breaking like glass in her mouth. "And because I don't want to love you anymore."

She turned, unable to look at him any longer, and left the room.

Chapter Fifteen

James scrubbed at his sore eyes. He didn't think he'd slept at all in the two days since his encounter with Talia. "What about early departure?"

"Doesn't look promising, I'm afraid," Mr. Graham said. "We can get the equipment loaded, but Dr. Yarrow's schedule prevents him from leaving London before the tenth, and you still need to secure a second medical officer."

"Find me someone quickly, then. I'll speak to Yarrow."

Graham blinked. "Don't you wish to interview the candidates yourself?"

"No. Just ensure he's qualified and understands the position." James jerked his head toward the door. "Go."

Graham gathered his belongings and stood, still looking baffled as he headed out the door. James tried to focus on the papers strewn across his desk, but the columns and rows blurred in front of him. His head ached.

He couldn't even grasp the things flying like gnats through his brain—snippets of details, tasks, plans…all sinking beneath the overwhelming, overpowering thoughts of Talia.

He stared at the papers. Graham had drafted a letter to the bank authorizing a sizable donation to the Ragged School Union, but James hadn't yet signed it. He had the sick feeling that as much as the union could use the money, Talia would find the gesture an utter insult.

Which, in some way, it probably was.

He groaned and pressed his hands to his eyes again. She'd kept his letters. She'd kept everything he'd ever brought back for her. Bloody hell. She'd kept his *coat*. He wished to heaven he had something of hers he could have kept close.

He wished above all else he had the courage to tell her he loved her. To confess that thoughts of her had only ever made him happy, that anticipation had flared inside him whenever he was going to see her again. He wished he could tell her the secret wish of his heart, the one he'd never dared to acknowledge until now, that some miracle would occur and allow him to live the rest of his life with her.

His throat constricted.

"Lady Sally, milord." Polly's voice broke into his thoughts.

James lifted his head and stood as Lady Sally entered the room. Polly dipped into an awkward curtsy.

Sally gave the girl an indulgent smile as she passed. "Good morning, James. The place looks wonderful since the last time I was here. Talia does have a nice touch, does she not?"

James swallowed hard. That was an understatement. His mind flashed to memories of Talia's slender fingers gliding over his chest, wrapping around his—

"You passed a pleasant morning?" Sally asked as she settled into a chair before the desk.

He struggled to nod. His morning had been bitter with regret and self-recrimination.

"Tea, Lady Sally?" he managed to ask.

"No, thank you, James. I'm on my way to pay a call on Lady Hamilton, but I wanted to stop and let you know that things are progressing well with Lord Ridley."

Bloody hell. The woman was going to talk to him about Ridley *now*?

"Er, my lady, I'm in the middle of—"

"Yes, yes. I'll be out of your hair in a moment, James." Sally leaned forward, her eyes crinkling at the corners. "Lord Ridley does seem to have taken to Talia. Why, he's coming this afternoon to take us to the British Museum, which led me to believe you must have informed him how Talia enjoys the Egyptian displays. Then he's taking us to the Albion afterward for tea. Isn't that lovely?"

James tried not to grit his teeth. "Lovely."

"Talia speaks of him quite often too, though she's still a bit guarded. To be expected, I suppose. Rushton isn't scheduled to return until the end of August, so we've plenty of time to get matters settled."

James clenched his jaw. "Settled, my lady?"

"To ensure Talia and Ridley's agreement. I'm certain Ridley and Lord Greenburg will wish to discuss the matter with Rushton."

"Perhaps it's best if it's not rushed," James said.

"Oh, Talia would never allow that," Sally agreed. "That's why I'm thankful we've another few months left. By the end of July, she might see what a good match she's found in Ridley. Except…"

Her voice trailed off. James looked up.

"Except?" he said.

"Oh, nothing." Sally waved her hand dismissively.

James's jaw ached. "Except *what*, my lady?"

"Well, it's a bit silly but…" Sally sighed. "I've spoken to Talia recently about my own marriage to my beloved Harold. You remember him, don't you? Wonderful man. And I'm afraid I might have given Talia the notion that *her* marriage should be one of mutual respect, love, and…well, passion."

"Passion?"

"Yes." Sally leaned forward, fixing him with her gaze. "And while Lord Ridley is delightful, I'm afraid I might have misjudged the degree of *passion* he inspires in Talia. I do fear she might hold out for a husband who will provide her with all three of those qualities…in *plenty*."

That notion sank into James like a claw.

Sally rustled around gathering her gloves. "I still would like to pursue this plan with Lord Ridley, James, but matters haven't progressed so far that we can't change our minds. If one of us happens to come up with another more suitable candidate, you know."

James narrowed his eyes. Sally gave him a bland smile.

"Keep thinking on it, would you?" she asked. "As will I, of course. Remember—mutual respect, love, and *passion*. Shall I write it down for you?"

"Er, no. No, that won't be necessary."

Sally waved her fingers at him and headed for the door. "Much obliged to you, James. No need to see me to the door. Do take a rest, if you feel the need. You're looking a bit peaked."

She bustled off. James rested his head in his hands. He didn't care if all of civilization were at stake. He *would not* seek out another man for Talia who could provide her with love and goddamned *passion*.

He shook his head. This business with Ridley was difficult enough. James tried not to imagine his friend with Talia, but of course it was impossible. He imagined them seated beside each other in the carriage, walking together in the museum, their heads bent as they discussed mummies and hieroglyphics...

A growl rumbled in his chest. Although she'd resisted the idea until now, Talia knew that marriage would be a benefit to her—she'd all but told James so. It was marriage to *him* that was an anathema.

Which was exactly how he should *want* her to feel.

James pushed away from his desk and paced to the windows. As frantically as he shoved things around in his fogged brain, he could discern no solution. He abhorred the idea of Talia going anywhere near another man, let alone marrying one, but there was no feasible way to make her marry *him*.

And if he tried to bully her into it by threatening to tell Alexander the truth of the Brick Street school... well, Talia would either call his bluff or resent him for the rest of their lives. Or both.

Which meant James had to leave Talia well enough alone. He gave a short nod as he convinced himself of that indisputable fact. He would leave London as scheduled—earlier, if he could arrange it—return to Russia and make a special trip to visit Northwood in St. Petersburg.

There he would fulfill his promise by giving North all the details of the Brick Street reformatory school; then he would return to his ship and set course for the Amur Valley. North could handle things as he saw fit, and Talia would contend with her eldest brother as she always had. Perhaps her possible engagement to Ridley would soften North's displeasure.

Good. And James would...

Run away.

He almost winced as Talia's voice whispered in his head. He clenched his fingers on the windowsill. Let her think what she wanted. If she blamed him for seducing her, for wreaking havoc in her life...fine. He'd take the blame if it would ensure her safety and security.

This time, he wouldn't fail. He would protect Talia the way he hadn't done for his own mother. Even if she hated him for it.

"Quite admirable, my lady." Lord Margate stepped closer to Talia. "Taking a boy like that under your wing. I hope he appreciates it."

Talia tried to smile. Word had gotten round that the magistrate had granted her guardianship request for Peter Colston. Rather to Talia's surprise, at this evening's ball, several members of the *ton* had approached her with remarks of approval, saying that such an act clearly demonstrated her commitment to the reformatory cause. Though the praise made her a bit uncomfortable, Talia wasn't so noble that she didn't foresee how this might turn opinion in favor of Brick Street.

"The House committee meeting is next week," she told Margate. "I hope I can count on your support."

"Of course. Perhaps we can discuss it in less public surroundings soon."

"Perhaps." Talia eased away from him with a murmured excuse and went to find Aunt Sally.

"Enjoying your evening, my lady?"

Talia smiled as Lord Ridley approached, extending a glass of champagne. Unlike Margate, Ridley was a very nice man in whose company she felt comfortable. He was handsome too, with a broad smile and twinkling eyes. He'd only ever treated her with the utmost respect and courtesy, which was certainly more than she could say for James Forester.

Her heart thumped at the thought of him. She ignored the hot flash of memory, the image of her body twined with his atop her white counterpane...

"Don't you think so?" Ridley asked.

"Oh, er...I beg your pardon?"

"I said the new exhibit at the Zoological Gardens ought to be interesting."

"Yes, of course."

"Perhaps you will allow me to escort you one day next week?"

Say yes!

The order shouted in Talia's brain. She was finished with James Forester. Ridley was a lovely man from a good family. She liked both his parents, who seemed more than pleased to accept her; Rushton would heartily

approve of the match; she would gain a respectable
union for herself and her family...

A tingle of awareness ran down Talia's spine. She
glanced over Ridley's shoulder to where James was
crossing the room. Her traitorous body surged with
heat at the sight of his tall, lean figure, her blood
warming at the thought of his fingers exploring between her legs...

God in heaven. She tilted her head back and downed
two swallows of champagne.

Surely James wasn't the only man who could make
her feel such things. Why, Ridley must have a similar
expertise, even if he didn't exactly inspire the flood of
arousal that James did.

Still, given some time and intimacy...of course she
and Ridley would be able to generate the same kind of
crackling attraction. Of course she would be aroused by
the sight of his bare chest; of course he would have her
moaning and gasping with one gliding touch...

"Poisonous frogs, they said, which shoot venom,"
Ridley remarked, plucking another glass from a server.
"Ought to be quite fascinating."

"Fascinating," Talia echoed.

She tried to focus on him again, feeling guilty and
annoyed with herself for even thinking about James in
Ridley's company, let alone remembering their hot intimacy. Very unfair to Ridley. It would be even worse to
encourage his courtship while still thinking of James.

Well. All would be fine once James left London
again. God only knew when...*if* he would return, so
Talia would be able to resume her life as it was. A life
devoid of James Forester.

"I've enjoyed the time I've spent in your company," Ridley said.

Talia felt his gaze on her face, and her stomach twisted at the sudden expectation surrounding him.

Her heart shriveled a bit. How she wished she could, in all good conscience, even consider the idea of marrying Ridley. Numerous marriages throughout the *ton* were founded upon mutual respect, if not love, and for plenty of other reasons—family unions, politics, business, finances. She would not be a horrible person if she married Ridley simply because he was a kind, respectable man who would offer her a good life.

In marriage, love didn't have to enter the equation...as her sister-in-law Lydia might have remarked. Except that for Lydia and Alexander, it eventually had. Just as it had for Sebastian and Clara. And Aunt Sally would forever cherish the memory of her blissful union with Uncle Harold...

"I'm sorry," Talia said, before Ridley could continue. "My lord, I'm very grateful for your kindness, but fear I must decline further attentions."

A hush descended between them. Ridley blinked. Talia became aware of an immense relief coursing through her at the knowledge that she had stopped matters from progressing. That she would not merely settle for a man she didn't love, regardless of how kind he was.

"I do apologize," she said again.

"Well." Ridley cleared his throat. "I admit that despite your beauty, I hadn't considered courting you until Castleford suggested it. Though perhaps your...ah, maturity isn't quite suited to—"

"I beg your pardon, my lord?" Talia shook her head,

her ears suddenly filling with a dull roaring sound. "Did you say Lord Castleford suggested you court me?"

"Yes, my lady. I thought he suggested the same to you."

Talia swallowed past the tightness in her throat. "No. He did not."

"Oh. I hope…well, I only meant that you weren't quite an obvious choice for me, but Castleford was quite laudatory about your virtues and suggested we might have quite a bit in common with—"

"Excuse me, my lord." Talia stepped away, prickles of cold erupting over her skin. "I must…if you'll… please excuse me."

Leaving a rather baffled-looking Ridley behind, Talia hurried from the crowded ballroom. Her lungs squeezed tight, making it difficult to pull in a breath. Desperate for air, she went to the doors leading to the terrace and stepped out into the cool spring night.

She pressed a hand to her chest as a riotous combination of dismay and sorrow rose inside her. Anger too, both at James and at herself for not recognizing his manipulations sooner. For secretly thinking that he would never want to see her with another man, let alone try to push her toward one…

She should have accepted Ridley, Talia thought as angry tears sprang to her eyes. At the very least, that would have shown James that she was no longer in love with him, that she could move on with her life as easily as he had.

"Out here alone, my lady?" a male voice inquired.

Talia swiped at her eyes, turning to see Lord Margate ʼaning against the doorjamb, his fair hair gleaming in the light. Talia's dismay intensified. A decent man had begun to court her, no matter the instigation, and she had rebuffed him because he could never offer her the type of marriage for which she secretly longed.

Yet other men like Margate would forever look at her with that knowing gleam, making no attempt to hide the salacious nature of their thoughts. A respectable marriage might provide some protection from such speculation, but never one contrived by James Forester.

Talia sighed. She could not win. And she was growing weary of the battle.

"Not enjoying the ball, are you?" Margate pushed away from the doorjamb to approach her, his stride casual. "The crush, the noise, the smell, the heat...I can't imagine why you'd want to escape all that."

Talia smiled without humor. She edged a little closer to the door, but didn't bother trying to escape his presence. Though Margate had always been a bit too arrogant for her comfort, he'd been the only person to express interest in supporting her testimony to the House committee.

"I confess I'd rather spend an evening at home myself," he remarked.

Talia rather doubted the truth of that statement. Another waft of cold washed over her, and she shivered. Margate glanced at her, then shrugged out of his coat to put it around her shoulders. The smell of smoke and brandy wafted from the material, and Talia slipped quickly away from his reach.

"Just trying to be polite," Margate muttered, tossing the coat onto the terrace railing.

"I need to find my aunt, as I'm certain she'd like to

leave soon." Talia turned to go back inside, wincing as Margate's hand closed around her bare arm.

"You'd prefer the crush to my company?" he asked.

"Yes, I would." She tried to pull her arm from his grip. "Please let go of me."

A hint of alarm spiraled through her when his fingers tightened.

"What is it you seek, Lady Talia?" he asked. "Surely you haven't attended so many soirees this season merely at the behest of your elderly aunt or because of your foolish school. You've gained quite a reputation as a recluse, haven't you? What…or rather, *who*…has brought you out into the world again?"

"Certainly not the likes of you," Talia muttered.

"It's your allure of mystery that intrigues me," Margate continued. He gave her arm a tug, which forced her a few steps toward him. "Other men as well. Everyone still speaks of the passion your mother appears to have possessed, which I'm certain fires your own blood in—"

"Let go of her." James's voice cut through the night air.

Relief flooded Talia when he stepped toward them, his expression dark. He reached out to unlock Margate's grip from Talia. "Go away before I kill you. And never touch her again. Don't even *look* at her."

Rather than react in defense, Margate smiled with amusement. "You're going to defend her, Castle? Word has it that she's visited your residence without the benefit of a chaperone…or perhaps it's *to* your benefit that she—"

Margate grunted as James's fist connected with his

jaw, his head snapping back. Talia's heart lurched. She grabbed James by the arm to stop him from throwing another punch, his muscles rock hard beneath her grip.

"Well." Margate straightened, swiping a trickle of blood from the corner of his mouth. "To her honor and all that sort of rot, eh, Castle?"

"Get out," James said through gritted teeth, his muscles bunching beneath his coat as he pulled back for a second blow.

Margate gave Talia another smile before sauntering back into the ballroom. Talia tightened her hand on James's arm. Her pulse raced with a combination of fear and exhilaration that he had defended her, as he always had before. James turned, his eyes simmering with anger.

"Are you all right?" he asked.

Talia nodded, forcing her fingers to unclench from his arm.

"Margate can't do anything to hurt me, James." She looked up into his dark eyes, wrestling with the wisdom of telling him the truth. Finally she did, because she had never given him anything less than the truth.

"You're the only man who can hurt me," she said, the admission making her throat ache.

James took a step back, as if she'd struck him. "What?"

Talia took a breath and sought for the words to explain. "After my mother left, I hid for a long time, not wanting to contend with men like Margate. Not wanting to endure sly glances and comments. I thought... I actually believed that such things would hurt me. And I'm just now realizing that they don't. They can't."

James frowned. "I will not have such—"

"James. They can't hurt me because men like him don't *matter*. I care nothing for Lord Margate or what he thinks of me. And his rudeness certainly can't compare to the storm my family has already weathered."

The ache in her throat spread through her chest and into her heart. "But you..."

"I never wanted to hurt you."

"And yet you have." The words broke apart in her mouth, bitter and cold.

James stared at her, his breath escaping on a rush. "Don't...don't tell me that."

"Why did you want Lord Ridley to court me?" Only as she asked the question did Talia realize there was another layer to her hurt. She'd thought that Ridley was actually pursuing *her*. Not because James had suggested it, but because he'd wanted to.

"Christ, Talia." James shook his head. "I *didn't* want him to. I never wanted him to. I tried to pretend I wanted him to because your aunt told me he'd be a good match for you."

"My aunt?"

"She came to visit me one afternoon and delivered quite a convincing speech as to all the reasons Ridley would make an excellent husband for you. Then she asked my help in arranging a meeting."

Talia's heart sank. She felt as if she were standing on a precipice with no idea how far she might fall if she took one step forward. "And you...you agreed?"

"Of course I agreed," James snapped. "What was the alternative? Tell your aunt that I wanted to strangle any man who even looked at you with admiration? Persuade her that no, actually, I am a better prospect than Ridley even though I'm so clearly *not*? What should I have done?"

"Oh, James." An ache expanded through Talia from the inside out. "You should have come to me."

James cursed, his shoulders slumping. Talia struggled to absorb the pain as she gazed at him—the gleam of light on his dark brown hair, the masculine planes of his features. His cravat had loosened, exposing the strong column of his throat that she knew felt warm against her lips and tasted like sea salt.

A surge of longing filled her, even as she turned away from him. Her longing for him would never fully die, much as she wished it would. But she'd told him the truth, as she always did, when she'd said that he was no longer the man she once knew. *That* James would never have thought so little of her wishes.

"Talia…"

"No."

"You must marry me. If word is out that you've come to my residence alone, and if Margate—"

"You had your chance, James." Talia stopped, resting her hand on the side of the door to steady herself.

You must marry me. A year ago she'd desperately wished she could say the same words to him. Of course Talia and James *must* marry. It could simply be no other way because they belonged together.

Until now.

Talia looked over her shoulder at him. She hardened her heart against the guilt in his eyes. "James, what if I did consent? How would anything change? You're still leaving in a fortnight."

"I won't go."

"And then I'll feel guilty for having forced you to stay." Talia shook her head, realizing with sadness that the fates would forever conspire to keep her and James apart.

No. She and James would forever keep themselves apart.

She straightened her shoulders and returned to the ballroom. He didn't follow her.

Talia went to find Aunt Sally and pleaded a headache as her reason to want to return home. She already knew her aunt's motives for going to James about Lord Ridley. Despite Aunt Sally's remarks about what constituted a blissful marriage, in the end she wanted Talia to find a husband as much as the rest of her family did.

"You were the one who told me what I should look for in a perfect marriage," Talia told her aunt, unable to keep the hurt from her voice. "Did you think I'd find all those things with Lord Ridley?"

"Possibly." Sally appeared entirely unrepentant. "Or that James would finally come to his senses about you."

"Nothing will ever happen with me and James, Aunt Sally."

For the first time, that statement quashed the flicker of hope that had never ceased burning in Talia's heart. Once back home, she asked Soames to fetch her an empty box from the kitchen. He returned with a wooden crate, which she took up to her bedchamber. She opened the desk drawer that contained James's letters and removed them all, dumping them unceremoniously into the crate.

Then, hands trembling and her eyes stinging with

tears, she opened her curiosity cabinet and took out all the artifacts and trinkets he'd sent to her over the years. A decade's worth of explorations around the world, all encompassed for Talia in polished stones, bright feathers, coins, seashells, figurines, shark's teeth, bracelets. She put them all into the box with the letters, then hefted it into her arms.

She pushed the door open and stepped into the corridor just as Aunt Sally came puffing toward the stairs, her white hair peeking out from beneath her cap.

"Oh, I thought you'd gone to bed already, my dear." Sally paused, her gaze going inquiringly to the box. "What on earth is that?"

"Just some old things I wanted to get rid of."

"It looks terribly heavy. Wait here, and I'll fetch Soames."

"No, I can—"

"I was going down for a glass of milk, anyway." Sally went toward the stairs, calling for Soames.

A few seconds later, the footman came to take the box from Talia.

"Put it out with the rubbish, please," she said.

"Yes, milady."

Talia fought the ache threatening to break open her chest as she watched him walk away with all her tangible memories of James contained in one old crate.

Soames's voice mixed with Aunt Sally's lilt as they headed down the stairs to the kitchen. Talia returned to her room and closed the door, swallowing hard against the tears. She'd cried enough for James Forester.

She rang for Lucy to help her out of her gown and into her night shift and dressing gown. She dismissed the maid with a word of thanks before climbing into bed. Despite the tangle of her emotions, she drifted into a welcome, dreamless sleep that restored some of her resolve. No matter what James did or didn't do, Talia still had work to do and an obligation to Brick Street and its students. Nothing could stop her from that.

In the morning, Lucy came in with a basket of muffins and a cup of coffee. She placed the tray on the table, then went to open the wardrobe. Talia realized she'd forgotten to put James's coat in the crate as well. After she'd dressed and Lucy left, Talia went to the wardrobe and took out the coat.

Suppressing the urge to run her hand over the soft wool, she tossed it onto the bed and sat at the table to eat breakfast. She'd taken one sip of coffee when there was a knock on the door.

"Talia?"

"Come in, Aunt Sally."

"Talia, come quickly." Her aunt bustled in, her eyes bright with excitement. She clapped her hands together. "We've a surprise visitor."

"Who?" A sudden apprehension filled Talia.

Sally smiled. "Come downstairs and see."

Talia pushed her chair back just as Aunt Sally hurried to ring for the maid. Sally paused when she saw the man's coat lying on Talia's bed.

"That's...er, I borrowed it from James last night." Embarrassment heated Talia's face. "It was chilly and I...I'd forgotten my wrap."

"Oh." Sally's confused—and somewhat intrigued—expression cleared. "James is so chivalrous, isn't he? Do hurry up, Talia."

"Who is here, Aunt Sally?"

"Your brother!"

"My..."

The words faded as Talia's throat closed over. A thousand thoughts flew through her mind—explanations, reasons, rationales—even as she knew the ugly truth to her very bones.

James had done it. He'd told Alexander her secrets, betrayed her to keep his promise. And now Alexander was here.

Chapter Sixteen

"Nicholas?"

Talia stopped on the stairs, shock flooding her at the sight of the disheveled, long-haired man standing in the foyer. He wore a ragged sailor's coat, torn trousers, and boots that had tracked muddy footprints over the marble floor. For a moment, she could only stare at him, hardly daring to believe he was truly back.

He lifted his head to look up at her, and then a wide, gleaming smile broke through the darkness of the bristly beard covering his jaw.

"Hullo, brat." His deep voice boomed through the foyer. "Aren't you a sight?"

"Aren't *I* a sight?" Talia hurried down the stairs, her heart racing with a combination of relief and excitement. "You look as if you've crawled from a swamp!"

Nicholas scrubbed a hand over his beard and chuckled. "Likely I have."

Talia reached the bottom step and threw herself at her

brother, laughing with delight as his arms closed around her and lifted her clear off the ground. Love filled her, washing away the despair she'd felt only a few moments ago.

"You smell dreadful," she remarked, hugging him tight and not caring that his filthy coat was sullying her dress.

"Fresh off the boat, milady. Just landed at the East India Docks not an hour ago."

"Why didn't you send word that you were coming?"

"I didn't know I was." Nicholas set her back on her feet and held her at arm's length to study her. "Intended to set a course for Greenland, but heard there's a prospect of a northwesterly gale so rather than risk the steamer transport, the commander ordered us back to London."

"How long will you stay?"

"Don't quite know." Nicholas shrugged out of his coat and tossed it to the waiting Soames, who barely managed to suppress a grimace as he caught it. "Commander might change his plans, so I'm to await orders."

"Come in, come in." Sally, who had followed Talia back downstairs, opened the morning room door to usher Nicholas inside. "Your father will be so disappointed he missed you."

"The old bird is out and about again, eh? Good to know."

"Shall I have a bath drawn, milady?" Soames asked dryly.

"Please." Talia wrinkled her nose at Nicholas, even as happiness and love buoyed her spirits. "Send tea in as well, Soames."

"And food," Nicholas added.

Talia followed her brother into the morning room, suppressing the urge to pepper him with questions until he'd had a chance to settle back in.

"Do you know when you'll receive your orders?" Sally asked.

"Should get word within a day or so as to what's planned next." Nicholas flopped down on the sofa and put his booted feet on the table, ignoring Sally's glare of disapproval. "Was hoping to have enough time to visit Bastian, meet his new wife." He scratched his bristly beard. "Has Alex returned?"

"He and Darius are both still in St. Petersburg," Talia said.

Nicholas paused to look at her. "They're all away?"

"They've been away for months now, and Papa left a few weeks ago."

"Left you alone?"

"I'm not alone. Aunt Sally came to stay until Papa returns. Everything has been fine."

Nicholas frowned at her. Talia frowned back.

"You left three years ago, Nicholas," she reminded him. "Not terribly concerned about leaving me alone then, were you?"

A sudden tension coursed between them, diluting the happiness of their reunion. Talia turned her attention to the tea tray when the maid deposited it on the table. Nicholas swallowed the tea in a few gulps and studied the plate of scones and muffins.

"Where did you last visit, Nicholas?" Sally asked brightly.

"The Malay Peninsula, my lady," he said, around

a mouthful of scone. "Charted the course of several rivers."

"Lord Castleford tried to secure an expedition there, but was unsuccessful," Talia said.

"Castle, eh?" Nicholas bit into a currant muffin. "Good man. Bit of a stick-in-the-mud, but worthy commander, from what I hear."

"You've not commanded an expedition yet?" Talia asked.

"Don't see the point, really. Too much responsibility. By hiring myself out, I can go where I please when I please."

And never stop anywhere, Talia thought. At least James had a place to hang his hat—when he chose to use it, of course. Nicholas would always be welcome at any Hall residence, but he had no place to call his own.

"I'll see about your bath and having a room prepared." Talia stood and embraced her brother again.

"You look well, brat." Affection softened the lines around his eyes. "I'm glad to see you."

Talia patted his bristly cheek. "And I you. I'll see if Papa's barber is available as soon as possible. I've little doubt you have small creatures living in that tangled beard."

She returned upstairs to see to the preparations for his stay, then let the servant Kinley take over to help get her brother into respectable shape again.

"Soames." She hurried to the footman as he passed in the corridor. "Send word to Lord Castleford's residence, please. Tell him that Mr. Hall has returned and he's welcome to call this morning, if he's available. If not, ask him to come for supper."

She knew James and Nicholas would like to see each other again, and certainly the two would have plenty to discuss about their various adventures.

Her spirits lifted for the first time in weeks, Talia asked the cook to prepare more cakes and muffins she knew both James and her brother liked. She returned upstairs to ring for Lucy again, wanting to wear something brighter and prettier than the gray dress she had on.

James's coat still lay on her bed. She hung it back in the wardrobe just as the maid appeared to help her change into a blue morning gown sprinkled with yellow flowers.

"Talia?" Aunt Sally emerged from the dining room as Talia descended the stairs again. "We've just got a note from James. He won't be able to visit this morning."

Disappointment speared through Talia. "Did he say why?"

Sally shook her head. "He didn't say he'd pay a call later today, either, and declined the supper invitation. I'd have thought he'd be eager to see Nicholas again. It's been years, hasn't it?"

"Years," Talia echoed, turning away from her aunt toward the morning room.

Her chest tightened. James had developed close friendships with all four of her brothers over the years, first with Alexander and then Nicholas, owing to their shared love of exploration. They'd spent many hours discussing shipping routes, maps of the colonies, weather conditions, expedition equipment, and provisions.

Any other time, especially with the two of them having just returned to London, James would have hurried over to see Nicholas and hear of his latest journey.

Which meant there could be only one reason for James to balk now.

Talia pressed her palms to her cheeks and closed her eyes. Images flashed behind her eyelids—James's hands on her bare skin, her lips against his chest, their legs twining together. Heat filled her veins.

"Can't decide if I feel like myself again or someone else entirely."

Talia opened her eyes at the sound of her brother's voice. She smiled. With his dark hair cut short again and his beard shaved to reveal the planes of his face and wide mouth, Nicholas looked like the handsome brother she remembered. His skin was darker, and new lines had formed around his mouth, but his eyes still held that mischievous twinkle that belonged only to him.

"I knew you were still somewhere underneath all that hair," Talia remarked.

Nicholas frowned and plucked at the sleeve of his gray coat as if it were some foreign material. "Bit of an adjustment, I'm afraid."

Talia approached and reached out to straighten the crooked knot of his cravat. "I hope you'll stay for a while."

Only as she said the words did she realize how much she meant them. She'd missed her brothers for a long time, but that ache had deepened since James returned. Her shaky relationship with him reminded Talia just how much everything had changed. Having at least one brother back at home might provide her with some much-needed stability, even if she didn't yet know how much she should reveal about Brick Street.

She dusted a nonexistent speck of lint from Nicholas's lapel and went to the fresh tea tray that the maid had left on the table.

"So tell me everything," she said, pouring him a cup. "Where you went, what you saw. I've loved the packages of books you've sent."

"I've got more for you too, somewhere in my trunk." Nicholas settled into a chair, folding one long leg over the other. "Thought you could use them for your schools. Last I heard from Bastian that's your primary charity these days."

"Has been for over a year now. I find it very fulfilling."

Nicholas accepted a cup of tea, studying her from beneath his dark brows. "Bastian also wrote that you've shown no intention of marrying."

Talia sighed. "Lovely to know my brothers are discussing such things with one another rather than me."

"I'm discussing it with you now, aren't I?"

"Very well, let's discuss," Talia said tartly. "You've not shown any intention of marrying either."

His grin flashed. "Touché, Lady Talia."

"Have you seen Darius recently?"

Nicholas shook his head, his gaze skirting away from her. If Talia hadn't been watching him closely, she might have missed the faint tightening of his jaw. Her heart sank at the thought that there might be tension between the twins. Different as they were, Nicholas and Darius had always had a strong bond.

"He's doing well." She smiled, anxious to divert his attention from any unpleasantness. "I saw him last fall in Russia before he returned to London for a short time. Something to do with a cipher machine."

"He's back in St. Petersburg now?" Nicholas asked.

"Yes, Alexander and Lydia live not far from his residence on the Fontanka." She paused. "You ought to pay him a visit."

Nicholas shrugged, shifting in the chair as if it were uncomfortable. He seemed bigger somehow, as if all that time spent on ships and trekking through unknown lands had expanded his position in the world. Hardly a wonder that he'd feel awkward sitting in the frilly morning room again.

He wouldn't stay in London long, Talia thought with a pang of sadness. Like James, he'd want to return to the open seas as soon as he could.

"What will you do today?" she asked.

"Pay a visit to the club, I suppose. Call on a few old friends." Nicholas rubbed his chin, then looked surprised by the fact that his beard was no longer there. "Castle is still at his Arlington Street place?"

"Yes, but he sent word that he couldn't visit today," Talia said. Irritation pricked at her suddenly. "I'll see if he can come tomorrow, perhaps. I'll have John ready the second carriage for you to use while you're here."

She stood and approached him. "Please don't be in too much of a hurry to leave."

A frown tugged at his mouth. "You all right, then, brat? Not been horrid for you, has it?"

Talia shook her head. Yes, it had been horrid, but there was no point in telling him that. She no longer wanted to dwell on the past.

"I'd just... I'd like having you here," she said. "Perhaps I can go with you to visit Bastian and Clara."

"I'll send word and see if they're available. Would be a good trip, eh?"

"Indeed. I'll see you at lunch."

Talia bent to kiss his forehead before she went to request the carriages be prepared. Pleased at the thought of having family around her after James left again, she went upstairs and collected her things.

She stopped at the printer's for a stack of notebooks and pencils, then the Exeter Hall offices of the Ragged School Union. Sir Henry wasn't in his office, so Talia left the supplies on his desk along with a note before returning to the carriage. She went to Mudie's Library for some new books and stacked them on the opposite carriage seat to bring to Brick Street.

After paying a visit to the modiste to check on a recent order, Talia found herself directing the driver to James's town house.

Anxiety clutched at her as she went up the steps and rang the bell. The maid, Polly, answered, a dishrag in her hand.

"His lordship is in the study," she announced importantly before allowing Talia to pass her.

Talia glanced around the house as she walked to the study. She was pleased to see that everything still looked neat and tidy after her decorating overhaul last week.

"James?" She knocked once and pushed the door open.

He was standing behind his paper-strewn desk, his hands clasped behind his back as he stared out the window at the back garden. At the sound of her voice, he turned with a frown. Talia's heart stuttered. He looked tired, his eyes lined with dark circles and his hair a disheveled mess.

"I knew it." She closed the door behind her and strode

to the desk, irritation biting at her. "I knew you didn't have any other plans, James. You wouldn't come to see Nicholas because of all that has transpired between us."

"Talia—"

"Did you think you wouldn't be able to hide it?" Talia snapped, her hands shaking as she put them flat on his desk and leaned toward him. "That Nicholas would somehow know we've been intimate? Are you ashamed of what we did, even though *I* was the one who initiated it, the one who proved yet again that you cannot resist me? For the love of God, James, what kind of *coward*—"

"Talia!"

She stopped short at the harsh note in his voice. James muttered a curse, dragging his hands over his face and through his hair.

Behind Talia, someone coughed.

Oh, no.

She stared at James, her pulse thudding. He grimaced. Slowly, Talia turned to find herself looking at Sir Henry, Lady Byron, and...Nicholas.

Hot embarrassment swept up her throat and stung her cheeks. She couldn't move.

"Lady Talia, I've..." James cleared his throat. "I had an appointment with Sir Henry and Lady Byron to discuss the patronage of the Brick Street school. Your brother just stopped by a half hour ago...unexpectedly."

Talia swung her gaze to her brother. Nicholas just looked at her, his face expressionless. A torrent of memories barraged Talia of all the vile gossip that had followed their mother's affair—whispers of her wanton behavior, her betrayal, her immorality. The scandal had driven Nicholas from London almost four years ago. Now he'd just learned that his sister...

"I'm sorry." The apology came out on a choked gasp as she ran from the room.

"Talia!"

Ignoring the simultaneous calls from Nicholas and James, Talia rushed past a dumbfounded Polly back to the carriage.

"Talia, wait!" James thundered, his boots ringing against the marble floor.

"Go, quickly. Anywhere." Talia snapped the order at the driver as she clambered into the carriage and slammed the door behind her.

She pressed her back against the seat and tightened her arms around herself, scorched from the inside out with humiliation.

How many times had she told herself that she would never be like her mother? How many advances had she fended off from men who believed that she was? How long had it been before she finally gathered the courage to stop hiding, to find a way to be useful to the world?

And yet that all slipped away with James, because no matter how often she tried to convince herself otherwise, she could not forget all he had been to her. She couldn't forget how wonderful it had felt to love him.

Now on the heels of Lord Margate's remark about Talia visiting James's house alone, and with Lady Byron and Sir Henry knowing that she and James had been intimate...

God in heaven.

"Milady?"

Talia blinked, aware that the carriage had come to a

halt on the side of the street. The driver John had descended the bench and was looking through the window at her.

"Any place in particular, or ought I continue driving round?" he asked.

"No." Talia fumbled for a handkerchief. "Er...sixteen Brick Street, John. Wapping."

He blinked. "Wapping?"

"Yes. Quickly."

Peter's stomach was tight with knots. He forced himself to approach Brick Street, though he dreaded having to face his sister. He knew Lady Talia had sent both Alice and his father word about her guardianship petition, but only Alice had responded with a note asking him to meet her at Brick Street that afternoon because their father would never allow him to return home. It was Saturday, so school was not in session.

It was yet another chance...one Peter didn't deserve. At the very least, though, he would honor his word to Lady Talia that he would testify about the conditions at Newhall. And he would try to make amends with his sister.

He climbed the steps outside the blacksmith's and entered the mildewed corridor. A man's voice came through the half-open door of the classroom.

Peter tensed, his footsteps silent as he made his way down the corridor. This time, he recognized the voice without needing to hear it twice.

He eased open the door farther. Against the far wall, he saw the back of a man's coat. Blond hair. A wide stance. The bastard Lawford.

Peter's heart plummeted into a sea of rage. He tightened his hands into fists, then froze as his sister spoke from behind Lawford.

"I won't tell anyone, Mr. Lawford." Her voice sounded tense, oddly high.

"I saw the way he looked at you. You're a beautiful woman, Miss Colston. I've known from the moment I saw you how neglected you've been, and I don't intend to let Fletcher stand in my way."

"Mr. Fletcher has treated me with nothing but respect." Her voice tightened. "Unlike you."

Peter's stomach clenched.

"I've helped you, haven't I?" Lawford asked. He reached up a hand, as if he were touching her hair. "You asked for my help."

"I never agreed to . . . to *this*."

Peter's fists tightened. He fought the urge to turn and leave. If Alice had gone to Lawford for help . . .

"I think you owe me, Miss Colston."

"Mr. Lawford, get away from me." A note of desperation threaded Alice's voice.

Do something! The voice shouting inside Peter's head was drowned out by a surge of fear. He hated Lawford. He was afraid of Lawford. He'd never been able to stand up to the man, and he couldn't think of what to do now.

"Stop!" His sister pushed Lawford's hand away.

Peter coughed. Lawford's shoulders stiffened. He turned, his eyes icy as he saw Peter hovering in the doorway. He stepped away from Alice.

"What the bloody hell are you doing here?" he snapped.

Peter saw Alice's face. She looked scared. Her hand was at her throat, and her skin was white. Peter knew all too well the kind of fear Lawford could inspire, and he hated that his sister felt it now.

"You're supposed to be in gaol." Lawford took two steps forward.

Peter swallowed past the tightness in his throat.

"I was…not anymore. The magistrate granted Lady Talia guardianship over me instead of a prison sentence."

Lawford stared at him for a second, then laughed. "That foolish woman doesn't know when to mind her business, does she? Apparently, neither do you, Peter."

Peter looked at Alice. "What's he done to you?"

"N-nothing. I was…he followed me here, but he hasn't hurt me."

"I would never hurt you," Lawford said.

"Peter…" Alice sounded desperate.

Peter couldn't move. The urge to escape surged inside him.

"Go away, Peter," Lawford ordered.

Peter stepped back. Even now, he couldn't imagine not following Lawford's orders.

Lawford's eyes narrowed. "I told you to go."

Sweat broke out on Peter's forehead. All thought drained from him. His skin crawled. He took a breath, locked eyes with his sister, and ran.

He crossed the room in four strides and crashed into Lawford with a grunt. His sister screamed. He and Lawford crashed to the floor. Lawford's fist hit the side of his jaw. Peter's vision blurred.

He gritted his teeth and grabbed Lawford's collar,

knowing he'd have to fight dirty. He slammed Lawford's head against the floor.

"Peter!" Alice grabbed the back of his shirt. "Peter, stop!"

Why the hell did she want him to stop? He was protecting her, dammit. He punched Lawford. Blood spurted from the man's nose. Alice gasped and yanked at his shirt.

"Bastard." Lawford seemed to gather his wits. He shoved Peter off him and got to his feet. Peter cursed, his muscles still weak from all those months at Newhall. He tried to wrestle Lawford to the floor again, but the man drew a booted foot back and kicked Peter between the legs.

Pain shot through Peter's body, all the air whooshing from his lungs. He cried out in pain, stars bursting behind his eyes as he clutched himself and tried to breathe. Alice sank to her knees beside him.

"You think you'll get away with this?" Lawford snapped. He grabbed a handkerchief from his pocket and held it to his bloody nose. "You're a lying, thieving little bastard, Peter Colston, and you'll never come to any good."

It was the same thing Peter had been telling himself for years, but he hated hearing it from Lawford again. He squeezed his eyes shut as the pain dissipated, feeling his sister's hand on his forehead.

"Neither will you," he gasped. He forced himself to open his eyes and look at Lawford. "You'll come to a worse end than I will, Lawford."

Lawford laughed, that cold, hard laugh that had echoed against the stone walls of Peter's prison cell. He fought the fear and tried to focus on the sensation of Alice's cool hand. He had a sudden memory of their mother touching his forehead like that when he was a child, if he'd gotten sick or hurt.

"You don't want anyone knowing what goes on at Newhall, do you, Lawford?" Peter asked. He managed to get to his knees. "That's why you wouldn't let Lady Talia visit. Why you don't want anyone speaking about it."

The second the words escaped his mouth, a strange sense of confidence filled him. He hadn't realized until this moment that he did have a way to stop Lawford. He'd been too blinded by fear to see it. He'd run away once too often.

He met Lawford's gaze, seeing comprehension dawn in the other man's expression. Peter grabbed Alice's hand and squeezed in warning. He knew Lawford carried a gun.

He got slowly to his feet, pulling Alice up with him. Aside from three small, dirty windows, the door was the only way out of the classroom.

Peter edged toward it, his hand tight on Alice's. Lawford stepped between him and the door, his expression implacable. Peter stopped. He could feel Alice trembling, her palm cold and sweaty against his. Lawford reached into his coat.

The corridor door slammed shut. Peter's heart thudded. Then the classroom door opened, and Lady Talia stepped in.

Chapter Seventeen

Talia felt the tension and fear before she even realized who was in the room. Her grip tightened on the books as she stared at Peter and Alice—both looking pale and shaken. Mr. Lawford stood between them and the doorway, his hand tucked into the lapel of his coat.

What...?

She retreated a step, seized by the sense that something was very wrong. She swerved her gaze to Peter, whose eyes burned with anger.

"Run!" he shouted.

Talia stumbled backward, her books falling to the floor with a thud. She turned to run, intent on the goal of getting help.

"Stop." Lawford's voice sliced the air like a blade.

Talia froze. Alice let out a cry. A shaft of sunlight came through the window and glinted off the gun in Lawford's hand.

"I've a cab outside," he said. He approached Talia and

took her arm, pulling her closer. He tucked the gun back beneath his lapel. Between the stays of Talia's corset, she felt the barrel of the gun pressing against her side. Pinpricks of sweat erupted all over her body.

"I want all three of you to walk outside and get into the cab," Lawford said. "Do nothing that will put Lady Talia in further peril."

He nodded at Peter and Alice. Together, they edged past Lawford to the door. Talia's heart hammered. She forced her legs to move when Lawford prodded her forward into the corridor. Surely he couldn't force them into a cab in the midst of the busy street. Even if he did, where did he intend to take them?

The noise of the blacksmith's workshop filled the air along with the acrid scent of coal. Lawford gestured to the cabdriver, who descended to open the door. The gun barrel pushed harder into Talia's side. Peter grabbed hold of the pull bar and started to haul himself up into the cab.

Then, in a blur, he turned, jumped from the steps, and crashed into Lawford. Lawford stumbled at the impact, but he was bigger than Peter. He shoved the boy away with a grunt. Workers from the workshop came toward the windows, lured by the sudden commotion.

Talia felt Lawford's sudden panic. He couldn't maintain control of all three of them. He pushed her forward, the gun still digging into her side. She clambered up the steps, twisting to find Alice. The other woman was running toward the blacksmith shop.

"Go," Talia shouted to Peter.

He turned and ran as Lawford shoved Talia into the cab and snapped at the driver to go. Breathing hard, he fell onto the bench opposite her and pulled the gun from his coat.

"You're not the one I want," he snapped, his features shiny with sweat. "But it's your own fault for interfering where you shouldn't. Did you really think I'd let you have guardianship over Peter Colston? Much less use him to further your own cause?" He shook his head. "It should have been easy to get him sent back to Newhall, but you couldn't leave well enough alone."

Talia gripped her hands together and tried to focus on the passing streets, to determine where they were going. Beneath her fear was the stark, growing realization that Lawford could never let her go now. He never *would*.

"Do not try to escape," Lawford said, his gaze on her face. "I've had more than enough experience with defiant boys, and I know how to subdue them. I would not like to see you as badly hurt."

Talia's heart pounded inside her head. After what seemed an interminably long period of time, the cab came to a halt outside the gates of St. Katharine's Docks. The stink of fish and smoke filled the air as Talia preceded Lawford out of the cab, his gun again concealed but pressing against her back.

He prodded her through the gates and onto the bustling quay. Talia tried to calculate the risk of screaming for help, of breaking away and running. The risk, of course, was that Lawford might shoot... and if the bullet didn't hit her, it could very well hit someone else and possibly kill him.

Her stomach churned with nausea. She tried to draw a breath into her tight lungs as Lawford steered her around a pallet filled with barrels of brandy. The warehouse doors were all open, like huge, gaping mouths. Wagons, carts, and horses shuffled in and out, transporting crates, bags, and casks.

Dark, narrow alleys lay between the warehouses, littered with rubbish and rotten food. It was her only chance. Before she could think or let the fear paralyze her, she yanked her arm from Lawford's grip and darted into an alley. Her feet sank into squishy piles of waste, the stench overpowering.

Half-expecting the ring of a bullet, Talia ran. She skidded on something slippery, righted herself, and kept going. If she could reach the back of the warehouse, she might be able to get in through the back door and—

Lawford grabbed her shoulder and pulled her back so fast she almost lost her balance. Talia shrieked. Panic clawed at her throat. She tried to wrest herself away again, but Lawford held fast. Then the hard butt of the gun slammed against her temple, and everything went dark.

Talia woke to the stench of rotting hay and fetid air. Her head throbbed. Her breath came in shallow gasps. She tried not to move, fear warning her that she should remain still until she figured out where she was.

Where *he* was.

She worked her jaw carefully and flexed her fingers. Her whole body ached, but nothing seemed to be broken. A sick feeling roiled in her belly. She cracked open her eyes. A thin stream of light shone from a lantern, illuminating a bare wall opposite her and a wooden floor covered with a brown, tattered mat.

A lock rattled. Talia closed her eyes again and didn't

move. Boots shuffled across the floor. She sensed him crouch beside her. Her heart hammered.

"I do wish you hadn't gone to Brick Street, my lady."

So did Talia. Except if she hadn't, who knows what would have happened to Peter and Alice?

Peter and Alice! They had escaped. They knew Lawford had her, and they would find a way to rescue her.

She hoped...except that they likely had no idea where she was. Deciding she had nothing to gain by feigning unconsciousness, she braced herself for Lawford's contempt and opened her eyes.

He was studying her, but his expression lacked anger. Instead he seemed concerned and a bit distressed.

"I'm sorry," he said. "I've got to leave you here while I go find Peter."

"Where is here?" Her voice came out cracked and rusty.

"The *Warrior*."

Talia's heart seized. "The prison hulk?"

Lawford nodded and got to his feet. "One of the few remaining. I served as a guard here several years ago before my appointment at Newhall. Horrible, filthy place. Must say the reform acts have done some good, at least."

Talia pushed to a sitting position, fighting off a wave of dizziness. A row of straight shadows fell onto the opposite wall.

Bars. She was in one of the ship's holding cells. She blinked to clear her vision. A wall of iron bars trapped her in the narrow space. On the opposite side of a narrow corridor, there was another empty cell.

"I don't yet know what I'm going to do with you," Lawford continued. He went to take a bucket and a bundle of white cloth from beside the door. "I can't have you telling anyone I've gone and abducted you or threatened Peter and Alice...but on the other hand, I never intended to hurt you."

"What about Peter?"

"Peter should have done what he does best, which is keep his mouth shut." Lawford unwrapped the bundle to reveal a loaf of bread, which he set in front of her along with the bucket of water. "I thought he'd learned at Newhall. More's the pity that he didn't."

Talia eyed him warily as he straightened, dusting the grit from his hands. Her head throbbed. "Where is Peter?"

"I don't know. I'm going to find him and Alice now. You'll be all right here until I get back and figure out what to do with you."

He turned on his heel and left, shutting the cell door behind him. Talia managed to get to her feet. Though she knew the futility of her efforts, she scoured the cell as if she could somehow find a way out. She strained her ears to try to hear something, but there was only a faint banging sound. She must be very far belowdecks indeed.

She yanked on the iron bars in despair. Only Lawford knew she was here. She had no idea if the *Warrior* would actually sail—transportation had been banned last year, though the few remaining hulks were still scheduled to depart over the next couple of years.

But why would Lawford lock her in a prison hulk if it wasn't going to set sail?

The answer came on a wave of dread. He wouldn't.

* * *

"She's not here." James stalked down the front steps to where Nicholas waited beside the carriage. Anger and worry churned through him. By the time he and Nicholas had managed to pursue Talia, her carriage had rounded the corner and gone. "I'll try the Ragged School Union offices."

He hauled himself into the carriage, snapping at the driver to go to Exeter Hall. Nicholas sat across from him, his expression set. Any other time, James would have tried to make amends, to provide some sort of explanation...except the only explanation he possessed was that he could not, for the life of him, withstand Talia Hall.

He suspected Nicholas did not want to hear such a blunt fact.

They rode in tense silence before arriving at the union building. James bounded up the stairs to Sir Henry's office, but the director was out for the afternoon and Talia was nowhere to be seen. James thought the only other place she might have gone was to Alice Colston's house or Brick Street. And he had no idea how much Talia had told Nicholas about either one of those places.

"Take the carriage and see if she's gone to Mudie's Library," he said, striding back down the stairs. "I'll go to the ragged schools. I've been there with her before."

To his relief, Nicholas didn't argue. James hurried to the cabstand and instructed the driver to head to Wapping. He hated the idea that Talia might have gone to Brick Street, especially since dusk had begun to descend. He tapped his fingers impatiently on his knee as the cab navigated the crowded streets. Smoke billowed from the blacksmith's workshop along with the smell of coal and noise of hammers striking iron.

He went into the classroom, but found it dark and empty. The dormitories? Without bothering to return to the cab, he ran down the street and around the corner to Gorham Street, where the lodging house dormitory was situated. He couldn't shake the feeling that something was terribly wrong...something beyond Talia's embarrassment over their intimacy.

He shoved the thought aside and grabbed a boy who was just going into the dormitory.

"Martin, have you seen Miss Hall?"

Martin peered at him from beneath a threadbare cap and shook his head. "She don't usually show up on Saturdays."

James passed him and entered the lodging house. Before he could ring for the housekeeper, the door to the kitchen banged open.

"Mr. Forester!" Peter Colston bolted into the foyer. "I saw you comin' up the street. We tried to send word to you. He's got her, sir. He's got Miss Hall."

"Who?"

"Lawford." Peter gripped his sleeves.

Three other boys emerged from the kitchen, their eyes wide. "Peter said he had a *gun*."

James went cold all over. "How do you know?"

"He was after my sister," Peter said. "She's gone to try to find our father, see if he can help. But I think I know where Lawford went."

"We need to rescue her!" Daniel shouted, and the other boys whooped in excited agreement.

"Come on, then." James spun on his heel and hurried

back outside. He and the boys returned to Brick Street and climbed into the cab. James didn't have time to think about the wisdom of bringing along four boys on his quest to rescue Talia. He'd have to trust that they might be able to help.

They descended at the gates of St. Katharine's Docks. James stood alongside the boys as they stared at the massive ship at the end of the basin. Moored by rusted chains, the hulk sprouted three tall masts, the gun decks pierced by cannon ports. The gangway was up, the ship shrouded in evening fog like a great, mythical beast.

"How..." James cleared his throat. "Why do you think he took her there?"

"Because he threatened to take *me* there when I was arrested," Peter said.

They all stared at the prison ship again.

"Ain't no way I'm goin' there," Daniel whispered fervently.

Martin pinched the other boy's arm. "It's Miss Hall we're talkin' about."

"Miss Hall oughtn't have got herself caught by Lawford ta begin with," Daniel muttered, shoving Martin with his elbow.

Peter grabbed one ear of each boy and gave them a hard tug. The boys winced.

"How do we even know she's there?" Martin asked. "You didn't *see* him take her aboard, did you?"

"She's there," Peter said.

James continued staring at the hulk. He'd been on dozens of different ships in his career, but never a guarded prison ship.

"What should we do?" Peter asked. A worried note threaded his voice.

"I've no idea."

Peter blinked. "You must have some idea. We can't just leave her there."

"We're not going to leave her there," James replied irritably. "But we need a plan."

He made plans all the time. Granted, they weren't plans to rescue the woman he loved from the hands of a madman, but...

His heart stuttered.

He didn't just love her beyond all reason. He liked her, admired her, cherished her, adored her...

A blinding image of Talia filled his head—laughing green eyes, her smile like sunshine, the way one look from her made his knees go weak...

"Sir?" Peter tugged at his sleeve. "Shouldn't we *hurry*?"

James pulled himself back to the present. His pulse raced. He sucked in a breath and nodded.

"Yes. Er...a plan. We need a plan." He paced a few steps. "We could take a boat out ourselves under cover of darkness, but we've no way of getting aboard."

"We could fight the sentries," Robert suggested, bracing his fists.

Peter thunked him on the head. "You against a sentry is like a tiger fighting a mouse. And you ain't the tiger. We've got to use our strengths."

James spun and pointed at the boy. "Good. Yes. What are your strengths?"

The boys looked at one another and squirmed.

"Uh, thievin'," Daniel ventured.

"Brawling," Robert added.

"I can read a little now," Martin said.

"That's not going to help," James muttered.

"That's exactly what I told Mr. Fletcher!" Martin replied. "Readin' ain't a help for anything."

"What about you?" Peter asked James.

"Me?"

"You're the biggest of us. What can you do?"

"I command expeditions around the world," James replied somewhat defensively.

"How can that help?" Peter asked.

Command. James knew how to make people do what he told them to.

One infuriating woman excepted, of course.

"All right, then." He dragged his hands over his hair as pieces began locking together in his brain. He also knew the push-and-pull rhythm of the docks, and though evening had descended, the workers would continue laboring until the light waned.

"We've got to get her out fast," Peter urged.

"We're not going to try to get her out," James replied, staring at the ship. "I've got to get *in*."

He turned to the boys and gave them instructions. As the sky began to darken, carts and wagons continued streaming in and out of the huge warehouse doors. Workers and sailors ambled toward the dock gates for payment and then got into a queue for inspection.

James and Peter exchanged glances as they moved forward to lose themselves in the throng of people clustered around the gates. As they were swept into the crowd, Peter gathered with a group of workers heading for the last warehouse on the quay.

James squinted through the evening fog at the *Warrior*. The gangway was down. Daniel darted past him en route to Warehouse Five. A few men began loading crates onto wheelbarrows to haul them up to the ships. James approached the dockmaster, a barrel-chested man who kept track of the incoming and outgoing vessels.

"*Warrior* going out soon?" he asked casually.

"Warping out to the river at midnight, then down to Gravesend before departing. Twenty-four hours hence."

Midnight. James glanced at the sun, which had just made its final descent behind the horizon. He calculated they had another hour or two as the workers would continue loading provisions for the ships setting forth the following morning.

"Got enough work for the cargo?" James asked.

"Chief warder took care of that." The dockmaster nodded toward a portly man with a bushy beard who was supervising the freight work.

When the foreman's back was turned, James slipped into the warehouse and found a man hefting bags of tea onto a pallet. He grabbed his pocket watch and took hold of the man's arm. A quick word about the cargo, and the man shed his coat and accepted the watch in exchange. James shrugged into the discarded coat, yanking the tight material over his chest. He took the man's place unloading the tea, then navigated the wheelbarrow toward the *Warrior*. A stream of workers moved up and down the gangway past the two sentries on duty.

James caught Martin's eye. He and Daniel were crouched behind a pile of crates that emanated the odor of fish.

"What's left to get on board?" Martin whispered.

"Flour, tea, casks of brandy for the officers, and potatoes," James said. "You both stay here."

The boys were vibrating with excitement, ready to do whatever James asked. He almost smiled. Not wanting to put them at risk, he had only asked that they keep an eye out for Lawford.

He couldn't, however, keep Peter out of the way. He piled a couple bags of flour onto the wheelbarrow as Peter appeared to help him push it toward the gangway.

Tension threaded James's spine. He'd put his trust in the boy's belief that Talia was actually on board the hulk.

They got the wheelbarrow onto the gangway and began rolling it upward. Closer...closer...

"Stop there!" the chief warder yelled.

Peter froze. James turned. The foreman was standing beside the gangway, his hands on his hips as he glared at them.

"Who the bleedin' hell—"

The crash of wood splintering against stone echoed through the dock. The warder jerked his attention to the warehouse. Several crates had fallen from the top of a pile. Broken wood and hundreds of dead kippers spilled over the ground.

The warder cursed, his face reddening as he ran toward the disaster. His foot skidded on the slippery fish and he went down with a thud. At his bellow of anger, the two sentries ran forward to help him.

Behind the remaining crates, Martin and Daniel raised their fists in victory and scurried off to avoid detection.

"Go," James hissed at Peter.

Peter grabbed a sack and started up the gangway. James took hold of the wheelbarrow and followed Peter up the gangway to the entry port. There was a bustle of activity on the main deck as workers opened the hatches to lower crates and barrels into the hold.

James motioned for Peter to stay concealed, then hurried off toward the stairs leading to the lower decks. He passed the galley, his heart jumping as he realized the cook was busy raking the coals of the fire just below a black boiler.

James held his breath until the man turned away from the door; then he darted past and made his way to the forecastle. He paused just outside a linen drying room, where shirts and stockings dangled from ropes strung up along the ceiling.

The hatchway by the top deck was barred and padlocked. A sentry's bayonet leaned against the wall, but the guard was nowhere in sight. James exhaled a slow breath. Sweat dripped down his neck. He had no way of opening the hatchway.

"Ho, there!"

James whirled, his fist striking out instinctively. The blow knocked the sentry's head back. He let out a yelp and stared at James in momentary shock. Before he could recover and strike back, James hit him again. The man's head banged against the wall, but he managed to lunge forward in a tackle. James grunted, the breath escaping him as he wrestled the sentry into the linen room.

With a muttered apology, he slammed the man's head to the ground, the blow stunning enough to give James time to grab a few shirts and stockings from above. He tied a gag around the sentry's mouth, then removed the jacket of his uniform and fastened bindings around his arms and legs. When he'd ensured the man couldn't escape, he pulled off his jacket, shrugged into the uniform, and took the keys from the sentry's belt.

After closing the linen room door, James unlocked the hatchway, grabbed the bayonet, and went down to the prisoners' decks. Two long rows of cells lined the top deck, filled with hammocks like gigantic cocoons. Snores and the rumble of conversation echoed against the wood. Lanterns hung outside the railings.

James grabbed a lantern, keeping his head bowed as a few of the men shouted at him. Fear seized him at the idea of Talia anywhere near dozens of rough prisoners.

He moved forward, his heart thumping as he continued down the hatchway to the lower deck. The air was hot and stale. The lower decks contained fewer prisoners, but surely not even Lawford would put Talia in their midst...

He kept going until he reached a narrow, whitewashed passage at the end of the lower deck. An unlocked door barred the passage. Gripping the bayonet, James pushed open the door.

Five solitary cells lined the walls. James stepped forward. Tension knotted his chest. A loud snore resounded from a hammock in one of the cells. He crept into the passageway, scanning the other cells. Empty...empty...*oh, God.*

Terror filled him.

She was lying on the floor of the last cell, her head buried in her arms, her eyes closed...

"Talia!"

She bolted upright so fast that James stumbled backward. His pulse pounded with a combination of fear and relief. Talia blinked, shoving her loose hair away from her face as she tried to orient herself.

"James?"

"Are you all right?" James set the lantern down and moved closer, gripping the bars of the cell.

"Yes...I...I think so." She pressed a hand to the side of her head, staring at him in disbelief. "How did you find me?"

"Peter knew Lawford would bring you here." He reached a hand through the bars. "I've got to get you out. The ship is leaving at midnight."

Talia's fingers tangled with his. An immense emotion coursed through him at the simple touch of her hand. He fumbled with the sentry's keys, not daring to hope that one of them might unlock this particular cell. After hastily fitting all the keys into the lock, he was forced to concede defeat.

"Do you know where Lawford went?" he asked.

"To find Peter and Alice. Are they all right?"

"Peter's fine. He's here. Alice is back at home, I think." James grasped the back of Talia's head and pulled her closer. He pressed his mouth to hers in a hard kiss, loath to leave her alone and yet having no choice. "I'll be back soon."

He grabbed the lantern and ran back down the passageway to the lower deck. The instant he stepped through the door, he crashed into Martin.

"What are you doing here?" James snapped.

The boy gave him a triumphant smile. "Part of thievin' is knowin' how to get around, right? Thought you'd want to know we spotted Lawford comin' along the quay."

James muttered a curse and grabbed Martin's arm. Together they made their way back to the upper deck.

"Where's Peter?" James whispered.

"Helpin' with the cargo loading, last I saw," Martin replied. "Guess he's such a good worker they don't care that he wasn't hired."

James didn't dare send Martin back down the gangway for fear he'd be caught by the two sentries standing guard at the bottom. Instead he opened the linen room door and pushed the boy inside. The sentry he'd tied up was still there, struggling against his bonds.

"Watch him," James told Martin, ensuring the man's bonds were still tight.

Martin gave a swift nod, crossing his arms as he stared at his captive. James left the lantern with Martin and ducked back to the hatchway door. He wanted to tell Peter to get off the ship. The boy might be able to do so easily, if he'd depart with a group of workers.

He started for the upper deck. The smell of boiled cabbage drifted from the kitchen. James turned the corner, then froze at the sight of William Lawford.

Lawford stared at him and grabbed for his gun. James darted forward, pushing the bayonet against Lawford's chest.

"Don't," he hissed. He fumbled to search Lawford's pockets and found the ring of keys. He got behind Lawford and prodded him toward the hatchway.

Silenced by the tip of the bayonet, Lawford preceded him down to the solitary cells. Talia rose to her feet, her eyes wary as she watched Lawford approach.

James nudged him with the bayonet. "Unlock it."

Lawford inserted the key into the lock and pulled open the door. Talia started to hurry out. Lawford stepped into her path. Alarm ignited in James's chest as he realized Lawford had gotten within touching distance of . . .

"Goddammit." The curse snapped from him the same instant Lawford shoved Talia back into the cell.

Talia's scream choked off as Lawford grabbed her neck. He twisted one arm behind her back and pressed his other hand to her throat, cutting off her air. James lunged forward, panic rushing through him.

"Stop," Lawford shouted. "I'll kill her, I swear."

He backed up against the far wall, his grip tightening on Talia's throat. She opened her mouth to try to suck in a breath. Terror lit in her eyes.

Stay calm. James battled the overwhelming fear, shoving it down beneath the certainty that the woman he loved was in danger and he was the only one who could save her. He lifted the rifle with a steady hand and aimed it at Lawford's head.

"Let her go."

"Back away," Lawford said. "I'm leaving this ship and locking you both up in here."

Talia grabbed Lawford's hand at her throat and tried to wrench his fingers away. Her face grew red. She fumbled at her skirts suddenly, her movements flailing and scared.

James backed up a step, but kept the rifle trained on Lawford. His finger twitched on the trigger. He ached to fire, to hit Lawford between the eyes. Only the fact that Talia was so close to Lawford stopped him.

Talia wrenched her hand from her pocket. A gleam of green shone in her palm. She brought her hand up frantically, scratching something deep along Lawford's cheek. He shrieked and released her, clutching at his face.

Talia sucked in a hard breath, gasping as she stumbled from the cell. James grabbed her and slammed the door, locking Lawford in. He took Talia's hand and ran back down the passage to the hatchway. They returned to the linen room, where Martin was still guarding the trussed-up sentry.

"How will we get out?" Talia whispered, nodding toward the guarded gangway.

"Leave it to us, miss," Martin said proudly, grabbing the lantern from the floor. "I'll get hold of Peter first."

He darted away. James shrugged at Talia's questioning look and led her back toward the kitchen. He put his arm out to indicate that she should stay behind him.

A sudden commotion broke out from the gangway. Martin and Peter ran from the upper deck, followed by a few of the other workers. James moved forward, his hand tight around Talia's arm.

Halfway up the gangway, Robert, who'd apparently been hiding between two casks of brandy, had rolled one of the barrels off the cart. It crashed to the gangway and broke, splashing liquor everywhere.

The sentries shouted and ran up toward the entry port as Robert pushed another barrel off. Close to the entry port, James caught Martin's eye. The boy lifted the lantern.

James suddenly knew what they had planned. He tightened his hand on Talia.

"Run," he ordered.

He dashed for the gangway, evading the sentries in the increasing chaos. Cold night air, laced with the smell of brandy, hit him as he hauled Talia down the gangway. They hit the quay just as flames burst from the gangway.

They turned to see the brandy flare into a spreading fire from the lantern Martin had thrown. At the entry port, the sentries and workers yelled to detach the gangway so the fire wouldn't reach the ship.

"There's Robert." Talia pointed to where Robert was racing away from the docks. "But where are Peter and...oh no."

James followed her line of sight to where Peter and Martin still stood on the deck of the *Warrior*. His heart sank. He started toward the ship.

The two boys jumped together and hit the water with a splash. Talia gasped. James ran to the edge of the quay. He dove into the water without thinking. The cold iced his blood. He fought for the surface and swam toward the spot where the boys had sunk beneath the water. Fear clawed at his throat.

He reached Peter first, grabbing the boy around the chest. "Where's Martin?"

"Don't know." Peter coughed up a lungful of water, his teeth chattering. "Went d-down."

James cursed. "Can you swim?"

"S-some. Go...go after him."

James released Peter and dove for Martin. The water was black and murky. He swam deeper, his hands skimming slimy plants and debris. When his lungs tightened, he swam up to grab a breath and went down again. Finally he sensed the boy kicking for the surface beside him, and he reached out to grab him. They came up together, sucking in air and spitting water. James hauled Martin onto his back.

They started back to the quay, the shouts and noise filling their ears again. James pushed Martin onto the quay before him as someone reached a hand down to help Peter clamber up.

Only when James had hauled himself out of the water did he look up to see that Talia was flanked by two river police officers.

Chapter Eighteen

𝒥t was all a terrible mistake." Talia kept her voice haughty as she eyed the officers. She had refused to speak to them or allow them to speak to Martin and Peter until they'd returned to the King's Street town house and gotten the boys and James into dry clothes. The boys were now eating soup and bread in the kitchen.

"I'm quite certain my father, the Earl of Rushton"—Talia paused to allow that illustrious title to sink into the officers' minds—"will be dismayed to learn that his daughter has been accused of something so heinous."

The officers glanced at each other and shifted with discomfort.

"I am equally certain," Talia continued, "that my brother, Mr. Nicholas Hall, who is at St. Katharine's Docks right now settling matters with the foreman, will be happy to compensate you both for treating me with such concern."

"As will I," James added.

"Er...just a bit of a mess, you know, milady," one of the officers muttered.

"Yes, I know." She blinked at them both. "I'm just so thankful no one was hurt."

The officers exchanged another glance.

"Er...perhaps we'll be off then," the second one said. "You're certain there's nothing you...well, if you've got anything to convey, you know where to find us."

"I most certainly do. Thank you so very much."

She walked them to the door, then called Soames and asked him to ensure that both Peter and Martin had had enough to eat.

"Then please escort Peter back to his father's house, and Martin to the Brick Street dormitory," she said. "And tell Miss Colston I will call upon her tomorrow."

"Yes, milady."

Talia returned to the drawing room, where James was sitting by the fire. Amusement creased his eyes as he looked at her.

"Well done, my lady."

Talia sank into the chair opposite him. She allowed her gaze to track over his hard-edged features, washed in firelight, the strands of sun-streaked blond still gleaming in his dark brown hair. An ache pooled in her chest.

"You came to find me," she whispered.

"Of course." He stared down at his clasped hands. "For the first time, I needed to run toward you. Not run away." He lifted his head, his eyes shadowed. "Because I realized I can't live without you. You've been...always, you've been a part of me, Talia, the good part. The reminder of family and dedication. Of courage. Everything I never had."

Talia's heart tightened. "You've always had those things, James. You just didn't want to admit it."

"I wanted to escape." He shook his head, his mouth compressing with self-disgust. "Bloody fool, I've been."

His words should have elicited some hope in Talia, but instead she just felt sad. As many times as she had thought about being with James, marrying him, she'd never been able to find a solution to the stark fact of their very different lives.

"Talia, dear, your bath is ready." Aunt Sally hurried into the room. "And Nicholas is on his way back."

Nicholas. Fear curled through her. She hadn't seen her brother yet, as he'd gone directly to the docks after James informed him of all that had happened.

She lifted her head to look at James, startled to find his gaze on her, somber but without apprehension. With Aunt Sally in the room, she couldn't bring up her embarrassment over bursting into his study and revealing the truth of their intimacy.

With a murmured excuse, Talia hauled herself upstairs to bathe. She let Lucy help her undress, then sank into the hot water with a sigh of relief. She soaped away all the grime and sweat, scrubbed her hair, and changed into a blue cotton morning dress.

Although she would have liked to sleep for a few hours, she knew she had to speak with her brother first. She returned downstairs, her nerves tensing when she heard Nicholas's voice coming from the drawing room.

She paused in the doorway. James was standing by the hearth, his feet apart and his hands clasped behind his back. His gaze locked with hers. A tremble swept her from head to toe at the resolute, determined look in his eyes.

"James—"

"I would very much like to marry you, Talia."

Although such a statement would have once sounded like magical bells to Talia, now they only filled her with dismay. She risked a glance at Nicholas, who was sitting on the sofa, staring down into a glass of brandy.

"Nicholas, I'm sorry. I..." Her voice faltered.

Nicholas set the glass down and rose to approach her. Gentleness softened the lines around his eyes as he settled a hand on her shoulder.

"Far be it from me ever to judge you, sister," he said.

Talia shook her head, tears stinging her eyes. "I've done just what she did."

"And what is that?"

"Disgraced our family. If people begin talking about me, about our family again...it's entirely my fault."

"I hardly think either Lady Byron or Sir Henry is apt to run around gossiping about what you have or haven't done with Lord Castleford," Nicholas said. "You haven't disgraced us, Talia, anything but. You've only ever been a blessing to this family. The only one, in fact."

Talia swiped at a stray tear as guilt stabbed through her. "I told myself so many times that I'd never be like her."

"And why do you think you are? Bastian seems to have concluded that she followed her heart, but at the expense of the rest of us. Have you done that?"

Had she? Talia stared at the knot of his cravat. She had followed her heart all those months ago at Floreston Manor, and she'd ended up hurting both herself and

James. And as much as she'd tried to deny she still had strong feelings for him, her heart still pulled in his direction, as if it alone knew the core truth of James Forester.

She looked past her brother's shoulder to where James stood. His expression was shuttered, but his eyes glittered as he watched her. Warmth spiraled through her.

"He's got the approval of us all," Nicholas murmured. "You know that."

He squeezed her shoulder and moved toward the door. Talia drew in a breath, her heart hammering as James approached. He reached out to touch a lock of her hair that had escaped its pin and curled it around his finger. Even with space still between them, Talia felt the warmth of his body.

"I meant it," he said. "I do love you, Talia. I'm only sorry it took me so long to understand that. To admit it." His eyes darkened with self-directed irritation. "I would give anything to keep you from being hurt, yet I'm the one who did just that. I want to make amends, Talia. I want to prove myself to you."

"You already have."

Hope sparked like fireflies in his eyes. Talia's heart ached. She reached up to put her hand on his cheek, rubbing her palm over the rough stubble coating his jaw. A thousand thoughts flew through her mind—all the dreams she'd once had about what their future together could be.

"I know who you are, James. I wouldn't have fallen in love with you if I hadn't. I've always trusted you, yes, but I've also always trusted myself."

He brushed his thumb across her lower lip, sending a

tingle across her skin. "Is that why you kept all the letters I wrote to you? The mementos? My coat."

Talia's throat tightened as she nodded. "I...I've thrown it all away, James. Once I realized there was no sense in clinging to the past. To what could never be."

"It *can* be, Talia." He lowered his head and pressed his warm mouth to hers.

"I want to marry you," he whispered against her lips. "Allow me to do everything in my power to make you happy. I swear upon my soul I will prove myself worthy of you."

"James, I will always count you as my dearest friend. But you were right when you told me you could never be married. I don't want to be the reason you're bound to London. And I don't want to be left behind while you travel the world."

"I don't want to go anywhere without you, Talia. I can't stand the thought of you in one place and me in another with only letters to bind us."

"You mustn't stop your work, James. Even if you said you would, I know you'd still have the urge in your blood. And I never want you to resent me for keeping you in London."

"I've already resigned from the southern Siberia expedition."

Talia stepped back in shock. "You what?"

"Yesterday. I sent word to the RGS that I'm unable to carry out my duties and they need to find a new commander."

"But...but that was the whole reason you made the agreement with Alexander. Because you wanted to carry it through."

James cupped her cheek, his eyes both serious and tender. "Since then, I have come to realize there is something far more important to me than an expedition to Siberia. I don't want to go any longer, Talia. I want to stay here with you."

Talia's heart gave a wild, joyful leap at his words, even as her mind warned caution.

"Are you certain of that?" she whispered.

"More than ever." James broke away from her suddenly and paced to the middle of the room. "You were right when you said I'm a coward, Talia. I've been running away ever since my mother died, ever since I discovered no one would help her. But I don't want to run anymore."

"If…" Talia took a breath, not wanting to wish too hard, to hope for too much. "James, if you stay here, what will you do?"

"I'll work with the RGS from the London offices. Perhaps finally straighten out my father's estate. Heaven knows I would love to turn over the running of the household to you, both in London and Devon. I can't remember the last time I visited the manor."

"And when you get the urge to travel again?" Talia asked. "What then?"

"I'll ask you what city you want to see, and we'll go there together." He turned to face her. "You used to love travel once, didn't you? Will you come with me?"

Love coiled like an embrace around Talia's heart at the expectation and hope in his expression. She could imagine without any effort at all a life like the one he described—the two of them spending the season in London and returning to Devon in autumn. She could see them traveling together, to the Continent, to Russia, even America. She could picture herself taking care of the household and perhaps, one day, their children...

She lifted her head to look at him. "And Brick Street, James? The ragged schools? What of them?"

A frown tipped his mouth. "I will not deny the importance of your work, Talia, nor will I prevent you from conducting it. I will, however, ask that you allow me to accompany you when you venture into districts such as Wapping."

Talia wasn't foolish enough to ask if he would actually help her, both practically and financially, but there would be time for that. There was still the possibility of Lady Byron's patronage, and for now that would be more than enough to find a new location for Brick Street and to start furnishing the school properly.

Silence fell as she and James looked at each other. Talia became aware that her heart was beating swiftly, like a wind-whipped leaf.

"Tell me..." He paused, his throat working with a swallow. "Tell me I have not done irreparable damage. Tell me somewhere, somehow, you still have a shred of love for me. Is that true... or false?"

Tears pricked Talia's eyes. "False."

He froze, his eyes darkening with despair. Before he could speak, Talia stepped forward and put her hand against his chest. Beneath her palm, his heart thumped.

"I don't have a *shred* of love for you, James," Talia said. "I have a... an *abundance* of love for you. It's never gone away, no matter how much I tried to tell myself otherwise. I love you, James Forester. I have always loved you."

He exhaled hard, relief easing the creases on his face. His eyes softened with tenderness as he slid his hand to the back of Talia's neck and drew her toward him. Their lips met with a soft, gentle touch brimming with the promise of the future. Talia closed her eyes and sank into the kiss, feeling as if a flower had bloomed open inside her. As if all the dreams she'd ever held for her and James had finally come true.

Lt. George Lawford, governor of Newhall prison, announced that his nephew, Mr. William Lawford, had taken a position with the prison hulks board and departed for New South Wales. The lieutenant further announced that, owing to a newfound "inheritance," he himself would retire and live out the remainder of his days in the country.

James dictated a letter to the governor of New South Wales, with whom he'd become acquainted during his recent expedition, and requested that he employ Mr. Lawford, who was on board the *Warrior*. Mr. Lawford would be well suited to overseeing convict labor in the stone quarries, James suggested, as he was unable to return to London owing to the fact that the Home Office would deny any request to return.

Once that matter was dealt with, James and Talia turned their attention to their upcoming wedding. Neither of them wanted to wait. Talia initially thought they should plan the wedding for the end of summer when her father returned, but she felt as if she had waited a lifetime for James already.

And once James set his sights on marriage to her, he immediately began making arrangements for their wed-

ding. Not a week after his proposal, Talia went downstairs one morning to find her brother Sebastian, his
wife, and his stepson, Andrew, in the dining room, having breakfast with Nicholas and Aunt Sally.

Talia threw herself into Sebastian's embrace with a
happy laugh. She hugged Andrew and hurried Clara upstairs with her to discuss the wedding gown choices the
modiste had sent the previous day.

A flurry of activity took place for the next few days,
and then finally Talia woke to the morning she would
marry James Forester. Clara and Lucy bustled around
helping Talia dress before they went to the nearby
church where James was waiting.

Her heart gave a happy leap at the sight of him—
tall and handsome in a dark blue morning suit and silk
cravat. His sun-streaked hair was brushed away from
his forehead, his brown eyes filled with warmth as he
watched her approach.

He bent to brush his lips across her cheek. "I love
you," he murmured in her ear as the priest called for
everyone to take their places. "And never will I tire of
telling you that."

His hands closed around hers as the priest began the
ceremony. She tightened her grip, their gazes locked together. *He will not let go. He will never let go.*

"I will," she murmured, when the minister prompted
her response to love and cherish James Forester. *I always have.*

He responded with his own vow, then lowered his
head again to give her what was likely a somewhat indecent kiss in front of the spectators.

"He's lucky another fellow didn't get to you first."

Sebastian smiled as he enfolded Talia in his arms. "Pater will be delighted. Old bird deserves to be delighted for a change."

"What do you think Alexander will say?" Talia asked.

"He's already sent a telegraph." Sebastian reached into his pocket for a piece of paper, which he gave to her.

Talia unfolded the paper with trembling hands. *Most excellent. Agreement settled beyond expectations.*

Pleased, Talia tucked the note away to put with her other keepsakes. They returned to King's Street and went into the dining room for the wedding breakfast before Sebastian and Clara excused themselves to take Andrew to the park for an outing. James left a couple of hours later, telling Talia he wanted to ensure his house was prepared for her arrival, and she spent the rest of the afternoon determining what she wanted to bring with her.

As supper neared, Nicholas strode into the drawing room.

"All right, brat, I'm off then." He gave her a big, warm embrace.

"You're really leaving again so soon?" Talia asked.

"Heard tell there's a ship heading off for a southern Siberia expedition," Nicholas replied, scooping his hat up from the sofa. "In want of a commander. Thought I might apply."

He clasped Talia's hands and bent to kiss her cheek.

"Castle will take care of you," he said. "We all know that."

Bittersweet love curled through Talia as she watched him stride toward the door. "Nicholas."

He turned.

"Visit Darius en route, would you? Tell him I miss him."

A shadow passed across Nicholas's face, but he gave a swift nod. "Take care, brat. Couldn't be more pleased about Castle, honestly."

Then he was gone. Talia stood in the empty room for a moment, remembering when her father's house had once been filled with her brothers' raucous shouts and laughter. She pressed a hand to her chest. This was the only house she'd ever known, and now for the first time ever, she was embarking on an entirely new life. With the man she loved.

With a smile, she started upstairs. She'd told James she would be *home* before supper, as soon as she finished organizing more of her belongings. She went to her bedchamber, where trunks and suitcases lay open and overflowing with dresses, petticoats, and shifts. Talia started toward the wardrobe, then stopped.

An old wooden crate sat on the floor beside her bed. Her heart thumped. She went to pry off the lid, then stared at the contents—James's letters and mementos. She picked up a seashell, running her thumb over the spiral grooves.

"Talia, did you want me to ask Madame Gaston to send your latest order to James's house?" Aunt Sally sailed into the room, her blue gown swirling like a whirlpool around her.

Talia straightened. "Aunt Sally, do you know how this came to be here?"

"What is it, dear?" Sally peered into the crate.

"Just some things I'd asked Soames to dispose of. You don't know why he brought them back here?"

"Why, no. Why should I?" Sally reached into the crate and removed a letter. "Why on earth would you want to throw away letters from James?"

"I was...er, well, I wasn't very happy with him at the time."

"Hmm." Sally dropped the letter back into the crate. "Considering he's now your husband, I imagine you're quite relieved to have such treasures back in your possession."

Talia narrowed her eyes suspiciously at her aunt. Seeming oblivious, Sally spun and headed to the door.

"Best get to James soon, dear. I'll have the rest of your things sent this week."

Talia looked at the seashell still cupped in her palm. A quicksilver flash of anticipation ran through her. She hurried to finish getting ready, then went to join James at his house. She found him in the parlor and happily submitted to his warm kiss. Her anticipation heightened as they ate a spare dinner of bread and cheese, neither one particularly hungry after the events of the day.

And then, finally, she was in his arms, free to surrender to the love and desire that had brewed inside her for so long. He kissed her gently, pressing his mouth to her lips, her cheeks, her eyelids, her forehead. Each touch sent shivers sparking through Talia's blood. She stepped back only to watch him undress, her heart pounding as he removed his shirt to reveal the expanse of his torso.

"I have a peignoir made especially for this night," Talia whispered, her gaze tracing the smooth muscles of his shoulders.

"You'll not be in it for more than two seconds if you put it on now," James warned, turning her to unfasten the row of buttons down her back. It took some time to divest Talia of her layers of clothing, and by the time she was left only in her shift, she was near trembling with urgency. She reached out and ran her hand over James's taut chest, heat flashing through her as she felt a shudder race through him.

Emboldened by the evidence that she affected him as much as he affected her, she stepped closer and placed both her hands on him. The warmth of his skin flowed up her arms, intensifying the desire uncoiling in her body. He lowered his head to kiss her again, his hands sliding down to grasp her hips as they moved toward the bed. Talia fell into the sensations—the press of their bodies together, the heat of James's breath as he traced a path across her cheek and down to her neck, the ridge of his erection against her thigh.

Talia closed her eyes, thrusting her hands into his hair. She'd thought it would be a hasty night, both of them too eager to prolong matters, but James seemed determined to take things slowly.

He pulled her shift over her head, his eyes darkening with lust at the sight of her nakedness, then proceeded to kiss every inch of her bare skin. His lips sent tingles traveling to her very core, and when he pressed his mouth to her belly, she arched instinctively against him.

Locking her gaze to his, she fumbled for the fastenings of his trousers and pushed them off his hips. He slid a hand down to her sex, his fingers working with a precise touch that sent flames licking through Talia's blood.

When James moved between her thighs, Talia softened and opened in response. She curved her arms around him, her heart hammering with both desire and trepidation. James placed his hand on the side of her neck.

"Look at me," he whispered, his gold-flecked eyes simmering with heat. "Never stop."

She sank into the depths of his gaze as he pushed slowly into her, his hands tight on her hips. Talia gasped, stunned by the sensation of him filling her, the exquisite pleasure wrapping them both in a haze of growing urgency. James captured her cries with the pressure of his mouth and slid a hand between their bodies to touch the knot in which her pleasure was centered. Any hint of apprehension slipped away, replaced by a sweet, churning need that grew more intense with every thrust of their bodies.

"James!" Talia sank her fingers into his back, gripping him tightly as bliss crashed through her. He pushed into her again, his groan vibrating against her skin as he surrendered to his own release.

He eased to the side, pulling her closer. Talia fit herself against the planes of his body and rested her head on his chest. The thumping sound of his heartbeat resounded through her. James pressed his lips against her hair.

"Remember I told you I'd gotten rid of all your mementos and letters?" Talia asked, running her hand over his damp chest. "They didn't get thrown away after all. I suspect Aunt Sally had something to do with that, though of course she would never admit it."

"After I'd discovered you'd kept all those things, I wished I'd had something of yours," James said, tucking

a stray lock of hair behind Talia's ear. "A silk handkerchief or a button from your glove...something I could
have kept in my pocket no matter where I was."

"You've always had something of mine," Talia said.

"Have I? What?"

"My heart."

Epilogue

Talia set the books on the tables and went to open the windows. The new Brick Street school classroom in Buckle Street was a large, clean room with rows of new desks and plenty of windows. There were bookshelves filled with textbooks, charts, maps, and a good supply of paper, pencils, and notepads. At the front of the room, Mr. Fletcher's desk sat in front of a wide chalkboard on which he'd already written out the day's lesson plan.

The door opened, and Peter and Alice Colston entered with a covered box.

"Mr. Blake suggested that we bring an array of items," Alice said, as Peter set the box on a table and pulled off the lid.

"He thought it would be useful for the boys to see how they're made." Peter removed a dozen mechanical toys from the box and lined them up on the table. "See, this one is the machine that controls the crank valve, so they can see how it works inside the automaton. And this is the mechanism used for movement, plus the bellows that we're trying to use for sound."

Talia and Alice exchanged smiles. At James's instigation, Peter had gone to work at Blake's Museum of Automata less than a month ago. Though Talia had been uncertain about how Peter would fare working with automata mechanisms, the arrangement had proven a resounding success. Mr. Blake was most pleased to have an apprentice, and Peter had taken to the work with both skill and enthusiasm.

Mr. Colston had allowed the boy to return home after learning of the respectable work and the possibility that Peter might one day earn a good living as a clock or toy maker. His testimony about the conditions at Newhall had also helped plans for another prison reform bill directed toward juvenile facilities.

"Peter, perhaps you'll come and conduct a lesson about this," Mr. Fletcher suggested as he approached the table. "It certainly would be useful for the boys to learn how such machinery operates."

Peter looked embarrassed but pleased at the idea. Mr. Fletcher turned his attention to Alice.

"And the dormitory provisions arrived, Miss Colston?"

"Indeed." Alice had taken over the management of the Brick Street dormitory, which was located on the upper floor of the building. In her role as supervisor of the staff and the boys, she'd proven most efficient. "I've started a teatime precisely at four, Mr. Fletcher, to show the boys how to conduct themselves properly. Perhaps you'll join us one afternoon?"

"I should be delighted."

Talia smiled as Alice and Mr. Fletcher held gazes for perhaps a second longer than was entirely appropriate. She turned to gather the books she intended to return to Mudie's Library.

"There's a note for you too, milady." Peter dug into his pocket and produced a wrinkled, folded piece of paper. "Arrived at Mr. Blake's with instructions to deliver it to you."

Talia looked at the paper, which bore her name in a distinctive scrawl. Pleasure coursed through her. She thanked Peter and said her good-byes before returning to the carriage.

After the carriage started back to Arlington Street, Talia settled against the seat and opened the letter.

My dear Talia,

This morning I woke to the despairing realization that you'd already gone. I had intended to bestow some very wicked attentions on your person. I hope upon receipt of this note, you will return home with all due haste...

Talia smiled as the carriage came to a stop in front of the town house. She found James waiting for her in the study. He held out his arms, a responding smile lighting his face as she stepped into his embrace.

"My dear love," he whispered, lowering his mouth to hers. "I missed you."

When their lips met, Talia's heart blossomed with happiness. Their three-week marriage was just beginning to unfold, showing her all that she and James were together, all they would be. It was true that their relationship wasn't as it was *before*—but now it was far richer and more beautiful than she could have imagined. And for the first time in her life, Talia looked forward with both eagerness and passion to the lovely promise of *after*.

The lovely Lydia Kellaway can solve the most complex puzzles. The one challenge she can't top? Managing the most infuriating man she's ever encountered...

Please turn this page for an excerpt from

A Study in Seduction.

Chapter One

London
March 1854

Every square matrix is a root of its own characteristic polynomial.

Lydia Kellaway clutched the notebook to her chest as the cab rattled away, the clatter of horses' hooves echoing against the fortress of impressive town houses lining Mount Street. Gaslights burned through the midnight dark, casting puddles of light onto the cobblestones.

Lydia took a breath, anxiety and fear twisting through her. She looked up at town house number twelve, the dark façade perforated with light-filled windows. A man stood silhouetted behind one window on the first floor, his form straight, tall, and so still that he appeared fixed in that moment.

Beneath the glow of a streetlamp, Lydia opened her notebook and leafed through pages scribbled with notes, equations, and diagrams.

She'd written his name at the top of a blank page, then

followed it with a numbered list of points, all related to the gossip and suppositions surrounding his family.

As she reviewed her notes, the back of her neck prickled with the strange feeling that she was being watched. She snapped the notebook closed and shook her head. Chiding herself for being unnerved by the shadows, she climbed the steps.

She reached for the bell just as the door flew open. A woman dressed in a vivid green silk gown stormed out, nearly colliding with Lydia on the front step.

"Oh!" The woman reeled backward, her eyes widening. In the sudden light spilling out from the foyer, Lydia saw that her eyes were red and swollen, her face streaked with tears.

Lydia stammered, "I'm . . . I'm sorry, I—"

The woman shook her head, her lips pressing together as she pushed past Lydia and hurried down the steps.

A curse echoed through the open door as a dark-haired man strode across the foyer, tension shimmering around him. "Talia!"

He didn't cast Lydia a glance as he followed the woman down the steps. "Blast it, Talia, wait for the carriage!"

The woman turned her head to glare at the man and tossed a retort over her shoulder. Lydia couldn't discern the words, but the cutting tone was enough to make her pursuer stop in his tracks. He cursed again, then went back to the house and shouted for the footman. Within seconds, the servant raced down the street after the woman.

"John!" The tall man turned to shout for a second servant. "Ready the carriage now and see Lady Talia home!"

He stalked up the steps and brushed past Lydia. He

seemed about to slam the door in her face, but then he stopped and turned to stare at her. "Who the bloody hell are you?"

Lydia couldn't speak past the shock.

Alexander Hall, Viscount Northwood. She knew it was him, knew in her bones that this was the man she sought, though she had not laid eyes on him before now.

Despite the hour and his anger, his clothing was precise, unwrinkled. His black trousers bore creases as sharp as a blade, and shiny gilt buttons fastened his silk waistcoat over a snowy white shirt.

His dark eyes flashed over Lydia. That look—keen, assessing, *close*—caused her breath to tangle in her throat.

"Well?" he demanded.

Every square matrix is a root of its own characteristic polynomial.

The locket. Jane. The locket.

"Lord Northwood?" she said.

"I asked who you are."

His rough baritone voice settled deep in her bones. She tilted her head to meet his hooded gaze. Shadows mapped the pronounced Slavic angles of his face, the sloping cheekbones, the clean-shaven line of his jaw.

"My name is Lydia Kellaway," she said, struggling to keep her voice steady. She glanced at the street, where the footman had stopped Lady Talia at the corner. A carriage rattled from the side of the house and approached. "Is she all right?"

"My sister is fine," Lord Northwood snapped, "aside from being the most obstinate, frustrating creature who ever walked the earth."

"Is that a family trait?" Lydia spoke before thinking, which was so contrary to her usual manner that her face heated with embarrassment. Not wise to insult the man from whom she needed something.

She almost heard Northwood's teeth grind together as his jaw clenched with irritation.

He followed her gaze to where the footman and coach driver had convinced Lady Talia to enter the carriage. The footman gave Lord Northwood a wave of victory before climbing onto the bench beside the driver. The carriage rattled away.

Some of the anger seemed to drain from Northwood, which bolstered Lydia's courage. Although she had no contingency plan for how to handle arriving in the middle of a family quarrel, she couldn't possibly leave now.

Her spine straightened with determination as she faced the viscount. "Lord Northwood, I apologize for the lateness of the hour, but I must speak with you. It's about a locket you purchased."

"A what?"

"A locket. A pendant attached to a chain, worn as a necklace."

He frowned. "You've come to my home at this hour to inquire about a *necklace*?"

"It's terribly important." She gripped the doorjamb so he couldn't close the door and leave her standing on the step. "Please, may I come in?"

He stared at her for a minute, then rubbed a hand across his chin.

"Kellaway." A crease formed between his brows. "Kin to Sir Henry Kellaway?"

Lydia gave a quick nod. "He was my father. He

passed away several months ago." Grief, heavy with the weight of the past, pressed down on her heart.

"My sympathies," Lord Northwood said, his frown easing somewhat as he glanced over her black mourning dress.

"Thank you. How did you know him?"

"We were both involved with the Crystal Palace exhibition in fifty-one." He stood looking at her for a moment, his gaze so protracted she could almost see his thoughts shifting. Then he moved aside and held the door open.

She stepped into the foyer, conscious of the fact that he did not allow her more space to pass, even as her shoulder brushed against his arm. The light contact made her jerk away, her chest constricting.

"What makes you think I have this necklace you seek?" he asked.

"I don't think you have it, Lord Northwood. I know you do. You purchased it from Mr. Havers's shop less than a week ago, along with a Russian icon." Her chin lifted. "It was a locket my grandmother pawned."

Pushing himself away from the doorjamb, Lord Northwood stepped forward. Lydia started before realizing he intended to take her cloak. She pushed the hood off her head and fumbled with the clasp.

He stood behind her, close enough that she could sense the warmth of his body, close enough that her next breath might have been the very air he exhaled.

"Come to the drawing room, Miss Kellaway. You'd best explain yourself."

Lydia followed him into the room and sat on the sofa, making a conscious effort not to twist the notebook between her fingers. Lord Northwood lowered himself into the chair across from her. A stoic footman served tea before departing and closing the door behind him.

Lord Northwood took a swallow of tea, then put the cup on the table and leaned back in his chair. His long body unfolded with the movement, his legs stretching out in front of him. Although his outward bearing was casual, a tautness coiled through him. He reminded Lydia of a bird of prey elongating its wings, feathers ruffling, poised for flight.

"Well?" he asked.

"I found the ticket in my grandmother's desk." She leafed through the pages of her book before finding a small slip of paper. "I hadn't known she'd pawned any of my mother's jewelry."

His hand brushed hers as he took the pawn ticket, the hard ridges of his fingers discernible even through the protection of her glove. She jerked away, curling her hand into a fist at her side.

"Your grandmother had a month to redeem her pledge," Lord Northwood said after looking at the slip of paper.

"I realize that. And I would have attempted to do so on her behalf had I known about the transaction to begin with. I thought Mr. Havers might not have put the locket up for sale yet, or if he had, perhaps it hadn't been sold. But when I arrived at his shop, he informed me he'd sold it last Thursday."

"How did you learn the name of the purchaser?"

Color heated her cheeks. "Mr. Havers refused—rightly so, I suppose—to divulge the purchaser's name," she explained. "When he became occupied with another customer, I saw his book of sales behind the counter. I was able to...borrow it long enough to look up the transaction."

A smile tugged at his mouth. She watched with a trace of fascination as a dimple appeared in his cheek, lending his severe, angular features an almost boyish glint. "You stole Havers's salesbook?"

"I did not steal it." She bristled a little at the disagreeable term. "I removed it from his shop, yes, but for less than ten minutes. I gave a boy sixpence to return the book to its proper place without Mr. Havers seeing him. You were clearly listed as the purchaser of the locket. Do you still have it, my lord?"

Northwood shifted, his hand sliding into his coat pocket. Lydia's breath caught in her chest as she watched him withdraw the silver chain, capturing the locket in his palm.

He studied the locket, rubbing his thumb across the engraving that embellished its polished surface.

"Is it a phoenix?" he asked.

"It's called a *fenghuang*, a bird of virtue, power, and grace."

He flipped the locket over to the design on the other side. "And the dragon?"

"When the *fenghuang* is paired with a dragon, the two symbolize the union of...of husband and wife."

His dark eyes moved to hers. "Of male and female."

Lydia swallowed in an effort to ease the sudden dryness of her mouth. "The...the *fenghuang* itself is representative of yin and yang. *Feng* is the male bird, *huang* the female. The bird and the dragon together speak of marital harmony."

"And the woman?" Northwood asked.

"The woman is yin, the bird called *huang*—"

"No." He flicked open the locket, turning it toward her to reveal the miniature portrait inside. "This woman."

She didn't look at the image. She couldn't. She stared at Lord Northwood. Something complex and strangely intimate shone behind his eyes, as if he knew the answer to his question yet wanted to hear the response from her.

"That woman," she said, "is my mother."

He snapped the locket closed between his thumb and forefinger. "She is very beautiful."

"She was."

The sine of two theta equals two times the sine of theta times the cosine of theta.

Lydia repeated the trigonometric identity until the threat of disturbing emotions had passed.

"Why did you purchase the locket from Mr. Havers?" she asked.

"I'd never seen anything like it."

"Nor will you again. My father had it specially made. It is pure silver, though I suspect you know that."

"I do recognize excellent craftsmanship." As he spoke, he lifted his gaze from the locket and looked at her. "And this locket must be very valuable, indeed, if it brought you here in the middle of the night."

Lydia nodded. She slipped her hand into her pocket and closed her fingers around a small figurine. She extended it to Lord Northwood. "My father brought this back years ago from a trip to the province of Yunnan. It's a jade sculpture of an elephant, quite well crafted. I'd like to offer it in exchange for the locket."

"Why didn't your grandmother pawn that instead of the locket?"

Lying would serve no purpose. Not with this man.

"It isn't as valuable," Lydia admitted.

"You expect me to make an uneven exchange?"

"No. My father also has several Chinese scrolls, one or two paintings—if you would consider several items in exchange?"

Northwood shook his head. "I do not collect Chinese art and artifacts, Miss Kellaway, so that would be of no use. As I said, I bought the locket because it was unique."

"Surely there must be something you want."

"What else are you offering?"

Although the question appeared innocent, the undercurrent of his voice rippled through her. Warmth heated its wake—not the tenderness provoked by emotions of the heart but something edged with wildness, lack of control. Danger.

Her eyes burned.

The locket. The locket.

"I...I have not the immediate funds to repurchase it from you," she admitted, "though I've been recently offered a position that involves payment, and I can offer you a promissory note in exchange for—"

"I trust no one to uphold a promissory note."

"I assure you, my lord, I would never—"

"No one, Miss Kellaway."

Lydia expelled a breath, unable to muster any indignation at his decree. She wouldn't trust anyone to uphold a promissory note, either. Almost twenty-eight years of life had taught her that well enough.

"Nor would I accept money that you...earned?" Northwood added.

The statement had a question to it, one Lydia had no intention of answering. If she told him she'd been offered a position on the editorial board of a mathematical journal, he'd likely either laugh at her or...Wait a moment.

"Lord Northwood, I understand you are in charge of a Society of Arts exhibition. Is that correct?"

He nodded. "An international educational exhibition, which I proposed well over a year ago. It's scheduled to open in June. Preparations are under way."

An international exhibition. Lydia's fingers tightened on the notebook.

"Is there by chance a...a mathematical element of the exhibition?" she asked.

"There is a planned display of different mathematical instruments used in various parts of the world."

"I see." She tried to ignore the shimmer of fear in her blood. If he did accept her offer, she would have no reason to take on any kind of public role. All of her work could be conducted before the exhibition even opened. Perhaps no one except Lord Northwood would even know.

"Lord Northwood, I should like to offer my assistance with your exhibition in exchange for the locket."

"I beg your pardon?"

"I have a talent for mathematics and am quite certain I could be a useful consultant."

"You have a *talent* for mathematics?"

He was looking at her as if she were the oddest creature he'd ever encountered. Lydia had been on the receiving end of such askance looks since she was a child and had grown accustomed to them. Coming from Lord Northwood, however, such dubiousness caused an unexpected rustle of dismay.

"Unusual, I know," she said, attempting to keep her voice light, "but there it is. I've spent most of my life with numbers, crafting useful theorems into solutions. I can advise you on the efficacy and value of the mathematics display."

"We are already consulting with a Society subcommittee composed of mathematicians and professors."

Lydia's heart sank. "Oh." She chewed her lower lip and flipped through the notebook. "What about the books? Do you need anyone to help with your accounting of the books?"

"No. Even if I did, I would not allow you to work in exchange for the locket."

"Well, I would still like—"

Before she could finish the sentence, Northwood rose from his chair with the swiftness of a crocodile emerging from a river. He crossed to her in two strides and pulled the notebook from her grip. Lydia gave a slight gasp. He paged through the book, his frown deepening.

"'Alexander Hall, Lord Northwood,'" he read, "'returned from St. Petersburg two years ago following scandal.' What is all this?"

A hot flush crept up Lydia's neck. "My lord, I apologize, I didn't mean to offend."

"A bit late for that, Miss Kellaway. You've been collecting details about me? For the purpose of retrieving the locket?"

"It was the only way I could—"

"'A *pompous sort*'? Where did you hear I was a pompous sort?"

Lydia's blush grew hotter, accompanied by a growing alarm as she sensed the locket swinging farther out of her reach. "Er...a friend of my grandmother's. She said you were known for moving about in rather lofty circles, both here and in St. Petersburg."

When he didn't respond, she added, "She also said you'd done excellent work building your trading company."

If the compliment mitigated the offense, he gave no indication. He turned his attention back to the book.

"'Scandal involving mother.'" Northwood's expression tightened with anger. "Did your research, didn't you, Miss Kellaway?"

She couldn't respond. Shame and dismay swirled through her chest. Northwood leafed through the rest of the book, his expression not changing as he examined the scribbled equations and theorems.

"What is all this?" he asked again.

"My notes. I keep the notebook with me so I can write things down as I think of them."

Northwood slammed the book shut.

"It's late, Miss Kellaway." His voice was weary, taut. "I believe John has returned with the carriage. If you'll wait in the foyer, he will ensure that you arrive home safely."

Lydia knew that if she left now, he would never agree to see her again.

"Lord Northwood, please, I'm certain we can come to some sort of agreement."

"Are you, now?" He stared at her so intently that Lydia shifted with discomfort. His eyes slipped over her, lingering on her breasts, her waist. "What kind of agreement?"

She ought to have been offended by the dark insinuation in his voice, like the low thrum of a cello, but instead a shiver ran through her blood and curled in her belly.

Yet she had nothing more to offer him.

"Lord Northwood," she finally said, "what do you propose?"

Alexander paused for a moment and stared at the woman before him. Who *was* she? Why did she make him so…curious? And why was embarrassment flaring in him because she knew about the scandal?

"I *propose*, Miss Kellaway," he said, his words clipped, "that you throw your infernal notebook into the fire and leave me the bloody hell alone."

Her eyes widened. "I'm certain you realize that is not an option," she said quietly.

He gave a humorless laugh. So much for attempting to frighten her off. "One can hope."

He could just give her the damned locket back. That would be the gentlemanly thing to do, though he suspected she wouldn't accept the gesture. For her, it had to be done through payment or exchange.

He rolled his shoulders back, easing the tension that lived in his muscles. His earlier frustration with Talia lingered, and now with Miss Kellaway here…it would be no wonder if he concluded women were the cause of all the world's troubles.

Certainly they were the cause of *his*.

"You're correct about this." He tapped the book with a forefinger. "My mother ran off with another man. Younger than she, even. Horrified society. Ever since, people have thought of us as rather extraordinarily disreputable."

"Are you?"

"What do you think?"

"I don't know. I give little credence to gossip. It's not easily proved."

"You require proof, do you?"

"Of course. Mathematics, after all, is built on foundations of proving theorems, deductive reasoning. It's the basis of my work."

"All in this book?" He paged through it again with disbelief. Scribbled equations, lists, and diagrams filled the pages, some smudged, some crossed out, others circled or designated with a star.

"Those are notes, ideas for papers," Lydia explained. "Some problems and puzzles I've devised for my own enjoyment."

Alexander laughed.

Lydia frowned. "What's so amusing?"

"Most women—indeed, the vast majority of women—engage in needlepoint or shopping for enjoyment," Alexander said. "You devise mathematical problems?"

"Sometimes, yes. May I have my book back, please?" Her frown deepened and she extended her hand. "You needn't find it all so funny, my lord. It can be very satisfying to craft a complex problem."

"I can tell you a thousand other ways to find satisfaction."

Her lips parted, shock flashing in her eyes as the insinuation struck her. He held out the notebook but didn't loosen his grip. Lydia grasped the other end of it and appeared to collect herself, her chin lifting.

"Well," she said, "I daresay *you* couldn't solve one of my problems."

He heard the challenge in her voice and responded as if she'd just asked him to place a thousand-pound bet. He let go of the notebook.

"Couldn't I?" he asked. "How certain are you of that?"

"Quite." She cradled the notebook to her chest.

"Certain enough to wager your locket?"

She wavered an instant before giving a swift nod. "Of course, though I'd insist upon establishing the parameters of a time frame."

The parameters of a time frame.

The woman was odd enough to be fascinating.

"If you can't solve my puzzle in five minutes' time," Lydia continued, "you must return my locket at once."

"And if you lose?"

"Then you may determine my debt."

He gave her a penetrating look that might have disconcerted any other woman. Although she bore his scrutiny without response, something about her demeanor seemed to deflect it, like tarnished silver repelling light.

"Lord Northwood," she prompted, her fingers so tight on the notebook that the edges crumpled.

What would move her? What would provoke a reaction? What would break through her rigid, colorless exterior?

"A kiss," he said.

Lydia's gaze jerked to his, shock flashing in the blue depths of her eyes like lightning behind glass.

"I...I beg your pardon?"

"Should you lose, you grant me the pleasure of one kiss."

A flush stained her cheeks. "My lord, that is a highly improper request."

"Not as improper as what I might have proposed." He almost grinned as her color deepened. "Still, it ought to give you proof of the theorem of my disrepute." He tipped his head toward the notebook. "You can add that to column four."

He knew he was being rude, but he'd spent the last two years holding himself, his words, even his thoughts, so tightly in check that something inside him loosened at the sight of this woman's blush. Something made him want to rattle her, to engage in a bit of bad behavior and see how she responded. Besides, wasn't bad behavior exactly what society expected of him?

"Do you accept?" he asked.

"Certainly not."

"All right, then. I'll tell John to take you home."

He started to the door, unsurprised when she said, "Wait!"

He turned.

"My lord, surely there is something—"

"That's my offer, Miss Kellaway."

Her hand trembled as she brushed a lock of hair from her forehead. The brown strands glinted with gold, making him wonder what her hair would look like unpinned.

Lydia gave a stiff nod, her color still high. "Very well."

"Then read me one of your puzzles."

"I beg your pardon?"

He nodded at her notebook. "Read one to me."

She looked as if she were unable to fathom the reason for his request. He wondered what she'd say if he told her he liked the sound of her voice, delicate and smooth but with a huskiness that slid right into his blood.

"Go on," he encouraged.

Lydia glanced at the notebook, uncertainty passing across her features. He'd thrown her off course. She hadn't anticipated such a turn of events when she'd planned this little encounter, and she didn't know how to react.

"All right, then." She cleared her throat and paged through the notebook. "On her way to a marketplace, a woman selling eggs passes through a garrison. She must pass three guards on the way."

She paused and glanced at him. A faint consternation lit in her eyes as their gazes met. Alexander gave her a nod of encouragement.

"To the first guard," Lydia continued, "she sells half the number of eggs she has plus half an egg more. To the second guard, she sells half of what remains plus half an egg more. To the third guard, she sells half of the remainder plus half an egg more. When she arrives at the marketplace, she has thirty-six eggs. How many eggs did she have at the beginning?"

Alexander looked at her for a moment. He rose and went to the desk on the other side of the room. He rummaged through the top drawer and removed a pencil, then extended his hand for the notebook.

He smoothed a fresh sheet of paper onto the desk and read her neat penmanship.

An image of her flashed in his mind—Lydia Kellaway sitting at a desk like this one, her hair unbound, a slight crease between her brows as she worked on a problem she expected would confound people. Perhaps it was late at night and she wore nothing but a voluminous white shift, her body naked beneath the...

Alexander shook his head hard. He read the problem again and began doing some algebraic calculations on the paper.

Odd number, half an egg more, seventy-three eggs before she passed the last guard...

He did a few more calculations, half aware of something easing inside him, his persistent anger lessening. He realized that for the first time in a very long while, he was rather enjoying himself.

Alexander scribbled a number and circled it, then turned the paper toward Lydia.

"She had two hundred and ninety-five eggs," he said.

Lydia stepped forward to read his solution. A perplexing surge of both triumph and regret rose in Alexander when he lifted his gaze and saw the dismay on her face. She hadn't expected to lose.

No. She hadn't expected him to win.

"You are correct, Lord Northwood."

He tossed down the pencil and straightened.

Lydia stood watching him, wariness edging her expression. Her skin was milk-pale, her heart-shaped face dominated by large, thick-lashed eyes. Her cheekbones sloped down to a delicate jaw and full, well-shaped lips.

She might have been beautiful if it weren't for the tense, brittle way she carried herself, the compression of her lips and strain in her eyes. If it weren't for the ghostly pallor cast by her black dress, the severe cut of which could not obscure the combination of curves and sinuous lines that he suspected lay beneath.

His heart beat a little faster. He went to stand in front of her. Lydia swallowed, the white column of her throat rippling. If she was fearful, she didn't show it. If she was anticipatory, she didn't show that either. She merely looked at him, those thick eyelashes fanning her blue eyes like feathers.

He reached up and touched a loose lock of her hair, rubbing it between his fingers. Thick and soft. Pity she had to keep it so tightly bound. He lowered his hand, his knuckles brushing across her cheek. A visible tremble went through her.

"Well, then?" Alexander murmured.

He grasped her shoulders, her frame slender and delicate beneath his big hands. He stared down at her, the muscles of his back and shoulders tensing. The air thickened around them, between them, infusing with heat. His heart thudded with a too-quick tempo and a vague sense of unease—as if whatever strange power vibrated between him and Lydia Kellaway contained a sinister edge.

He inhaled the air surrounding her. No cloying scent of flowers or perfume. She smelled crisp, clean, like starched linens and sharpened pencils.

Her lips parted. Her posture remained stiff, her hands curled at her sides. Alexander wondered if she ever allowed herself to lose that self-contained tension. He continued to grip her shoulders, and for an instant they were both still. Then he slipped his hand to the side of Lydia's neck just above her collar.

She trembled when his thumb grazed her bare skin, brushing back and forth against her neck, the only movement within the utter stillness surrounding them. Color swept across her cheekbones, the same reddish hue as a breaking dawn. Her throat rippled with another swallow, but her expression didn't break; her posture didn't ease.

If anything, she grew more rigid, her spine stiffening. Alexander's thumb moved higher, to that secret, intimate hollow just behind her ear, his fingers curving to the back of her neck. His palm rested in the juncture of her neck and shoulder. Her skin was as smooth as percale; tendrils of her dark hair brushed the back of his hand.

Want. That surge pulsed through him, hot and heavy, the desire to strip her dull clothes from her body and touch her bare skin. As if in response, her pulse quickened like the beat of butterfly wings against his palm.

A soft thud sounded on the carpet as her notebook fell to the floor.

He lowered his mouth to hers. She didn't move forward, but neither did she back away. Her flush intensified, her chest rising as if she sought to draw air into her lungs. Multiple shades of blue infused her eyes. Her breath puffed against his lips. His hands tightened on her shoulders, the side of her neck.

The cracks within him began to smooth, the fissures closing. Instead he was filled with the urge to prolong this strange attraction, to savor the mystery of what would happen when their mouths finally met.

"Later."

His whisper broke through the tension like a pebble dropped into a pool of still, dark water. Lydia drew back, her lips parting.

"What?" Her question sounded strained, thin.

Alexander slipped his hand away from her neck, his fingers lingering against her warm skin.

"Later," he repeated. "I will require the payment of your debt at a later date."

Lydia stared at him before stepping away, her fists clenching. "My lord, this is unconscionable."

"Is it? We never determined payment would be immediate."

"It was implied."

"Ah, that's your mistake, Miss Kellaway. It's dangerous to assume your opponent holds the same unspoken ideas. Dangerous to assume anything, in fact."

He almost felt the anger flare through her blood. For an instant, she remained still, and then something settled over her expression—a resurgence of control, of composure.

She started for the door, her stride long and her back as stiff as metal. Just before she stepped out, she turned back to him.

"Though I prefer a more systematic approach to proving a theorem, my lord, I appreciate your assistance."

He watched her disappear into the shadows of the foyer; then he smiled faintly. He picked up her notebook from the floor and slipped it into his pocket.

THE DISH

Where Authors Give You the Inside Scoop

♥ ♥ ♥ ♥ ♥ ♥ ♥ ♥ ♥ ♥ ♥ ♥ ♥ ♥ ♥ ♥

From the desk of Jennifer Haymore

Dear Reader,

When Lady Dunthorpe, the heroine of THE SCOUNDREL'S SEDUCTION, came to my office, she filled the tiny room with her presence, making me look up from my computer the moment she walked in. The first thing I noticed was that she was gorgeous. Very petite, with lovely features perfectly arranged on her face. She could probably be a movie star.

"How can I help—?" I began, but she interrupted me.

"I *need* you," she declared. I could hear the smooth cadence of a French accent in her voice. "My husband has been murdered, and I've been kidnapped by a very bad blackguard...a...a *scoundrel.*"

I straightened in my chair. "What? How...why?" I had about a million questions, but I couldn't seem to get them all out. "Please, my lady, sit down."

She slid into the chair opposite me.

"Now," I said, "please tell me what exactly is going on and how I can help you."

She leaned forward, her blue eyes luminous and large. "My husband—Lord Dunthorpe. He was killed. And his murderer...his murderer has captured me. I don't know what he's going to do..." She swallowed hard, looking terrified.

"Do you know who the murderer is?

She shook her head. "*Non.* But his friends call him 'Hawk.'"

Every muscle in my body went rigid. I knew only one man called Hawk. His real name was Samson Hawkins, he was the oldest brother of the House of Trent, and I'd just finished writing books about two of his brothers.

Yet maybe she wasn't talking about "my" Hawk. Sam was a hero, not a murderer. Still, I had to know.

"Is he tall and broad?" I asked her. "Very muscular?"

"*Oui*...yes."

"Handsome features?"

"Very."

"Dark eyes and dark hair that curls at his shoulders?"

"Yes."

"Does he have a certain...*intensity* about him?"

"Oh, yes, very much."

Yep, she was definitely talking about Sam Hawkins.

I sat back in my chair, stunned, mulling over all she had told me. Sam had killed her husband. He'd kidnapped her...and was holding her hostage...*Wow.*

"I need your help," she whispered urgently. "I need to be free..."

"Of course," I soothed.

Her desire to be free sparked an idea in my mind. Because if she truly knew Sam—knew the man inside that hard shell—perhaps she *wouldn't* want to be free of him. She was beautiful and vivacious—she'd lit up my little office when she'd walked inside. Sam had certainly already noticed this about her. Now...all I had to do was work a little magic—okay, I admitted to myself, a *lot* of magic, considering the fact that Sam had killed her husband—and I could bring these two together.

Sam hadn't lived a very easy life. He *so* deserved his very own happily ever after.

This would be a love match born in adversity. *Very* tricky. But if I could make it work—if I could give Lady Dunthorpe to Sam as his heroine—it would probably be the most fulfilling love story I'd ever written.

With determination to make it work, I turned my computer screen toward me and started typing away. "Tell me what happened," I told Lady Dunthorpe, "from the beginning…"

And that was how I began the story of THE SCOUN-DREL'S SEDUCTION—and now that I've finished it, I'm so excited to share it with readers, because I definitely believe it's my most romantic story yet.

Please come visit me at my website, www.jennifer haymore.com, where you can share your thoughts about my books and read more about THE SCOUNDREL'S SEDUCTION and the House of Trent Series. I'd also love to see you on Twitter (@jenniferhaymore) or on Facebook (www.facebook.com/jenniferhaymore-author).

Sincerely,

Jenny Haymore

♥ ♥ ♥ ♥ ♥ ♥ ♥ ♥ ♥ ♥ ♥ ♥ ♥ ♥ ♥ ♥

From the desk of Kristen Ashley

Dear Reader,

As a romance reader from a very young age, and a girl
who never got to sleep easily so I told myself stories to get
that way (all romances, of course), I had a bevy of "starts"
to stories I never really finished.

Not until I finally started to tap away on my
keyboard.

One of them that popped up often was of a woman
alone, heading to a remote location, not feeling well,
and meeting the man of her dreams who would nurse
her back to health. Except, obviously (this *is* a romance),
at first meeting him, she doesn't know he's the man of
her dreams and decides instantly (for good reason) she
doesn't like him all that much.

Therefore, I was delighted finally to get stuck in Nina
and Max's story in THE GAMBLE. I'd so long wanted
to start a story that way and I was thrilled I finally got
to do it. I got such a kick out of seeing that first chapter
unfold, their less-than-auspicious beginning, the crackling dialogue, Max's A-frame (inside and out) forming in
my head.

But I had absolutely no clue about the epic journey I
was about to take—murder, assault, kidnapping, suicide
and rape, trust earned and tested—and amongst all this,
a man and a woman falling in love.

The focus of the book is on Nina's story—oft-bitten,
very shy, to the point where she's hardly living her life

anymore, feels it, and knows she needs to do something about it even as she's terrified.

But whenever I read THE GAMBLE, it's Max's story that touches me. How he had so much from such a young age and lost it so tragically. How he took care of everyone around him in his mountain man way, but also was living half a life. And last, how Nina lit up his world and revived that protective, loving part of him he thought long dead.

The struggle with this, however, was Anna, the love Max lost. See, I knew her well and she was an amazing person who made Max happy. They were very much in love and neither Max (in my head) nor I wanted to give her short-shrift or make any less of the love they shared even as Max fell deeply in love with Nina.

I didn't know if this was working very well, for Nina was so very much *not* like Anna, but, at least to me, I found her quite lovable. This was good; you shouldn't try to find what you lost but simply find something that makes you happy. But still, it was important for me that the love Max shared with Anna wasn't entirely overshadowed by the love he had for Nina because Anna was in his life, she was important, and being so was part of what made him the man he turned out to be.

In a book that has a good deal of raw emotion, one line always jumps out at me and there's a reason for that. I was relieved when a friend of mine told me it was her favorite in this whole, very long book. So simple but also, by it being her favorite, it told me that I'd won that struggle.

It was Max saying to Nina, *"I see what I had with Anna*

for the gift it was but now that's gone. With this act, are you sayin', in this life that's all I get?"

In a book where grave tragedy had consistently struck many of the characters (as life often hands us our trials), I love the hope in this line. I love that Max finally comes to realize that the beauty he had and lost was not all he should expect. That he should reach out for more.

And he *does* reach out for more.

And in the end, he finds that it isn't all he would get. Being a good man and taking a gamble on a feisty woman who shows up in a snowstorm with attitude (and her sinuses hurting), he gets much, *much* more.

So I was absolutely delighted to take his journey.

Because he deserves it.

From the desk of Nina Rowan

Dear Reader,

What is the worst part of writing a historical romance? Once upon a time, I might have thought it was most difficult to unravel the plot and character motivations, but the more I write, the more I realize the truth. It's the research! And I don't mean that in a moan-and-groan-it's-homework way. I mean that the more I research for the sake of a book, the more I get flat-out distracted by all the little golden nuggets I find.

When I start researching, I tend to trawl the *London Times* archives, which has a searchable database that is so beautiful and easy to use that it almost makes me cry. For A DREAM OF DESIRE, I started by looking up articles about prisons and juvenile delinquency, but got quickly distracted by other things like the classified advertisements. The *Times* was full of ads for polka and mazurka lessons, "paper hanging" sales, tea companies, and job openings for schoolmistresses and butlers. The "prisons" search term appeared in the classifieds in an advertisement for "prisons supply of coal, meat, bread, oatmeal, barley, candles, and stockings." The ad requested that suppliers submit an application to the keeper of the prisons to be considered for the position.

I also get distracted by other articles about criminal court proceedings (a goldmine of story ideas), new laws, intelligence from overseas, and details about royal court life, like the state ball of 1845 at Buckingham Palace, which was attended by over one thousand members of the nobility and gentry and where Her Majesty and the Hereditary Grand Duke of Mecklenburgh Strelitz danced the quadrille in the ballroom, which was festooned with crimson and gold draperies and lit by a huge, cut-glass lustre.

I find that fascinating. But distractions aside, it really is within the pages of the newspapers and magazines published in the nineteenth century that the most vivid details of a story can come to life. When I first started writing A DREAM OF DESIRE, I thought surely the term "juvenile delinquent" was a historical anachronism, but it was used often in Victorian-era *Times* articles about "juvenile destitution and crime."

I've come to accept the fact that rather than being a dedicated, focused researcher, I'm more like a magpie whose attention is caught by shiny objects. But I've also learned to appreciate how much all those little tidbits of information come in handy when crafting a story—what might happen if the hero and heroine were in attendance at Her Majesty's state ball? What if the heroine was having a clumsy moment (or better yet, was distracted by the hero's rakish good looks) and tripped over the Grand Duke in the middle of the quadrille? What if she found herself face-to-face with a rather irate Queen Victoria?

Must go. I have some writing to do!

Nina Rowan

From the desk of Jane Graves

Dear Reader,

I like wine. Any kind of wine. I've learned a lot about it over the years, but only because if you use any product enough, you'll end up pretty educated about it. (If I ate

147 different kinds of Little Debbie snack cakes, I'd know a lot about them, too.) I can swirl, sniff, and sip with the best of them. But the fourth S: spit? Seriously? The theory is that one should merely taste the wine without getting tipsy, but come on. Who in his right mind tastes good wine and then spits it out?

My husband and I once went to a wine tasting/competition where we took our glasses around to the various vintners' booths and received tiny tasting pours, which we were to sip, savor, and judge. By the time we sampled the offerings of about two dozen vineyards, those tiny pours added up. At first we discussed acidity, mouth feel, and finish, then thoughtfully marked our scorecards. By the end of the event, we'd lost our scorecards and were wondering if there was a frat party nearby we could crash. Okay, so maybe that spitting thing has some merit.

In BABY, IT'S YOU, the hero, Marc Cordero, runs an estate vineyard in the Texas Hill Country that has been in his family for generations. As I researched winemaking for the book, I discovered it's both a science and an art, requiring intelligence, intuition, willpower, and above all, heart. The heroine, Kari Worthington, feels Marc's pride as he looks out over the grapevine-covered hills, and she's in awe of his determination to protect his family legacy. For a flighty, free-spirited, runaway bride who's never had a place to truly call home, Cordero Vineyards and the passionate man who runs it are the things of which her dreams are made.

So next time I go to a wine tasting, I'm going to think about the myriad challenges that winemakers faced in order to present that bottle for me to enjoy. But I'm still not gonna spit.

I hope you enjoy BABY, IT'S YOU!

Jane Graves

JaneGraves.com
Twitter @JaneGraves
Facebook.com/AuthorJaneGraves

♥ ♥ ♥ ♥ ♥ ♥ ♥ ♥ ♥ ♥ ♥ ♥ ♥ ♥ ♥

From the desk of Adrianne Lee

Dear Reader,

I have a secret to confess: I'm not creative with my hands.

My mother and sister inherited an artistic gene that I did not. My mother drew a Christmas scene on the mirror over the fireplace every year. Drawings I create look as though they were done by a toddler.

My sister can wrap a present that is too pretty to open. Gifts I wrap look as though I've hired a chimpanzee and given it ten rolls of Scotch tape, though that is probably insulting to chimpanzees.

I have zero skills at flower arranging. People think I'm joking when I say that, but it's actually true. If I set out to arrange a bouquet of my favorite blooms, by the time I'm done, I end up with two-inch stems. And if a food item needs to look as appealing as it tastes, I'm in trouble.

Therefore, when I set out to write the Big Sky Pie series, I had to imagine pastry chefs with the skills of sculptors, who create masterpieces, not with clay, but with pie dough. Molly McCoy is at loose ends after the sudden death of her husband. She has always dreamed of opening her own shop, a venue to sell her blue-ribbon pies, and she decides life is too short to not act now. But just as her dream is about to become a reality, Molly suffers a life-threatening health crisis. Worrying about the pie shop might be the end of her—if her son and his about-to-be-ex-wife don't step up and take over.

When my mother passed away unexpectedly, I was thrown off kilter so badly I lost forty pounds in six weeks. So I really understood how Quint McCoy could lose himself after his beloved dad died suddenly. Up to that point, Quint had always had a sense of who he was and what he wanted. He just didn't understand that work wasn't as important as family until after his grief caused him to push away everyone he loved.

Callee had grown up unable to trust that anyone would ever love her. Quint's rejection proved her right. She didn't fight for their marriage; she just went along with his request for a divorce. And that divorce is almost final when Molly collapses. She tricks Callee into agreeing to work with Quint to open her pie shop, but can this sizzling hot couple work together without their emotions setting flame to the Big Sky Pie kitchen?

I hope you'll enjoy DELECTABLE, the first book in my Big Sky Pie series. All of the stories are set in northwest Montana near Glacier Park, an area where I vacationed every summer for over thirty years. Each of the books is about someone connected with the pie shop in one way or another. So come meet the couples whose relationships grow from half-baked into a love that will melt your heart. Also, each book offers a different delectable pie recipe. What more could you want?

Adrianne Lee

Find out more about Forever Romance!

Visit us at
www.hachettebookgroup.com/publishing_forever.aspx

Find us on Facebook
http://www.facebook.com/ForeverRomance

Follow us on Twitter
http://twitter.com/ForeverRomance

NEW AND UPCOMING TITLES

Each month we feature our new titles
and reader favorites.

CONTESTS AND GIVEAWAYS

We give away galleys, autographed copies,
and all kinds of exclusive items.

AUTHOR INFO

You'll find bios, articles, and links to personal websites
for all your favorite authors—and so much more.

GET SOCIAL

Connect with your favorite authors, editors, and
other Forever fans, and share what's important to you.

THE BUZZ

Sign up for our monthly romance newsletter,
and be the first to read all about it.